NIL

Lynne Matson

NIL

SQUARE
FISH

HENRY HOLT AND COMPANY | NEW YORK

SQUARE
FISH

An Imprint of Macmillan
175 Fifth Avenue
New York, NY 10010
macteenbooks.com

Square Fish and the Square Fish logo are trademarks of Macmillan and
are used by Henry Holt and Company under license from Macmillan.

Square Fish books may be purchased for business or promotional use. For information on
bulk purchases, please contact the Macmillan Corporate and Premium Sales Department
at (800) 221-7945 x5442 or by e-mail at specialmarkets@macmillan.com.

Library of Congress Cataloging-in-Publication Data is available.

ISBN 978-1-250-05702-0 (paperback)   ISBN 978-0-8050-9772-6 (ebook)

Originally published in the United States by Henry Holt and Company
First Square Fish Edition: 2015
Book designed by April Ward
Square Fish logo designed by Filomena Tuosto

10 9 8 7 6 5 4 3 2 1

AR: 4.2 / LEXILE: HL570L

FOR STEPHEN
I WOULD FIND YOU IN ANY WORLD

TIME IS THE FIRE
IN WHICH WE BURN.

—DELMORE SCHWARTZ

CHAPTER 1

CHARLEY
AUGUST 10, NOON

Heat.

Inexplicable, consuming heat—choking like smoke, burning like fire.

That was my last memory before the invisible flames spiked into icy nothingness, along with the crazy thought that if I survived this bewildering bonfire, my dad would freak when I was late returning his new car.

CHARLEY
AUGUST 10, 11:56 A.M.

Dang, it's hot.

I'd been out of the car for all of one minute, and I was already roasting like a skinny rotisserie chicken. The asphalt radiated heat. Shifting my feet, I fumbled with Dad's keys, dying to climb back into his Volvo with its arctic air-conditioning and new car smell.

Instead, I grabbed the plastic bag from the back seat and slammed the door. I had fifty dollars' worth of clothes to return. Fifty dollars of my hard-earned summer babysitting money, wasted on two silly skirts I never should've bought in the first place. The minis were crazy short, and on me, they looked downright skanky. I'd never wear them, and had Em or Jen been with me, they wouldn't have let me put the darn skirts in the cart.

But yesterday, like today, it was just me.

Well, crap, I thought, biting my lip as I stared at the empty car. I hated being alone. I always had, and I hated that I hated it. I mean, I'd never even gone to see a movie by myself and secretly envied people who could. The truth was, I'd never had to be alone. My sister, Em, was always around, or Jen, my best friend since second grade. Or both.

Until now.

A fresh wave of loneliness washed over me with the heat; it was the same wave I'd felt when we'd dropped Em off at college last week, and again yesterday when I'd watched Jen board a plane bound for Milan. My two favorite people, gone.

Not forever, I reminded myself. I refused to pitch a pity party in the Target lot. *It's just a few months, four at the most.* Jen's study abroad program ended in December. By Christmas, life would be good, and our senior spring would rock. Until then, I had volleyball. Practices would keep me busy, and games would keep me focused. And I'd visit Em in Athens every chance I could.

Feeling slightly better, I locked Dad's car and faced the open lot. Asphalt as black as coal stretched before me, broken only by lonely white lines. *Park in the far corner,* Dad had said, tossing me his keys with a wink. Catching the keys, I'd smiled. *I love you too, Dad.*

Of course I'd parked in the far corner. No other car was anywhere close.

Now that I was walking, *far* wasn't the word. It was like I'd parked in dadgum Egypt, and I'd swear it was just as hot. Not that I'd ever been to Egypt, but I couldn't imagine it was any hotter than Georgia in August. The Target bull's-eye flashed like fire in the distance. Near the lot's center, the asphalt shimmered in the heat. I watched the ground blur, absently thinking of a desert oasis. It was the kind of shimmer that moves with you . . . moves away, always out of reach.

Not this one. This shimmer stretched into the air, rippling like a wall of wavy glass. Then it rolled.

Swiftly.

Strangely.

Toward me.

In the time it took to blink, the air in front of me melted. It undulated, like a wave of liquid crystal, and before I could breathe, the wave engulfed me in a silent rush.

Hot air gripped me like a vise, then burst into flames. Every speck of skin screamed; every nerve ending exploded.

I'm being flash-fried in the Target lot! The thought ripped through my brain as the invisible flames drove deeper. I tried to scream, but choked on the heat; it was in my mouth, in my lungs, in *me*, like a living darkness I couldn't shake. Blistering tar coursed through my veins, then filled my chest, stealing my air and slicking behind my eyes.

A darkness blacker than asphalt rushed at me; I fell to meet it. My last sensation was of icy cold. A biting cold as raw and as painful as the heat had been seconds before, and then—nothing.

No light. No sound.

No air.

CHAPTER 2

THAD
DAY 267, DAWN

Two days ago, Kevin went renegade, bolting to Search alone.

Yesterday his clock ran out.

And today—well, today seriously sucked. Maybe for him, and definitely for us, because one day later, we still didn't know if Kevin had made it or not. All we knew was that today was his Day 366, and on the island of Nil, no one got a Day 366.

Swallowing bile, I realized my brutal beach run had done absolutely nothing to clear my head. If anything, I felt worse. Now I was exhausted *and* edgy. Not the way to start a Nil day.

One meter from the tree line, I stopped, and in a move that would've stunned my coach back home, I forced myself to breathe. To consciously take in air. *Focus the breath, focus the mind*—it was my coach's classic send-off before we hit the mountain, not that I'd ever really listened. I inhaled through my nose, breathing from my gut. *Breathe in . . . hold . . . breathe out.* Coach always swore that if we were doing it right, our breath would sound like a roaring ocean. Ironically, all I heard *was* a roaring ocean. Behind me, potent liquid avalanches crashed into shore, crumbling one after another.

Breathe.

A black streak flashed on my right. Instantly amped, I pulled my knife and spun, fully aware I might already be toast. The blur dropped something near my toes, and my adrenaline rush died on the spot.

"Nice." I stared at the dead bird at my feet. "Burton, you shouldn't have." Of all the cats on Nil, Burton stood out the most. A jet black cat, his paws were pure white. They looked like they'd been dipped in snow.

Sheathing my knife, I nodded at Burton. "Really, you keep it."

Now the cat looked annoyed, like he'd hoped for more. Burton and I had come to a truce months ago. I tossed him fish scraps, he hissed in return, and occasionally he brought me dead stuff to show he actually cared.

Nothing like starting the day with a corpse, even if it was just a bird.

Abruptly, I felt like the bird. Dead on my feet, like I'd spent the day shredding fresh powder, but here on Nil, the day had barely begun. And thanks to Nil, I hadn't touched a snowboard in exactly 266 days.

Dwelling on snow and corpses and breathing exercises not worth a crap, I trudged down the path, the one that led to the Wall.

I found my name and touched the letters like a blind man reading Braille. I did this every morning. Part of me knew it was borderline obsessive; the rest of me didn't care. After nine months on the island, I'd earned the right to a few whacked-out rituals. The Wall was a memorial, *our* memorial, even for those of us still here.

The longer I traced, the calmer I felt, and by the time I finished my name a third time, I was almost Zen. Then I glanced at Kevin's name and my near Zen shattered: five letters, then a blank space. His empty space screamed at me, begging to be filled. But to fill the space, I had to know what to carve; the ugly void was a cruel reminder that

I did not know. I closed my eyes. My head felt ready to explode. And if I felt this crappy, I couldn't imagine how Natalie was holding up.

Not so great, I thought, picturing her face as she lurched into the City last night. Both hopeful and hopeless, she was a different kind of lost. And the worst part—the part that made me want to slam my head against the Wall—was that there was nothing to do but wait. Wait to grieve, wait to celebrate, wondering if Kevin's fate was a sneak peek at our own. This was Nil's favorite game, the one where she messed with our heads.

I prayed Kevin had won. But either way, he was gone, and he wasn't coming back. There was no overtime on Nil.

"Thad!"

Hearing my name, I turned away from the Wall. Rives was walking toward me, his dreads tied back, his face all business. A sleek wooden board rested against one hip.

"Any word on Kevin?" His eyes darted over my shoulder.

"Not yet."

"Maybe today." Rives looked as frustrated as I felt.

"Maybe." We might as well have been discussing the weather. *Think it'll rain today? Maybe.* Meaningless small talk about something over which we had no control.

I glanced at his board. Remembering this morning's monster swells, I frowned. "You going out alone?"

"You know it," Rives said, breaking into a grin. "Unless you're game."

For a half second, I actually considered it. Then I sighed. "I can't."

Rives gave me a long look. "You sure, bro? I'll wait."

"Thanks, but I'm out. I promised Natalie I'd do sweeps."

There was no way Rives would argue with that. As he walked away, I called, "Rives!"

He turned. "Yeah?"

"Be safe. Watch your back, eh?"

"Always." Grinning again, he threw me a quick salute.

Rives vanished into the trees. The sky was clear, and the clean air smelled like salt. It was like every other morning for the past 266 days—and yet it wasn't. A cagey vibe hung in the air. More than just the anticipation of the verdict on Kevin, it was something else. Something new, something I couldn't quite nail. But it was there; I felt it. And it was something to do with me.

What are you cooking up now, Nil? I wondered, stifling a twinge of dread. Looking around, I saw nothing but leaves shifting in the wind.

Nil says wait, she giggled in the breeze.

Like I had a choice.

CHAPTER 3

A sharp pain in my hip woke me. When I opened my eyes, I saw red.

Literally.

Jagged rocks the color of rust stretched as far as I could see. Boulders as big as buses, small chunks like cars, and a million smaller rocks the size of balls—golf balls, baseballs, volleyballs, you name it. All were uneven, with weird serrated edges, and all were the same exact shade of burnt red. I lay on a raised outcropping, on my side.

And I was *naked*.

Outside, in a creepy rock field I'd never laid eyes on before in my life.

I scrambled to my feet, and brushing off grit, I stumbled toward the edge. Spiky gravel covered the rock like sprinkles on a cupcake. *That explains the pain in my hip*, I thought randomly. I slipped twice but didn't fall.

My rock, shaped like a mushroom with a fat stem, was mashed against a clump of smaller rocks masquerading as petrified red cauliflower. Using the smaller rocks as stairs, I worked my way down, moving as fast as the prickly rock would allow. At the bottom, I scrunched into the wisp of shade.

Frozen against the rock, I listened.

The only noise came from me. Air whistling in and out of my lungs, blood slamming against the chambers of my heart. The surrounding silence was so vast, so complete, it had a presence all its own: it was eerie, almost otherworldly. And with the desolate red landscape stretching for miles, I felt like I'd woken on an alien planet.

An. Alien. Planet.

I began shaking, violently, with the kind of icy fear I'd felt only once before, when Em and I were T-boned by a drunk driver and I'd seen Em sandwiched behind the wheel, bright red blood running down her forehead into her closed eyes. She'd turned out to be fine. I couldn't say the same for myself right now. Stark naked, goodness knows where, wherever *here* was. My last memory was of scalding heat, burning cold, and pain.

Jerking my head down, I expected my skin to be fried, but it looked fine. All of it, which I could see, because I was *naked.*

Slowly, I pressed my head back against the rock. The red rock landscape stayed silent, and still. At least the sky was blue. Brilliant, clear blue.

Maybe I'm dead.

I thought I'd passed out, but maybe I had actually *passed.* Did that awful heat mark the entrance into death? Absorbing my God-forsaken surroundings, I abruptly thought, *Hell.* Hell was a red rock desert, where you woke up naked and alone. I'd always thought Hell was an underground cavern teeming with the moaning damned, but maybe we all got our own personal Hell, crafted just for us, because mine sure looked a lot like this: no clothes, no people, and definitely no clue.

But it didn't feel like Hell. And even though I'd skipped church lately, I was a pretty good kid. Sneaking out at night to drink beer on the local golf course with Em was the worst thing I'd ever done, and that really wasn't so bad. Not bad enough to wind up in Hell anyway. My gut told me I was alive, then my gut told me I should be afraid. Very afraid.

My Em-bleeding-behind-the-wheel fear was back. Was the air thinner here? I couldn't seem to get enough air.

Around me, nothing moved.

I swept the area, looking for something to tell me where I was, or wasn't, but all I saw was rock. It coated the ground, hunkered in clumps, and giant piles of it blocked my line of sight. If I wanted to see anything, I'd have to climb. But I knew if I could see past the rock hills, then anything lurking out there could also see me.

Trapped, I thought humorlessly, *between a rock and a hard place*. Revealing myself seemed like a really bad idea. On the other hand, I couldn't stay plastered against this rock forever.

Hunching over, I crept toward the largest pile and started up. Scaling the rocks was like walking barefoot over spiky balls from our giant sweetgum tree—uncomfortable, but doable, as long as I watched my step. Near the top, I peeked over the edge. All I could see was more rock. I hesitated, hearing my volleyball coach's voice in my head. *Use your height, Charley. Make it work for you.* Okay, well, on the court in a uniform is one thing, outside stark naked was another.

I took a deep breath—and then I climbed. On the summit, I stood, but I couldn't help covering my chest with one arm and my privates with the other. Feeling like an idiot, I surveyed the broken landscape.

A blue haze rose in the distance, speckled with green. *Mountains*, I thought, feeling a spark of hope. Green meant life, and more importantly, water. *Are there mountains on Mars?* I wondered. Then I wanted to slap myself. I didn't—because that would mean flashing more of my already overexposed self—but I wanted to, because mountains or not, there was no oxygen on Mars, and I was definitely breathing oxygen-filled air. This wasn't Mars.

But that didn't mean it was Earth.

The sun—only one, thank heavens—hung high in the cloudless sky. Feeling heat on my bare shoulders, I knew I needed to find cover. Even with my olive skin, eventually I'd burn, especially certain parts that had never seen the sun.

I looked left. West, perhaps. The ground sloped gently away. No mountains, but I sensed that direction was safer. *Follow the lead,* my dad would joke as he tapped his nose, his golden-brown eyes twinkling. Along with his looks, I often thought I'd inherited his lead. Heading west *felt* right.

I turned and my breath caught. Twenty yards out, the red ground was shimmering. The air lay still. And if it was quiet with the wind, without it, this place was dead calm.

The shimmer lifted into the air, and then it moved—straight toward me.

I scrambled right, aiming not to outrun it but skirt *around* it, likening it to a tornado; we'd had one in Georgia once. Running over the crumbly rocks and leaping to hit flat spots, I missed. Pain slashed across my heel, making me stumble, and when I looked back up, the shimmer hovered fifteen feet away and closing. Not speeding up, not slowing. Just drifting . . . toward me.

Kicking into high gear, I sprinted across the rocks, leaving a trail of red on red. A flat portion of rock caught my eye; behind it was a small cave—more like a scoop carved out of the rock face, just big enough for me. I darted toward the opening. Folding like an accordion, I tucked inside the shallow hole.

Shade dropped like a curtain. I pressed my back against the cool rock, letting my eyes adjust.

The shimmer approached, silent and sinister.

Seconds later, the wall of wavering air drifted so close I could reach out and touch it, not that I did. But I couldn't look away. Glistening like water under glass, a million pinpricks of translucent light winked at me. Every color was there, rippling and moving, filled with an unnatural iridescence.

Then the shimmer's edge hung directly in front of me. A razor-thin streak of silver back-lined in black onyx, the air in front and behind was clear and as blue as the sky above. I sat completely still, afraid to move, afraid to breathe, terrified the shimmer would suck me in and take me goodness-knows-where.

The shimmer kept moving, drifting out of sight.

A second ticked by, then two.

Outside my hole, the wind was back. It blew fine dust across the landing near my toes, miniature funnels of red.

I stared at the funnels, thinking of tornadoes and shimmers. Tornadoes were definitely bad. I didn't know whether the shimmers were good or bad, but I felt I should avoid them. One had obviously brought me here, which was bad, or at least not good. It was like some twisted Wizard of Oz experience, minus the red sparkly shoes to take me home.

I uncurled myself in time to see a second shimmer form off to my right, in virtually the same place that the first one had appeared.

Without hesitation, I ducked back into my cave. The dust lay flat. This shimmer drifted farther out than the first, and when it passed, its edge lurked yards away, not inches. Like the first one, the second shimmer passed without stopping.

Tucked into a silent ball, I watched the dust, waiting.

The wind stalled; the dust funnels collapsed. A third shimmer swept across the red field in my line of sight, this one farther out than its predecessors, much farther. It, too, disappeared off to my left, shrinking into itself in the time it takes to blink, and then was gone. The shimmers looked less ominous in the distance, less sentient. Most important, they didn't seem intent on finding me, but they were still as freaky as Dorothy's tornado.

And that's when I thought, *If one shimmer brought me here, maybe one will take me back*. So when a fourth shimmer appeared, I ran for it. I loped toward the wall of wavering air, ignoring the pain in my heel, feeling ridiculous in my galloping nakedness but hell-bent on catching the shimmer anyway. It moved slowly across the red rock, hovering inches from the ground and stretching ten feet high and half as wide.

As I gained on the shimmer, I wondered exactly what would happen when I hit the roiling air. *Will it burn? Feel like ice?* In ten feet, I was about to find out.

Five.

Two.

I was inches away when the shimmer crumpled into a black dot. Then the dot vanished. The wind instantly returned, whipping my hair with a vengeance.

The shimmer was gone.

I stood naked on a strange rocky plateau, feeling a sense of failure for something I didn't even understand. I'd missed it, whatever it was. And with the distance between the shimmers widening, I knew I couldn't run fast enough to catch the next one.

But unable to help myself, I waited, my eyes scouring the ground for movement.

No new shimmers appeared.

Did the shimmers come in sets like waves? How often did they come? I'd no idea. And I had no clue what they really were.

Without warning, I was totally aware of my vulnerability without clothes or cover. *Get out!* my gut screamed. *Out of this field, out of the sun, and out of sight*. Something told me this field was a dead end, and to *move*.

I spun, took a step, and buckled in pain. Glancing at my heel, I winced. It was shredded, bathed in blood, and there was nothing I could do—except keep moving.

The going was slow, and painful. I fell into a pattern of taking several steps, then pausing to get my bearings, not that I really had any. I took two awkward steps to my left, then hopped forward, aiming for a flat spot and feeling like I was playing Stephen King's version of naked Twister. I was so intent on my footing that I almost missed seeing it: a flash of cream among the red.

Hobbling over, I found two sandals and some cloth. No, *clothes*.

Beside a deep crevasse, a pair of shorts and a bandana lay in a heap. Both were a strange off-white. Giddy with hope, I snatched up the shorts, and something bright went flying; it whistled past my ear, disappeared into the crevasse, and landed with a muffled *crack*. I wondered what it was, but I wasn't about to peer into the dark hole to see what fell. At the rate I was going, I'd probably fall in myself. Whatever it was, it was gone.

I held up the shorts. The fabric was soft and worn. Straight cut with rough stitching and a jagged lace-up fly, they looked like primitive boys' Bermudas. One side was torn, but they were definitely wearable.

"Sweet," I said.

The word rolled through the open air like a shout. I stopped, instantly freaked out, realizing these clothes belonged to someone.

Someone who might be watching.

A fresh jolt of panic made me shake. Clutching the shorts like a thief caught red-handed, I scanned the rocks, every muscle taut as I waited for someone to leap out shouting, "Those are mine!"

No one did. The land stayed silent.

This morning I would've never picked up random clothes off of the ground and put them on, but then again, this morning I was not stranded buck-naked in a creepy red rock desert. *Beggars can't be choosers*, I thought, slipping on the shorts. Then I laughed, because in some weird twist of fate, they actually fit.

I'd always been skinny, built like a boy, with a boy's name to match. When all the girls grew curves, I'd just stretched, growing like crazy until I hit six feet. Recently my chest had made a small effort to catch up—the key word there was *small*—but I still had no hips. The boyish Bermudas were perfect.

I wrapped the bandana around my chest like a contestant on *Survivor*. *Where the heck's my tribe?* I joked. Glancing around the silent rocks, I realized that if there was a tribe here, I might not want to meet them. They might not be friendly.

No longer naked, I felt a million times better.

The sandals were big but better than nothing, and with protection for my feet, I moved quickly through the sea of red. Some rocks slid, others held firm. Soon the back of my right sandal looked like I'd dipped it in red paint. *Lookin' good*, I thought wryly, watching my step. These rocks seemed made for snakes. But nothing moved, except me.

Working my way around another deep crack, I slipped. Shards of red skittered away, like they were running, too. One looked like a dagger. I picked it up, hefted it once to gauge its weight, then whacked it against a boulder to test the dagger's strength. It held; if anything, the dagger scraped the boulder. *Like rock, paper, scissors*, I thought. *Dagger beats boulder.*

I tucked the shard into my waistband, thinking it might come in handy. *Dagger beats snake—or worse.* Then, the idea of me engaging in hand-to-hand combat, armed with a piddly rock dagger, was so absolutely ridiculous that I laughed, which was better than crying, but both emotions were so raw, so powerful, like two sides of the same coin, I feared too much laughing might flip me into tears and if I started, I wouldn't be able to stop. I stopped laughing, took a deep breath, and trekked on.

But I kept the dagger, just in case.

Eventually the red rock gave way to wavy black, like asphalt that had been poured but never flattened. Cracks split the black like snakes, but other than the cracks, this rock was fairly smooth. Best of all, it didn't shift under my feet.

Scrub brush popped up, dotting the black like dry tinder. As I passed an especially large thicket, a zebra peeked out. *Do zebras charge?* I wondered. Unsure about zebra aggression, I took a slow step backward.

I blinked and the zebra was gone.

Of course I'd hallucinate a zebra. Why couldn't I dream up Robert Pattinson or, better yet, a river of Gatorade? My mouth felt as dry as the cracked ground under my borrowed sandals.

The flat black rock gave way to rocky black earth with strange trees, trees with gray skeletal trunks and crispy green leaves dripping off branches like rain that wouldn't fall. Odd trees like skinny pines cropped up, and then I heard a familiar sound: the ocean—distant, but real. Before I could celebrate, the ground flashed like a mirror, and for one agonizing second, I thought it was a shimmer ready to rise. I was still conflicted as to whether the shimmers were good, or bad, or both.

Then I realized I was watching water. A pool of clear water, the size of a Ping-Pong table, nestled in the black rock. I scooped up a handful and smelled it. Fresh, or possibly brackish, the hint of brine could have been from the pool or blowing in from the sea. Figuring I had nothing to lose, I tried a sip. Cold and crisp, it tasted like heaven. I gulped handfuls until I was no longer thirsty. As I sat up, a blur of white glinted in the sky.

I ducked into the nearby thicket and pressed deep. Keeping completely still, I watched. To the east, two white-winged creatures soared high overhead, too far away to see. Other than the possibly imaginary zebra, these were the first creatures I'd seen. I spied legs—human legs—which totally creeped me out.

Bird men?

Where *was* I?

Twenty minutes later, I knew. I was in the most beautiful place I'd ever seen.

I stood at the tree line, gaping at the view. There was the ocean, dappled in late-afternoon sunlight, rolling into a black sand beach tucked into a small bay. Black rocks sprouted near shore, glittering like dark crystal. On each side, black cliffs rose in the distance, covered with patches of green. Close to me, majestic palm trees swayed in the breeze.

It was the kind of awesome beauty I'd only seen on the Travel Channel, when I'd watched a show about private islands owned by people with more wealth than everyone but God.

Holy crap, I thought, watching a towering wave roll and break. *I'm totally lost.*

I took another step, and my toe hit something hard. My sandal caught and stuck. I looked down, and when I realized what I'd kicked, I screamed.

It was a human skull.

CHAPTER 4

THAD
DAY 267, LATE AFTERNOON

What a waste of a day.

Despite three solid flyovers, we saw nothing. *Make that nothing good*, I thought, remembering the black rhino foraging near the groves. Another two tons of fresh Nil fun, complete with a built-in deadly weapon. Lucky us.

Right.

I dreaded the look on Nat's face when we came back empty-handed.

Shutting down that visual, I focused on the wind. In the first stroke of good luck today, the afternoon gusts blasted onshore, giving us the brakes we needed. Right now I'd take any advantage Nil offered. My arms were spent, and my eyes felt gritty. I was done, and if I had to guess, so was Jason.

Our landing site stretched less than half a kilometer ahead, sprawled between twin fissures of black. *Aim straight, drop nose, hold steady.*

Slowing in the headwind, we glided over the rocks about seven meters off the ground. Jason cruised ahead of me. Landing was its own little rush, not quite like takeoff, but close.

Then I heard it: a snap; it echoed through the air like a fire-cracker. A half second later, Jason's glider dipped erratically and nearly pitched him off.

"Jason!" I shouted. "Shift your weight!"

Jason slid right, switched his grip, and landed like a seasoned pro, even though he was only thirteen. And thanks to his cool head, he still had a chance to see fourteen.

I landed a wingspan away, my adrenaline pumping like I was still fifteen meters high.

"You okay?" I called.

"Yeah. Support rod broke." He held up his glider. One side bar dangled limply, like a broken arm.

As I stared at the wounded flyer, I had the weirdest sense that the break was a message from Nil. A not-so-subtle reminder of how close death really was—like we could forget. After all, the support cracked high enough to scare, but not high enough to kill. First the dead bird, now a broken glider.

Message received, I thought grimly. Nothing like a little Nil overkill.

We hiked back, hauling the crippled glider, knowing Natalie was waiting. Unfortunately, Bart found us first. He ambushed us as we approached the Shack.

"Thad," he started, his nasal whine sending my annoyance level off the charts, "we need to talk. I haven't been on Search in almost a month. Twenty-nine days."

"Hello, Bart," I said, peeling off my fly rig. "No, we didn't find Kevin. Or his clothes. But thanks for asking."

"Sorry," he said. His eyes flicked over Jason before circling back to me. "But I'm due, Thad, you know I am. It's not fair."

"It's not fair," I repeated, working to keep my voice level. "Really?" Sarcasm seeped in, and then for the first time since Kevin bolted, I lost it. "In case you haven't noticed, nothing about Nil is *fair*. It's not *fair* that you landed here. It's not fair that leaving is a crapshoot and that every damn day brings you closer to death. And it's definitely not *fair* that our past Leader, who spent months working her butt off for everyone else, is sitting by the fire, wondering if her boyfriend is dead, terrified she might never find out."

Bart sputtered, waffling between agreement and protest, neither of which I wanted to hear. *Why am I wasting my time?* I wondered.

I held up my hand. "You're right. It's not fair. But that's how it is. I don't pick the teams. So if you want someone to pick you, I'd suggest you pull your weight and then some." I looked evenly at Bart. "And hey, if you don't like the City rules, you can always leave."

Bart paled. "Fine." He turned, then spun back. "You know, losing the knife was an accident. It wasn't my fault."

"Yes, it was." Talla stepped out from the Shack, her blond hair tied in a hard knot. "You didn't secure it. And you lost it. Your fault."

"Of course you take his side. Everyone knows you're after his job. Or maybe you're just after him." Bart smirked.

Talla nearly snarled. "All I want is to get home. The sooner the better. Isn't that what *you* want?"

"Enough," I snapped. I was too drained from sweeps to handle much more. "Drop it, both of you. I need to talk to Natalie."

"Too late," Talla said. She pointed to the fire, where Jason stood beside Natalie, his arm wrapped around her shoulders and her head hung in defeat.

God, I hated this place.

CHAPTER 5

CHARLEY
DAY 5, LATE AFTERNOON

I should have been a Girl Scout. Or a ninja. Or better yet a Girl Scout ninja with a black belt in self-defense.

That was my latest epiphany as another juicy fish darted past my outstretched fingers. I could forage through the local Kroger and cook up a mean feast of shrimp and grits, but I'd never caught a shrimp or ground a grit in my life. I'd never fished, camped, identified edible plants, or learned how to start a fire without matches. And I sure as heck had never taken karate.

Volleyball camp suddenly seemed lame.

Exhausted, I flopped down on the sand. This morning I'd collected bamboo and palm fronds to craft a shelter at the tree line, something to give me much-needed shade from the midday sun. I'd remembered my geometry teacher rambling on about triangles being the strongest shape in nature, and it turned out he was right. Using bamboo as scaffolding and fronds as coverage, construction had taken most of the day, but the result was pretty awesome, not that there was anyone to see it. The effort had turned my arms to jelly. I was bone tired, and I was hungry. And I was still totally freaking out.

The last five days had been the longest of my life.

I didn't know where I was or how to get home. I'd seen no ships, no planes, and most disturbing of all, no people. *At least none alive,* I corrected myself reluctantly. The human skull was never far from my thoughts. A bleached-white skull, half buried in dirt, with my sandal wedged in the empty eye socket. I'd yanked my foot out and run away, and I hadn't gone near it since.

What happened to the dead-skull person? Did he starve to death? Was he killed? If so, by what? None of these thoughts brought me to a happy place, but then again, right now nothing did. It was like I'd fallen into my own personal *Twilight Zone* episode, and I had no clue how to get out. It had everything to do with that shimmer; I knew it. But I hadn't seen any shimmers since the red rock field. And believe me, I'd been looking.

At least I'd found food. Strange green fruits hung on trees to the north. I'd watched a bird eat one, so I figured it wouldn't kill me. I'd picked and peeled two. Although they were as sour as lemons, I'd devoured the green fruit anyway, eating everything but the rind.

Rounding out my all-fruit diet were pineapples and coconuts. Using my rock dagger, I could mutilate a pineapple in a quick minute, but the coconuts were tougher. I'd pierce the shell, tip back the fruit, and chug the milk like I was swigging a Sprite, then after drinking it dry, I'd bang the husk against a rock. But so far every single coconut had refused to break, and I'd been through at least eight. Not even my rock dagger could crack one, and shards of that stuff could slash through almost anything, including my heel, which was still tender and swollen. Soaking my foot in the ocean seemed to be helping, but each time I sat in the sea, fish teased me mercilessly, flaunting their edible selves.

I really wanted fish, even if it meant eating sushi. Unable to capture a fish by hand—I mean, who does that?—I made a spear using materials left over from my shelter project. Okay, less a spear, more like a bamboo rod with a sharp rock tied to the end with a green palm frond strip. I figured maybe I could whack a fish.

But like cracking coconuts, spearfishing with a crappy, homemade spear proved impossible. Maybe it was my spear, maybe it was my poor technique. It didn't matter; the result was the same: no fish.

Frustrated, I picked up my worthless spear and chucked it into the sea. The spear flew over the water, skipped once, then sank. *Super,* I thought, instantly regretting my impulsive throw. If I didn't find some decent food, I'd disappear, too.

Leaving the water, I wandered south. *Maybe I'll find a nut tree,* I thought optimistically. Then I prayed I'd know an edible nut if I saw one.

I passed the thick stand of bamboo, then the grove of palms, but desperate for more than coconut milk, I kept going, venturing farther south than ever. The vegetation thinned as the bay curved toward the sea, ending at a stern cliff. Black and massive, the cliff was bare rock. Near the base, a small bush with glossy green leaves grew alone. Tucked inside the leaves were bumpy yellow fruits.

More fruit, I thought without enthusiasm, but at least this fruit offered variety. The bush looked healthy, the warty fruit less so, and as I went to pluck a yellow fruit, the unmistakable stench of vomit hit me in the face. Gagging, I stumbled away, working not to retch.

Leaving the stinky plant, I climbed. The cliff was riddled with openings, perfect for hands and feet. I fell into an easy rhythm, and after turning the bend, I found myself inside a series of massive rock arches.

The view was stunning.

Blue sky filled the openings, perfectly framed in black. Below me, water hissed and spit against rocks, churning white on black. I turned in a slow circle, and something caught my eye. Something smooth in a wash of crags.

The largest arch, still a volleyball court's distance away, boasted a large flat spot at eye level. No, not flat, at least not totally. Fissures graced the rock face, too uniform to be natural.

Intrigued, I hiked closer. A carving decorated the rock face: a maze, etched in a perfect circle, with a human figure in the very center. *Like a primitive cave drawing*, I thought. But the longer I studied the carving, the more I realized the maze was too symmetrical to be primitive; it was more like one of those freaky designs that pop up on cornfields overnight. But that wasn't right either. Given the level of detail, this glyph was no overnight sensation. The human figure at the epicenter suggested the carver was human, or maybe that's what I wanted to believe. What I *needed* to believe. Despite my gruesome skull discovery, I hadn't shaken my alien planet worry.

I wasn't sure how long I stood there, tracing the rings and trying to discern meaning from their existence. Long enough for my legs to cramp. Long enough for my stomach to rebel. Long enough for the air to turn cool.

The chill snapped my reverie. Looking up, I saw that the sun had dropped, and I couldn't scramble away fast enough. I didn't want to be caught out here at night.

Leaving the rock arches took longer than I expected. My original pathways were blocked by the tide, forcing me higher to avoid being crushed against the rocks by churning water. By the time I made it back to my hideout, I was shaking and sweating. And I was *starving*.

Unfortunately, coconuts were the only choice I had.

I drained one quickly, but gagged on the sweet milk and fought to keep it down. Wracked with stomach cramps, I longed for a bagel, or toast. And a Sprite. A fountain Sprite, on crushed ice, lemon-limey sweet with just enough bubbles to settle my stomach. Holding my stomach, I shuddered. Then, watching the sun drop close to the water, I shuddered again.

The nights were a million times worse than the days.

Nights were pitch-black, full of claustrophobic, creepy darkness.

Nights were when the shakes came, from cold, and from fear. I was absurdly terrified of nighttime critters, not just weird bird men or potential aliens. My greatest fear was snakes. I'd developed an almost paralyzing fear of them, ever since I'd found a cottonmouth sleeping in my Rollerblade when I was six. I knew my snake phobia wasn't totally rational—that I had more to worry about right now than snakes—but for all I knew, the dead-skull person had died of a snakebite. I'd spent the last four nights huddled against a tree, armed with my rock dagger, waiting. I'd been stood up, at least by anything creepy, but I'd barely slept.

And now the darkness was back.

I jogged over to a large black rock on the sand and curled beside it, soaking up the residual warmth from the sun. For the first time, I stayed on the beach as night fell, watching the stars come out. As the constellations took shape, I blinked. There was the Little Dipper, glowing brilliantly against the clear night sky, with Polaris shining brightest of all.

I was on Earth, but I had no idea *where* on Earth I was. Or when.

I was totally alone.

Like a rubber band stretched past its limit, I broke. I bawled, like Em after the car accident, but not like Em, because there was no one to hold my hands and tell me everything would be okay. Nothing was okay, especially me. I wept until I was as empty as the beach around me and then I lay there, spent. Still cold, I no longer shook. I was oddly numb.

I'd just dozed off when a crunching sound echoed like an alarm.

The noise intensified, then stopped. Silence rushed in, louder than before. Pressed tight to my rock, I listened. A twig cracked, then another, snapping as crisply as the break of dry bones. A whoop, guttural and plaintive, reverberated through the night air.

Something was moving through the trees behind me. Something that didn't sound human.

Something that just might be as hungry as me.

CHAPTER
6

"Nat—"

"No." Her face was set, like her mind. It wasn't the first time she'd reminded me of my kid sister, Holly.

"Look, you've got Priority," I said. "You need to go."

The firelight made Natalie's cheeks as hollow as her eyes. They'd been that way ever since her Search team came back without Kevin.

When Natalie stayed silent, I tried a different tack. "Plus, it'll give you something else to think about, eh?"

Natalie turned to me, shadows falling across her face. "You think going on Search will take my mind off Kevin?" She laughed, a lifeless sound. "It's all I think about. Every minute of every day. How much I miss him, how much I want to be with him, how much I hope he made it. But if I go on Search, I might never know. And worse, what if I find—" Pressing her lips into a tight line, she shook her head.

"Okay," I agreed, like I had any say in her choice. "But soon, Nat, okay? You won't get anywhere sitting here."

"I hear you," Natalie said.

But are you listening? I thought. *Because Nil sure as hell is.* Surely this was part of Nil's fun. Watching veterans squirm as our days ran out, crowing as we lost time to indecision or, in Nat's case, grief.

"Promise you'll think about it?" I asked, using my gentlest big brother tone. "About going?"

Natalie lifted her haunted eyes to mine. "It's all I think about."

Don't we all? I thought. The wind sliced through the trees, and I swear I heard Nil laugh.

Rives came over and gave Nat a silent hug, then sat on the rock beside her. No one had much to say, and within minutes Natalie stood.

"I'm out. See you guys in the morning. Another dawn, another day." She didn't even try to smile.

"Chin up, twin," Rives said. "It's not over till the fat lady sings." He cupped his hand behind his ear, making an exaggerated show of listening. "Nope, don't hear a thing." Rives dropped his hand and grinned. "Definitely no singing."

Nat looked at Rives, her eyes weary. "There are no fat ladies on Nil, you know that." She squeezed his shoulder. "But thanks."

"I hate this," Rives said after Natalie walked away. He stared at the darkness where Natalie disappeared. "God, I hope Kevin made it. That's a good girl right there."

"I know."

For a minute, we just sat there, watching flames cut into the night. A Nil cat, a tiny gray one I'd never seen before, rubbed against a fire-warmed rock, arching her back and purring. Cats were everywhere on Nil. Some harmless, some not. This one was so small I wondered if it was a native. Watching the cat, I thought of Burton. He'd been conspicuously absent since I'd dissed his dead bird offering. That random train of thought shot me straight back to Kevin, and the mental ride sucked.

Rives leaned back on his elbows and looked at the stars. "Do you ever get used to it?" he asked quietly. "The waiting?"

"Nope," I said. "Sucks every time."

Rives nodded. "That's what I thought."

That night, it took forever to fall asleep. I lay there, thinking about Kevin, and about Natalie. But mostly I thought about Nil.

Nil's like that girl you spot in the lodge after a full day of kick-ass boarding, when you're stoked and high on life. She looks good, freakin' hot. Long hair, tight body, killer smile. Has a name like . . . Mallory.

But once you really get to know her, the truth rips your guts out. The truth is, she's cruel. Heartless. The kind of girl who sleeps with your best friend when your back is turned. And once the mask falls off, so does the glamour. That's the island of Nil in a nutshell. Blow-your-mind gorgeous, until you peel away the façade and see her for who she really is.

It wasn't the first time I wondered what she had in store for me.

CHAPTER 7

CHARLEY
DAY 12, DAWN

I hadn't slept in three days, and the mere thought of a coconut made me gag. I knew that if I could just eat some protein, I'd feel better—or at least not starve. So for the past few miserable hours, I'd been crafting a net from palm fronds.

I glanced at my net, decided it looked ridiculous, and kept weaving anyway.

The air was cool and dark; the stars were just beginning to fade. Huddled beside a rock, I worked robotically, totally aware I was in a mental free fall. I felt nauseous and shaky, like I'd downed too many energy drinks at once. Two nights ago, I'd heard a distinct roar, throaty and wild, like a lion in the Atlanta zoo. But for all I knew, the roar belonged to a dinosaur. At this point, anything seemed possible, except sleep.

Last night had been the worst yet. First I'd heard roars, then sounds I couldn't identify. Not a roar, not a howl, but more like an inhuman cackle. It lasted forever, echoing through the darkness. I didn't know what the heck it was, and I didn't want to find out. All I knew was that *something* was out there in the woods, something other than just the random goat that kept sneaking up on me in the night. Something I didn't want to meet.

As I forced another frond into place, I tallied my personal scorecard. Eleven nights of freaky darkness. Five with visits from the nocturnal goat, two with prehistoric roars, and one with creepy cackles. And eleven long days without solid food, decent sleep, people, or shimmers. I thought I'd seen a shimmer yesterday, moving south on the black sand, but I wasn't certain. I wondered if the zebra was real. If any of this was real. There'd been no rain, and the weather didn't change. Each day was sunny, clear, breezy, and quiet.

Worse than the silence was the isolation. I thought again of Hell. Or purgatory. Or something else, possibly worse, and I was in it. And yet it was the most beautiful nowhereland I could imagine. The sunsets were gorgeous: brilliant fire shooting across the water until the sun fell into the sea, and the sunrises were just as stunning. Naturally I was awake for both since I couldn't sleep. The sand was as black as coal, the water as clear as glass. Farther from shore, the water turned to glittering aquamarine as it stretched toward the sky, vast and breathtaking.

It was too beautiful to have all to myself, and yet I did.

Whose clothes are you wearing, Charley? my mind whispered. *Whose skull did you find?* Maybe I wasn't alone, but I sure felt like it. Home seemed light-years away.

I wondered what my mom and dad were doing right now. Were they putting up flyers with pictures of me? What about Target? Did the parking lot have security cameras, and if so, what would they show? The shimmer? Me fainting? I prayed they hadn't captured me naked. Then I realized it didn't matter, because whatever the Target-cam had recorded, it wouldn't help anyone find me here. The only person who could get me out of here was me.

I stared at my wilted net in shock.

When had I switched from escape to survival? I hadn't explored in days. I'd stuck near my shelter, conserving energy and spending the heat of the day out of the sun.

No more.

I'd leave. I'd go back to the red rock field and look for shimmers; they were the only clue I had. But if I wanted food, I'd better grab it now.

I gave myself one day. *This* day. To gather food, then either way, I was gone.

The sun woke, rising quickly. A bird soared overhead, and in a flash of survival brilliance, I decided to hunt for nests. If I could steal some eggs, I could suck out the insides like I'd been draining coconuts, a primitive version of a protein shake.

After stashing my net, I strode along the tree line, heading south. To my dismay, my goat broke from the trees and followed me. Yesterday I'd made the mistake of tossing him fruit rinds, and he'd escalated his stalking ever since.

"Shoo!" I scolded.

The goat looked at me like I was crazy. Determined to ignore him, I continued walking, scouring the trees for nests, but each time I glanced back, the goat was still there. With my luck, he'd scare off the very birds I was trying to track.

Down the beach, a handful of birds circled, lazy and watchful. More clustered on the black sand—like vultures, but smaller. They were pecking at something on the ground. Mindful of the skull, I approached warily, but the goat charged ahead and startled the birds. One dived at my face. Jumping back, I screamed.

On the sand, the birds shifted. Through the gap, I saw a horseshoe crab carcass.

Just a crab, I thought with a rush of relief.

Could I eat raw crab? I gagged at the thought; the answer was no.

I moved toward the sea, giving the crab and its scavengers a wide berth. My persistent goat took the high road, trotting along the tree line.

The rising sun spread across my shoulders. I walked slowly along the water's edge, soaking up the warmth, and I'd just geared myself up to head back into the cool shade of the trees when a spotted animal leaped from the tree line. The size of a large dog, it moved like a cat, low and fast, like a crazed mutant cheetah. Still airborne, the cat-dog sank its teeth into the goat's flank, flicked its jaw once and threw the goat to the ground. The birds scattered; the goat went down without a fight. The spotted animal tore into the goat like this was a National Geographic special.

WHAT WAS THAT? my brain screamed.

I backed into the water, terrified the animal would decide my goat was just an appetizer to the main course of me. Submerged to my neck, I moved parallel to the beach, willing myself invisible and keeping an eye on the cat-dog. It was wholly focused on its goat feast. When the animal was a mere speck, I left the water and raced to my hideout at the edge of the trees.

Forget eggs, fish, and my plan to leave in the morning.

I'd had enough of this secluded bay, where animals roared and people died and goat-killing animals leaped from the trees without a sound. I was getting the heck out of this freaky place *now*, before the next predator came after me. I. Was. Done.

I took off my chest wrap, squeezed the water out, and put it back on, thankful the cloth dried quickly. Moving with desperate efficiency, I ate my last greenfruit and washed it down with water stored in my hollow coconuts. I drank them dry, knowing I'd refill them on my way. My half-finished net lay under a bush at the sand's edge. I dragged it out, found my dagger, and, peering through the leaves, I cast one final look at my beach.

Then I nearly fell through the bush in shock. Two boys were walking down the beach. *My* beach.

And they were coming straight toward me.

CHAPTER 8

THAD
DAY 278, DAWN

The mood in the City sucked. Even for Nil, it was a new low.

I lay there, hating Nil for the torture. For the constant mental merry-go-round. For the current City vibe, which was one body short of a burial. The wait for news on Kevin was killing us, which was probably the point.

After grabbing breakfast, I strode to the Wall. So many names, too many names. All gouged into the wood, first names only. I checked out Kevin's, like maybe good news had come in the night, even though I knew it hadn't. Of course the space beside his name sat empty. Waiting, like us.

Finding my name, I tapped each letter, too restless today to trace. Then I tapped my blank space. No cross, no check. *I'm still here.* Then I glanced back at Kevin's. No check, no cross. But he's gone.

Like Ramia.

Please not like Ramia.

Eight months after she vanished, Ramia was still MIA. No body, no clue. And eight months later, her final words still weirded me out.

For the first time, I wondered if Ramia had predicted Kevin's fate, too.

It doesn't matter; it means nothing. It was the same pep talk I gave myself whenever I thought of Ramia, which happened more often than I cared to admit. Pushing Ramia and crosses and every other Nil negative from my head, I ditched the Wall and went to collect my board.

The Shack was deserted. I didn't go inside; I didn't need to. All our boards were racked outside, and right now I had tunnel vision. But as I hefted my favorite plank, I sensed I was being watched. Turning in a slow circle, I scoped out my perimeter.

Clear. No movement, no people.

I chalked my jitters up to lack of sleep and went to find Jason.

He was down by the water, chunking rocks into the sea, lips in a line. Jason was the oldest thirteen-year-old I knew. Kevin had looked after Jason like a big brother, and nearly two weeks after Kevin bailed, I still wasn't used to seeing Jason alone.

"Hey, man," I said when I was in range. "You ready?" I gestured to my surfboard.

"Yeah." Jason hauled off and threw his last rock. The black piece flew and fell. He watched it disappear, then without a word, he picked up his board and followed me into the water.

The waves were solid five-footers, but a relentless crosswind made them bumpy. As I made the drop, if I closed my eyes, just for a second it was like shooting down a double black at Whistler. It didn't scratch my snowboarding itch, not even close, but this was Nil, and I'd take what I could get. Still, I kept my closure to an extended blink. Like Kevin told me on Day One, Nil demanded eyes wide open.

The current moved fast, pulling us south. At this rate, we'd end up down by Black Bay, a long trek back with a board—especially one made of solid wood like ours were—and we still had to fish. I'd just made the call to go in when a faint scream sliced across the water. Then it vanished, disappearing like backspray gusting off a wave.

Board held tight, I searched for the screamer.

Talla was paddling out, mouth closed. One look at her typical game face told me it wasn't her.

Back on the beach, Rives led a crew in wind sprints, running balls to the wall, working on speed. Nothing unusual there. No one screaming like a girl.

Then I realized if someone had screamed, I wouldn't have heard it over the surf.

Get out of my head, Nil.

I signaled to Jason and pointed toward shore. He gave me a thumbs-up. As I dragged my board through the froth, I glanced toward Black Bay, the scream lingering in my ears like water I couldn't clear. Or maybe that was Nil. New teams had launched, Kevin was still MIA, and Nat refused to budge. And then there was me, wired so tight that I was hearing things.

Ten minutes later, nets in hand and minds on edge, Jason and I made tracks for the pools.

Our fish pools are ingenious, no credit to me. They were here when I got here, and they'll stay when I leave. Black rock pools that fill with the tides. Slam the reed door traps, and spearfishing's as easy as shooting fish in a barrel, which essentially was the plan.

But something pulled me to the Bay.

"How 'bout this," I told Jason. "Let's head to Black Bay first, look for redfruit, then we'll fish on the way back. Sound good?"

Jason nodded, and in that moment, I knew he wanted to avoid the City as much as I did.

We cut inland, took the path through the cliff, then popped out near the Bay. The first clump of redfruit trees was loaded, but the fruit was still green, so we kept walking. Sand crunched under our feet, like an endless stretch of broken shark's teeth. Chunkier than the white sand near the City, this sand was as black as night, as black as death. Classic Nil beauty.

"It's mighty quiet," Jason commented, his head on a swivel.

I stopped immediately. "Hold up," I said, raising one hand.

We stood perfectly still. Without our footfalls, the beach was cemetery quiet. Possibly Nil-up-to-something quiet. I swept the air, then the trees, looking for movement. *Eyes wide open.*

Up ahead, a bush jerked and snapped back, a motion too sharp to be wind.

"Jason," I said, pulling my knife, "movement. Ten meters, straight ahead. Come to my other side, okay?"

Jason moved immediately. "Person?" he whispered. "Or animal?"

Person, place, thing, or animal? my mind asked. A game I played as a kid. Not so fun on Nil. I'd take person over animal any day, and both over a thing. Like I'd figured out early on, it was the things that could kill you. Place was the only category not in question. That answer was always Nil.

"Don't know," I said. "Something. Maybe nothing."

Walking again, I kept my eyes trained on the spot where I'd seen movement.

The same bush swayed. A definite movement, more like a parting. My fingers choked down on my knife.

"Something's coming," I told Jason.

The bush shifted sideways, and a figure stepped out. A girl. Tall, lean. Long legs, long muscles. Great shoulders. Full lips. Even though she looked island-thin, she was hands-down the most gorgeous girl I'd ever seen.

And she was wearing Kevin's clothes.

CHAPTER
9

When I stepped onto the sand, I got my first good look at the boys.

Each one carried a brown net—I felt a sharp pang of net envy right then—and a gourd strung across one shoulder. Both wore shorts made of the same white material as mine; neither wore shirts or shoes. And both were really tan, without any body fat. Considering my own nutritional predicament, I could see why. The shorter one had curly brown hair and freckles. His nose was peeling, badly. He looked fifteen, at most.

I was captivated by the taller boy.

He looked eighteen, maybe nineteen. Blessed with high cheekbones and sandy blond hair that brushed his broad shoulders, he looked like he'd just stepped off the cover of a cheesy romance novel in the grocery store book section. Definitely human, and totally hot.

He stared at me like I was a ghost. His stance next to the younger boy was protective. I thought of the goat-killer, then noticing his slightly raised hand clutching a knife, abruptly I thought, *Maybe he's wary of me.* For a second, I saw myself through his eyes: gaunt, sunburned, not a speck of makeup, looking like some six-foot wild child from the bush after twelve days of oceanside camping. I was a tropical freak show.

"Hey," I said, trying to smile. It seemed I'd forgotten how to form one. I made an effort to wave and look less threatening, but ended up feeling like a goofball as neither boy smiled.

The shorter one pointed his spear at me. "Those are Kevin's clothes." His dark eyes were accusing.

The taller boy reached out and gently lowered the first boy's spear. "Did you see him?" he asked. "A guy? Dark hair, about your height?" He rested his hand on the younger boy's shoulder, and his voice softened. "Or his body?"

They think I stole these clothes! From a dead body!

Horrified, my words spilled out in a rush. "No! I didn't see anyone! I mean, y'all are the first people I've seen! I found these clothes, in a pile, way back there"—I waved my arm wildly toward the red desert, then grabbed my top as it slipped. I'd grown so skinny, there wasn't much to keep it up—"in the middle of a red rock field."

Relief washed over the boys' faces like sunlight. They grinned at each other, and the taller boy clapped the shorter one on the back as the short one threw a fist-pump and shouted, "Yes!" Then, as if they'd just remembered I was there, they turned back to me.

"I'm sorry," the tall, golden-haired boy said. His features were no longer wary. His eyes were a rich sapphire blue, lighter than I'd first thought. "I'm Thad, and this is Jason."

The younger boy smiled and waved. "Hi."

"Hey," I said, struck by the shift in their expressions. "I'm Charley."

"Nice to meet you, Charley," Thad said, flashing a cover-model grin. "Welcome to paradise."

For a moment I couldn't think. Then I regrouped, speaking fast. "There's an animal. With spots. Back there." I pointed down the beach. "It jumped from the trees and ate my goat."

"You have a goat?" Thad raised one eyebrow, something I'd always wanted to do but couldn't.

"Not really." I felt like an idiot. "It was stalking me."

"Was." Thad nodded.

"Right. It's dead. Because *something* attacked it and ate it for breakfast."

Thad nodded again, looking oddly unconcerned, which was crazy since *a giant cat-dog just ate my goat.*

I glared at him. My adrenaline rush was fading fast, but I had a spark of fire left, and I leveled it at Thad. "Look, something ate that goat. Sort of like a big dog, but it moved like a cat, and it had *spots.* What *was* it?" I demanded.

"Hungry," he said, breaking into a grin.

"Well"—I floundered a bit as I stared at his smile—"are there more of those things? Like a pack?"

Thad shrugged. "I doubt it. If I had to guess, I'd say it was the lone hyena we've seen lurking around the City. Usually it goes after rabbits or a Nil cat."

"Rabbits?" I frowned. "I haven't seen any rabbits. Or cats."

"Maybe the hyena ate them." As he grinned, his eyes sparkled. Gracious, was this boy *hot.* And slightly infuriating.

"Charley, do you know how long you've been here?"

I didn't hesitate. "Twelve days."

He did that eyebrow thing again. "Twelve?"

I nodded. "I've counted the days by marking a tree at sunrise, so I'm pretty sure I'm right, unless I was out for a day before I woke up, but I don't think so. I would have burned, because I was—" I broke off, realizing I was babbling out loud. I never babbled. *Did solitary confinement make people babble? Or just Thad?* I couldn't think straight.

"Let me guess. You woke up naked, eh?"

I had the terrible thought that *he'd* seen me naked.

He chuckled. "Everyone does, not just you. But hey, now you've got Kevin's clothes, eh?" He pointed to my borrowed Bermudas.

"Right," I said, embarrassed. Something nagged at me, but my lethargic brain refused to cooperate. Thad spoke before I could find my question.

"Charley, do you remember the date? When you passed out, before you woke up here?"

"August tenth."

"And the year?"

When I told him, he nodded, as if I'd confirmed what he already knew. I wanted to ask him what he thought the date was, but my head was full of sludge. Like circuits weren't firing, or pathways weren't connecting. Distracted, I watched his hair brush his shoulders, his question echoing in my head. *Do you remember the date . . . before you woke up here?*

"Where's *here?*" I asked, latching on to that word like a life preserver. "Where am I?"

"Black Bay."

Thad's answer threw me. Before I could rephrase, he kept going, like some gorgeous island interviewer. "Charley, sorry for getting so personal, but how old are you?"

"Seventeen." I raised my chin. "How old are *you?*"

He smiled. "Seventeen."

"Really?" I said, unable to hide my surprise. "You look older."

Thad laughed. "That's what a little island living does for you. Speaking of island living, don't take this the wrong way, but you look like you could use some food. And sleep. Why don't you come with us to the City? We've got plenty of food and beds, and you can meet everyone when you're ready."

I stared at him. I didn't know him, and now I was thinking about going off with him, to a strange city who knows where. After twelve days in isolation, the thought was a huge relief. I couldn't believe I hesitated, and yet, I did.

"It's okay, Charley," Thad said quietly. "We've all been where you are."

"Not all," Jason spoke up. "Samuel came from the east, and Talla came from the groves—"

"Jason." Thad looked at the younger boy. "Enough. You know what I mean."

Grinning, Jason drew his fingers across his lips in a zipping motion. Thad turned back to me. "Charley?"

Looking into Thad's eyes, I decided to trust him—as if I had any other option. "Okay," I said, feeling shaky and weirdly overwhelmed. My adrenaline high was gone.

I thought of my dagger, my pitiful half-woven fishnet, and hollow coconuts. It wasn't much, but it seemed important to take them—to have something of mine. Of *me*, of whatever was left of me, which judging by my hip bones, wasn't much. "Let me just grab my things."

Thad looked curious. "Need any help?"

"I've got it." I wanted a minute to gather my thoughts, because my head was scary out-of-sorts.

I turned, moving so quickly my brain sloshed in my head. Behind me, Thad kept talking to the boy whose name I'd already forgotten. The boys' voices faded. My legs felt heavy; each step took more effort than the last. The coconuts became bricks. Black spots danced in front of my eyes, blurring like spots on a hungry hyena.

I had a moment of absolute clarity when I knew exactly what was about to happen. And just like before, I was powerless to stop it.

CHAPTER
10

THAD

DAY 278, LATE MORNING

As Charley turned, I wondered what she had to grab. She'd only been here twelve days. Longer than most rookies lasted slumming solo, but still, not a lot of time to start a collection.

I looked at Jason. "Stay put. And stay alert, okay?"

Jason nodded. "I'm on it."

I followed Charley to the edge of the brush. Watching her move, without warning, my mind flashed back to the moment she'd stepped onto the beach. She'd stood on the black sand, chin raised, Kevin's shorts slung low on her hips and his bandana wrapped around her chest, her dark hair whipping around her shoulders, like a kick-ass character from a graphic novel.

I'd been shocked.

Shocked by her looks, shocked by her clothes. I was so shocked that she'd beaten me to the meet-and-greet, which was a first. Her accent was thick, like honey. I liked the way words dripped off her tongue, but what I liked the most right now was that she'd found Kevin's clothes—just his clothes.

Back in the present, relief and elation slammed through me

again, two waves of a tight set, washing away days of worry. *You did it, man.*

I couldn't wait to give Natalie the good news. I'd let Jason tell her, I decided. Let him relive it again. And I'd tell Rives about the hyena.

A bamboo lean-to blended into the trees, sleek and impressive. Beside it, Charley moved slowly. Maybe she was reconsidering coming with us. When I'd asked her to come to the City, she'd looked at me like I'd asked her to go skinny-dipping. She wouldn't be the first to bail on the City, but the thought of her scouting Nil alone made me cold.

She picked up a rock, some green strips, and two coconuts. The coconuts were small and underripe, and I was about to tell her to leave them when she took an odd step sideways.

"Charley, you okay?" I stepped closer, wondering what was up with her.

She didn't answer.

I hesitated. "Charley?"

She dropped the rock, then the coconuts, like a juggler who's lost control. Green strips fell like confetti. Charley crumpled to the ground, where her head struck a boulder with a sickening crack.

I ran over, way too late. *C'mon, Thad.* I wanted to kick my own ass. *You can time it better than that.*

Charley was out cold. Bright red blood dripped down her temple. I kneeled beside her, not sure what to do. Moving head trauma victims was never a good call, but neither was sending Jason back alone for help. And leaving her here wasn't an option. It'd be like a sacrifice to Nil.

I picked up Charley, thinking she was too light for someone her height.

Jason came over as I stepped onto the beach. "What happened?" he asked.

"She passed out. Hit her head on a rock."

"She's bleeding."

"Really? I hadn't noticed." I scowled at Jason. "Let's hustle. Watch the tree line. And keep a hand on your spear."

We strode in silence, retracing our steps. Charley didn't stir, which scared me.

"Thad, look!" Jason's shout was excited. "See it? Near the high-tide mark!"

"What?" I panted.

"Gate at two o'clock!"

Now I saw it. Up ahead, glittering air rose from the ground, writhing like a sheet of living ice.

"Go, Jason!" I said. "Run!"

"What?" He looked stunned. "No way! It's yours!"

"No. I'm taking Charley back. Now go!"

Indecision flickered across Jason's face.

"Go, dammit! *Run!*"

He shed his gear, then took off like a shot. Digging deep, arms pumping, Jason bolted like a beach sprint, only this time it was the real deal. Seventy meters out, the iridescent wall of air rolled away from us, racing toward the trees.

"Angle up!" I shouted.

Jason didn't acknowledge me, but I knew he'd heard. His head stayed down, his feet flying over the black sand.

Run, Jason. Get there. He had the speed, the distance. The angle.

Victory roared in my chest. Jason was less than a meter away.

Then the gate collapsed, dissolving into a shimmering line, then a black dot. And then it was gone.

Only one victory today, Nil teased, shaking her polished finger, her island eyes laughing. *Not two.*

Jason stood near where the outbound had vanished, his hands on his knees, his chest heaving.

"Any more?" I yelled. My gut said no, the first one was too fast, but you never knew what Nil might have up her designer sleeve.

"Nope. A single," Jason shouted.

Damn, I thought. Because if it was a double, Jason would make it. But it wasn't his day. Or mine. Or anyone else's. It was a single gate, with no takers.

His face flushed from his sprint, Jason strolled back, catching his breath. No need to run now, not for another twenty-three hours and fifty-nine minutes.

Charley's eyes stayed closed.

"Hang on, Charley," I murmured. "We're almost there."

Leaving the black sand, I wove through the trees, grateful for the shortcut through the cliff. Almost running but not, I kept one foot on the ground, trying not to jostle Charley. Soon I saw the ring of A-frames. Close enough to see people by the water, too far for them to hear. I'd just left the cliff behind when Jason caught up with me, loaded with his gear and mine. And Charley's.

"Now what?" he huffed.

"Find Natalie," I said. "Tell her about Kevin and Charley. Tell her we need help. Tell her about Kevin first!"

With a nod, he took off, running almost as fast as when he chased the gate. But this time his head was high, and he was grinning like a fool.

I looked down at Charley. Her golden eyes were still closed.

"Hey, Charley," I whispered. "Welcome to Nil City."

CHAPTER 11

THAD
DAY 278, AFTER NOON

The sound wave hit us before we reached the City's edge. Whoops and cheers blasted through the air; news of Kevin's success was spreading fast.

Charley didn't move.

Natalie came running, tears streaming down her smiling face. But when she got a solid look at Charley, her grin faded. Eyes on Charley, Nat shifted into full-on command mode, one step shy of barking orders.

"That's a lot of blood, but head injuries bleed so much, it's hard to tell how bad it really is," Natalie said as we walked toward the A-frames. "She might have a concussion. Someone needs to stay with her tonight and wake her every few hours."

I almost interrupted to tell her I knew all about concussions, but she was on a roll so I let her go. I'd smacked my head into a tree snowboarding when I was thirteen, knocked myself out, then spent the entire night throwing up—and that was with a helmet. Without one, I'd have died for sure. I still wear a helmet when I board. Or did.

Nil had snow, but I'd never touched it. It dusted the peak of the tallest mountain, and we didn't have the clothes or the gear to play on it. A snowcapped mountain, a total Nil tease.

Charley moaned, and I cut Natalie off mid-sentence. "Let's get her settled," I said, praying I hadn't shaken Charley on the way back and made her concussion worse. The sooner I could lay her down, the better. "Where?"

"My house," Natalie said. "I'll clean up her head and stay with her."

"I'll stay," I said quickly.

She looked at me, curiously. "Not yet. Rives needs you. He and Bart got into it about watch. Someone needs to settle Bart down." Natalie grinned. "As in you."

Bart. Charley and Bart, two polar opposites—the contrast was vintage Nil. Bart was like a gnat, the kind that buzzed around your ear, persistent and annoying, regardless of how many times you swatted it away. Right now the last person I wanted to deal with was Bart, and he was the one pulling me away from Charley. Classic.

Slipping into Nat's A-frame, Charley in my arms, I moved toward the bed on the right.

"No!" Natalie jumped to block me. "Not that bed. This one." She pointed to the other bed.

"Nat, you're killing me," I groaned as I stumbled to the other bed, which looked exactly like the first. My forearms were dying; my quads weren't much better. Sometimes Nat's leadership slipped into irritating bossiness, like now. The bed didn't matter; Charley did.

Once Charley was settled, Natalie went to work treating Charley's gash. Neosporin and Motrin would have been great, but we were stuck with salt water and deadleaf. I watched Natalie wrap a cloth around her own hand, then pick up a handful of mashed deadleaf and press it against Charley's wound. Throughout Natalie's doctoring, Charley never moved.

"Do you think she's okay?" I stared at Charley's closed eyes. "She's totally out."

"I think so. Her cut's not that bad. She's really thin and probably dehydrated, not to mention exhausted. Twelve days is a long time." Holding the deadleaf compress steady, Natalie used her free hand to gently brush hair away from Charley's eyes. The simple kindness of it made my throat tight. Like Rives said, Nat was a good girl.

As if she'd read my thoughts, Natalie looked up, smiling. "When I saw her earlier, it took me back to the day I stumbled into the City, and I'd only been wandering three days. Twelve! No wonder she's so skinny. I'd kill for her legs, though."

I couldn't help glancing at Charley's legs. They were covered by a thin sheet, but I remembered them being long, lean, and sexy as hell. My mind flashed back to Charley on the beach, then bloody in my arms.

Open your eyes, I thought. *Open your eyes so I know you're okay.*

"Thad?"

Natalie was staring at me.

"Yeah?" I cleared my mind, or tried to.

"Anyone else back?"

"Not that I know of. But I saw today's gate. It flashed at Black Bay. Jason almost caught it. He was close."

Natalie sighed. "Close doesn't count. And if you saw the gate, it means Samuel didn't catch it either. Or Li."

"Nope. Or anyone else." I shot Natalie a pointed look. "So you'll head out tomorrow?"

"The next. I want to stay for the Nil Night."

"Okay." I looked back at Charley, who was either unconscious or asleep. "Anything I can do for her?"

Natalie cocked her head at me. "Not right now. She needs rest and water. Tell you what. How about I sit with Charley until you get back? You go take care of business, then take over. Deal?"

"Deal."

As I rose, Natalie said, "Thad. One more thing." Her soft voice was choked. "Will you carve for Kevin?"

The tightness in my throat was back. "I'd be honored."

She nodded her thanks and gave me a silent wave.

It was my second trip to the Wall today, only this one was eminently more satisfying than the first. Going straight to Kevin's name, I took pleasure in carving a check beside it. His empty space had been waiting long enough. *Congratulations, man. You did it.*

The edginess was gone.

Off to find Rives, I bumped into Samuel, my roommate who'd left early this morning to Search near the lava fields. His dark skin dripped water, and it wasn't rain, not on this side of the island.

"Sorry, man," I said, reaching out to clasp his hand. "Maybe tomorrow."

"Maybe." Samuel nodded, reflexively. "I thought I saw one. I went at it, hard." He shook his head, his disappointment still fresh. We'd all run for false alarms. "But hey"—he forced a grin—"I've got time. Twenty-nine days, but who's counting?"

"Right." We both laughed, because the answer was *everyone.*

"You hear about Kevin?"

"No." Samuel's face closed. "What's the word?"

I grinned. "He made it. A girl found his clothes in the red lava field."

And just like that, hope was back. "All right." Samuel nodded, cracking a smile. "That's what I like to hear."

"Absolutely. We'll make it." I clasped Samuel's hand.

"We've got to, man," he said, his smile fading, his grip crushing. "We've *got* to."

I nodded, feeling abruptly intense, like he'd handed me his urgency.

"I'm gonna surf." Samuel looked at the water. "Wanna go?"

"Already did. It's choppy, but decent."

Samuel waved. I watched him go, knowing there was nothing Samuel could do until tomorrow's noon. Nothing but wait.

And surf.

Behind Samuel, a head-high swell pitched and rolled. It peeled down the line, crisp and full, cleaner than this morning. Much cleaner. *The wind*, I realized. It had shifted. The crosswind was gone, taking the chop with it, like the ocean was celebrating Kevin's verdict too.

As I scanned the ocean, I spotted Rives. The sooner I could talk to Rives and deal with Bart, the sooner I could get back to Charley.

"Wait up, man," I called to Samuel. "I'm in."

We trotted over to the stash of boards propped by the Shack. Finless wooden planks, made by someone who was here before me and which will be used by others after I'm gone—unless I break the board, which I sure as hell better not do. Breaking a board feels like bad karma, and God knows we don't need any more of that.

I grabbed my favorite, the thinnest one, about two and a half meters long. No fins to carve with, but that's okay. My Burton boards back home don't have fins either, and they shred the snow just fine. Water, snow. Whatever. Give me a board, and I'm good to go. It's the best part of Nil.

Or was.

I thought of Charley and her golden eyes full of fire. I replayed the morning until we hit sand.

"Time to thread the needle," Samuel said.

"Absolutely." I nodded.

There were two heaps of black rocks, like bookends, where we always put in to paddle out. You get a sick rush heading out that way, because you have to time the waves or risk getting crushed, and if there's one thing about Nil that I get—I mean really get, way down deep in my core—it's that she's all about the timing.

I shot through the walls of black, scoring a surge of survival stoke, and worked my way through the swells. Close to shore, Rives bailed in the flats. Bart was nowhere in sight. Not surprising since he didn't surf, but I'd guessed he'd be around, trying to make his case to Rives. Or worse, to me.

Beyond the break, I waited for Rives to paddle back out. For the first time in days, the lineup was packed. With people, with energy. With the heady vibe that Kevin had made it. It was killer, and yet I couldn't stop thinking about Charley.

Charley, standing on the beach, chin raised in defiance.

Charley, studying my face, ready to bolt.

Charley, lying on the bed, knocked out cold.

"Rives!" I waved him over.

"Hey, bro," he said, pulling up on his sled. "Already heard. Good news travels fast." He grinned.

"Definitely. Listen, what's the deal with Bart?" I asked. The sooner I could settle it, the sooner I could get back to Charley. "Nat said you guys got into it about watch?"

Rives nodded, looking pissed, which was rare. "Last night I couldn't sleep, so I came outside. Bart was sacked out by the fire. I'm talking full-on REM. All but two torches were out. I woke him up, told him to get his butt in bed, that I'd finish watch myself. Told him I'd talk to him after I cooled down. So this morning we had a little come-to-Jesus meeting. I told him he was off watch duty. That for someone so eager to get out on Search, he was doing a piss-poor job of showing he was worth taking. I mean, would you want Bart as your support? When he sleeps on watch?" Rives shook his head, disgusted. "Especially when, for all we know, the tiger's still out there, prowling around. And by now that kitty's hungry."

Rives shrugged, his anger waning. He never stayed pissed for long. "Anyway, that's how we left it. He's still whining. I'm just over it. But, listen." Now Rives looked uncomfortable. "There's something else. And it happened last night, on Bart's watch."

CHAPTER
12

CHARLEY
DAY 13, DAWN

I opened my eyes, and for one terrifying minute, I had absolutely no clue where I was.

Then yesterday rushed back. The encounter with Thad ... me falling. Glimpses of Thad and a girl with strawberry-blond hair intermingled with pain and thirst, all locked in a fog of exhaustion. Snippets of Em's sweet voice wove through my memories, coupled with the taste of fruity Sprite and liquid grass. Apparently I'd hit my head harder than I thought.

I sat up gingerly. My head felt sore, but I'd expected worse. I lay on a bed made of who-knows-what, covered by a thin sheet in a small house with open sides. Half walls of black rock supported wood framing, topped with a thatched roof. Air brushed my cheek, cool and salty. It smelled like morning.

To my left was another bed, where a girl with strawberry-blond hair was curled under a speckled blanket, sleeping. Her eyes were closed, and her hands were tucked under her cheek. She looked fragile and, if possible, more tired than me.

The only other furniture was a primitive chair and a small table.

Resting on top was a gourd and a half of a coconut, which I realized was a cup. Suddenly my mouth felt drier than a box of cotton balls, and I forgot about the ache in my head. *Please be water. Please be full.*

Lifting the gourd, my hands trembled. I tipped the gourd toward the coconut-shell cup, thrilled to see water pour out. Crisp and fruity, it was nearly as refreshing as Sprite.

After drinking my fill, I slipped outside.

I stood at the edge of a ring of open thatched huts. A massive firepit sat center stage, its embers smoldering. Several lit torches surrounded the fire. The ocean wasn't far; I could hear the waves. The sky was a hazy greenish blue, the color that seeps through the night just before the sun burns the darkness away. The air was cool, slightly breezy, and silent, reminding me of every breaking dawn for the last twelve days.

But for the first time, I wasn't alone.

Past the last hut stood a boy, his back to me. He faced a massive wooden sign made of long boards stretching between tall posts and bearing rows of carvings. The boy was tracing the carvings with one hand. The confident slant of his broad shoulders was familiar; so was the golden hair touching his shoulders. His bare back formed a perfect V. At the same moment I recognized the boy as Thad, he turned around.

Seeing me, he smiled and walked toward me. I just stood there gawking, not speaking. It was like I'd had too many shocks and could no longer regroup, especially not this early. Thad didn't say anything either, which seemed kind of weird. He just kept walking, his eyes on mine.

"Morning, Charley," he whispered. He was so close now that I could touch him, not that I did, and suddenly I understood his silence had been in consideration for everyone sleeping in the open rock houses. "How's your head?"

"It feels like I hit it with a rock." My soft tone matched his.

He smiled. "More like a small boulder."

"I'll have to take your word for it," I whispered, returning his grin. "I don't remember."

Thad's grin faltered. "Yeah. I figured. I'm sorry I wasn't there when you woke up."

A flash of Thad sitting beside me filled my head. "Did you sit with me last night?"

He nodded. "Natalie and I took turns checking on you."

"Natalie?" I frowned. "Was that the girl in the other bed?"

"Yeah. She doctored you up last night." He paused. "Hey, do you want to take a bath?"

"With you?" I blurted, shocked.

He fought a laugh. "No, not with me, although I think I should come along to make sure you don't pass out again and drown."

I couldn't tell if he was serious. I'd never been good at gauging sarcasm.

"Natalie thought when you woke up you'd like to take a bath. And now you're awake. So . . ." Thad grinned. "Bath?"

Did I stink? It was too horrible to think about, especially since Thad looked like he was ready for an island photo shoot. Even without a mirror, I knew I looked scary dirty.

"Okay, but I didn't pack any soap," I whispered.

"Got it covered. As long as you don't mind smelling like a coconut. We're out of guava."

Again, I couldn't tell if he was teasing me.

"Gee, I really was hoping for guava," I said. "Or at least kiwi."

"Kiwis don't grow on the island, at least not that I've seen. Hang on. Be right back."

Where would I go? I wondered, watching Thad duck into the hut beside mine. *What island?*

Thad reappeared. Now he carried a brown satchel, its strap slung across his chest, making his shoulders look even broader.

Ignoring his shoulders, I asked, "Thad, where am I?"

"The City," he said. "We're still on the western shore of the island, the dry side. If you've noticed, it never rains here, but the east gets tons of rain. There's literally a rain forest over there. There's also a volcano—"

"Thad, stop." My voice was sharp. "I mean what island."

"Nil," he said flatly. "You're on the island of Nil."

"Nil?" I asked, combing my memory. I'd paid attention in social studies. Not to mention I had a weird fascination with maps. One entire wall of my room was covered with a giant world map. I'd studied it for hours, dreaming of all the places I'd like to go. Distant countries, famous cities, remote islands. None were named Nil. "I've never heard of it," I said.

"Neither had I until I got here."

"But where is *here*? What is this place?"

Thad ran his hand through his hair. "To be honest, I don't know. It just is."

It just is.

A chilling scene burst behind my eyes: my broken body lying on the pavement, my head cracked and bleeding, the Target bull's-eye sparkling in the distance as a handful of EMTs stared down at me, shaking their heads.

"Am I dead?" My voice was strangely calm. "Or am I dreaming? Is any of this real?"

"You're not dead, Charley," Thad said quietly. "And it's definitely no dream." Then he smiled, his tone forcibly lighter as he pointed to my feet. "How are those sandals working out?"

Thrown by his random question, I answered automatically. "Fine."

"Really? Because they look too big."

"They're a little big," I admitted. "But it's better than nothing. That red rock was awful."

"Sharp, eh?" Thad nodded. "C'mon, let's get you some sandals that fit." He motioned for me to follow. As we walked, Thad barely made a sound. He had an athlete's grace—strong, fluid, and confident.

Thad disappeared inside a small rock hut at the edge of the camp. A minute passed, then Thad popped his head back out. "Are you coming?" He looked amused. "I don't bite."

I smirked, then followed him inside, searching for a snappy retort, but by the time I thought of one, the moment was gone.

Like the other huts, this one had black rock as a foundation, topped with open wood framing and a thatched roof. Shelves lined the sides and back, filled with neat stacks of ivory-colored cloth, baskets of rags, balls of twine, knives, satchels, more gear I didn't recognize, and sandals. Lots of sandals.

"This is the Shack," Thad was saying. "It's where we store our gear. Sheets, clothes, tools, gourds, rope, you name it. And most important for you, sandals. It's no Sport Chek, but it works."

"What's Sport Chek?" I asked, then instantly felt stupid. Sport Chek sounded like Dick's Sporting Goods, only with a much cooler name. Either my brain was still asleep or I'd whacked my head harder than I'd thought.

"A sporting goods store back home," Thad said conversationally, as he sifted through a row of sandals. "Okay," he said, handing me a pair identical to the ones I was wearing. "Try these. See if they fit better."

I slid one on. It fit perfectly.

"Impressive," I said. "You've got a future in ladies' footwear if this island gig doesn't work out."

"I'll keep that in mind. I have other plans, but it's good to have a backup." Grinning, he held out his hand. "I'll take your old ones."

I passed them over, and as Thad went to stash them on the shelf, he stopped, frowning. Bloody sandal in hand, he looked up. "Are you hurt, Charley?"

Light bounced off his cheekbones, making his face more chiseled than ever, but it was his expression that took me aback. Worried, oddly protective. His blue eyes caught mine, and I stuttered, "No. I mean, I was. I cut my foot my first day here. It's better now. I soaked it in the ocean."

"Good call." Thad set the bloody sandal aside. "Ready?" He tipped his head toward the exit and smiled. My brain was mush.

The fresh air outside cleared my head. "Okay, about Nil." The word felt foreign on my tongue. "What is this place? How'd I get here? Tell me everything."

We started away from the camp, and the ocean rumble faded. I paid attention, keeping my bearings as we walked, and I was about to repeat my question when Thad answered.

"Have you ever seen the reality television show *Survivor*?"

I nodded. "Yeah."

"Okay, well, Nil's kind of like that, except no one shows up with bags of rice, and no one gets letters from home. And of course, no one gets voted off."

Again, I couldn't tell if he was being sarcastic.

"So how do we leave? I mean *can* we leave?" Before he could answer, I blurted out, "I found a skull."

"A skull?" Thad stopped walking. "Where?"

"Near the bay, just off the beach. I"—I paused, swallowing—"I tripped over it."

Thad looked thoughtful.

"It looked old," I added. "Like it had been there a while." When he didn't say anything, I spoke quietly. "Thad, what happened to that person?"

He shook his head. "I don't know." The honesty in his voice was pained.

"So, can we leave?" I repeated.

"Sure. Everyone leaves, eventually." The flatness in Thad's voice was back.

"Really?" I asked, suddenly skeptical. "How? How do we get home?"

"Same way you got here, Charley. A gate. Catch one, and you're gone."

"A gate?" I frowned. I hadn't seen anything that looked like a gate, or even a door. Then a lightbulb went off. "Are you talking about the shimmers?"

"Shimmers?" Thad smiled. "I haven't heard that term, but yeah, same thing. Shimmer. Liquid wall. Air boil. Heat wave. Wormhole. Portal. Gate." He paused. "Call it what you want, but it's all the same thing. It's the only way off the island."

I had a million questions about the gates, about Nil. Each question waved its hand, begging to be called on first, so naturally I asked something else. "You said Sport Chek was a store back home, but I've never heard of it. Where's home?"

"Whistler, British Columbia. Just north of Vancouver in Canada. You?"

"I'm American. I live near Atlanta, in a town called Roswell."

We were moving again through the trees, parallel to the ocean. The only sound was our footfalls; there were no crickets, insects, or animal noises at all. *Weird*, I thought. *The silent island.*

"Roswell? Like the town with all the alien stuff?" Thad was asking.

I laughed. "Yeah. That's Roswell, New Mexico. I live in Roswell, Georgia." I paused. "But after the shimmer in the parking lot, Roswell, Georgia, doesn't seem too normal either."

"Let me guess. It was noon, really bright sun. The ground melted, took flight, and the next thing you knew, you were burning and blacked out. And then you woke up naked." His tone was so nonchalant he may as well have been describing the menu at the local Chick-fil-A.

"Pretty much. Is that what happened to you?" I asked.

"Different verse, same song."

I shot Thad a puzzled look.

He smiled. "Everyone's story is pretty much the same. Different places, different countries, but it's always noon, it's always sunny. There's always a gate and then—poof. You wake up naked. Here on Nil."

You forgot alone.

"Okay, Charley, it's just through these trees."

The trees were green and lush. The ground sloped down, then the trees gave way to a vast pool nestled in black rock, like some exotic swimming hole straight from a Hollywood movie. The water was clear and sparkling, except for the ripples of white stretching from the far side where a waterfall at least three stories high cascaded down a wall of black; it poured into the pool with a steady roar—like the ocean, but more constant, less rhythmic.

"This is it," Thad said. "Crystal Cove."

"It's beautiful," I whispered. Another piece of my tropical paradise, worthy of a postcard, not that I could send one from here. I thought of Em, and a lump rose in my throat.

"You okay? You look pale. Did we walk too far?"

"No. I'm fine. I just"—I swallowed—"I wish my sister could see this." I pictured Em tilting her camera, the one with the fancy lens she got for her birthday, snapping shot after shot. The lump in my throat grew. "She'd love this."

Thad's voice was quiet. "She's better off where she is."

I looked at Thad. He was reaching into his satchel, his face hidden.

"Okay," he said, looking up with a grin. "I've got coconut soap, a towel, and new clothes. The pool's shallow. But be careful. Over by the waterfall, it drops fast to overhead. Behind the waterfall is a small ledge. I'll leave your stuff at the edge here, then I'll turn around." His deep blue eyes turned playful. "I promise not to peek."

My cheeks burned. "Definitely no peeking." My mouth felt dry and yucky, and suddenly I felt icky all over again. "Crazy question. Do y'all have any toothbrushes?"

"Sort of. They're rough, but they work." Thad pulled a contraption from his satchel. It was a stick with some spiky things on one end. "The bristles don't last that long; they're plants. This one's yours. Natalie made it."

"Thanks." I felt incredibly grateful to a girl I didn't even know. Then I had a thought. "Do objects come through the gates too? Like toothbrushes?" I smiled.

"Nope. No objects. Just living things, like people. Everything here in Nil City has been made by us or those who have come before." His voice was unmistakably proud, but sad, making me wonder what he was thinking.

He looked down, and a ray of light glinted off his hair, gold on gold. And in that moment, I'd never felt filthier in my entire life.

I took one step toward the pool and stopped. Rocks lined the edge, full of nooks and crannies—perfect hideouts for water moccasins. "Thad," I said slowly, eyeing the water, "are there snakes in there?"

"Nope." He grinned, and the mischievous glint in his eyes returned. "No snakes. Not in the Cove, not anywhere on Nil."

"*None?* Are you sure?"

"I'm sure. There's nothing cold-blooded on the island. No snakes, no lizards. No reptiles of any sort. Only warm-blooded creatures make it to Nil."

"Huh. No snakes." Nil instantly was less scary. I took another step toward the Cove, then turned back again.

"Aliens? What about aliens?"

"There are no aliens in the Cove," Thad answered straight-faced.

"Not in the Cove. I meant on Nil." I rolled my eyes. "It's just—the first day I was here, I saw some creatures, flying. Like birds, but I swear they had heads. Human heads. And well, with the freaky way I got here, I've been wondering what they were. And if they're dangerous."

Now the corners of Thad's mouth curved up. "That was me and Jason, using gliders." He cocked one eyebrow, his grin spreading. "So nothing dangerous, eh?"

I think you're plenty dangerous. "Well, I did fall and hit my head within minutes of laying eyes on you," I said.

"I'm sorry about that," he said, running his hand through his hair.

I snorted. "Why are you apologizing for me fainting?"

"I'm sorry I didn't catch you."

An awkward silence fell between us; the crisp morning air was suddenly heavy. Thad cleared his throat and pointed to the Cove.

"Word of warning, Charley. The water's chilly. It's spring-fed, so when you first walk in, it's a bit of a shock." He grinned, a lazy grin that stole oxygen from the air. "I'll turn around now."

With Thad's back to me, I stepped into the pool.

The water wasn't chilly. I know chilly. The early November air that brushes your face first thing in the morning is chilly. The can of Sprite when you pull it from the refrigerator is chilly. The water in the shower before the hot side kicks in feels chilly.

The pool water was *freezing.* Stepping into the Cove felt like stepping into an ice bath, something I'd done once after an intense volleyball workout at the suggestion of our overzealous coach who thought ice baths were great for muscle recovery. I'd thought it was pure torture. And right now I was thinking my dreamy island bath with coconut soap would be the shortest one in history.

But the longer I sat in the icy water, the better I felt. I scrubbed my skin with the milky soap, feeling sand scour my skin, rubbing until my skin turned red and was tender to the touch. Until it felt clean.

Then I tackled my hair. I could feel the cut, and took pains to avoid it.

"You doing okay, Charley?" Thad called. "Still conscious?"

"Fine."

"Let me know if you need help." I heard the laughter in his voice.

"I've got it, thanks. You know, I *have* taken a bath before, even though I may not have looked like it."

Now Thad laughed out loud.

After I rinsed my hair, it felt like wet straw, and I knew it would be a nightmare to untangle without conditioner. Then I realized I didn't even have a brush. But maybe Thad did. His handy satchel seemed full of tricks, like an island version of a magic hat.

I left the water, toweled off, and dressed quickly in the fresh clothes. Same material as before, only this time it was a halter top and a piece of cloth that I guessed was a skirt. No underwear. *Does everyone here go commando?* I wondered, wrapping the skirt around my waist. As I tied it tight, I laughed. It was shorter than the ones I was returning to Target, the crazy-short minis that had landed me here in the first place.

"What's so funny?" Thad asked.

"I think Nil has a sense of humor," I said as I gave my skirt a dirty look. "A twisted one."

"You catch on fast."

I looked back at the clothes I'd been wearing, wondering if I could wear the shorts instead, but now that I was clean, I saw how filthy my old clothes—or rather, Kevin's—were. Too yucky to be an option, that was for sure. The shorts were so grimy they made my island mini look good by comparison: a sad fact if there ever was one.

"Are you dressed yet? Clearly these trees are fascinating, but if you're decent . . ." He trailed off.

"I'm decent." *Sort of, excluding my teeny mini.* "You can turn around now."

"How're you feeling?" Thad's eyes went straight to my legs. *Embarrassed.*

"Better," I said. "It feels great to be clean. Thanks for the help."

"I didn't help. But I offered, remember?" He grinned.

I groaned. "You know what I meant."

He grinned wider.

Definitely dangerous.

Changing the subject, I said, "I take it there are cows on the island?" I pointed at my sandals. "And goats? And . . ." I hesitated, not wanting to sound like a looney tune. "Zebras?"

"Could be." Thad shrugged. "We've got cows, chickens, goats, and for some reason, lots of cats. I'm not sure who made the sandals. Lately we've been focused on making more clothes. We're low. We use paper trees."

"Paper trees?"

"I'm sure there's some proper botanical name, but no one here knows it. We use the bark, for paper and cloth. It's not the easiest thing you've ever done, so we take care of the clothes we have because it's tough to make more. There are grass skirts, too, but those don't last long."

"Grass skirts." My voice was disbelieving. "Please don't tell me there are coconut tops."

Thad laughed. "Only if you want to wear them."

"No thanks." I was actually thinking, *Hell, no*, but my daddy was firmly against swearing, except in the most dire of circumstances, like when the Bulldog quarterback got sacked. On second thought, maybe a coconut top did merit a *Hell, no*. Too late now.

Thad picked up the dirty clothes. "Let's wash them while we're here, eh?"

I snatched them back. "I'll do it."

"What, you think guys can't do wash?" He did that eyebrow thing again.

No, I'm embarrassed to have you touch my smelly clothes. Thad's offer felt strangely intimate and more than a little awkward. But before I could protest again he'd already flicked the bandana out of my hand and was expertly scrubbing it in the water.

Following his lead, I washed the shorts. Soon everything smelled like coconut-lime shower gel from Bath & Body Works.

"Who makes the soap?" I asked.

"Li. She's crazy good with floral stuff. She's from Beijing. She doesn't speak much English, but we get the gist of it. Her sandsoap's the best. I'm not sure if she already knew how to make it, or if she learned from Ramia, but no one makes soap like Li."

"Where's Ramia?"

"Gone."

Thad wrung out the cloth as he stood. I did the same, but when I got to my feet, the world swayed.

He caught my elbow. "Don't fall down on me again."

"I won't." I said, trying not to snap. I hated feeling weak, although I was. The pressure of Thad's hand on my elbow competed with the pulse in my temple, then the wooziness passed. "I'm okay. Just stood up too fast."

The pressure on my elbow vanished.

I changed the subject, determined to get myself under control. "Hey, you don't happen to have a brush, do you?"

"How about a comb?" He reached into his satchel and pulled out the most beautiful wooden comb I'd ever seen. Hand carved, it had thick tines, rubbed smooth.

"Wow. I've never seen anything like it." I ran my fingers over the silky wood.

"Miguel's handiwork. He's the best carver in the City."

"Who else is in the City?" I sat on Thad's rock and began wrestling with my hair. "And how many other cities are there?"

"None. Just Nil City. The island's not that big. And the number of people changes. Right now there's me, Natalie, Rives, Jason, Li, Talla, Raj, Heesham, Samuel . . ." Thad counted on his fingers as he spoke. "And you make twenty-one."

Taking a break, I rested my shaking hands in my lap, wondering exactly how hard I'd hit my head. I was *tired*.

"Charley, no offense, but you look like you're gonna collapse. If you want, I'll finish combing your hair." He stuck out his hand, gesturing for the comb.

I stared at his outstretched hand, totally floored.

I *loved* getting my hair brushed. More than getting my back scratched, more than getting a massage, more than anything, and I'd always dreamed about having a cute boy brush my hair.

Thad had just served up my secret fantasy on an island platter.

CHAPTER 13

It was a serious WTF moment in my own head.

I couldn't believe I'd just offered to comb her hair. But she did look ready to take a header any second. Make that another header. She still had a nasty lump from yesterday. Her coloring had paled, or maybe that was because I'd just offered to comb her hair. *Seriously, Thad, WTF?*

Charley's eyes were glued to the comb, like she was weighing whether to say yes. Like she was wondering why the hell I'd asked.

Maybe she thinks my post-Nil plan is to become a professional hairstylist.

It took all I had not to laugh, but I didn't want Charley to think I was laughing at *her*. My post-Nil plan involved boards and snow, sponsors and races, not a monotonous job that stuck me indoors doing the same dull crap, day in and day out, like crunching numbers or styling hair. But after nine months on Nil, my well-crafted plan felt more like a fading pipe dream. Blurry, and distant. And possibly already shot.

I no longer felt like laughing.

Charley looked up and smiled. God, she was beautiful. "Okay." She handed me the comb. "Thanks."

I moved behind her, glad she couldn't see my face. She didn't say another word. I had no clue what she was thinking; she was impossible to read.

This was a first for me, combing a girl's hair. I really didn't know why I'd offered, and as sure as the Canucks need a decent defenseman, nine months ago I never would have. But it felt . . . right. And after 278 days here, I didn't have much to lose. Just a no.

But Charley had said yes.

I swept her hair away from her neck. Drying quickly, her dark hair fell in soft waves around her shoulders. I worked slowly, sucked into the moment. Her head was tilted slightly to one side, but she didn't move. I combed until Charley's hair was perfect, like her.

"All done," I said.

"Thanks." Her voice sounded thick, like she'd been thinking of home.

"Ready to head back?" *Say no. Say not yet. Say anything but yes.*

Because I wasn't ready. Not ready to leave this moment. Not ready to introduce the ugliness of Nil. I wanted to hang out with Charley—just Charley. I wanted to know this cool girl who'd survived solo for twelve days, and who'd made me laugh more in twenty-four hours than I had in months. And suddenly I wanted it more than anything else I'd wanted in the last 278 days.

"Ready," she said. *Damn.*

"So," I said as we walked back, "where were you when the gate hit?"

"In the Target parking lot. I was about to return some stuff I didn't need," she said, pulling on her skirt. "You know how Target sells everything." She cocked her head at me. "Or maybe you don't. I don't know if Target's in Canada, but they sell everything from board games to bikinis. Half the stuff they sell is as useful as a back pocket on a shirt, my dad says, but before you know it, your cart's full." Charley grinned, but my thoughts were stuck on the potent image of her in a bikini.

"Anyway"—she waved her hand—"it was hotter than an Easy-Bake Oven. That's Georgia in August for you." She laughed, then her smile faded. "I remember seeing the ground shimmer, like a desert oasis. Then it *moved*, and the next thing I knew, I was on fire. Burning, then freezing, and then I was here. Well, not here." She swept her hand around us, her grin wry. "But you know what I mean."

"I know what you mean." I returned her half grin.

She looked thoughtful. "It's one of those weird moments you'll never forget. I mean, it's so clear. The Target sign, the heat. Like I remember exactly where I was when I heard about the mega quake that leveled most of LA. I'll never look at Target the same."

"An earthquake hit LA?"

Charley nodded. "Last month. It was huge, seven point something. It was awful."

"Wow." I thought about the quake, another event in the real world I'd missed. "You wouldn't happen to know how the Canucks finished last season, would you?" I joked.

"I don't know how they finished, but I do know they beat the tar out of the Thrashers. Our team got pounded. It was bad."

I stared at Charley. *Our team*, she'd said. Like she actually cared. "You follow hockey?"

"Just the Thrashers. We go to tons of games. They're really fun."

"Yeah." *Charley likes hockey.*

"Thad." The smile was gone from her voice, bringing my thoughts to a halt. "What do you think's happening back home? I mean, does anyone know about Nil? Is anyone coming to find us?"

Time for some hard Nil truth. Just one piece. If you get it all at once, it's too much to swallow, and I didn't want Charley to choke.

68

"I don't know," I said with complete honesty. "I don't know what they know, but here's the thing: I wouldn't count on any help from back home. There're no ships, no planes, nothing ever even washes up here. There're nothing but what's on the island." I paused. "There's one way in and one way out. A gate."

She nodded, no doubt letting the zero hope of rescue sink in. "What about you?" she asked quietly. "Where were you when your gate hit?"

Snowboarding, and pissed. "I was on top of a mountain. I'd gone heli-boarding." I paused, wrenched back to the moment. "There were four of us." *Me, Jonas, Finn, and Carter, my best friend who'd just spilled his guilty guts about sleeping with my girlfriend.*

"Everyone else had taken off, I was catching my breath." *And giving Carter some space before I beat the ever-living shit out of him.* "The sun was bright. I remember sweating in my gear. Then the snow went liquid, and I was more than sweating; I was burning. I passed out. When I woke up, I was here."

"I passed out, too. I'd never fainted before in my life. And now I've fainted twice in two weeks." She looked surprised.

Don't be, I thought. Nil was full of surprises. And to give Charley credit, she didn't look like the fainting type. She actually looked like she might kick some ass if she got something to eat.

Charley was watching me. "Did you wake up in the red desert, too?"

"Nope. I landed at the base of the mountain." I pointed.

"So gates can show up anywhere."

Even though her statement wasn't a question, I nodded.

"And they only come at noon?" Charley was connecting the dots. *It won't be long,* I thought.

"Outbounds only flash at noon," I said. "But incoming ones flash anytime. Mine dumped me here at night."

"At night?" She looked horrified. "That's awful. I can't imagine waking up here in the dark."

We walked in silence. I was gearing up to break the ultimate bad news.

"So the outbounds," she said. "Do they always come in sets like waves?"

I wondered exactly how many gates she'd seen in her twelve days. "No. Singles are the most common, and the fastest. They're racers, tough to catch because of their speed. Doubles are less frequent, but not by much. They move slower and are easier to catch. Triples are rare, but they happen. They tend to be drifters, even slower than doubles."

"What about quads?"

"Quads?" I shook my head. "I've never seen one."

"I have."

"Hey, quick question," I said. "Do you wear contacts?"

She laughed. "My vision's fine. Twenty-twenty. And I did see a quad, in the red rock field, the day I arrived. It wasn't moving that fast, but I didn't catch it either." She looked chagrined. "I didn't think to chase it until the last wave. By then it was too far out."

"I'm impressed. Most people run from gates at first, not after them."

"Oh, I did that, too. Don't forget—it was a quad. I had a few minutes to consider it."

"Not that many minutes." I still couldn't get over the idea of a quad. *Giving us more chances, Nil, or are you playing the tease?* Now I had the hope of a quad, as well as the knowledge that we'd missed four solid chances to get off this rock. Surely Samuel could have made one of four. Or better yet, Li.

Charley was looking at me, expectantly.

"Since we're talking about gates, let me give you the scoop on the City. We Search for gates in teams, and the longer you've been here, the greater your priority. And someone's your Spotter."

"Spotter?"

"Spotter." I nodded. "We all show up naked, so glasses don't make it. Or contacts. Some people wouldn't see a gate five meters away, let alone fifty. You have to see the ground turn liquid in the distance, then watch it rise and roll. And you need to know which direction to run to intercept it. That's the Spotter's job—to spot the gate rising and tell you which way to go. All you do is run." I paused. "Search teams are three or four people, five at the most. It gives the Spotter company on the return trip to the City, plus help carrying the gear."

Ask it, Charley. Tell me how much you're ready to swallow.

She frowned. "Why doesn't the whole team go through the gate?"

Atta girl. One down. Two to go. "Because only one person can take a gate at a time. One person, one gate. Nil's rules."

Charley was island quiet.

Surely it's part of Nil's fun. Seeing rookies squirm as they put the pieces together. Watching as they finally see through the island's façade. For Charley, Nil's mask was just starting to crack. For some people, it all crumbles at once; for others, it falls one piece at a time. Either way, it disappears for everyone, eventually. Because it has to.

"And the gates take us back?" Charley asked, her voice remarkably steady. "Back home, back to the Target lot? Or do they take us somewhere else? Some other world?"

That's two, I thought. *One to go.* "I don't know, Charley. No one does. But we know every incoming gate comes from our world, so it makes sense that outbounds take us back, like a loop. But the truth is, we don't know. Not for sure." I watched emotion whirl across her face, so fast and furious that I reached out to stop it.

"Hey," I said, tilting up her chin with my finger, "it'll work out. You'll see your family again. I can't promise it, but I believe it." I sounded as fierce as Samuel the day before.

Charley's golden eyes searched mine, like she was hunting for truths. For the last truth, the one that cracked Nil's beautiful mask for good. She nodded, but her eyes stayed troubled.

"It's okay." I whispered the lie, the same one I told her yesterday.

Her eyes stayed on mine. "I have one more question," she said.

Here we go. The final question, breaking Nil's mask to bits.

"Shoot," I said, braced and ready.

"When I woke up this morning, I swear there was a cheetah pelt on that girl—Natalie's—bed. Y'all have cheetahs here?"

Her question was not the one I was expecting. "Not that I know of, but there could be." I smiled. "We've had the occasional cheetah, lion, and tiger, along with cows and goats."

"Don't forget the zebra," she said, forcing a smile.

"Too right. We don't want to leave him out."

"How do you know it's a him? It could be a her."

"Point conceded."

Charley's eyes swept the trees. "Thad, my point is, Nil has dangers, like cheetahs, that we might not know about, right? Things we can't see?"

"You got it," I said. *Person, place, thing, or animal.* It's always the things that are the toughest.

"Just trying to figure Nil out," she said. She wasn't smiling.

I knew I should tell Charley about the days. But I hesitated. Maybe because I didn't want to ruin the morning. Maybe because once you know, it's always on your mind, like a leech on your brain, sucking out hope. Or like a clock, counting off the minutes, only in my head it sounded like a detonator. The tick-tock, just before the *boom.*

Soon enough, I thought. *You'll see Nil for what she is soon enough.*

I didn't tell her.

Charley filled the silence before I could. "So what's the deal with the carving? The one on the black rocks, south of where we met?"

"The Man in the Maze?" I asked.

"The Man in the Maze," she repeated, like she was feeling the way it sounded. "Exactly. Who carved it?"

"Don't know." I shrugged. "There's an identical carving on the eastern side, near the rain forest, only that one has a woman in the middle."

"What do they mean?"

"No clue," I said.

She was quiet. Then, "What do you think they mean?"

"That we're rats in a maze?" I said, grinning.

"I'm serious," she said.

"So am I."

For a long moment, the only sound was leaves crunching to dust under our sandals.

Then she stopped and looked straight at me. "Do you know anyone who's made it out? I mean someone you know personally, Thad, not just someone you heard about?"

"Yes," I said softly. "I do. I promise there's hope, Charley." Because I knew that was what she was asking. *Is there a chance? Or am I screwed?* "For all of us." This time I wasn't sure whether my words were for her or for me.

She nodded.

"So tell me about your family," I said, desperate for a change of subject. "Is your sister older or younger?"

"Older. By ten months." As Charley spoke, the words rolled off her tongue like sugar. I'd never met anyone like Charley, not on Nil, not anywhere. Her long legs matched mine stride for stride, and I liked that, too. I wondered if she liked to run.

She'd better, Nil laughed.

In that moment, I knew Nil had made her move and that now she was playing dirty. Because as much as I hated Nil, I liked Charley more, and I couldn't wait to know her better.

But I was leaving.

Nil says go. Nil says stay. Nil was totally screwed up, or maybe that was me.

Charley had stopped talking.

"What were you saying about Em?" I asked, moved to fill the sudden silence.

Her head was tilted to the side. "Is that breakfast? Something smells delicious."

"Definitely. I'm guessing roast fish, warm pineapple. It's a break from yesterday's roast fish and warm pineapple." Smiling, I stole another look at Charley. She looked hesitant, almost nervous. I watched her lift her chin, like she was steadying herself.

"Hey," I said, drawing her golden eyes. They were almost level with mine, another hot Charley-fact. But they were guarded, like when I'd first met her.

"I know it's weird, coming into the City. Meeting people. Like a roller coaster of new. But don't forget, everyone's been in your sandals. If you want, I'll stick close. Be your personal island guide." I grinned.

Just say yes.

CHAPTER 14

"Okay," I said. "I've always wanted my very own island guide." I was just happy I didn't say island *god*, which is what I was thinking.

Then I smelled a wave of something yummy, and all I could think was *food*.

The fire ring hummed with action. Fish hung across the coals, and green cabbage-like leaves lay stacked in piles to one side. People milled around, maybe a dozen. Guys wore no shirts, showing off decent physiques, but most were on the thin side. One looked almost skeletal. The girls were similarly trim. Clearly the island diet was a hard-core weight loss plan, especially when you threw in the physical demands necessary to survive. Most girls wore wrap skirts like mine, and almost all had a cloth wrapped around their chest like I'd done with Kevin's bandana. One girl had a halter like me, tied the same way, which was a relief. I'd never cared much about clothes, but that didn't mean I wanted to wear them backward either.

Thad put his fingers in his mouth and whistled. As all heads turned toward us, he called, "Morning, everybody. Meet Charley."

I felt like the new kid being introduced in the middle of the school year.

"As some of you know," Thad was saying, "she found Kevin's clothes. She's been here thirteen days."

Feeling all eyes on me, I automatically waved and smiled. "Hi, y'all." Heads nodded, faces smiled. I recognized the girl who'd been under the cheetah quilt, Natalie. She waved back.

"And in case you didn't hear, Charley's not our only new arrival. Heesham roped a cow yesterday." Several boys whooped and shouted. Thad smiled, raised his hand, and kept talking. "Jason says she's a Holstein—that's a dairy cow, people—so fresh milk is on the menu. Feel free to ask Jason for a lesson in milking. Last but not least, tonight's a Nil Night."

More whoops and smiles from the crowd. I was grateful he'd introduced me first, then the cow and the Nil Night, whatever that was. I was no longer the center of attention. If that had been his plan, it was awesome.

"So let's get busy, and get lucky." Thad saluted. As the conversations resumed, a boy strode over to us. Tan and wiry, the boy had dark hair that fell to his shoulders like Thad's. *The standard male island haircut,* I thought.

"Hola, Charley." The boy's voice was soft. "I'm Miguel." The carver, I remembered.

Before I could say hello, he turned to Thad.

"I need you, amigo. There's something you need to see." The intensity in Miguel's voice gave me chills.

Thad nodded at Miguel. "Okay." Turning to me, Thad's eyes were dark. "Charley, why don't you grab a bite? I know you're starving. I'll be back in a minute." Then he smiled. "Watch for zebras, okay?"

Look for them or watch out for them? Because somehow zebras seemed the least of my worries. Thad was already walking away, listening to Miguel, who spoke too fast for me to catch. My eighth-grade Spanish was weak to start with, and it hadn't aged well.

And my island guide was gone.

Unsure what to do, I stood there in my ridiculously short skirt, feeling self-conscious and oddly alone. *Here's your tribe,* I thought, looking around. But I felt like I was joining after the merge, late in the game.

Not a game, my mind corrected sharply. Nothing here felt like a game.

Natalie came over, along with the other girl I'd noticed wearing a halter like mine. Taller than Natalie and thinner, with deep ebony skin, the girl's collarbones jutted against the halter. I wondered if my shoulders looked as bony as hers; I almost looked down but didn't.

"Hi, Charley!" Natalie smiled up at me. "You probably don't remember, but I'm Natalie. How's your head?"

"Better. And I remember a little. Thanks for yesterday."

Natalie waved it off. "Please. Like I really did anything. This is Sabine. Sabine, Charley."

Sabine smiled. "Welcome, Charley. I'm rather new, like you. Fifty days and counting." Her speech had a delightful lilt. She pointed to my shirt. "Nice wrap."

"Thanks," I said. "I'm just happy I didn't put it on backward."

"If you had, no one would have cared." Still smiling, Sabine shrugged.

Following Sabine, more people introduced themselves. I found myself nodding and smiling and saying nice to meet you and privately wondering how the heck I would ever remember all their names and when I'd get to eat.

"I'm Jillian." Dark-brown hair, freckles, two long braids tied with twine. "Day One Hundred Fifty-two."

"Bart. Day Ninety." Cocky smile, sunburned shoulders. Close talker.

"Samuel." Strong grip. Quick nod. Massive shark tooth around his neck. "Too long."

"Stop." A girl stepped up—the only person I'd noticed who was even slightly heavy—and elbowed him lightly in the ribs before turning to me with a huge grin. "I'm Macy. Been here sixty-one days."

"Julio." Young, with a baby face. He mumbled three numbers in Spanish; I caught one. Literally, *uno.*

Odd, I thought. They wore their days like a badge of honor. Names and numbers began to blur.

"Raj." At least I think that's what the next boy said as he bobbed his head. Focusing on his introduction, I missed another girl's altogether.

"Talla." Straight blond hair, knockout body. I missed her day count because I was so distracted by her chest. No one should get boobs and muscles, but Talla had gobs of both. Her spear seemed out of place.

A tiny Asian girl with chin-length hair bowed. "Li," she said softly. "Day Three Five Four." Her accent was so thick it took me a minute to register the number.

Day Three Five Four.

She'd been here 354 days.

I smiled at her, privately shocked by the idea that I could be here in a year. Recalling Thad combing my hair, I silently admitted being here a while might not be so bad. But a *year*! Holy crap, that was a long time.

Gates must be harder to catch than I thought.

The group dispersed as quickly as they came. Only Natalie stayed behind. I watched Li go, still grappling with the fact she'd been here nearly a year. When I was certain Li was out of earshot, I turned to Natalie. "Did I hear Li right? That she's been here three hundred fifty-four days?"

"Yeah." Natalie sighed. "Awful, isn't it?"

"Totally. Has anyone been here longer than Li? I mean, is there some fifty-year-old island man wandering around, still looking for a gate?"

Natalie laughed. "You're funny. Nope. Li's been here the longest." Then she shot me an odd look. "Thad took you to the Cove this morning, right? And he gave you the scoop?"

I nodded. For an instant, Natalie looked troubled, then she smiled so fast that I wondered if I'd imagined her concern altogether.

"Well, I'm glad he found you. I'd planned to help you get a bath, but I ended up sleeping in. Of all days, right? Anyway, I still remember how good it felt to get that first bath after wandering around in jungle dirt." Her eyes drifted up to my scalp. "Let's eat and then we'll check your head. Here." She held out a piece of bread, and it was all I could do not to snatch it from her hand. The bread was sweet and moist. And it was *bread*.

"I don't think I've ever tasted anything so good," I said, savoring the last bite.

Natalie laughed, making her eyes sparkle. "Julio's family owned a bakery. He's been experimenting since he's been here."

"Charley."

I turned and found Sabine holding out a wooden plank with fish and some pineapple chunks. "Here you go," she said.

"Thanks."

"I'll grab drinks," Natalie said. "And more bread." She winked at me. "Be right back."

I followed Sabine to a heap of black rocks—four giant boulders shaped like beanbags, but as smooth as granite and just as hard. Natalie returned, carrying three coconut-shell cups and another piece of bread, which she dropped on my plank. After passing out the cups, she took a full plank from Sabine and sat.

"Cheers," Sabine said, lifting her cup. "It's nice to meet you, Charley, even if it is under these circumstances."

"It could be worse," I said. "At least we've got breakfast and fire."

Sabine chuckled. "I forgot. You've been meandering for twelve days." She leaned forward. "Did you see any gates?"

"One, I think. Oh, and I saw some my first day here."

She nodded, then picked up the fish with her fingers. I copied her, happy to have a crash course in island etiquette.

White and flaky, with a hint of citrus, the fish melted in my mouth. I'd never had fish for breakfast before, but then again, I was all about new experiences these days. Before I knew it, my fish was gone. I started on my pineapple, forcing myself to slow down.

The fire crackled, the ocean rumbled in the distance, and voices and laughter blended into comforting background noise. It was the most surreal breakfast of my life.

Sabine's face lit up. "I see Heesham," she said, setting down her plank. "Be right back."

"Where's Sabine from?" I asked Natalie as Sabine hurried away. "I can't place her accent."

"Switzerland. No—wait, that was Andrea. Sabine's from . . . Belgium? No." Natalie shook her head, groaning. "Crap. That was Stella. I'm totally blanking on where Sabine is from." Natalie rubbed her temples. "I should know this, right?"

"What about you?" I asked. "Where's home?"

"The United States. A little town in Minnesota called Rochester. Not to be confused with Rochester, New York." She smiled. "You sound Southern. You're American, too?"

"Born and raised. I'm from a little town outside Atlanta called Roswell, not to be confused with Roswell, New Mexico." I smiled as Natalie laughed. But she still looked tired, and despite her smile, she seemed blue.

"Hey, are you okay?" I asked.

"Yeah." She looked down, twisting a tiny shell bracelet on her wrist. "I just really miss Kevin. All I can think about is getting home and finding him."

"But how do you *know* the gates take us back?" I regretted my comment immediately. *Way to go, Charley. Burst Natalie's bubble when she needs it to float her.*

Natalie didn't seem fazed. "We don't, but it makes sense. They bring you here, and they take you somewhere. Why not back home?"

"But how do we know they don't dump us on another island? Or in another time?" Desperate for answers, I couldn't stop, but to her credit, Natalie didn't seem to mind.

"We don't," she repeated in the same matter-of-fact tone. "But all the people and animals here are from Earth, and we're definitely still *on* Earth—you can tell by the stars—so we figure the gates take us back home. Whatever this anomaly is, it's tied to Earth. To *our* Earth, and from what we can tell, to the same time. Time on Nil tracks time back home. Didn't Thad ask you for the date when he found you?"

I nodded.

"Well, it's because we keep checking to see if there's a variation, if our calendar still holds. So far, so good. It's August twenty-third on Nil, and August twenty-third back in our world."

August 23. I should be in school right now. Studying calculus, reading Plath, playing volleyball, planning to visit Em on the weekend. But I wasn't, I was here on Nil. Wherever—or whatever—Nil was.

"So what is this place? Nil, I mean." I knew I was asking her the same questions Thad had already answered, but I couldn't help it. I needed answers as much as I need food, and Natalie seemed more forthcoming than Thad. "A parallel world? An alternative universe?"

"Parallel world, crimp in space. Who knows." She shrugged. "We get older here just like we would back home. Days pass, just the same. It doesn't matter what Nil is. It just is."

It just is. Thad's exact words. No one seemed as desperate for understanding as me.

I played with my last piece of pineapple as Natalie finished her fish. *Fish.*

"Stupid question, but if only warm-blooded things come through the gates, how come there's fish?" I pointed to her plate.

"We don't know," Natalie said. "The ocean's full of cold-blooded creatures, but there aren't any on the island. Not one. Only warm-blooded things come through the gates. So maybe the ocean was here before the island; maybe they appeared at the same time." She shrugged. Her tone of voice was identical to when she said *It just is.* "But we do know that the gates are the only way out."

"How do you know?"

"Every so often, someone takes a sea kayak or builds a raft, trying to escape. But the current brings them back. It's pretty clear that if you want to leave Nil, you'd better catch a gate."

If you want to leave Nil. I shivered.

"Why Nil?" I rubbed my bare arms. "I mean why is that the name?"

"Because it's no-man's-land, Charley," Natalie said quietly. "A place that doesn't exist. It's nowhere, and yet we're here."

"Uh," I said, feeling more creeped out than ever, "I meant how do you know it's *named* Nil?"

"Oh, that." Natalie waved her cup. "It's carved into the top of the Naming Wall." She pointed to the sign I'd seen Thad tracing this morning. "You'll put your name up if you want to stay."

"What do you mean, want to stay?" I asked, surprised.

"You're so right." She laughed, but it sounded hiccupy. "We all want to leave, the sooner the better. That's why we set up the Search system, to give everyone the best chance at escape." Her thoughtful look was back. "Did Thad explain Search?"

"He said the City supports the Search teams."

She nodded, then looked over at Sabine, who was talking to a tall boy with jet black hair, mocha skin, and a thick beard. I assumed he was Heesham, the boy she'd jumped up to greet. He looked like he'd just stepped off a powerlifting mat; his muscles were ginormous. He wore a loincloth, the kind I'd only seen in movies. Then I realized there was no way his massive thighs would fit into a pair of shorts. Grinning broadly, he cradled something green and leafy in his massive hands, holding it carefully as Sabine inspected the leaves. But Heesham was watching Sabine's face, not his hands.

Abruptly I felt like I was intruding on something intimate and looked away.

Natalie was still watching the couple. "Sabine's amazing. She knows tons about herbs and medicinal plants. Her mom was into alternative medicine. I've been showing her what I know, which isn't much." Now Natalie looked at me. "My dad's an ER doctor. Everyone comes to our house after falling off a bike or whatever, so I know enough to be helpful. Or dangerous." She smiled. "Anyway, if you're good with blood, you might want to think about learning a little island medicine. That's what we call it. An inside joke."

Neither of us laughed, and Natalie's small face turned Em-kind. "Take some time. Get to know everyone and what everyone does. Be thinking of what you're good at or want to do. Some people fish, some hunt. Others tend the crops. There's not many, just yams, other root veggies, and herbs. Make sure to meet Jillian, she's the best at identifying paper trees, and Julio, he's our baker. Macy's learning how to make soap—it's pretty easy—but we could use another baker, or a seamstress. Can you sew?"

She talked so fast I felt slow. "Um, sew? No."

"Crap. Me either, and we haven't had a good tailor since Han left. Just think of any skills you have and keep an open mind, okay?"

I nodded. I wondered what Thad's job was.

"Did Thad mention the Covenant?" Natalie changed topics like most people blinked.

"No."

"Well, if you put your name on the Wall, you're agreeing to abide by the Covenant. It's just a pledge to do your part, to support the City and the Searchers. There's plenty of food on the island, but we've got to catch it, pick it, and sometimes cook it, and that takes time. Other people repair gliders, make clothes, whatever. We all support the Search teams. That's the whole point of the City. So, if you want to stay here in the City, you've got to figure out something to contribute. It's just the way the City is."

She must have read my face because she said, "It's not as scary as it sounds. It's just that there aren't that many of us, so to support the teams, those staying behind keep the City running. It's more like a camp than a City, but it's ours." There was pride in her voice, the same pride I'd heard in Thad's earlier this morning.

"Does anyone not stay?" It sounded like a really bad idea.

"Occasionally newbs go off alone. Sometimes they come back, sometimes they don't." Her matter-of-fact tone gave me chills. "It's a personal choice, but I hope you'll stay." She smiled.

After being alone for twelve days, I had no urge for a solitary jungle quest. And part of me worried that Nil harbored secrets making snakes look downright warm and fuzzy.

"I'm in," I told Natalie. "I'll figure out something to contribute."

Easier said than done. I couldn't spear fish, weave a stupid net, or make fire. I'd no clue how to bake island bread. At home I made cakes from a box.

Maybe I could make soap.

"Charley," Natalie said hesitantly, "would you like to bunk with me? It'd be nice to have a roommate again."

Somehow I knew who her old roommate was. I'd been wearing his clothes.

"Sure. And—I'm sorry about Kevin."

"I'm not." Her voice was fierce. "He made it."

I meant I'm sorry you miss him. But feeling awkward, I let the subject drop.

"So how long have you been here?" I asked.

"Too long." Natalie traced the edge of her coconut cup with one finger. "So long that home seems like another life."

Sabine came back, a welcome diversion.

"Sorry," she said. "Got caught up with Sham. He found a plant I've been looking for." Sabine babbled on about plants and herbs, most of which I missed; her accent was entrancing. So was her grin.

"Sabine's the one who found the deadleaf," Natalie offered, smiling. "If you crush the leaves, it makes a numbing salve, which is a huge help. The fruit's poisonous, but Sabine uses the seeds to brew a tea that works like a sleeping potion after it ferments. It's what knocked you out last night, when you were hurting after you started to wake up. It's the closest thing to Tylenol PM that we've got." A wistful look passed over her face. "Would've been nice for Kev to have had some when he broke his arm. But at least now he's home, in the land of Motrin and orthopedic surgeons. Sometimes I think that's the best thing I've ever done here. Setting his arm, making sure he didn't lose it. He wants to be a surgeon. Anyway"—she took a deep breath—"let's take a look at your head." Natalie talked *fast*; I had to work to keep up.

Natalie's fingers danced across my scalp. "Looks good. Just don't mess with it, okay?"

"Okay." As if I wanted to touch blood. Dried, fresh, mine, someone else's, it didn't matter. Blood gave me the willies, in any form. No island medicine for me.

Soon the breakfast area cleared, of food and of people. Again I felt grateful to Natalie, a stranger who took care of me last night and kept me company today. But I couldn't help noticing that my island guide was still missing.

Sabine stood. "Let's go see how things are shaping up for tonight."

"Tonight?" I asked, feeling lost, again.

"Tonight's a Nil Night," Natalie said, smiling impishly. "We have one to celebrate whenever someone makes it home. Like Kevin." She positively beamed. "And to welcome newcomers—like you." Seeing my face, she laughed. "Don't worry. It's no big deal."

Big deal or not, I hoped the spotlight stayed on Kevin rather than me. As the newest contestant, I felt conspicuous enough.

As we cut through the trees, the unmistakable smell of roasting meat filled the air. "Someone's smoking something," I said, taking a deep breath. Even though I'd just eaten, my mouth watered like I'd just walked by a pregame tailgate at UGA.

Sabine made a face. "It's the hog. Don't worry, Charley, you don't have to eat it."

"Have to? I *want* to. I haven't smelled anything this good in weeks."

Natalie laughed. "Sabine's a vegan, Charley. No meat."

"I take it you're not?" Sabine asked, crinkling her nose. But she was smiling.

"Nope. I'm a Southerner. Barbecue is its own food group for us."

The trees fell away, dumping us on the beach. White sand shifted under my sandals, finer than the black sand I'd been walking on for the past two weeks. But the sand was nothing compared with the scene before me.

The sun sparkled, rising into a cloudless sky. The ocean lay ahead, stretching until it met the horizon, blue kissing blue. Close to shore, the waves broke and retreated. But for the first time since I'd set foot on Nil, the beach was full of people and activity. A firepit wafted lazy smoke into the air. Around the fire, kids laughed and talked. Two shirtless boys were playing catch with a coconut, throwing it like a football, their shoulders and backs rippling under a sheen of sweat. The girl built like a Playboy bunny was sprinting down the beach beside a tall boy with dreadlocks, like an advertisement for island athletic wear. Other kids floated on surfboards past the whitewater. It looked like an island retreat, like the perfect Hawaiian vacation spot.

Something twanged, like when a violist strikes a sour note.

"Natalie," I said, turning, "where are the adults? The little kids?"

CHAPTER
15

I hated to leave Charley, but the look on Miguel's face left me no choice.

"What's up?" I asked. Miguel was usually chill. My-English-is-choppy-so-I'm-just-gonna-listen chill, but still chill. Right now his face was anything but chill. He looked seriously disturbed. "Is it about the Shack?"

"No." Miguel kept his voice low. "Elia's team. They bring something back. Something you need to see."

Something bad. Miguel's face said it all. My stomach felt like I'd swallowed rocks.

"Behind the Shack," he said. "Come."

Sy and Johan lounged on a flat rock at the City's edge. Johan's hair was so filthy it looked more brown than blond, and both boys' skin was streaked with dirt. They were Search-dirty and then some. Elia was nowhere in sight.

"Welcome back," I said.

Sy stood. "Thad, check this out."

He walked over, handling a piece of cloth as if it held delicate crystal. Beside me Miguel crossed himself and whispered in rapid-fire Spanish. Johan looked ready to throw up.

As Sy slowly peeled back one corner, I'd have sworn Nil giggled. Inside the cloth was a bracelet, an ivory-colored cuff, about two inches wide and perfectly smooth.

I knew that cuff.

It'd taken the owner months to craft it—to smooth it using a fine mixture of sand and salt. I remember sitting beside her, watching her rub the cuff. I'd thought it was creepy then. Hollow and empty, it was beyond creepy now.

"What is it?" Bart's voice came over my shoulder. I'd forgotten he'd followed us.

"A bracelet," I answered, irritated. Then I looked at Sy. "Where'd you find it?"

"Near the groves." He swallowed. "Whoever she was, she didn't make it. I, uh, had to take it off her wrist. Or what was left of her wrist." Sy looked ashamed.

"I told him to leave it." Speaking for the first time, Johan's words were like nails. "That to bring it back was bad karma, but he insisted." Johan shot a dark look at Sy, who visibly withered. "He doesn't get it." Johan's troubled face matched Miguel's. "We buried the body, and we should have buried the bracelet with it."

No argument there.

"Look, I thought we should bring it back," Sy said. "So you or someone else could ID her. I didn't think just telling you about it would be enough to make a positive ID. She deserves a cross, man. On the Wall."

I couldn't argue with that either.

"But to disturb someone's final resting place—" Johan broke off. He shook his head and crossed himself.

"I don't see what the big deal is," Bart offered.

"Thank you," Sy said, emphasizing each word.

Johan exhaled heavily and leveled his eyes on Sy. His voice was a mix of frustration and pity. "The deal is," he said softly, "we didn't see a single gate after you took the bracelet. Not one."

Sy stiffened. "It's not like a gate's guaranteed to flash. It's all chance anyway. Pure luck."

"Bad luck," Johan shot back. "Which you brought upon us. You should have left it."

"No," Sy said. "I did the right thing. She deserves a cross."

The argument felt stale, getting nowhere but here.

"Enough," I snapped. "What's done is done." Rattled, I couldn't stop staring at the cuff.

"What's it made of?" Bart asked, his voice curious. Unsuspecting.

"Bone."

Sy dropped the cuff like it was on fire.

I lurched forward. The brittle bone fell toward the charcoal rock, and just before the cuff hit and shattered, I caught it.

Johan was beside himself. "Holy Mary, Mother of God! Sy, are you *trying* to bring us bad karma?" He ran both his hands through his hair, pulling at the roots.

Sy stared at the cuff in my hands, his mouth slightly open, as Johan spun to me. "Do you know who it belonged to?" he asked, his eyes wild and worried.

"Ramia," I said quietly. "Her name was Ramia."

Sy found his voice, but his eyes remained locked on the cuff. "Bone?" he asked. "Who carves stuff from bone?"

"Ramia," I said.

"Yeah, I got that," Sy said. "But, man, that's messed *up*."

I shrugged. "Ramia made the bone fish hooks, too." *And she had a disturbing knack for predicting people's fate, including her own.* I closed my eyes, blocking the memory of her prediction for me. "She left my third week here."

"She didn't get far," Bart said at the same time Sy said, "That sucks."

Suddenly I couldn't wait to be rid of the bracelet. It felt heavy in my hands. "I'll take care of this, okay?"

"You'll bury it, right?" Johan's eyes were twitchy.

"Definitely."

Johan stood. "I'll come with you. Sy, you come, too." Johan's tone left zero room for Sy to worm out. "We buried her, we should bury this, too. And we'll pray." Briefly, he turned to Bart and Miguel. "No offense, but you two should leave. Thad makes three, and right now we need all the luck a trinity can bring."

Miguel didn't need to be asked twice. Crossing himself repeatedly, he took off. Bart lingered, then left.

We walked in silence, past the Flower Field, to the burial ground. Johan and Sy used flat rocks to dig a hole. I wrapped the cloth around the bone like a shroud, then placed it in the hole, and Johan filled the tiny grave with dirt. The cloth disappeared, Nil reclaiming her own.

Untying a small sack from his waist, Johan shook out a handful of bleached coral. One by one, he placed pieces on the raw dirt until he'd formed a cross.

Still on his knees, he said, "Let's pray."

Eyes closed, I listened to Johan's deep voice.

"Heavenly Father, we come to you on our knees. We ask you to bless this bracelet. And bless its owner, Ramia. May she rest in peace, and give her family strength. Your strength, wherever they are. And, Father, please help us. Please protect us from Nil and get us safely home. Amen."

"Amen," I murmured.

"Jeezy Pete, Johan, was that a prayer for the dead girl or for us?" Sy asked as we stood. "Are you supposed to dump all your prayers together like that?"

Johan shrugged. "Can't hurt. Might help." He looked at me,

worry darkening his eyes. "Thad, I've got a bad feeling. We shouldn't have taken that bracelet."

Johan was by far the most religious and most superstitious person in the City. But I had a bad feeling myself. Finding a body was never good, and stripping it of a bracelet—a bracelet made of *bone* of all things—felt even worse. Especially *Ramia's* bone bracelet. Holy Nil-nightmares-waiting-to-happen.

"At least it didn't come back into the City," I said, looking for the good. "And in the end, Ramia gets her cross."

Johan nodded, but he still looked worried.

"What kind of bone was that?" Sy asked. "Please don't tell me it was human."

"Cow."

"Well, that's something," Johan said.

That's all we said the entire way back.

At the edge of the City, Sy cut right. "See ya," he mumbled. Then he scurried toward the Cove. Johan hung back with me.

"I'll carve for Ramia," I said.

Johan nodded. "Thad." His voice was firm. "I won't go out with Sy again. I know he's new, but he doesn't listen. And he doesn't get Nil." Johan paused. "About an hour before we found Ramia, an inbound flashed twenty meters away. A hippo fell out. Big one, too. My shout gave us plenty of warning, but Sy panicked. He dropped the supply pack as he bolted to hide, and guess who trampled it? You know it, the hippo. Our last two days of food, gone." Johan snapped his fingers for emphasis. "That's why we're back early. And then the bracelet. We shouldn't have taken it. But Sy wouldn't listen."

"I hear you," I said. "I'll talk to Sy."

"Good," Johan said. "Maybe you can open his eyes."

Doubtful, I thought. If the bone bracelet—hippo combo didn't sway Sy into recognizing Nil's bad karma, I couldn't imagine what words would.

"I'll try," I said. It was the best I could do.

I strode to the Wall, ready to rid myself of Ramia and find Charley. Going straight to Ramia's weathered name, I carved a cross beside it. Then, out of habit, I glanced at my name. The day I'd carved those letters was still fresh: I remember gouging the wood, sealing the deal, and I remember my confidence, tinged with relief. The weird truth was, when I first landed here, I was secretly kind of stoked. Primed for a break from the grind and the pressure, I'd viewed Nil as a forced vacation, a mandatory mid-season break. I figured I'd be back on the mountain in no time. Back battling my dad over my dreams or his.

I couldn't have been more wrong. And judging by the crosses littering the Wall, plenty of other people had been wrong, too.

Except Ramia. She'd been dead right.

I closed my eyes, abruptly repelled by the Wall, by the crosses, but mostly repelled by Ramia, whose prophecies I couldn't shake.

Spinning around, I nearly knocked Li down.

"Ramia." She pointed to the cross. "How you know?" Li made a slicing motion across her throat.

"Sy and Johan, they found her."

"No. How you know it Ramia?"

"Her bracelet." I wrapped my hand around my wrist. "The cuff. It was her."

Li nodded, her eyes back on Ramia's fresh cross. "Nil crazy," she whispered.

"Thad! Incoming!" Macy shouted from the tree line. "On the beach!"

I dashed toward Macy, pulling my knife. The handle was still warm. I hit the sand at a full sprint, just in time to see the inbound gate flash brilliant and blinding. I had seconds, at best.

Charley, Sabine, and Natalie stood between me and the gate. Just ahead, Raj held a knife; Samuel and Rives gripped spears.

Blade low, I sprinted toward Charley. Her eyes were on the gate. It glittered over the sand, like a two-dimensional disco ball, and for an instant, the beach was perfectly reflected in the sparkling air.

Then every speck went black.

Rider. I tensed. *Person, thing, or animal?*

Natalie stepped slightly in front of Charley as a blur of red fell from the air.

Person, I processed with relief. A boy. Nothing with fangs, nothing with claws. My knife slid back into hiding as the gate collapsed and winked out completely.

Slowing, I jogged up behind Charley, in time to hear her murmur, "Another kid."

Before I could speak, Charley looked at Natalie. "What do you mean, no adults? No children?" Her voice was measured, carefully deliberate; it was the same tone I recognized from this morning as Charley worked to connect Nil's dots. "Not in the City, or not here at all?"

"Not on the island," Natalie said. She'd already ripped off her chest wrap and was draping it over the boy's groin. He was still out cold. "The youngest person is Jason, who dropped in at thirteen. The oldest person to come through was nineteen. All of us fall somewhere in the middle. Like this guy." Her arms folded across her chest, Natalie tilted her head at the boy. "Didn't Thad tell you?" she asked Charley, her expression perplexed. "Only teenagers come through the gates."

"And the occasional mountain lion," Charley muttered.

"Don't forget African lions," I said. "We get those, too."

She whipped her head around. "You're kidding."

"Nope. We're pretty sure gates regularly roll through the African plains."

"The zebra." Charley nodded. "Right."

Rives tossed Natalie a piece of fabric. "Nice move, twin. You just made my day."

"Then my work here is done," Natalie told Rives, tying the material around her breasts in a flash. But her eyes stayed on Charley.

"Lions and zebras and teenagers, oh my," Charley said in a tight voice. She was staring at the boy.

The boy moaned, drawing everyone's attention but mine. I stayed locked on Charley, who frowned.

"Is he burned?" Charley asked. "I mean, can gates burn you? Mine felt like it. And he looks fried."

Now that I looked, the boy did look a little crispy. His face was bright red, like his hair. Ditto for his shoulders.

"If the gate roasted him, it'd be a first," I said. "I think he had a head start on his Nil tan."

Charley nodded. "Poor kid. Now I know why you didn't add *alone* to your 'same song, different verse' intro this morning. I guess not everyone wakes up naked and alone, just the lucky ones."

"Lucky?" Natalie's voice was sharp. She raised an eyebrow at me, and I mouthed, *Not yet.*

The boy moaned again and blinked.

"Seeing how you're still introducing Nil to Charley, I'll take this one." Nat's voice had a dangerous edge. "Unless you want to."

"All yours," I said.

The boy jerked up, making the wrap slip and exposing himself. Snatching back the cloth, he stared at us, shocked.

"Hey," Natalie said in her gentle-but-firm Leader voice. "It's okay. You're okay."

"Bloody 'ell." His eyes flicked to Natalie. "Who the fuck are you? And where the 'ell's my bathers?"

I actually felt bad for the guy. Charley had a point. His entrance on the beach in full view had to suck, worse than just waking up in a dark meadow by yourself.

"You nicked my clothes?" The boy looked incredulous. "And my watch?" He scooted backward on the sand, but struggled to stay covered.

"We didn't take your clothes." Natalie's voice was soothing. "I'm Natalie. I know this sounds crazy, but you came through a wormhole, and your clothes didn't make it. I'll answer all your questions in a minute, I promise. But first, where were you when the heat hit?"

The boy flinched. "How'd you know that?" His accent was tough, like a brogue. He narrowed his eyes at Natalie. "Wha'ja do to me?"

"I didn't do anything." The edge crept back into Nat's voice. "The heat, it's a gate. A portal. A wormhole, and it brought you here. But where were you?"

The boy blinked. "Mykonos. On holiday."

"Okay." She nodded, smiling like normal Nat. "Do you remember what day it was?"

"What day?" The rookie looked thrown.

"Try to remember," Nat urged, gently. "What day was it?"

He told her, and she nodded. "And the year?"

She nodded again. "Okay, like I said, I'm Natalie. What's your name?"

"Rory."

"Welcome to Nil, Rory," Natalie said.

"Nil?" Rory frowned. "Where the 'ell's Nil?"

"Good question," Charley said.

Rory jerked his eyes to her, lingering on her legs before traveling north. Watching his lip curl into a smile, I fought the urge to knock him back unconscious.

"Who're you?" he asked Charley.

"Charley. Been here thirteen days." Her response killed all

thoughts of Rory. How would Charley know the days were so important? "Just thought you'd like knowing you're not the only one new to the freak show," she added, smiling.

She doesn't know, I thought, strangely relieved. *She's just being kind.*

Natalie spoke back up. "Nil's an island. We all got here the same way you did, and we're all trying to get home. Gates go both ways." She smiled wryly. "Welcome to paradise."

"Bloody 'ell." The boy looked from Charley to Natalie, then swept the rest of us. When he passed over Heesham and Rives, he stiffened, and his eyes flew back to Natalie and settled, hard. "You think I'm a fucking *eejit?*" He glared at her. "That I'll buy this Alice in Wonderland shit yer selling? What're you blokes really after? Money?"

"Hardly." Natalie sounded disgusted. "What we've told you is the truth. It's up to you what you want to believe."

"Bloody 'ell," Rory said. "I've got no bathers, no mobile, no idea where the fuck I am or who the fuck you nutters are." His fingers gripped the wrap so tightly they turned white; freckles popped out like dirt. "Fucking fairy-tale nut jobs."

"Like I said, you're on Nil," Natalie snapped, "and it's no fairy tale, let me tell you that. And if you wouldn't mind, would you please stop using the word *fuck* so much? It's getting on my fucking nerves." Then she stormed away.

I was shocked. I'd never heard Nat cuss, let alone ditch a rookie.

"Be right back," I told Charley. Then I glanced at Rives, who was eyeing Rory with a mix of contempt and pity. "Rives, you got this covered, eh?"

"Yeah." Rives nodded. "Go."

I had to jog to catch Natalie. "Nat, you okay?"

She turned, and I was stunned to see tears streaming down her face. "I can't take it anymore. People come, people go. Jerks drop in, and Kevin's *gone.*" Her voice cracked. "I'm done. I want out. I want Kevin, and I want to go home."

She looked ready to break, or maybe she had.

"I know. Hey—" I moved to hug her, but she held up one hand. "No. I'm fine," she said, sounding remarkably steady. "Get back to Charley."

Charley. I sucked as an island guide. I'd left her twice now.

"You'd better tell her." Natalie's eyes narrowed. "And I mean now. She needs to know."

"I know. I was just giving her some time. To, you know, get adjusted."

Natalie sighed. "There is no time. You know that." She paused, then hit me with a hard Nat stare. "If you don't tell Charley, I will."

CHAPTER
16

The boy named Rives led Rory away, steering him by the shoulder. Lips pursed, Rory looked like a mad blowfish, or maybe it was just his sunburn.

As I turned, Thad reappeared by my side.

"I think I need a new island guide," I teased. His face kind of fell. "Kidding," I said. "Is Natalie okay?"

"She misses Kevin."

"I figured." Then I remembered something. "Hey, what did Miguel show you?"

"A cow bone."

"A cow bone," I repeated. "Why?"

"I had to bury it."

"Okayyy," I said. "Did something bad happen to the cow? I mean, obviously the cow died. But was it bad?"

"Actually, no. The cow fell off a cliff. Everyone had steak for dinner." Thad grinned.

"Huh." I didn't know what else to say.

I looked around the beach. The surfers had come in. I recognized one as Jason, the curly-haired kid who'd accused me of stealing Kevin's clothes. The boys had stopped throwing their coconut football; the group around the fire had split up. Anticipation hung in the air as thick and heavy as Atlanta humidity in August.

And then it hit me: it was nearly noon.

"Is everyone looking for a gate?" I asked. "An exit gate?"

"Yeah." Thad's eyes roamed the beach. "They always come at noon, but that's all we know. They pop up anywhere, but never the same spot two days in a row." He ran his hand through his hair, clearly frustrated. "It sucks. Like trying to hit the lottery."

I noticed no one watched the ocean.

"Do they ever come from the water?" I asked.

"Nope. Just across land." Tension rolled off Thad in waves.

Heesham stood closest to us, about twenty feet away. Sabine stood near Heesham, her eyes as busy as Thad's. Two other boys—one I recognized as Miguel—stood at the tree line; others were fanned to the right. Just as Natalie walked out from the trees with Li, the wind stalled, the sun felt hotter, and everything happened at once.

The sand at Sabine's heels melted. Shimmering sand rose into the air behind her, then the sand fell, leaving wavering, iridescent air stretching over her head. Recalling the gate that brought Rory, I immediately saw the difference. This gate was like the ones in the red rock field: more translucent, less reflective—more like glass than a mirror, and this gate rose from the ground, whereas Rory's gate had popped midair and dropped. This gate was an outbound. And it was right behind Sabine.

The gate was still rising when Heesham shouted, "Sabine! Run!"

Other voices: "Li! Gate!" It was a chorus. "Li! Li!"

To my surprise, Sabine leaped *away* from the gate, not toward it. At the same time, Li broke from Natalie, sprinting toward Sabine. Sabine twisting; Li running. The shimmering air streaked forward and rolled over Sabine. She cried out, the outlines of her body rippled and faded, the gate collapsed inward—and then it was gone.

So was Sabine.

Li stood five feet away, her face pale.

Heesham let out a cry like a wounded bear, shattering the weird silence. His face set in furious stone lines, he strode to the ocean, where he launched something small into the sea. Without waiting for it to drop, he took off running, up the beach. Alone.

The shift in the mood was shocking.

No one smiled. No one laughed. Other than Heesham, no one even moved. Only on Nil does a naked boy fall from the sky and no one bats an eye. And yet when that gate swallowed Sabine, everyone looked shocked.

I turned to Thad. "What's wrong? Why aren't people happy for Sabine? Did something bad happen to her?"

"No. It's just—Li's been here so long, that gate should have been hers. And Sabine's a huge loss." Thad shook his head. "Huge."

Miguel and a blond boy I hadn't met yet walked up. The blond boy's face was a mixture of fury and defeat—like Heesham's, but different. Less angry, more frustrated.

"Thad," he said, in an accent I couldn't begin to place, "you see? Our best healer, gone." The boy snapped his fingers, then clenched his hair at the roots. His eyes sparked. "Sy brought this upon us. You talk to him. Make him *see*."

Thad sighed. "I hear you, Johan. I'll try."

The boy nodded, slightly mollified.

Miguel cocked his head at the angry boy. "Ready, amigo?" After a quick triple count, they took off at a fierce sprint.

"My money's on Johan," Thad said. His tone was dull.

"You don't have any money," I said. "At least not here."

"No, I don't." His voice still flat, Thad watched the boys race.

"Thad, look at me." That got his attention. "You said everyone wanted Li to catch that gate. That it should've been hers. What did you mean?"

Thad glanced back at the boys, but not before a shadow flickered across his face, a soul-wrenching darkness at odds with the brilliance of the day.

"C'mon," he said, "let's walk."

I didn't move. "No. I don't want to walk. I want to know what's going on. And I want to know now."

Thad looked at me, his golden hair falling into his eyes, his face set in hard lines. Then he sighed, and his face melted into the same defeat I'd just seen on Johan. "You're right. You have to know. I was just—" Shaking his head, he gave a humorless laugh.

"Just what?" I asked.

"Being an idiot. Hoping to delay the inevitable, pretending for a minute it didn't exist. But it does."

"What?" I frowned, frustrated.

"Nil." Thad sighed. "Okay, here's the deal. You get here, as a teenager, somewhere between thirteen and nineteen. You have one year. To catch a gate, or—" He stopped, his sapphire eyes so full of fire I thought he might go up in flames.

"Or?" I prompted.

"You die."

The bright blue sky remained cloudless, and the aquamarine ocean still crashed gently onto the white sand beach, but the scene was suddenly warped. Twisted, as I processed Thad's words.

"What do mean, you die?"

"You die." Thad's voice was heavy; the fire was gone. "It's like everyone has a personal window of time that the gateway to Nil stays open for them. It's always one year. Exactly three hundred sixty-five days. If you miss that window, you're done."

"What do you mean, you're done? You *die?* How?" I'd always been a stickler for details, and these seemed pretty darn important.

"I'm not really sure. I've never been with anyone on their last day, and most people Search alone at that point. Then we either find their clothes or their body." Thad looked sick. "That's why I asked you about the days, because it's important to keep count."

"Tick-tock," I said, doing some quick mental math.

"You okay?" Thad's eyes searched mine.

"Peachy. Eighteen is overrated."

"Don't tell me you're giving up." He sounded shocked.

"I was kidding. I've still got three hundred fifty-two days." I looked at Thad. "What about you? How many do you have left?"

Thad's grin was wry. "Eighty-six. But who's counting?"

Me. Em-bleeding-behind-the-wheel fear shot through me. I couldn't imagine Nil without Thad, but it was more than that. It was something deeper, something raw, something that I didn't expect or understand, something I just *felt.*

Me.

CHAPTER 17

I'd swear she said, "Me."

Maybe I'd read her lips, or maybe it was what I wanted to hear. When I'd told her the truth, horror flickered through her golden eyes—and something inside me let go. Not broke, but gave in. Made me *want*.

To fight.

To stay.

To be with Charley, a girl I didn't know but wanted to—more than I'd wanted anything in months. For the first time since my feet hit Nil dirt, there was something I wanted more than leaving: time. Time without limits, time to get to know the girl who made me feel alive again. And in that moment, I hated Nil all over again, because she'd given me something she could snatch away, or worse, keep for herself.

I swallowed, fighting the rush of emotion, then a surge of guilt. I hated that I'd deceived Charley. Maybe not outright lied, but certainly hadn't told her the full truth from the get-go. It was a total Bart move.

"I'm sorry, Charley." I felt like a slimeball.

"Did you just say sorry, Charley?" A smile lit her face, like she was happy to not be talking about death anymore. "Like I've never heard that one before. What are you sorry for?"

"For not telling you sooner. I didn't because once you know, you start watching the days, and you never stop, but it's no excuse. I should have told you this morning." I scanned her face, trying to figure out where I stood.

For a minute, she looked far away. Then she smiled at me, her eyes warm and clear. "It's okay," she said. "I'm kind of glad you didn't. Hey, still up for that walk?"

Looking at Charley, her chin slightly raised, looking more gorgeous and full of quiet fight than any girl I'd ever met, I grinned. "Not anymore. Rain check?"

She looked taken aback. But more than anything, she looked tired.

I chuckled. "You look beat. I don't think a long beach walk is what you need right this second. I might have to carry you back."

She glared at me. "No one asked you to carry me."

"True. And hey, I'd do it again. But there's something I want you to see." Something to counter the ugliness of Nil, something I had a hunch Charley would love.

We cut through the City, then through the trees.

"So I can't walk down the beach, but I'm strong enough for a woods hike?" Charley asked. Her face was pale, a fact I didn't miss— or like.

"It's close. Two minutes, tops, but I could use a snack." I paused, giving her a chance to take a break. "What about you?"

"Sounds great," she said, sitting on a black rock. "I'm thinking a peanut butter and jelly sandwich, chips, and a Snickers. And a Sprite." As she talked, her hand crept to her head.

"How 'bout a pineapple?" I pulled the fruit from my satchel. "It's almost a Snickers. Minus the chocolate, the caramel, nuts, and nougat." With my knife, I sliced the pineapple in two and cored each half. After cutting a half-moon slice, I speared the yellow fruit on my knife and offered it to Charley.

"Wow," she said, plucking the fruit off my blade. "Where'd you get the handy tool? I gutted a poor pineapple with lava rock. It didn't go so well."

"The Shack. There's a stash of knives in there. Most are wood. They're stronger than you think, and there's a few rough metal ones, too, like this one. Someone before us made them. Our job is to sharpen them and not lose them." *Thanks again, Bart.* Leave it to the biggest tool to take one on Search and come back without it. I made a mental note to talk to Bart again later, along with Sy. Then I focused on Charley.

The two of us ate quietly, tossing rinds into the woods and licking juice off our fingers.

"Best Snickers I've ever had." Charley smiled. "Thanks."

I laughed. "Just wait. It gets better."

We walked in easy silence. Blue sky shone ahead, and when we broke through the trees, an open meadow burst with color: purples, blues, pinks, reds, yellows, and lots of white. Riding the breeze, the colors shifted in gentle waves.

"This is the Flower Field," I said. "I don't know what kinds of flowers they are, but—"

"It's gorgeous," Charley said simply.

For a minute, we just stood there. As they always did, my eyes drifted to the brightest patch of white. Not in the field, but high to the right, on the mountain peak. White covered the summit, like confectionary sugar, full of icy goodness. My mouth watered; I could almost taste the snow. I closed my eyes and let myself go, feeling a sick powder rush. This was my favorite spot on the island, and my most hated.

Then the wind whispered, making me open my eyes and look at Charley.

Her eyes were on the field. The wind played with her hair, pushing it around, making the ends tickle her shoulders. Her head was tilted to one side, and her expression was strange.

"What is it?" I asked.

She looked at me and smiled. "Nothing. Thanks for showing me this." But when she looked back at the field, the weird expression returned. It bothered me that I couldn't read it.

"Charley, what's wrong?"

Charley laughed, a subtle sound that said *everything*. "It's funny," she said, still watching the Field. "Everything's so beautiful here. Too beautiful. Like it's not real. And it really isn't."

"Oh, it's real," I said.

She shook her head. "I've never seen such beauty. The black sand beach, the Crystal Cove. The Flower Field. Even the red lava field was beautiful in its own freaky way. But it's not really real. Because in three hundred fifty-two days, it will all disappear, right?" Charley turned to me, and her golden eyes were haunted.

The façade was gone. For Charley, Nil's mask had finally cracked, this time for good.

That afternoon, I pulled Rives aside and told him about the skull Charley had found.

"Take Miguel, Heesham, and Nat and anyone else you want. Go to Black Bay, try to find it. If you do, try to make an ID. Look for a necklace, a bracelet. Anything." I handed him a bag of bleached coral. "Then bury it."

Rives nodded. "Will do, bro."

As Rives walked away, I thought about the skull. *Can we leave?* Charley had asked, her golden eyes troubled. *Everyone leaves, eventually*, I'd said. And it was true. Now, whether you made it out alive or dead, that was a different question, and the answer was up to Nil.

Nil crazy, Li had said.

She was so right. And right now, she was exactly the person I needed to see.

CHAPTER 18

CHARLEY
DAY 13, EARLY EVENING

I sat on the bed while Natalie messed with my hair. It was the latest surreal Nil moment of the day. Less *Survivor*, more like *America's Next Top Model*, island edition, but I still felt completely out of place.

Outside Natalie's hut, twilight approached, flickering like torchlight. Using the final moments of daylight, Natalie was crafting an island updo, so intent on her work that she didn't speak, although I sensed that her thoughts dwelled on something more important than my hair. She'd barely spoken since I'd returned from the Flower Field. I had no idea what to say to make her feel better, because the thing was, I didn't feel so great myself.

Eighty-six days.

Three hundred fifty-two days.

Eighty-six days.

The numbers flashed like neon signs in my head. *Once you know, you start watching the days, and you never stop.* Thad was right. But it was *his* days that I was stuck on. Three hundred fifty-two seemed like a lifetime compared with eighty-six.

"Natalie." I turned, and she hit me in the nose with her comb.

"Sorry!" It was the first smile I'd seen from her this afternoon.

"Listen, Thad told me about the days."

"I know. He had to." Her voice was hard.

"I've been wondering. How many do you have left?"

"Thirty-three."

"Thirty-three?" I jumped up. "Why aren't you on Search?" From what I knew, it seemed pretty darn clear she should be out hunting shimmers, not sitting here combing my hair.

"Yeah. But when Kevin left, I kind of lost it. I had to know if he made it, and I was afraid to leave, afraid I'd miss the news, or find—" She stopped, her free hand fingering the shell bracelet on her wrist. "I'm leaving in the morning. I just confirmed my team with Thad."

Thad. Thad, with eighty-six days, busy taking care of me and apparently everyone else—like Natalie, who looked less than excited about going on Search.

"Don't you want to go?" I frowned.

"I do. But today, it was a reality check, you know? A reminder of how tricky it is to catch a gate. Sabine's gone, and she wasn't here long enough to get a haircut. And then there's Li, who's got less than two weeks." She twisted her bracelet so hard the shells dented her wrist. "I might not make it, Charley," she whispered. "I might not see Kevin again. There's no guarantee. Not here."

"Not anywhere," I said. "But you can't think like that."

She stared at her bracelet.

"Natalie, I haven't been here long enough to know how you feel, and I'm not going to pretend I do. But Kevin made it, and you can, too. You can't give up. You've got thirty-three chances, and more than that if you think of how many doubles might be out there, too, not to mention triples or quads. But you can't catch one if you don't try."

Now she looked up. "Quads?"

"Yup. I saw one on my first day here. My point is, don't quit. Not on Kevin, not on yourself. And not on me, okay? You kind of remind me of my sister, Em—unless you quit." I squeezed her hand, thinking I pretty much stunk at the whole rah-rah thing. *This is why you were never a cheerleader, Charley,* I thought. *That and the fact that you're six feet tall.*

She hugged me so fiercely it was like she'd channeled Em. "Thanks, Charley. I'm so glad it was you who found Kev's clothes." She paused. "You didn't find anything with the clothes, did you?" The hope lighting Natalie's eyes belied her casual tone.

"Just sandals. Why?" Thad's words from this afternoon popped into my head. *Our job is to sharpen them and not lose them.* "Oh, are you talking about a knife? Is that what I missed?"

Natalie looked taken aback. "A knife? No. It's nothing." Then she regarded me with the same critical eye my mom gave me when I'd cut my bangs in sixth grade. "Now, we'd better get to it if we're gonna finish that hair before tonight."

Thirty minutes later, Natalie announced, "Done."

Using two thin sticks, she'd swept part of my hair into what Natalie assured me was a very a fashionable 'do. The rest trailed down my back. Then she'd smudged my eyes with charcoal and glossed my lips with something that tasted like pomegranate. Stepping back, she looked at me like a painter studying her canvas. "You look amazing. I'd kill for your coloring, not to mention your legs. There's just one thing missing." She raised one finger and grinned. "Got it." Reaching over, she broke a single white blossom off a wreath by her bed and tucked it behind my ear. "There," she said, nodding. "No bunches of flowers in the hair, too fussy for you. But this"—she adjusted the flower—"is perfect."

Her eyes dropped to my clothes, and she frowned. "Well, at least they're clean. It's not like I can pop into Anthropologie and get you something else, right? But I can make these fit better." In a flash,

Natalie adjusted my halter; the uncomfortable knot of fabric at my back vanished. Then she retied my skirt, making it shrink by inches.

"Stop tugging on it, Charley." She intercepted my hand, grinning. "It's not as short as you think. Plus, you only live once." Her own words caught her off guard. I saw her stiffen, then close her eyes, fighting herself.

This time I hugged her.

"Natalie, it's okay. You'll make it."

For a minute she just held me tight. Then she let go and wiped her eyes.

"Okay, that's enough mushy gushy," she said. "Otherwise we'll smear our charcoal, and I worked hard on that." Smiling, she draped the wreath of flowers around her neck. Then, like she'd done it dozens of times before, she grabbed a handful of tiny white blossoms from a small bowl and tucked them into her hair in three seconds flat, like pearls sparkling within the strawberry blond. "Thanks, Charley. I'm glad you're here, even though I'm sorry you're here." She smiled, a real Natalie smile.

"Am I interrupting?" A voice at the doorway made my insides jump.

"You always are," Natalie scolded Thad, grinning. "But don't let that stop you." She looked at me and winked.

Thad eased inside, and the A-frame suddenly seemed small.

"Hey," I said.

"Hey." Thad smiled at me, and for a second, there was no air. Same bare chest, same ripped abs, same golden hair touching his shoulders. He wore the twine necklace he always had on, but tonight it boasted a single caramel shell that blended with his skin; I'd have sworn it held a piece of black rock before. His eyes swept over me, lingering on my legs.

"You look"—he swallowed—"underdressed."

"Really." I lifted my chin, determined not to pull on my skirt. "You think so?"

"Definitely. And I know just how to fix it." Pulling his hands from behind his back, he held a necklace of white flowers, woven together with a bright green vine. Simple, and gorgeous.

"May I?" he asked. For the first time, he looked uncertain.

I could only nod.

Thad moved closer. Inches away, he smelled like coconut and something fruity. With a movement so gentle it was almost a caress, Thad slipped the flower necklace over my head. "It's a tradition that a veteran welcomes each rookie. Charley from Georgia, consider this an official welcome to Nil City." His blue eyes were playful. "Last time I said that, you were unconscious."

My skin registered the cool touch of flowers as I tried to sift through yesterday's fog, again. Thad lifted my hair to settle the lei on my shoulders and the sensation pulled me back to the present.

"I hope you'll stay." Thad murmured, then he blinked heavily, like he'd said something wrong. "In the City, that is. Not go off hunting gates alone." His eyes locked on mine.

"A solo island quest sounds like a really bad idea," I said truthfully. "Lions and tigers and zebras, remember?" *And no you.*

Thad grinned. "Do you want to make it official? Carve a little graffiti, Nil style?"

I had no idea what he was talking about.

"The Naming Wall. Follow me." Taking my hand, he led me out of the A-frame.

I loved the feeling of Thad's hand wrapped around mine. I half expected to wake up, remembering the strangest dream about a hunky island guide, tailor-made just for me. Combing my hair, holding my hand—it was all as unreal as the freaky Friday trip that landed me here in the first place. The sweetness of this moment scared me, just a little. Or maybe a lot. I was in too deep to tell.

Thad stopped. Turning to look at me, he said, "I forgot to tell you. You look gorgeous." His voice caught. "More beautiful than anything else on Nil."

"How's your vision?" I asked. I was awful with compliments, especially when they seemed impossible.

He laughed. "Perfect." Pulling my hand, he said, "C'mon."

The fire ring simmered on low. No one was around. Torches were lit, and laughter and music drifted from the beach, but up here, it was just me and Thad, wrapped in night air.

When we reached the Wall, Thad let go, leaving my hand extraordinarily empty.

He pulled out his pineapple slicer, and with slow, deliberate strokes, Thad carved the first five letters of my name. Then he paused. "Tell me how to finish . . . *i-e* or *e-y?*"

"*E-y,*" I answered.

He chuckled. "So right."

"What's that supposed to mean?"

Thad finished etching the *y* and blew on my name. Without turning, he said, "Because for your name to end in a *lie* doesn't fit. You're the most real girl I've ever met, on or off Nil."

I didn't know what to say to that.

Thad's fingers brushed the wood, sweeping away the last shavings from my name. Seven letters, etched forever, then a space. I knew that whether I wanted it filled or not, in 352 days, my spot would no longer be blank. Two names above me, a fresh check followed Sabine. Other spots were blank, like mine. But it was the crosses that gave me chills. Scattered across the Wall, they reminded me of the random crosses I saw when I was driving—the ones hammered into the ground marking a roadside death. Simple, and haunting.

The empty space beside Thad's name was bracketed by two crosses, each beside a name I didn't recognize.

"Does a cross mean what I think it means?" I asked, staring at the pair of crosses. "That those people didn't make it?"

"Yup." Thad said. He turned to me, his eyes pleading. "But let's not think about that right now. Not tonight. Please?"

"Not tonight," I whispered, feeling the weight of the lie as it passed my lips. Because I couldn't promise not to think about those twin crosses near Thad, advancing like they wanted to swallow him, too. *Eighty-six days.*

I forced myself to focus on the "right now" part: right now Thad was right here.

"Thanks," I said.

"For what?"

"For carving my name. And for this." I touched my lei, careful not to crush the flowers.

"You're welcome, Charley with an *e-y*." Thad's voice was husky. He grinned, and my mouth went dry. "Ready for a Nil Night?"

"Ready," I managed.

"Lead on," he said, gesturing for me to go first.

The beach gathering reminded me of an old-fashioned luau. I'd been to one at the Polynesian resort in Disney World, which was as artificial a luau as you can get. But this one felt like the real deal. There was a pit in the sand, lined with coals and an honest-to-goodness pig. There was a bonfire surrounded by black rock. Fish and crabs steamed over the fire, and yams baked near the crabs. Julio had concocted more sweet bread; it sat beside bowls of pineapple and mango on a makeshift table.

Girls wore flower leis or blossoms in their hair, or both. Others wore necklaces made of shells, nuts, or things I couldn't identify. Same for the boys. Some necklaces matched; more often they didn't.

And there was music. An Asian boy played reed pipes. Samuel, the dark-haired boy with a massive shark-tooth necklace blacker than his skin rocked a set of drums that look worn and weathered. A freckled girl with two long braids—*Jillian*, I recalled—sat beside him, singing and playing a primitive guitar.

Rory, the angry boy who'd fallen out of the gate dropping f-bombs, stood apart from the group. He leaned against a tree, arms crossed, watching. Even in the dark he looked sunburned and wary.

Natalie handed me a coconut cup, then gave one to Thad. "Drinks on me," she said, smiling.

"Thanks." I took a sip and found the same fruity water I'd had yesterday. "Yummy."

A boy came over and draped his arm across Natalie's shoulders. As tall as Thad, with skin like my favorite latte and bleached-out dreads, I placed him immediately: he was the athletic boy I'd first seen running on the beach, the same boy who'd led Rory away. But for the life of me, I couldn't remember his name.

"Hello, Charley." He grinned. His eyes were strikingly light. "I haven't had the pleasure. I'm Rives. Rhymes with 'leaves,' but it's R-i-v-e-s on the Wall, in case you're looking." He winked. Rives's smile was infectious; it put me at ease. So did the fact that Natalie didn't throw off his arm.

"Nice to meet you, Rives-who-rhymes-with-leaves," I said, smiling back.

"Even if it is under these circumstances." Rives's grin widened.

Natalie leaned into Rives, which made her look even smaller. "Charley, stay away from this boy. He's trouble with a capital *T*."

Rives feigned outrage. "What? Nat, you're my girl. Where's the love?" He wrapped his arms around her, giving her a squeeze.

Natalie laughed. "You know I love you, twin. But I've got to protect Charley."

"Nat's right," Thad said, "watch out for Rives." But like Natalie, Thad was smiling.

"Gotcha," I said. "I'll add him to my list of Nil dangers."

Rives hooted. "Flattery will get you everywhere." He planted a kiss on Natalie's cheek, then let her go. "Later, twin." Grinning like the devil, he said, "See ya, Charley. Thad."

"Later, man," Thad said.

"For twins, y'all don't look a thing alike," I told Natalie as Rives walked away.

"You don't think so?" Then she burst out laughing. "We share the same birthday. A weird Nil-incidence." She shrugged, then sipped her water. I wondered how long Rives had been here. *Long enough to be chummy with Natalie*, I thought. And Thad.

Beside me, Thad whistled, making everyone turn.

"Grab a cup, everybody." He waited for everyone to get situated. "First, to Kevin, who made it. Here's to you, brother." Thad raised his cup as shouts of "to Kevin" and random woots cut the night. "And to Sabine, who gave us heaps to be thankful for while she was here, stuff that'll still help even though she's gone. And even better, she's not just gone, she caught a gate." He raised his cup. "To Sabine." Sabine's name drifted through the night as cups filled the air.

"And to Charley, and Rory, welcome. We're glad you're here, even though we're sorry you're here." He raised his cup to me and smiled. "Cheers."

The crowd fell away; it was just us, inches apart, and the warmth I felt had nothing to do with the fire.

Thad took a sip, then as he turned back to the group, his smile vanished. "As some of you've heard, the Shack was trashed again last night. Nothing was taken, just messed up. But we can't afford to lose supplies, so for now, we've set up watch on the Shack."

Reading between the lines, Thad's words held a warning. *If it's one of us, we're gonna catch you.* For the first time, it occurred to me that perhaps not everyone was thrilled with the City.

Thad kept talking. "Three Search teams will roll out at dawn. Li's got Cassie as Spotter, Quan and Raj as support. Samuel chose Maria as Spotter, Heesham as support. And Nat's heading out, with Jason as Spotter . . ." This last announcement triggered loud hoots and *yeahs*, drowning out Thad's words. Natalie looked almost happy. I hoped Jason was a good Spotter.

"So that's it. Focus on the good, live in the moment. To now." Thad raised his cup. Cups filled the air, and the chorus of "to now" was deafening.

"Ready?" he asked, turning back to me.

CHAPTER
19

Charley looked better than ever.

With rest and a few decent meals, her coloring had improved, and when she smiled, her golden eyes sucked me in, like a potent Nil swell. Even better, there was never a lull as we talked, and we clicked in too many ways to count. Charley made me feel real again, and she made me *feel*.

It was a sick Nil joke.

Of course I'd meet the perfect girl here. Here where I had no future, where I only had a now. Here where hoping too much hurt like hell, so I'd tried not to hope at all.

"Thad?" Charley asked.

"Yeah?" I shook off my mental slush.

She was looking at the beach. Groups were scattered like shells. Laughing, talking, eating, being together. Just another cookout at the beach—and yet it wasn't. I wondered if Charley saw that, too. Had she figured out that Nil Nights were our way to blow off steam, to release some pressure before we imploded for good? Because even with a daily dose of sports, the reality was exhausting. Each day was a sprint. We chased food and hunted gates, staying one step ahead of hunger and every fresh Nil threat. Running toward freedom and away from Nil, gunning to survive this day, because the next one might bring the gate with your name on it.

Or not.

Charley's thoughts did not track mine.

"The thing with the Shack," she said, turning toward me. "So it's an inside job?"

I raised an eyebrow. "Did I say it was an inside job?"

"You didn't have to. I assumed that since nothing was taken, someone's trying to cause trouble, or maybe it's just an animal. But either way you want to find out, right?"

Charley was incredibly perceptive.

"You got it," I said.

She nodded, still looking thoughtful. "So are you in charge?" she asked. "I mean, is that your job? You're the one who talked tonight, and everyone comes to you with questions."

"For now. It's a hand vote thing. Before me, Natalie was Leader; before Natalie, it was Omar, and so on. It's just someone to help settle differences and to coordinate teams."

"Why did Natalie quit?"

"She got Priority." *And once you have Priority, that's all you do. Search. Pray. And run like hell.*

"Priority?" Charley frowned.

"You get Priority at sixty days out. Then you're off job detail. You've paid your dues, so all you do is Search, with full City support. People with Priority pick their teams first."

"I thought you picked the teams." She sounded frustrated.

"Nope. The Search Leader does, which may be a person with Priority, but not always." One look at her face told me I was talking in circles.

"Okay, let me lay out the whole Search team deal. When a person goes on Search, they pick who they want to take. Jason's the best Spotter, so he gets picked almost every time. Timing gates is tricky. Jason's got a natural instinct for how gates roll, the speed, stuff like that. Plus, he's the youngest kid here, and people want him to make it. That's the other reason he gets picked, to give him a solid shot when it's his turn."

"And Spotters are the eyes, right?"

"Yup. Gates always roll north, never east—west. But you need all the eyes you can get to spot a gate rising and track its roll. Every second counts. And like I said, the rest of the team is backup. Like sherpas."

Charley digested this information. "Do the gates appear in one spot more than others? I mean, is there a go-to spot to catch one?"

"Nope. Nil doesn't make it that easy. There're a few hot spots right now, but gates jump around. It's like trying to catch lightning."

"That stinks. It'd be good if we knew where gates were more likely to hit. If there's a pattern."

"Yeah, a schedule of outbounds would be great. We're still waiting on Nil to deliver one."

Charley smirked. "I'm serious."

"So am I. If anyone's ever figured out how to increase the odds of getting off this rock, they took the secret with them when they left." *And it doesn't help us now, and now is all that matters.*

"There's something I don't get. Y'all didn't know if Kevin made it or not. If Jason's the best Spotter, why wasn't he with Kevin when Kevin caught a gate?"

"Because Kevin was down to his last forty-eight hours. He wouldn't let anyone go with him, especially Natalie. He said he had to make it alone, and if he didn't, he wanted her to remember him alive. His words."

Charley was quiet, no doubt pondering Kevin's choice. *Good luck*, I thought. I still didn't understand why Kevin went renegade. In the end it worked out, but it seemed to me that Kevin caught a gate despite his choice, not because of it. Ditching his team made no sense. It was like cutting off your hand because your fingers hurt. And Nat still went through hell.

"Okay, one more thing." Charley spoke slowly. "When groups go out, what stops someone else from taking a gate? From skipping in front of the person with Priority?"

"Nothing," I said. Her eyes widened, then narrowed. "It happens," I continued, "but it's rare. Stealing someone's gate is island manslaughter. You may not pull the trigger, but you're damn close, because you're stealing their best chance to leave—and to live. And if you make it off, you've got to live with knowing you might've just sentenced someone to death, especially if that person had Priority. Some people might be able to carry that weight around, but not most. Especially if you've stayed in the City. You get to know people. You want them to make it."

Charley stared at her cup, running her thumbs over the rim. "I saw the look on Sabine's face when the gate grabbed her. It was pure horror, and the last thing she would've heard was everyone yelling for Li. Poor Sabine. But there wasn't anything she could do." Her voice had dropped to an agonized whisper.

"No, there wasn't. Because it wasn't Li's gate after all; it was Sabine's. Nil made the choice."

I couldn't help thinking it was because of Ramia and that creepy bone cuff. Because Nil had left Ramia and her bracelet exactly how Nil wanted, exactly how Ramia predicted: bone on bone. Maybe Nil wanted us to wonder about Ramia's fate; maybe we weren't meant to know. We were Nil's pawns, her playthings. This was her sandbox, and it didn't matter if we didn't want to play. Thinking of Charley, I felt a spike of fear.

She was looking away. I followed her eyes to where Heesham sat by himself, staring at the sea where he'd thrown the bracelet, a gift meant for the girl who taught him how to say *love* in French.

"Is Heesham okay?" Charley asked.

"He will be," I said. "Tonight's tough. He'd fallen pretty hard for Sabine."

She nodded, like she understood.

Do you, Charley? Do you see how screwed up Nil really is? But I pushed Nil's cruelty from my head, because I didn't want to think about it tonight. Just one night.

"There's something I want you to see," I said, standing.

"What is it?" She tilted her head to look at me.

"You'll see." Smiling, I held out my hand, hoping she'd take it. *Needing* her to take it.

She took it.

I grabbed a torch and led her down to a stretch of black rocks, the same black rocks Jason had been chunking into the sea the day I met Charley. Some were tiny, like black diamonds. Others were pebbles, like slick gravel, or chunks. But one was as big as a table and just as flat.

"Cool rocks," she said. "Thanks for the beach tour. I give it five stars."

I laughed. "Five? Man, I was hoping for ten. But I do like these rocks."

"Uh-huh," was all she said, in that same velvet voice.

Chuckling again, I said, "Have a seat."

She let go as we sat, which pretty much sucked, although it did help to have both hands to wedge the torch into the sand. Then I sat beside her, so close our hips touched, which was a fresh rush all its own.

The sun was a brilliant orange ball. It hung over the water, centimeters from the horizon. The fading light licked the ocean's surface like fire.

"I don't know if you've noticed," I said, "but when the sun sets here, it sinks fast. After it touches the water, it disappears in seconds. And just before it drops out of sight, you'll see a green flash. Watch."

For a few minutes, we sat side by side. Not talking, just being.

Now, Nil whispered.

The orange ball tapped the water, dropped, and dipped from sight. And there it was—the emerald flash. Then it was gone, like the sun.

"Wow," Charley breathed. "That was cool."

"Yeah. It's like the sun's last stand, like the day wanted to live a bit longer."

I wanted to kick myself. I'd asked her not to talk about death, and here I was, doing it for her.

Charley faced the water, biting her lip, and I didn't know her well enough to read her. But I knew I'd ruined the moment.

"Hey," I said quietly, "you okay?"

She turned to me. Torchlight flickered in her eyes, like flames on the sun. "Yeah. I was thinking about the green flash and how gorgeous it was, like everything else on Nil. More surreal island beauty. And I was thinking that you're a heck of an island guide. First the Crystal Cove, then the Flower Field, and now this. You do this often?"

"Never," I said.

"So I'm just lucky?" she teased.

Not if you landed here, I thought. But I couldn't bring myself to say it. Then I had the weird thought that right now, I *felt* lucky, which wasn't just weird, it was insane.

"Hey, other than your family," I said, "is there anyone special you're missing back home?" *'Cause if there is, I bet he misses you more.*

"Are you asking me if I have a boyfriend?" Her smile was mischievous.

"Subtle, eh?" I laughed. Usually I wouldn't come right out and ask, but here, I had nothing to lose but ignorance. "Well?"

"No."

"I find that hard to believe."

She shrugged. Her dark hair blew off her shoulders, making my breath catch.

"What about you?" she asked. "Any girl back home you're missing?"

"No."

"I find that hard to believe." Her light tone matched mine.

"It's true. There's no one for me back home."

Watching Charley smile, I was dying to kiss her. Hell, I was eighty-six days away from dying anyway, but something held me back. Something in her eyes.

Then she shivered.

"You're cold." I fought the urge to wrap my arms around this girl I'd just met less than forty-eight hours ago. "Told you that you were underdressed." I grinned.

"I didn't see any jackets in the Shack," she said. "And the Gap was already closed."

As she rubbed her arms, I made myself ask, "Do you want to head back to the fire?"

Say no. Say you'll stay with me. Or better yet, kiss me, and you'll forget all about being cold.

CHAPTER 20

CHARLEY
DAY 13, NIGHT

Thad was so close I could make out the individual lashes framing his eyes. A small scar perched over his left eye. Shaped like a tiny mountain, it dipped into his eyebrow, and my fingers itched to touch it. Watching his lips curve into a lazy grin, I wanted to kiss him—more than I'd ever wanted to kiss any boy, ever.

But he'd just asked me if I wanted to go back, which meant he probably did. And I was not about to make a fool of myself by throwing myself at a boy looking for an escape.

"Okay," I said, but I didn't move. I was too overwhelmed by the moment and, frankly, by Thad. There were no boys like Thad back in Roswell, and I was definitely not in Roswell anymore. I was on Nil, where you watched the days, counted them down, and lived like you were dying.

Which we were.

Maybe I should kiss him after all.

"Ready? Or did you change your mind?" His voice was teasing.

The burning torch cast shadows on his face, highlighting his lips and jaw, and I nearly kissed him right then.

But I didn't. Because he was the one who'd asked to go back.

"Sorry." I smiled, swinging my legs over the rock's edge. "Just letting everything sink in, I guess."

He nodded. "Yeah. It's like it's too screwed up to be real. But it is." Looking away, he got to his feet.

Night air flooded the space he'd left, leaving me colder than before. As I climbed down, he offered his hand, but let go the instant my feet touched sand. Feeling foolish, I crossed my arms to give my hands somewhere to go. Thad strolled beside me. Each step brought us closer to the crowd, and I found myself wishing I'd said no. *No, I don't want to go back. No, I don't want our moment alone to end. No, I don't want to share you with anyone.*

And, as it turned out, I had to share Thad with everyone.

For the rest of the night, we were never alone. People came up constantly, sometimes to meet me, more often than not to talk to Thad. About nets, about gliders. About Search team choices and Search strategies. About prawns and crabs, about deadleaf and something called taro root. He had answers for everyone, which I noticed because I rarely left his side, or maybe he rarely left mine. And when he did, every so often he'd look over at me and smile, even as someone else stepped up to fill the space.

Like now.

I'd just refilled my drink when a boy with stringy hair approached. I remembered his face, but not his name.

"Charley, I'm Bart."

As he thrust out his hand, I automatically stepped back. Bart was one close talker. "So twelve days by yourself. I made it a week before I ran into Julio, but I was holding my own . . ."

Sandwiched between Bart and the fire, I felt trapped.

". . . landed by the volcano . . ."

Tuning Bart out, I overheard a girl thanking Li for her flower necklace. Thad's words drifted through my head. *She's crazy good with floral stuff.* Li bowed to the girl, then as if she sensed I was watching, she turned toward me. Our eyes met, she gave me an almost imperceptible nod, and in that moment, I knew she'd made my lei. The girl with less than two weeks to live had taken some of her precious time to weave a necklace of flowers for me.

Sometimes it's like it's too screwed up to be real. But it is. Thad was so right.

"Excuse me"—I interrupted Bart, smiling to counter my rudeness—"there's someone I need to talk to."

As I walked away, he said, "Charley." His voice was sharp; the cordial Bart was gone. I turned, wondering what brought on the abrupt change.

He closed the distance between us—*too close!* my mind cried; I couldn't help leaning away—and his eyes were shrewd. "About Thad. He's not all that you think he is. He loves to give newcomers the intro, especially girls. Ask Talla if you don't believe me."

Talla. Her name brought a flurry of images. Big boobs, flat abs, lethal spear. Check.

"Just a little friendly advice." Bart grinned.

But we're not friends, I thought.

I stared at Bart, wondering what motivated his "friendly" advice. Something felt . . . . off.

"Everything okay?" Thad's voice broke in. The animosity between the two was palpable.

"Fine," I said quickly, glad I'd already excused myself once. "I was just going to talk to Li."

I left the boys, avoiding their eyes and, hopefully, their drama. By the fire, Li sat alone. She was tiny, with the most beautiful eyes that I'd ever seen. As dark as night, they were rich with emotion.

"Li," I started, then I faltered, feeling the weight of my flower lei.

I'm sorry you didn't catch today's gate. I'm sorry you watched Sabine leave instead. I'm sorry you only have eleven days left. I'm sorry for what you must be going through.

I'm sorry.

But I didn't say it. Because I really didn't know what she was going through. Not yet, and maybe not ever. And I didn't say it because I didn't know *her*, and I'd never have the chance.

I was sorry for that too.

She was watching me expectantly, no doubt wondering why I was smiling like a greeter at Walmart but saying nothing.

"Thank you," I said. "For this." I touched my flower necklace. "It's beautiful."

"For tonight," she said. "Enjoy." Li smiled, but I sensed she was thinking, *Enjoy it now, sister, because it's temporary.* Like how I'd felt at the Flower Field. Enjoy the beauty because it's fleeting; it can vanish in an instant, and it will definitely disappear in 352 days, whether I want it to or not.

I nodded.

She bowed her head slightly, then her dark eyes returned to me.

I didn't bow back, unsure what etiquette called for. Afraid of insulting her, I simply nodded again.

The move made me dizzy. The heat from the fire felt like a pulsing wall—like a freaky nighttime shimmer—only instead of sucking me in, it pushed me away. From the heat, from Li, from Bart. From the whole Nil Night, which had been festive and exhausting. Days on Nil seemed longer than days back home. I knew they weren't, but they sure felt like it.

I looked around. Natalie was nowhere in sight. Thad was deep in conversation with Samuel and Rives. The night air vibrated with energy, shared by everyone but me. Me, the newcomer. Me, the latecomer.

Suddenly I felt more tired than a flag on July fifth.

I'd made it two steps down the path when Thad's voice boomed behind me. "You ditching me already? I know, I suck as an island guide. Sorry, Charley."

"I thought we agreed. No more *sorry, Charley*s." I stopped, letting Thad catch up. "Listen, it's okay. You've got a full plate, and to be honest, I'm a little worn out." I hated admitting it, but it was true. I was so tired my legs trembled. I began walking again before I fell down. No more fainting for me.

"So did y'all get the Search plans all worked out?" I asked.

"What?" Thad frowned.

"You and Samuel. And Rives. Y'all have been talking for forever, about tracks and hot spots and who knows what else."

"And here I didn't think you noticed," he said, smiling.

Was he kidding? I'd spent the whole night knowing exactly where he was. I couldn't tell if he was teasing or not, but I was too tired to figure it out.

We reached my hut or, rather, Natalie's.

"Thanks for the company. And for this." I touched the delicate lei. "It's beautiful."

"Not to sound totally lame, but it doesn't compare with the girl who's wearing it." Then he kind of groaned and laughed, both at once. "Man, that did sound lame, but it's true."

"Very lame," I agreed. "And I hate to break it to you, but I think your vision's going."

"My vision is just fine." His voice was husky. "Like I said, it's perfect." He reached over and brushed a strand of hair out of my eyes.

"Sleep well, Charley with an *e-y*. I don't want you to pass out on me again tomorrow."

"Not a chance," I shot back.

He laughed. "Night." Then he melted back into the darkness.

Inside the hut, Natalie was curled on the bed, smiling like Em. Moonlight seeped in, an island nightlight.

"You should have kissed him," she declared.

"Were you listening?" I asked, collapsing onto the empty bed. Nat was worse than Em. No, she was *exactly* like Em.

"Of course I was listening. And you totally should've kissed him. You only live once, remember?" She smiled broadly. Hope had replaced the earlier shadow.

"Maybe," I said. "But it seems like if Thad wanted a kiss, he would've kissed me. I'm not sure I'm his type." *And I'm not sure he's mine*, I thought, remembering Bart's warning. I had no intention of being one of many.

Natalie's jaw dropped. "Exactly what type is that? Tall and exotic? Geez, Charley, are you really that oblivious or are you fishing for compliments?" Now she looked annoyed.

"I'm definitely tall." I reflexively tugged on my skirt. I'd always heard my looks were "unique," which meant absolutely nothing. Unique's one thing, exotic's another.

Natalie stared at me. "Okay, you really are that oblivious. Look, I've known Thad since his Day One. You should know that he's there for everyone, but at the same time, he's kind of distant. He's different with you." Watching me, she frowned. "I'm serious, Charley. Thad's never paid attention to any girl here. He's been all business, until now. Until *you*."

"Really?" I said. "That's not the idea I got from Bart."

Natalie snorted. "Ignore Bart. Everyone else does. Listen, just be good to Thad, okay?"

I stayed quiet.

"Is there someone back home?" she asked sharply.

"No."

"You answered fast. Are you sure?"

"Positive. I have this funny thing about height. I don't like guys shorter than me, which ruled out most of the school. Plus, most guys had issues with dating a girl who towered over them, especially if I wore heels." *And the rest looked at me differently after Matt, and I had issues with that.*

She snorted. "I bet you just intimidated the heck out of them." Then her eyes gleamed. "But Thad's taller than you. Or hadn't you noticed?"

"I noticed," I admitted.

"That's what I thought." Natalie grinned. "Like I said, be good to him. Don't break his heart."

"Please." I rolled my eyes, but Natalie didn't laugh.

"I'm serious," she said quietly. "He's a good guy."

Good guys are dangerous, because you can't tell when they're being bad. I knew that firsthand. Lost in thought, I curled up under my thin sheet, absently wishing I had socks and pulling on my skirt. The micro-mini wrap seemed determined to shrink at every opportunity.

Frowning, Natalie sat up and studied my face in the dim light. "Haven't you ever had a serious boyfriend?"

"Not really."

"Either you have or you haven't." She sounded Em-direct. "Which is it?"

I sighed. "There was this one guy. Matt Kilwin. He was two years older, and hotter than the sun. I'm talking tall, rocking bod, the whole works. The summer before my sophomore year, we hung out." I flashed back to buried memories.

"Did you love him?" Natalie asked, curious.

"No." I shook my head. "I didn't know him well enough to love him. Talking to Matt was like talking to a mannequin. Or maybe he was so good-looking I couldn't think of anything to say," I admitted.

"Anyway, we didn't do much talking. Em called it the 'summer movie-make-out marathon.'" I smiled, but the memory stung. My mind had already leaped ahead—to Stacia. Five feet of cheer captain fury, leveled at me.

"What happened?" Natalie prompted.

"The girlfriend he'd supposedly broken up with came back from her summer in Spain. They got back together, if they were ever apart. She told everyone I'd tried to steal Matt by sleeping with him—which was so not true, all we did was kiss—but the truth didn't matter." My sophomore fall was a total nightmare. Clumps of senior girls, whispering in the halls. *Six-foot slut. Amazon whore. Who does she think she is? Matt Kilwin!* I closed my eyes to the memories. Matt was forgettable; it was the Stacia fallout that was tough to erase.

"Witch. What did Matt do?"

"Played football, got voted Best-Looking."

"No, I mean did he stick up for you? No, of course he didn't; I can tell from your face. What a jerk." Natalie shook her head, then smiled. "Hey, got you something." She pointed to the table, where a folded cloth lay beside the gourd pitcher. "Shorts. You pull on your skirt every five seconds, and I figured you'd be more comfortable in shorts." She shrugged. "Most of us just wrap the skirt tight enough so we don't flash anyone, and to be honest, after a few weeks here, you really don't care. But then again, I'm only five foot three."

A lump had formed in my throat, but Natalie was still talking, in that same rapid-fire pace I'd noticed her use when she was explaining island business. "We're low on shorts right now, but seeing as you're taller than most of the guys, I guarantee no one will care. Everyone wears what fits them best." Now her smile turned mischievous. "And it's better than a loincloth. They're worse than the skirts."

I hugged Natalie tight, so overwhelmed by her thoughtfulness that a thank-you seemed insufficient. But it was all I had.

"You're welcome. Now go change," Natalie said, breaking our hug. "I know this pair will fit." Without pausing, her voice softened. "They were Kevin's."

Of course they fit perfectly.

We talked until we grew sleepy. Being with Natalie was like being with Em, like a slice of home on Nil. And yet it was Nil, and Thad was never far from my thoughts. I felt something with him I'd never felt with any boy, ever, even Matt Kilwin. Especially Matt Kilwin.

You do this often? I'd teased Thad after he'd showed me the green flash. *Never*, he'd answered, sounding surprised himself.

Natalie was right. Thad *was* a good guy.

Dang it, I thought. *I should've kissed him.*

I'd just dozed off when Natalie's voice crept through the darkness.

"France," she said quietly. "I just remembered. Sabine was from France."

CHAPTER 21

I'd risen before the sun, eager to see Charley. But so far, I was the only one up.

It was just me and hundreds of faceless names on the Wall. I thought about the skull Charley had found. Maybe it belonged to someone on this Wall, maybe not. *No necklace, no clue,* Rives had reported last night. *Maybe he was a loner, maybe he was before our time. The skull was as clean as the skeleton in my science lab. I don't know if he got a cross on the Wall, but he got one back at the Bay.*

My fingers skimmed the wood, tracing my name. One cross above, one cross below, and my space empty, like Nil's whacked-out version of tic-tac-toe. In eighty-five days, one of us would win. And one would lose.

There was no draw on Nil.

Ramia's name caught my eye. So did her fresh cross, but I refused to start the day with Ramia. A new name begged for attention: Charley, with an *e-y.*

I wished I'd kissed her. Then I remembered the hesitation in her eyes, the reason I hadn't. *Damn,* I thought. *I wish she'd kissed me.*

"Thad!"

Talla burst from the trees, her blond hair flying behind her. A red mark on her face stuck out like a burn.

"Rory," she gasped. "He came in. I had watch at the Shack. Told him what he could take—a spear, a water gourd. A week of food." Slowing, Talla took a breath. "He told me to eff off, that he'd take what he wanted. He grabbed knives, the last metal ones. I tried to stop him, but—he's gone." She looked beyond pissed. "With knives and a net and God knows what else."

Talla's words hit home, and the reality cut deep. *The last two metal knives, gone. Knives we can't replace, knives we need.* The only one left in the City hung at my waist.

"When did this happen?" I asked, already calculating my route. "And what happened to your face? Don't tell me he hit you."

"He hit me." She nodded, her face furious. "Maybe twenty minutes ago? I'm not sure. I was out." Her hand went to her cheek, which was already swelling.

I wished I'd punched Rory yesterday after all.

"Get Rives," I told her. "Tell him I'm on it. And lie down, okay?"

Talla nodded, my cue to take off. The clock was ticking.

I took the easy trail out, the one by the Shack, the same one Charley and I had walked yesterday when we went to Crystal Cove. The other paths were narrow and rough, or so open they didn't look like a trail. Worn and marked, this trail was like hiking for Cub Scouts. Rory looked more resort-coddled than survival-campy. He'd go Cub Scout all the way.

Keeping low, keeping quiet, I jogged down the path, working through what I would say when I found him. Trees came and went. Nil listened quietly as I tracked Rory.

I passed the Cove, and when I was out of waterfall range, I paused, sifting through the stillness, searching for sounds of Rory.

Wind whispered, leaving echoes of silence. No ocean now, which was telling. No animal noises, which was neither reassuring nor remarkable. And no human sounds, which was disappointing.

The path narrowed, snaking inland through clumps of trees, toward the mudflats. I was at least two kilometers from the City now, maybe more. I was about to turn back when I heard him—crashing along like a hippo, which initially I thought he was.

Rory was lumbering along, swinging both arms, a bulging bag slung across one shoulder. Occasionally one of his arms would strike a branch, whacking it away, only for it to snap back, like Nil wanted to whip his ass, too.

I padded up the path, careful to avoid twigs or anything that might crack under my feet. I was only four meters behind him now. He'd never make it alone, I realized, not if he let me get this close without turning.

"Rory," I said.

He spun. Seeing me, his eyes narrowed, and one hand flew to his satchel. "Whaddya want?"

To kick your sorry ass as payback for Talla. Restraining my temper, I tried diplomacy first. "Five minutes," I said.

"Two," he snarled.

Whatever, I thought, already tired of his tough-guy routine. "Fine. Two. So here it is. I know you want off the island. I get it. But you can't steal, dude." I pointed at his bag. "Not the net, and not the knives. So cough 'em up." My voice went hard. "Now."

Rory's sunburned face sparked like an angry tomato. "I don't think so. I'm not in your little island cult. I can do as I please."

It took all my restraint to only use words. "You can't knock girls out and steal crap that's not yours. You can take clothes, a water gourd, a week's worth of food. And a spear. Basic survival gear. But not the knives. They're City property. Same for the net."

Rory's face went nuclear; his thin smile was gone. "Who the 'ell do ya think you are, telling me what I can and cannnot do? If ya think I'm gonna dodder around and sing campfire songs with ya, you're out of your fucking mind. Do you *know* who my dad is? He's George O'Whirley, of O'Whirley Enterprises, a fucking Fortune 500 company. A *transportation* company. If there's a way to get me out of here, my dad'll find it." He looked smug. "And he didn't make his bloody fortune lolling around singing 'Kumbaya.' "

Fury welled in me like lava, ready to blow. "I don't give a flying *fuck* who your dad is. Because he's not *here*, and no matter what you think or how much money he has, he's not gonna get *here*. All that matters is what goes down between us, right here, right now. And right now you're going to give back what you took." I paused. "Now."

Rory looked amused, then his face slid back into a condescending sneer. "No can do, Holy Joe. I'm taking the knives and—"

A muffled noise at one o'clock caught my attention. Behind a pile of black rocks just past Rory, something rustled, then scratched. Something weighty. Listening intently, I tried to gauge what it might be, but it was hard to filter the sounds through Rory's rants.

Rory was shouting now. "I don't give a bollocks, you hear me?" A vein had popped out on his neck, and his flushed face splotched white.

"Whatever," I said, wholly focused on Rory again. "Hand over the knives. Then you can go. I won't stop you."

"No." Rory gripped the bag harder.

"Seriously. Don't do this." It was like a bad junior high moment when the kid says *make me*. "Give me the knives."

Rory laughed. "Fuck you." He spat at my feet, then turned and crashed up the path.

"Rory!" I yelled, dreading the coming fight. "Last chance!"

"Go to hell!" he roared over his shoulder.

"Already there," I muttered.

I'd taken two steps when a massive creature exploded from the trees and landed on the path in front of Rory. Snorting and squealing, with two sets of stained tusks, bristles for hair, and patches of bare skin, it was the ugliest beast I'd seen on Nil.

Thing, I thought, pulling my knife. A mutant, scary Nil plaything.

As Rory skidded to a halt, the beast lowered its head. With a surprising burst of speed, it charged.

Yelping, Rory backpedaled, arms wild. I raced forward, angling right, gunning to intercept the beast from the side before it reached Rory. My attack window narrowed; Rory's feet were slow.

Then Rory tripped and fell. The beast kept coming, barreling forward like a wild boar on 'roids. Too close to Rory, too far from me. Rory lay sprawled flat on his back, his legs at odd angles, but at least they were moving.

Get up, I willed Rory silently as I arced around the beast's side. It's impossible to fight when you're not on your feet.

Still on the ground, Rory scrambled backward like a crab.

"Get up!" I shouted at Rory; I couldn't help it. "GET UP!"

His eyes wide with terror, Rory struggled to find his feet. The shoulder strap circled his neck like a noose, and trapped beneath him, the loaded satchel pinned him to the dirt. Rory was still horizontal when the animal butted him with two quick strikes.

Rory screamed and threw his hands up to protect his face; at the same time, I targeted the beast's side. The animal squealed and thrashed, its tusks flashing like weapons, making it tough to get a lock on its chest.

I lunged and barely nicked hide.

Before I could regroup, the beast charged Rory again, its head down, tusks in play. This time the animal struck Rory with enough force to toss him a meter through the air. As Rory flew backward, I struck the boar's chest, then hacked down, and when I ripped my blade out, blood spurted from the wound, a weak plume.

Not enough, I thought, spinning out of tusk range. Not enough to kill, just enough to draw its attention to a new threat: me.

I sprinted sideways, certain the animal would follow, but when I looked back, it hadn't moved. Torn between Rory and me, its head vacillated erratically, its legs clumsy in indecision. Taking advantage of the animal's confusion, I ran back, directly toward the animal this time, and drove my blade deep into its chest with everything I had. This time I felt my knife grind on bone.

Roaring, the beast swung to face me. I leaped back, but my knife jerked me to an abrupt halt. Hot pain slashed across my forearm as I wrenched my knife, hard.

Abruptly, the blade released. I stumbled away, bobbling my knife, watching blood gush from the animal's chest. This time it was a geyser, a fountain of red.

The beast squealed in fury, and turning full on me, it charged. I cut right, moving fast, fighting to grip my slick knife; my hold was dangerously weak, but I was determined to draw the boar away from Rory. I cut right and the animal faltered. It was less than a meter away when it teetered and fell. The ground shook. The beast twitched violently, then lay still.

Silence dropped like fresh snow.

The animal was easily three hundred pounds, maybe more. Definitely more. Resting on its side, its bloody belly was exposed. The thing was female, and a mommy thing at that.

Rory lay on his back, gripping his thigh with both hands and moaning. Scratches and cuts crisscrossed his face and forearms, defensive wounds, weeping blood. His shorts were torn, and near his waist, a dark red spot was spreading ominously. More red ran down his leg. Bright red ran through his fingers, and curses flew from

Rory's mouth faster than the blood. One quick look told me all I needed to know: Rory needed more help than just me.

"Hang in there," I told him. Moving quickly, I ripped a cloth from my waist, tore it in half, and then wrapped part around Rory's thigh in a makeshift tourniquet. My hands were coated with blood. Red was everywhere. I'd just cinched the knot tight when a mewling squeal split the silence behind me.

Snatching up my bloody knife, I turned. A small piggy creature crept from the trees and skittered toward the dead boar. It nosed the beast's belly, trying to suckle. *A baby*, I thought, lowering my knife.

Rory moaned. His hands were back on his leg. "Fuck, it hurts."

Kneeling, I pressed the extra cloth to Rory's hip. Red saturated the material and matted the cloth to his skin, making me wish I had something more, knowing I didn't. I hefted Rory over my shoulder in a fireman's carry, angling his body to put pressure on his hip wound.

"Hang in there," I said, gritting my teeth against his weight. "You're going back to the City, at least for now."

Rory moaned again. "Fuck."

"A cluster," I agreed.

The walk back sucked, more than I could have imagined. Each step felt like I was hauling a two-hundred-pound sack of cement. My forearm throbbed, and my quads burned like I'd spent the day boarding. Soon I was huffing like I was high on a mountain, climbing into thin air with my backpack and board, just before it got good and I flew downhill.

Only there was no flying today; no good would follow. My foot slipped in my shoe, sliding on something warm. Sweat, blood, I had no clue. My hands were wet and sticky, too. With my sweat and maybe with my blood. Or Rory's, or the beast's. Or maybe all three.

Rory stopped cursing, a bad sign. I picked up my pace.

"Stay—with—me," I panted.

When I caught sight of the Shack, Sy was outside, stretching pulp out to dry.

"Sy!" I gasped. "Get Rives! Miguel!"

He took one look, dropped the pulp, and took off, shouting. Rives came running, with Johan. Bart trailed behind, with Charley and Talla on his heels.

Johan and Rives lifted Rory off my shoulders; the abrupt loss of weight made my legs buckle. "Need line," I managed, watching them lay Rory on the ground. "For stitches."

I collapsed, wishing we had Sabine or Natalie or anyone else with a clue about island medicine. At least Miguel could string line for fish. "Where's Miguel?"

"Fishing," Charley said, kneeling beside me.

"Who else can stitch?" I directed this question at Rives and Johan. They were taking Rory's pulse and assessing the damage. Rory was out cold.

"Li," Bart offered.

"He meant who's around," Talla snapped.

"The City's pretty empty right now," Charley said softly. "I think it's up to us." Eyeing Rory, she took a deep breath. "What can I do?"

"He needs blankets," I said. "And bandages. I think he's in shock. And we need Miguel or someone else who can stitch." I looked at Bart, who hadn't moved. "Now!" I barked.

Rives leaned back on his heels. "Thad, I'm sorry. He's gone."

"Who? Miguel?" I said, confused.

Rives shook his head. "Rory. He's gone."

"Gone?" I was stunned. "Check for a pulse. Again."

"I did." Rives's light eyes were shadowed. "There's nothing. He's dead."

"Check again," I said, feeling sick. Feeling responsible. For chasing him. For interfering. For doing too much and for not doing enough.

"Sorry, bro." Rives didn't move. Johan was making the sign of the cross over Rory, then he crossed himself, his lips moving in silent prayer.

"Are you sure?" I asked Rives. "He's dead?"

"I'm sure. Whatever got him ripped him wide open. He just bled out."

I stared at Rory, thinking he should look worse, thinking there should be more blood. The ground around him was pristine. Green growth, brown dirt. No red. But Rives was sure, and I trusted Rives.

He's gone.

"What was it?" Sy blurted. "What got him?"

"I don't know," I said, knowing he had to ask but still feeling like it disrespected Rory. Rory, who lay a meter away, a fresh Nil kill, his satchel slung uselessly across his shoulder. Silver knives spilled out, glinting with accusation.

He'd never tried to pull one out.

The knives winked at me as I spoke. "Some kind of wild boar. At least three hundred pounds of ugly, with two set of tusks. And it was female." I paused. "I think it was protecting its baby. Or babies." Who knew how many more little beasties were growing up on Nil? More fun for the future.

"A pig did this?" Bart asked, his voice an annoying mix of amusement and disbelief.

Charley's golden eyes flashed. "Thad didn't say a pig. He said a 'wild boar.' With tusks, two sets, and mean. That doesn't sound like a pig to me." Even her sugary accent didn't warm her words.

Bart blanched. "Right," he mumbled.

Rives ignored Bart completely. "Where was this?" he asked.

"A couple kilometers past the Cove. The boar jumped from the trees and charged. It was fast."

Rives frowned, looking thoughtful. "Fast and ugly, two sets of tusks. Sounds like a warthog. They're bad news; kill lions and shit in Africa. Did it take off?"

I shook my head. "No. It's dead."

"Are you hurt?" Charley asked, gently turning over my hand. Her skin looked incredibly clean against mine. The blood on my hands and forearms had started to dry, making it blacken and crack, and fresh red oozed from a gash near my wrist. More blood coated my legs in sticky rivulets, mixing with sweat and dirt, a hideous collage of Nil death.

"Thad?" Charley's voice was worried.

"Huh?"

"Are you hurt?" she repeated softly, her eyes searching.

"Not really." Suddenly I couldn't wait to wash off the blood. I pulled back my hand; I didn't want Charley to touch it. To let any more of Nil's blood touch *her*.

Getting to my feet, I addressed Rives. "Two things. First, we need to bury Rory. Second, we need to salvage that hog. It's too much to waste. I'll help with the burial, then a team can go get the hog."

"No." Rives shook his head. "You've done enough. Go get clean. We'll take care of Rory, then the hog."

I hesitated, torn between wanting to help Rives and wanting to be rid of the blood.

Rives's voice was soft. "We've got this, bro. Now go."

As I started away, Rives threw out an arm to stop me. "Not the sea. With all that blood, you'll be chum. Go to the Cove."

You've done enough, Rives had said.

But not enough, I thought, glancing at his eyes full of pity. I'd

failed Rory, and now I'd brought back a dead body for Rives to bury.
I couldn't bear to look at Charley.

Like I'd told Rory, it was a total cluster.

Whipping around, I broke into a run, back up the same bloody
path I'd just carried Rory down. Blood on the ground. Blood on me.

Bloody hell, cackled Nil.

There would be no escape today.

CHAPTER
22

CHARLEY
DAY 14, MID-MORNING

I sat on a rock, waiting.

So far, Thad had been behind the waterfall for at least an hour. I knew he was alive and long since clean, but just needing that quiet space, that quiet time. I pictured him sitting on the slick black ledge, breathing crisp air, hearing only the roar of the water cascading down in front of his face. A wall like a shimmer, but just water. A wall that was exactly as it appeared to be.

I wondered if Thad was cold. I would be freezing under there. Inside the A-frame at night under thin covers, I no longer shook, but I was still cold. The only time I felt warm was in the sun, like now.

When Thad emerged, he looked exhausted.

"You pruney yet?" I asked.

His head whipped to me. "What are you doing here?" His voice sounded strange. Vacant, and distant.

"I thought you might like some fresh clothes and a towel." I pointed to the Cove's edge, where Thad had left the same offerings for me. "I'll turn around. I promise I won't peek."

"It's okay. I won't mind if you do." Thad's tone was detached, like his thoughts were anywhere but here.

I turned around and studied the trees. Light crept through the branches, making each leaf pop with color. Nil was breathtaking, no question, but there was ugliness, too. The beauty was everywhere; the ugliness subtle. But it was there all the same. I'd never been more aware of it than when I'd seen Thad stumbling back with Rory, covered in blood. Despite the sun, I shivered.

"I know those trees are riveting," Thad's deep voice came from behind me, "but you can turn around now."

Wearing a clean version of the shorts that had been soaked with blood, Thad stood there, drying his hair with the thin towel, which was more like a cloth. Because, as I'd figured out, every bit of cloth was some version of the same, all made from the paper trees.

"How long were you waiting?" he asked.

"Not long."

"Liar," he said, almost breaking into a smile.

"How would you know? Were you watching?" My voice was teasing.

"Actually, no," he said, and the light left his eyes. "I was just thinking. And trying not to think."

"How'd that work out?"

"Not so great." Thad sat beside me. The gash on his forearm looked raw. It would leave a scar, but at least it had stopped bleeding.

"Your arm looks better," I offered.

"Yeah. That's what washing off blood will do, eh?" He clenched and unclenched his fists so hard I wondered if it hurt.

"Thad, I know I just got here and that I'm way behind the curve. But I've figured a few things out." I paused, watching his knuckles turn white. "One is that everyone looks to you. For help. For advice. It's why you won the hand vote for Leader. It's why Talla came to you today. It wasn't right that Rory stole stuff. You went after him because it was the right thing to do, and then everything went to hell in a handbasket. It's not like you knocked him out, took the stuff back, and left him there." I stopped, feeling like I was rambling, but needing to finish. "So you can't beat yourself up over what happened."

Thad studied his hands. "I didn't like him. From the get-go. But I didn't want him dead."

"Of course you didn't. That's why you carried him back. You did all you could."

"Did I?" Thad lifted his head. His eyes were tortured. "I missed, Charley. I had a shot, but I missed. If I'd gotten it the first time, maybe Rory would have made it. I'm pretty sure it was the animal's last strike that killed him. And what if I'd just let him go? Not gone after Rory in the first place? He went ballistic. I think the noise drew the hog." He looked away. "I think our fight triggered the attack."

"Maybe, maybe not," I said, my tone purposefully no-nonsense. "You can play the what-if game all day, but it won't change what happened. You aren't responsible for Rory's death. You tried to save him, in more ways than one. And you tried to protect the City. No one blames you, so stop blaming yourself."

Thad didn't reply. I could tell he didn't expect me to say anything, which was good since I had no clue what else to say. The waterfall echoed like rain through the silence.

"Do you know that he didn't use any of the knives that he took?" Thad said finally. "Not one. He didn't even try to fight back."

"But you did," I said, refusing to let him wallow in self-doubt or, worse, self-hate. "Don't you see? You fought for him, and that means something. And you could've gotten killed. Wild hogs can be really mean."

Now Thad looked over, one eyebrow raised. "Do you run into lots of wild hogs in Georgia?"

My face felt hot. "Well, I haven't, but they've made the papers. There was this one, named Hogzilla. It was huge, like, a thousand pounds." Knowing I sounded Southern crazy, I got back on track.

"My point is, wild hogs can be dangerous, especially when they're protecting their babies. And if you want to play what-if, what if the hog had gored you, too? When you came back, covered in blood, I thought—"

I broke off, remembering Thad staggering down the trail, drenched in red. My voice shook. "I'm really glad you're okay."

"Me too." He sounded choked. "Thanks."

Thad's eyes dropped to my lips.

Finally, I thought. I felt guilty for wanting Thad so much, especially right now, but heaven help me, I did. My lips tingled in anticipation. As I leaned closer, I tucked a strand of hair behind my ear.

Reaching over, he took my hand. With his thumb, Thad rubbed the inside of my wrist, then my palm, making me shiver—until I realized he was rubbing away blood. Dried blood, staining my skin like a macabre tattoo, from the few seconds I'd held Thad's arm.

My skin burned; he was rubbing too hard.

"It's okay," I said, covering his hand with mine. "It's okay."

Thad jerked his hand back, and my hands fell together, empty. As I tucked them in my lap, Thad put his hands on his knees and closed his eyes, like he was fighting something—maybe himself. "Charley, I—"

Thad broke off, listening. As Thad stood, I heard the sounds of people. Moments later, Miguel, Johan, and Rives came into view.

"What's up?" Thad asked.

"Just getting dinner," Rives said. "Julio wants to get the pig on the coals ASAP."

Thad nodded, then turned to me. "Charley, thanks for the shorts and towel. And—for what you said. I'll catch you later, okay?" The distance was back.

Rives spoke up. "Thad, we've got this, bro. You don't have to come."

"Yes, I do." Thad's jaw was hard.

He looked back at me, but he was already gone, withdrawn to a place I couldn't reach and wasn't sure I wanted to. Then, without another word, Thad took off, striding down the trail alone. Miguel and Rives exchanged a long glance, then jogged after Thad. Johan lagged a few yards behind.

Ten quick steps later, the group was gone.

Thad's bloody clothes lay by the bank. Using a stick, I flicked them into the Cove, into the same spot where Thad and I had washed Kevin's clothes. I swished and rinsed, repulsed by the blood seeping from the cloth, and grateful I'd thought to bring soap. When the cloth finally rinsed clean, I wrung out the shorts and tucked them in my bag along with Thad's towel. Then I wondered what to do next.

Oddly enough, I didn't feel like company.

I headed west, winding through thick foliage. Eventually the path shifted north, and as the ground rose, I came to a junction. One route cut hard left, toward the ocean, I guessed; the other veered slightly east. *Inland*, I thought. I thought of the prehistoric roars—roars I hadn't heard since I'd come to the City—and without hesitation, I hooked left.

I'd just spied the ocean through the trees when a boy popped into sight, his back to me. He lunged toward the beach, like a sprinter bursting from the blocks, and recognition hit me like a rock.

At the same moment I said, "Bart?" a burst of noise cut the quiet; it was a girl, barking commands like a Spanish general.

Bart spun toward me, startled. "Charley! You scared the crap out of me!" Color flooded his pale face as he waved for me to follow. "C'mon, let's go!"

Three more commands, then a shout. More like a whoop.

Bart broke through the trees. A few steps behind, so did I, and I nearly ran smack into a dark-haired girl.

Heesham stood a few feet away, on a white sand beach I'd never seen. Both wore grins brighter than the sun. Seeing us, the girl threw both hands in the air in triumph. Dangling from her fingers was a twine circle, holding the biggest shark's tooth I'd ever seen.

"Samuel!" she cried. "He's gone!"

"Awesome," I said, watching Bart slap Heesham's giant palm in a sloppy high-five. "Where was the gate?"

"Near the trees." Heesham grinned. But even before he pointed to the spot, I knew.

It was precisely where Bart had been hiding.

CHAPTER
23

THAD
DAY 280, LATE MORNING

I tracked the blood, rewinding the morning. Everything I'd said, everything I'd done.

Echoes of Charley rang in my head. *You did all you could.*

Echoes of Rives. *You've done enough.*

Echoes of Li. *Nil crazy.*

Li was right. Nil was freaking nuts.

The blood trail darkened, and then the blood was thick, because I was there. The scene was fresh in my head, like a low-budget horror flick. Only all that was left were scattered entrails—the beast was gone. By the looks of it, something had dragged it away. Something bigger than the hog.

Nil crazy.

"It's gone." My voice was flat. "Something took it."

"Whoa," Rives said, walking over to the trail's edge, where heavy drag marks scraped the rocks and lines of blood told the story. "Something hungry."

"Not anymore," I said.

"Amen to that," Johan said.

Knife out, I jogged to the black rocks, where I'd first heard the squeals. Behind the largest rock was a dark hole, almost a cave.

"Rives," I called. "Check it out. I think this is where it lived."

To the left of the burrow, something snorted. Rives and I spun at once, knives out. A small beastie cowered, bloody and whimpering.

"Warthog for sure," Rives said. Then with one swift slice, he killed it.

I wasn't really sure why I went back. Maybe to purge the nightmare from my system, maybe to reassure myself the nightmare was real. But now having gone, I felt better—and worse. Strangely numb, to the badness that was Nil.

I needed a breather.

I needed to get off Nil—*right now*—and I knew just how to get the relief I craved.

"Let's go," I said. It was all I could do not to run.

Near the Shack, Macy and Maria flanked Heesham. Full of life, Heesham was talking fast.

"—flashed right there. A short sprint, twenty meters, tops. Samuel stepped in and that was it."

Catching Samuel's name, I stopped. "Samuel made it?" I asked.

"Sure did." Heesham grinned. "First day of Search, too. Good karma, man. A good day on Nil." He hugged Maria, who squeezed him back and laughed.

I didn't respond. I couldn't. Stretched to my limit, I ran.

Paddling out, I left Nil behind. For the next hour, I focused on the waves and the rush, and absolutely nothing else.

There was no blood in the water.

CHAPTER 24

CHARLEY
DAY 14, TWILIGHT

The festive air of the previous night was gone.

A small hog roasted on the beachside firepit, and the torches were lit, but the similarity to last night ended there. With three Search teams gone, fewer people were around, and the ones who remained were subdued. Rory was gone, but he wasn't forgotten.

But he will be, I thought. Because when I passed the Wall, I noticed he'd never carved his name.

I scanned the beach for Thad. I hadn't seen him since the Cove. I'd worried about him all afternoon, wondering if he still blamed himself for Rory's death. Plus, there was something I needed to talk to him about—something that had nothing to do with Rory. Unfortunately, Thad was nowhere in sight.

Seeing Jillian and Talla, I waved, but it was Bart who caught my eye. I gave him a noncommittal wave and turned around. Bart was the last person I wanted to talk to. I was certain I'd caught him just as he was about to make a dash for Samuel's gate, and even though I didn't mention it, I sensed Bart knew that *I* knew. He'd followed me around all afternoon like a puppy, obviously trying to make a better impression.

It hadn't worked.

Talla intercepted me as I left the beach. Her hair was tied in a tight ponytail, making the bruise on her cheek more prominent.

"Charley, aren't you going to eat?" Talla never wasted time with hellos.

I shrugged. "I'm not hungry."

"Doesn't matter," she said. "You need to eat when food's around, especially the good stuff." She cocked her head. "Or are you avoiding someone?"

Direct, as always, I thought. "Maybe."

"Well, better confront him now. Don't let the problem fester. Not here, where time is short."

Bart was watching us, and for a second, I actually considered taking Talla's advice. Then I dismissed the thought. I'd spent too long with Bart today as it was, and my gut said confronting him wouldn't do any good. Sometimes the better course of action was to do nothing, letting worries work themselves out.

Talla made a frustrated sound. "Don't think, go. Thad's over there." She pointed to where Thad stood with Johan in the shadows.

Before I had a chance to tell Talla she'd misunderstood, Thad looked up and our eyes caught. For one long moment, we stared at each other. With a dismissive nod, Thad turned away.

My cheeks burned. I felt eyes on me, but none were Thad's.

"Thanks, but I'm worn out," I said. "See you tomorrow."

Talla followed me. "Charley, stop. Whatever it is, handle it now, before you get hurt." Her voice hardened. "Or before it hurts someone else."

I whirled, wondering who she was talking about. *Bart? Or Thad?* It didn't matter either way; right now I didn't want to talk to either one. I just wanted to get away—from the boys, from this night. From Talla. From this entire place.

She stared at me expectantly, arms crossed.

"Thanks for the advice," I said, doing my best to sound civil and failing. "I'll keep that in mind."

True to my word, I weighed Talla's words. Like my nana always says, you get what you pay for, and in the case of Talla, her advice was free. Worthless. I tossed it out and decided to take my own. I'd let things work themselves out.

It was a terrible call.

CHAPTER
25

I dripped with sweat from hauling black rock. "I think we're good," I told Rives, nodding at the pile. "Let's clear the loose rock first, then mix paste."

For the last few hours, we'd been prepping to repair the base of the last A-frame, the one anchoring the left corner of the City ring. The rear wall had crumbled, and no one could camp there until it was secure. Now that we had the rocks, we just had to build it back. Not an easy task, since we weren't the ones who'd built it in the first place.

Voices carried across the open air, and Charley's stood out. Part of a group headed to the groves, she was walking past the firepit. Long legs, tight lines, and chin lifted like it was her against the world. Against Nil's world.

"Thad." Rives cleared his throat.

I forced myself to look at Rives. "Yeah?"

"Take off, man." He nodded toward Charley's group. "We'll finish later. I told Julio I'd help him with the pits anyway."

"If you need to go, go." I resumed methodically stripping away loose rocks. "I've got a ton of crap to do. No time for field trips today."

Rives was quiet, and he didn't move.

"So are you helping me or Julio?" My voice was unexpectedly harsh.

"You," Rives answered, dropping beside me. "Let's get it done."

We worked in silence. I focused on the rocks, or tried to.

Rives spoke first. "Listen, Thad, if you want to talk—"

"I don't."

"Okay, bro," Rives said. "But if you don't want to talk to me, then you at least need to talk to you know who."

Wrong, I thought. Charley was the one person I *couldn't* talk to. And that was the problem.

I felt Rives's eyes on me, waiting, but it was a grating nasal whine that shattered our silence.

"Thad!"

I looked up to see Bart striding toward us.

"Have you seen Charley?" he asked, his eyes sharp.

"Why?" I couldn't help snapping.

"Does it matter?" Bart asked with a slick smile. In that moment, I could tell he was enjoying this conversation way too much.

"Not really," I said, shrugging. "I just like knowing where everyone is jobwise. And come to think of it, aren't you supposed to be harvesting taro right now?"

"We're going this afternoon," he answered quickly.

"Really," I said. "In full sun." I didn't take my eyes off Bart.

He nodded. "We thought it'd go faster if we gathered a crew. That's why I'm looking for Charley."

"Well, you're out of luck. She already took off on her job detail. Like most everyone else."

Bart's eyes narrowed as my words hit their mark.

Rives spoke up. "Bart, buddy, now would be a good time for you to remember the little heart-to-heart we had the morning after I busted you sleeping on watch. Like I said, no one's making you stay in the City. But either you're in or you're out. There's too few of us as it is. We can't afford to pull dead weight. You hear?"

"Are you threatening to kick me out?" Bart looked incredulous.

"No." Rives shook his head. "But you keep complaining about Search, that no one picks you. I wonder why."

Bart stared at Rives.

"Bart," I said, drawing his eyes, "taro." I pointed toward the fields. "Find a crew or not. I thought Sy and Raj were helping you anyway. For all you know, they're already in the fields working, waiting on you."

Bart's face looked pinched. "You love being Leader, don't you, Thad? Being big man on the island, telling everyone what to do. Can't get enough, can you?"

I sighed. "If you want the job, Bart, ask for it. But considering no one will pick you for Search, I wouldn't count on getting the vote for Leader. And feel free to nominate someone else anytime."

"If you say so." Bart grinned. Then he turned away.

"What a tool," Rives said as Bart sauntered past the firepit.

"Only not so handy," I said.

"True. But he's sharp enough to be dangerous," Rives said. He was still watching Bart.

"Only when he slacks off. He's more annoying than anything else." Turning back to the rocks, I had no intention of wasting more mental energy on Bart than I already had.

Bart disappeared, and for me, it was out of sight, out of mind. With Charley, it was the complete reverse. The longer she was out of sight, the more I thought about her. And the more I tried *not* to think about her, the more she occupied my every thought. It was only when she returned from the groves—looking exhausted but uninjured—that I relaxed. Night had already fallen. Along with Rives and Talla, I helped Charley's group unload packed satchels in the dark, filling baskets and shelves with fruits and nuts. They also brought back a chicken, a fresh food find. Eggs were a welcome change from fish any morning. So was Rives's chatter, which filled the awkward gaps in the polite small talk between me and Charley. While Charley talked to Jillian, I slipped away.

I was checking the chicken pen for gaps when Talla strode up.

"Thad, who's got Shack watch tonight?"

I'd forgotten to set it up. "Me," I answered.

Talla crossed her arms. "You took it two nights ago. Why do you have watch again?"

"Because I can't sleep." I coughed up this honest answer before I thought of a better one; it was the same reason I'd taken watch the night Rory died. When I wasn't reliving the boar attack, I was thinking of Charley, knowing she was a few A-frames away, wondering if she was lonely or, worse, scared. My head was all over the place.

Talla gave me a long look, then nodded. "Okay. I'll relieve you at dawn."

True to her word, as the stars faded and pink streaks split the air, Talla appeared at the Shack.

"Anything?" she asked.

"Nothing," I said, stretching. "Not a peep, not a roar. And no visitors."

"I don't know if that's good or bad," Talla said. "But you're done. Get some sleep."

Knowing I'd just lie there and think, I opted for exercise instead. I hit the beach, ran a series of hard interval sprints, and was bracing to go again when—like my thoughts made her real—Charley stepped onto the sand. Wearing Kevin's shorts and a simple chest wrap, she wore her hair long and loose; it blew around her shoulders, like the first day I'd met her. I wanted to go to her, to spill my guts. But I didn't know what might come out if I opened my mouth. Nil and Charley, both in my head, making it spin so fast I couldn't separate my thoughts from my fears.

So I ran. Away from Charley . . . going for speed . . . going for pain. Pain and more pain, because maybe if I hurt enough, Nil would let me sleep. And not feel.

Mental pictures crashed in with the waves. Charley wearing Kevin's clothes; Charley's hair falling through my fingers; Charley's hip against mine; Charley's lips inches away; Charley's hand covered with blood; Charley with Rives by the fire; Charley's name on the Wall.

It's too late, Nil sang over the surf.

My legs screamed for mercy, and my chest ached. A deeper ache than the need for air, and in that moment, I knew Nil was right. It was too late.

But I still didn't know what to do.

CHAPTER
26

I'd ignored Talla's advice, and three days later, mine had turned out to be a complete bust.

Worry was eating me alive.

I stepped outside, and disappointment hit me with the morning breeze. No one stood near the Wall. Only a handful of people were near the firepit, and Thad wasn't among them. I couldn't help feeling like he was avoiding me, or at least making no effort to see me, and I'd no clue why. All I knew was that my island guide was missing.

And I missed him.

And I hated that I missed him, because he obviously wasn't missing me.

After grabbing a wrap from the firepit, I sat alone on the black boulder, the same one I'd shared with Natalie and Sabine. *Was it really only four days ago?* Natalie was gone, on Search. And Sabine was just plain gone. Remembering her face flickering like a horrified hologram, I hoped she was home. Maybe she was with her family right now, eating pastries or whatever they eat for breakfast in France.

Here in nowhereland, I was having a mystery meal wrapped in a thick green leaf.

Expecting fish, I was thrilled to find shrimp. The only thing better would've been a big ole pile of cheese grits on the side, but shrimp was shrimp, and this shrimp was *good*. Plump and tasty, it was seasoned with coarse sea salt and chopped fruit.

Six bites, and the shrimp were gone. Nothing remained but wilted greens.

"You know, you can eat the leaves," a smooth voice said.

I looked up. Rives stood there grinning, holding a plank piled high with wraps and slices of yellow fruit.

"Good to know." I rolled up a green leaf and took a bite. "Tastes like spinach," I said, making a face.

He laughed and plopped down beside me. "It's not spinach. I don't know what it is; I just know it's edible. And it's better with shrimp. Hold out your board."

I did, and he dumped some fruit slices on it and another wrap.

"Thanks," I said.

"No problem. And if you want fresh cow's milk, just ask Jason. It's warm, but tasty." Rives raised his cup. "So," he continued, smiling at me, "what's your story?"

"The short version? I was in the Target parking lot in Atlanta and a gate grabbed me. Then I woke up here, buck-naked."

Rives nodded. "The long version?"

I shrugged, smiling. "Now that I think about it, there is no long version. That's it."

"You're wrong." Rives wiped his mouth. "Everybody has a long version."

"So what's yours?" I asked.

"Short or long?" Rives's light eyes twinkled, in that cocky way a guy's eyes flash when he knows he's good-looking. And Rives was.

Perfect latte skin, model-worthy dreadlocks, and striking green eyes the shade of summer limeade.

"Either."

"Grew up everywhere and nowhere, all over Europe and Asia. My dad's American, my mom's Swiss-French, but they're both journalists, so we travel a lot. I was in Phuket when the gate hit. Now I'm here." Rives popped a fruit slice into his mouth.

I waited for him to finish chewing.

"How old are you?" I asked. Rives seemed older than everyone else.

"Seventeen."

My age, I thought, surprised. *And Thad's.*

"And you're Thad's wingman?"

"Wingman?" Rives raised one eyebrow like Thad.

I nodded. "You back him up, like with the wild boar thing."

Now Rives laughed. "I'm one of his Seconds."

"Maybe." I smiled. "But I still say you're his wingman."

Rives grinned, then wolfed down the rest of his wrap.

"Where is he? Thad?" I tried to sound casual.

"Teaching Talla how to fly a glider."

Talla. Talla with big boobs and flat abs, Talla the girl whose honor Thad flew to defend after she was struck by Rory. I knew he was busy, that as Leader he juggled lots of jobs. I'd just hoped island guide was still near the top of his list. But I was either selfish or stupid. Or both.

"Hey," Rives was saying, "you still there?"

"Sorry." I switched gears to a more pressing worry. "Rives, there's something I need to tell you. As one of Thad's Seconds."

"Shoot," he said.

"The day Rory died, I went exploring. I hiked north, and just before the north cliffs, I ran into Bart. He was crouched at the tree line, just off the sand, like he was hiding. Then Samuel caught his gate. The thing is, it looked like Bart was dashing out when I saw him—like he was about to steal Samuel's gate."

Rives's face went hard. "Really."

"I know, it sounds crazy. But that's how it felt. Bart played it off, like I'd surprised him just as he was about to cheer Samuel on. But, Rives, I'm telling you, it felt weird."

Rives nodded, his expression thoughtful. "I'm on it. Thanks for the heads-up, C."

We finished our wraps, chatting easily. Relieved after unburdening my Bart worry, I did most of the talking, picking Rives's brain about Search strategies and gate timing.

"Rives—" I hesitated, unsure how to frame my next question. "The carving. The one Thad calls the Man in the Maze. Do you know what I'm talking about?"

"Yeah. The one at the Arches."

"What do you think it means?"

Rives shook his head. "I'm not sure."

"Me either. But I think it's important. When I asked Thad about it, he said we're all rats in a maze." I paused. "I know I just got here. But I can't shake the feeling that there's more to it and that we need to figure it out, especially since there's a second carving on the other side of the island."

"Maybe," Rives said. "But unless it's going to point us to a gate, I don't see how it's gonna help."

"Good point," I admitted. "But think on it, okay?"

"Will do. And hey, except for the Bart part, it was fun." Rives tapped his empty plank against mine and smiled.

I smiled back. "Thanks for listening."

"Anytime." He stood, took a step, then he turned back. "Charley—about Thad." My stomach did a little flip at his name. "Don't give up on him, okay?"

"Okay," I said. But I thought, *You've got it backward.*

"I mean it," Rives said, watching me. "He's solid. Give him a chance."

My emotions were obviously as clear as the Cove, because Rives said, "Look. Thad's done a lot for the City. Since he's been Leader, no one's been hungry and no one's gotten seriously hurt—until Rory. Thad's all business, twenty-four seven. But with you, it's different."

Wrong again, I thought. *He treats me* exactly *like everyone else. And that's what hurts.*

"You're a great wingman," I told Rives. For the first time, I saw a resemblance between Rives and his twin, Natalie. Both cared for Thad like a brother. That thought made me smile. "Listen, Thad and I are fine," I lied. "He helped me get settled, and now I've got my hands full figuring out how to pitch in. No time to waste."

"True." Rives nodded. But his usual grin was gone.

An hour later, Julio was enthusiastically explaining the baking pits when Thad and Talla returned, walking side by side, laughing. I feigned interest in baking, but at that moment I couldn't have cared less about sweet bread. I just wanted to get away.

"Thanks, Julio," I cut in, forcing a smile because Julio was a nice guy, and to land here at fifteen would have killed me. "I've got to go. See you later."

Talla caught me before the beach path. Thad was, of course, nowhere in sight.

"Charley." Talla's voice was tight, like her overfull chest wrap, like her abs. "I don't know what's going on with you and Thad. And part of me doesn't care. But you need to talk to him, because he's kind of a mess."

I stared at her, stunned. "*I've* got to talk to him? He's avoiding me, in case you haven't noticed."

"Really? Because you're the one who stalked off when we got

back." Her gaze was intense, and I realized I'd never seen her look any other way. Talla had a fierceness about her, a competitive spark that spilled over into even the most average moments, like now. "All I'm saying is that you two need to work it out, because he's so distracted that he's not helping anyone, especially himself."

I felt defensive, and I resented it.

"Talla," I said, keeping my voice level, "I don't know you. And while I think you're trying to help, there's nothing to help with. Really."

Talla cocked her head, making the muscles in her shoulders ripple like cords. "You're as bad as he is. Freaking awesome." She sighed. "Well, this is going nowhere. C'mon, let's run. Jillian's waiting. Maybe a good workout will clear your head."

My *head is just fine*, I thought, but surprising myself, I agreed. It felt good to push my legs and focus on running, or rather, adopting Talla's pace, sprinting like a swarm of yellow jackets was on our tail. I held my own, but Talla was faster.

Jillian quit first, and although I didn't admit it, stopping was a huge relief. "I've got to check the pulp," Jillian said as she slowed. "See how it's drying. I'll see you two later." With a warm smile and a wave, she turned toward the Shack.

Talla nodded to me. "Good run." Without waiting for a reply, she jogged away, no doubt ready to tear into someone else about the latest City infraction.

I grabbed a firewood sling and headed south, down a path I'd never seen. Collecting tinder as I went, it felt good to explore and be productive. The path ended at an opening in the cliff. Light glinted at the far end.

A tunnel, I thought.

It was more a cavern than a tunnel. Dim light came from both ends, bouncing around the walls, making them glitter. Halfway through, I slowed, totally awed. Crystals lined the walls; they winked at me, playing tag with sunlight. More crystals lay scattered on the ground, some muddy, some clear. One loose piece near the exit looked like a perfect cube of sugar.

With my mind consumed by Thad and Talla and rock cave crystals, it wasn't until I spotted the black sand beach that I realized I'd emerged near where I'd camped my first days on Nil.

I looked back, observing how easily the cavern blended into the cliff. *A shortcut*, I realized, making the City closer to Black Bay than I'd thought. The irony of the City's proximity was as laughable as the island mini I'd first sported.

Pausing to listen, I picked out muffled ocean sounds, the occasional bird, and the rustle of wind. I thought of the skull, and shivered. I'd just decided to walk to the Arches when Natalie's words rushed back. *Make sure to meet Jillian, she's the best at identifying paper trees.*

An idea burst into my head, fully formed. I spun around, and taking the same shiny shortcut, I ran straight to the Shack. Jillian stood exactly where I'd hoped she'd be.

"Jillian!" I said, eyeing the sheets of pulp. "Quick question. How do I get some paper?"

CHAPTER
27

CHARLEY
DAY 24, LATE MORNING

I looked down in disgust.

What should've been soap looked like curdled milk. Not exactly what anyone would want to rub all over their body, especially me.

"Nice try," Macy said encouragingly. "Just takes practice."

"I don't know," I said, watching Macy unwrap her bark mold to reveal a perfect square. "I'm not sure soap's my thing."

I didn't know what my thing was, but I was determined to figure it out, and soon. I was working on something—something unique—but at this point, it was still rough.

As I rinsed my hands, I thought about Jillian stripping paper trees and Heesham beating the pulp to make cloth. I thought about Macy's perfect soap molds and Julio's mouthwatering bread. I thought about the teams collecting firewood, harvesting yams, picking redfruit, or wrapping fish. I thought about Li making delicate leis of flowers that began dying as soon as they were picked, but most of all, I thought about Thad.

We'd barely spoken since the day Rory died. Thad was everywhere, and yet, missing. Behind the scenes, in plain sight, Thad had been working almost feverishly—discussing island medicine, repairing gliders, plotting Search team makeups and patterns, and organizing food: plantings, harvests, fishing, and who knew what else. Talking to everyone and anyone. He was both present and distant, even with me.

Especially with me.

Or maybe it was just that I always noticed where he was. Sometimes I felt his eyes on me, even when he was with someone else, but before we could talk, he'd vanish. Once I'd caught him openly staring, looking like he was about to say something—and yet he hadn't. Twice I'd woken early and seen him sprinting alone on the beach, pushing himself like he was training for the Olympics. I didn't join him.

I ran by myself.

And explored by myself.

And worked on my secret project by myself.

Good times, I thought miserably.

At that moment, I realized I was lousy company. My mom would be horrified at my lack of Southern graciousness.

"So, how long do Search teams stay out?" I winced at my puny effort.

"Usually a week," Macy said. "Sometimes less, sometimes more. Natalie's should be back any day. Same for Li's."

I nodded.

"Hey." Macy grinned. "Cheer up, girl. It gets better."

"Thanks." I returned her smile, not sure exactly what was going to get better, or how. "What do you miss the most? About home?"

"You mean besides a decent razor and a DQ dip cone?" Macy laughed.

"I'm serious."

"So am I." She smiled, a real smile, unlike my forced one. "I miss my family, and I miss my church. I miss all kinds of little stuff. But right now I'm missing football season. I'm a majorette, and football season is the best part of the year. And I'm missing it." Macy squeezed my hand. "You'll make it, Charley. You still look like you need to eat, but you'll make it." She chuckled. "I believe everything happens for a reason. I believe I'm supposed to be here, and I believe I'll get back home. Same for you. Same for all of us."

I decided against bringing up Rory. He wasn't going anywhere.

"Thanks," I said. "For the lesson, and the pep talk."

"Anytime." Macy smiled. Serenity surrounded her like a bubble. As we carried our sandsoap back to the Shack, the walk was peaceful, like I'd finally taken a deep breath, long overdue.

After leaving Macy, I ran into Jillian and Talla. One look from Talla and my Macy-bubble burst on sight.

"We're going running," Talla offered. "Want to come?"

"Thanks, but I already went."

"So go again," she said. "We'll take it easy on you."

Talla grinned, but it was her same competitive grin that grated on my last nerve. Whenever I ran with her, I had the perverse urge to beat her and found myself pushing my legs past their limits and getting annoyed when I lost. On the flip side, my victories didn't make her too happy either. I'd developed a grudging respect for her, but I wasn't up for Talla right now. It was because of Talla that for the past week, I'd chosen to run alone.

"Thanks, but I'm good."

"Okay, we'll catch you tomorrow." Talla took one step, then spun back. She stood ramrod straight. "Charley, you're not good. And neither is Thad. You two need to work out whatever is *not* going on between you two, because it's getting to the rest of us."

"Talla—" Jillian started, her tone warning.

"No," Talla snapped. "I'm sick of it. It's not just about them. And she needs to hear it." Talla shot me a look that would've frozen Hell. "Work it out, Charley. One way or another."

Then she strode away.

I felt like a child being reprimanded, and I was furious. Determined to steer clear of Talla, I took the shortcut to the rocks where Thad first showed me the green flash nearly two weeks ago. Thankfully, the spot was deserted. Grateful to be alone, I climbed out onto the largest rock, thoroughly frustrated by both Thad and Talla—one distant, one bitter, neither of which I understood. What did Talla mean, *It's not just about them?*

I wish I could ask Em.

And just like that, my fury fizzled.

I missed Em. I missed home. I missed my life—and I was missing it. I was just another Nil visitor, living a surreal time-out from life, losing time I couldn't get back. If I even got back at all.

"Charley." Bart's nasal voice jarred me from my private pity party. Skin sloughing off his shoulders fluttered in the breeze, and I couldn't help leaning away. "Want some company?"

Hell, no. "No, thanks. Just having some quiet time."

"Suit yourself." Today Bart had a bandana tied around his head, like how Rives wore his. Only on Bart it somehow looked like he was playing dress-up, and it looked ridiculous. "If you change your mind, we're about to play island ball." He pounded his hairy chest like a pale, peeling gorilla. "It's hard-core, but mixes things up."

"Thanks." With a smile to counter my rudeness, I turned away. Bart always left me with the feeling I needed to take a bath, even if I'd just stepped out of the Cove.

The Cove. Beautiful water as clear as glass, cascading into a black rock pool as cold as ice. Trees with deep green leaves the color of lush magnolias, kissing an Easter egg blue sky, lime green moss clinging to life on damp charcoal rock that will never burn—unless I happen to be standing on it when a shimmer rolls through. The Cove was a perfect snapshot of Nil's beauty. Beauty so intoxicating that if I weren't careful, I could forget the danger. But the danger was there. Always lurking, and very real.

I closed my eyes, and like it did constantly, my mind wandered to the Man in the Maze. I'd visited the carving earlier this week. No sign of the hyena or anything else dangerous, although I'd startled a camel and managed to freak myself out, and probably the camel, too. But during my latest visit, I'd made a discovery: the number twelve carved at the top, centered directly over the maze. I'd missed the number my first time around, probably because it was packed with dirt. I had no idea what the twelve signified, or, for that matter, the maze itself. Despite my heavy scrutiny, the Man in the Maze had refused to give up his secrets. And no one else was as obsessed by the carving as me.

I returned to my List of All That I Was Missing.

My senior year, although all I really missed was volleyball. I wondered how the team was faring without me and whether my scholarship hopes were already sunk. I missed playing, but I didn't miss homework or school without Jen.

Instead of sitting in calculus, I sat by the sea, with nowhere to be. And nowhere to go.

Bart was gone, leaving me alone.

As in all by myself.

My mind ping-ponged between the good and the bad, and I fought to keep the volley alive. I wasn't sure settling on one side of the Nil net was a good thing.

Ping-Pong. Since Em had left for college, I'd played with my dad. The last time I'd seen him, he was tossing me the keys to his first brand-new car ever, trying to cheer me up. My throat constricted at the memory. *Did I even tell Dad good-bye?*

"Charley." Thad's voice startled me.

"Hey," I said, turning. He stood behind the rock, looking cover-model gorgeous—until I got to his eyes. They looked haunted.

"You okay?" he asked.

Are you? I thought, watching his ghosts dull the blue.

But I didn't ask. I might have a few days ago, but not now.

"Yeah." I nodded. "Just thinking."

"About what?" he asked, climbing up to sit beside me. The rock shrank under us.

"About home. It feels far away, which is crazy." I paused, twisting my hair into a roll, determined not to gnaw on my lip. "I can't even remember what the last thing I said to my dad was. Something about his new car. Something stupid."

Thad didn't answer right away.

"I got in a fight with my dad. I wish I didn't remember the last thing I said."

"Whatever it was, I'm sure he knew you didn't mean it."

"Oh, I meant it. I just wish it wasn't the last thing I said."

I tilted my head at Thad. "Then it's a good thing you'll catch a gate soon so you can finish the conversation."

Thad raised an eyebrow. "What makes you so sure?"

"Because if anyone will catch a gate, it's you. Something tells me you get Nil better than anyone. And when your time comes, you'll make it." I shrugged. "Just a feeling."

Thad chuckled. "I like your feelings, Charley with an *e-y*."

For an instant, his eyes were light, the way I remembered them, but then a veil fell and the ghosts were back. "But I don't think it's up to me, not really," he said. "I think Nil has her own agenda."

"Wow," I said. "That sounded all deep and dark."

"Dark." He half smiled. "You nailed it."

"What's that supposed to mean?"

Thad didn't answer.

"Thad, don't make me guess here." My voice was unexpectedly sharp.

"Sorry." Thad watched water crash against our rock. "Lately, maybe it's because I've been here so long, I feel like I finally get Nil. The darkness of it. Like with Rory. He was so pissed, and I can't stop thinking that our yelling attracted the hog. Like Nil was drawn to the hate, you know?" Then he laughed, an empty sound. "I know, it sounds insane."

"No, it sounds like you feel guilty." I paused. "Thad, Rory's death was not your fault. Yes, y'all yelled. Yes, Mama Hog got angry, or felt threatened, or whatever. But Rory's the one who fell out of the sky mad and sour, and he's the one who set that awful day in motion. It's totally terrible that he died, but *his death wasn't your fault*. But hey"—I stopped long enough for him to look up at me—"if you want to beat yourself up about it, go ahead."

When Thad stayed quiet, I grinned. "You know I'm right."

"Maybe." He smiled slightly, then dropped his eyes to his hands, which, thankfully, weren't clenched in knots. "I'm just tired of the bad stuff. The death, the blood. The waiting."

"The tick-tock," I said.

"Exactly." His voice was oddly choked.

For a few minutes, neither of us spoke. Darkness lingered over Thad like a cloud, and I didn't know what else to say. We hadn't spoken this much in almost two weeks.

"Look, I know I've been preoccupied lately," Thad said. "Since Rory, I've been trying to get my head straight."

I looked at him, abruptly overwhelmed by all Thad had gone through. Not just watching a boy die after carrying him for miles, but dealing with Nil, day in and day out, for 290 days. Watching people come, watching people go. Watching people die, and maybe not just Rory. Probably not just Rory. And here I was, thinking his distance was about me. I'd never felt more shallow or foolish.

"It's okay." I laid my hand on his arm. Despite myself, I got a little thrill when he didn't pull away. "I've only been here twenty-four days, and sometimes it gets to me. I mean, I was just sitting here, thinking about everything I miss. But when I thought about what I didn't miss, it made me feel a little better. So—well, not going all sunshine and daisies here, but maybe try focusing on the good stuff for a while so the bad isn't so dang overwhelming. Like you said yourself, 'focus on the good, live in the moment.' Samuel made it; so did Sabine. Natalie and Li are on Search, and we haven't seen any gates around here, so maybe they've caught one wherever they are."

Thad regarded me with an unreadable expression. I almost stopped, thinking again how crappy I was with the whole rah-rah thing, but I was determined to finish.

"I'm not saying ignore the Dark Side, and I'm not saying it's not here. I'm not blind, or stupid. But there's bad stuff everywhere, not just on Nil, and you can't let it all in. Plus, it's not all bad. I mean, look. How many other people are sitting by the ocean right now with this amazing view?"

"None." His eyes were so blue, it almost hurt to look at them. Almost.

"Sorry for getting so deep," I said, feeling stupid even though I'd just said I wasn't. "You started it."

"I did." Thad smiled. This time it reached his eyes; the ghosts were gone. The shift was subtle, but definitive. "Hey, sorry I've been such a crappy island guide lately. After Rory, I realized how thin we are. We need more than one person who can stitch, more than one person who can fix the gliders, that sort of thing. A little cross-training, eh?"

No more tormented Thad. Now it was determined, all-business Thad.

"And thanks for giving Rives the heads-up on Bart," he said. "He's one to watch out for."

Funny, I thought. *Bart said the same thing about you.* Then I had a thought. "You think he's the saboteur? The one who messed up the Shack?"

"Maybe. It hasn't happened since we set up watch, and that's all that matters. But back to what you told Rives, I wouldn't worry. I doubt Bart has the balls to steal someone's gate."

"I don't know," I said slowly. "Doesn't seem like stealing someone's gate takes guts. Seems more cowardly to me."

"Could be." Thad didn't look worried. "But either way, he's got to prove he's worth taking on Search, and that's part of what I've been working on. Not babysitting Bart, but organizing work details, educating everyone on hot spots, spreading information."

"Two things." I spoke carefully. "First, I noticed you've been on a tear, helping everyone. But sooner or later, you'll have to look after yourself."

"I know." His voice was quiet. "That's what I'm planning for. I've got Priority soon."

For a second, Nil looked gray, like Thad's eyes full of ghosts. Nil without Thad was unimaginable.

"You said two things. What's the second?" he asked.

"No more sorry, Charleys. I was fine on my own."

"Oh, I know that." He flashed his easy grin. "So are you saying you don't need an island guide?" His tone was teasing, but I heard the flicker of disappointment, or maybe that was just what I wanted to hear.

"Need or want?" I copied his tone, smiling.

"Either," he said.

"I wouldn't mind an island guide, if that's what you're asking."

"Sounds like want," he whispered.

Our eyes locked, and as Thad leaned forward, a shout from the beach ruined the moment.

"Thad!" Heesham's voice. "You ready, man?"

Thad closed his eyes, then turned to Heesham. "Five minutes," he called. When Thad looked back at me, his eyes were playful, the way I remembered them from my first day at the Cove.

"So, Charley with an *e-y*, what do you miss the most? What are you wishing you had that's not here?"

Nothing, I thought, watching humor flash inside Thad's sapphire eyes. *Absolutely nothing.*

"Power," I managed.

"Too general," he said. "Try again."

I thought for a second. "Okay, hot showers. This morning, when I took my latest Cove bath, I couldn't stop shivering. I used to take showers so hot the whole bathroom would steam up. Once the steam actually set off the smoke detector in my room. I'm serious," I said as Thad laughed. "What about you? What do you miss the most?"

Thad watched the white foam curl around his ankles. "Riding up the lift with my board hanging from one foot. Seeing the white below me, knowing I was about to shred it." He paused. "The first run of the day, when the snow's like powder and the sun's so bright it hurts. Launching down the mountain, flying so fast nothing can catch me. I miss that."

The ache in his voice was palpable. I stayed quiet, feeling sadder for Thad than me. Nothing I'd missed for 24 days could hold a candle to being denied for 290.

Thad kept going. "A cheeseburger, thick and juicy, with bacon. And fries."

My mouth watered.

"Sprite," I said. "Fountain Sprite, on crushed ice, the kind you can crunch in your mouth when the Sprite's gone but the ice still tastes sweet."

"Barbecue chips."

"French toast. With butter and syrup."

Thad grinned. "Chocolate bars, preferably a Crispy Crunch."

"Umm," I said, tasting imaginary chocolate. "Chocolate chip cookies. Warm from the oven, when the chocolate's still gooey. With milk."

Thad groaned. "When we get back, can I come to your house? Because I really want one of those cookies. How did we get stuck on food?"

When we get back, he'd said. I lifted my eyes to his. *We?* I thought.

"What?" he asked.

For a second, neither of us spoke. Then I said, "Socks." I smiled.

Thad looked surprised. "Socks?"

"Socks." I nodded. "I miss socks. My feet freeze at night."

"Watching or catching a Canucks game. Hell, I just miss hockey, period."

I laughed. "My iPod."

"Echo that," Thad said nodding. "Got Nuffin here."

"Did you just quote Spoon?" I asked.

"So Charley knows Spoon." Thad grinned. "What else do you have on your iPod?"

Thad and I had similar taste, which was cool, but we both had lots of bands neither of us had heard of. I wished I could look them up on iTunes, but of course, I couldn't.

"Hey, listen, I could talk tunes all day, but Heesham's setting up island ball and I said I'd play. Come with me?" His voice was anxious, like he wasn't certain I'd say yes. *Boys.*

The minute our feet hit sand, Thad smiled devilishly.

"Race you back," he said. "Winner bakes the other a chocolate chip cookie when we get home."

"You can bake?" I asked.

"I have hidden talents." He grinned.

I laughed. *I'll bet you do.* "You're on."

We lined up beside each other, two track stars toeing an invisible line.

"On your mark," Thad started, "set . . . go!"

I hung with him until the end, when Thad easily pulled away.

Huffing and puffing, I jogged up to Thad, who was breathing hard, hands on his hips. "Did you quit on me?" he asked.

"Did you hold back?" I shot back.

"Nope. You quit. Or at least you didn't kick it at the end." He laughed as I made a face.

"No way. You're just fast."

"Well, we'll have to work on that. Fast is good on Nil." Thad's jaw hardened despite his smile.

"I'm getting that idea."

Looking away, Thad pointed. "Perfect timing."

Up the beach, Heesham and Rives were pounding two wooden poles into the sand. A net stretched across the middle. Talla held a green ball; it appeared to be woven from the same green strips I'd tried to fashion a net from on my second week here, only these strips were cross-hatched in a tight pattern, perfectly forming a ball.

A *volleyball*.

Heesham cupped his hands. "Court's ready. If you're game, bring it."

"Is he talking about volleyball?" I asked cautiously. Nothing here was exactly what it seemed.

Thad nodded. "Yup. Nil style. Be my partner, and I promise to bake you a full batch of cookies when we get home." Thad's devilish grin was back.

"You're on."

"Ever played before?" he asked.

"A little." I smiled.

"Oh, yeah," Thad said, his grin widening. "Let's bring it."

CHAPTER 28

THAD
DAY 290, AFTER NOON

"We're in." I called.

"You a team?" Rives asked.

As I nodded, Rives took point. "First game," he announced. "Charley and Thad against Bart and Talla."

Talla shot Rives a hard look, then trotted onto the sand, loosening up her shoulders.

"Hey, Charley," Bart called. "I'll take it easy on you, seeing as you're new and all."

"No need," Charley said. "I'm a big girl."

"Oh, I know," Bart said. "What are you, like, seven feet?"

Charley's cheeks flushed. I guessed her height was a sore spot. I wanted to tell her it just made her sexier, but I left it alone.

"You want to serve?" I asked her.

"All yours." She stared at Bart. But now her chin was raised, and her look was calculating, almost dangerous.

I served to open the game. Talla connected, setting up a sweet shot for Bart, who sliced a weak shot across the net. The ball fell like a wounded duck, and Charley spiked it home with the force of an

Amazon warrior. The ball landed at Bart's feet, where he yelped and fell.

Fighting a smile, I turned to Charley. "You play *a little?*"

Grinning, she pinched her thumb and forefinger together. "A little."

I laughed.

We pounded Bart and Talla. They never scored once. Sy and Jillian lost, too. Jason and Heesham put up the best game, but we still won handily. Talla had just called for a rematch when the ground rocked, violently.

"Quake!" I shouted, grabbing Charley's hand.

The net sagged as the ground shifted. People dropped to the sand or gripped rocks for support; Charley's hand held mine in a death grip.

Game over, Nil giggled. The quake was as subtle as a brick.

The tremor ended as quickly as it began.

"Earthquake?" Charley asked in the postquake stillness. "Do these happen often?"

"Nah. Just when Nil decides to shake things up a bit."

"Funny," she said without smiling.

"I thought so." My tone was grim.

"Hey, Thad!" Heesham yelled. He was already rolling up the net with Jason. "You didn't tell me you had a ringer, man!"

"Didn't know," I answered. "Heesham, take Jason and check the Shack. Make sure everything's secure, then scout the Cove for slides. Sy and Jillian, find Julio and check the fire ring, then the baking pits. Rives, take Bart, Macy, and Talla. Sweep the perimeter and make sure everyone's okay. Charley and I'll start checking foundations."

Rives saluted, and everyone split.

Working methodically around the City ring, Charley and I

inspected each A-frame foundation for cracks. The only suspect one was the last A-frame, the one Rives and I had just repaired. Our patch had crumbled, and the entire corner was in shambles. It needed a full reconstruction. At least we had the rocks.

I showed Charley how to mix wet sand with root gum and crushed shells, making island cement. *Please hold*, I thought as we set the first rock in place. We didn't need this A-frame now, but tomorrow was another story. Some days I felt like we were barely holding the City together.

As I reached for a second rock, Charley stopped me, her eyes on the construction, her hand on mine. "If we reset it the same way, it'll crumble again. What if we reinforce it?"

I set the rock down. "How?"

"I have an idea. Give me a sec." She jogged to the Shack, and when she returned, she carried a small stack of bamboo. She laid the bamboo rods on the ground in a crisscross pattern. "We need to cut a few down, but if we wedge these rods between the rocks like this, I think it'll support the corner weight better, and we can set the rocks around it." She looked up. "What do you think?"

I stared at the bamboo, seeing what she did: island rebar.

"I think you have hidden talents. It's brilliant."

"Not hardly," she said. "It just makes sense. Plus, my uncle's a civil engineer. He builds bridges."

"Like I said, it's brilliant."

Following Charley's lead, we wove the bamboo into the corner, creating a lattice pattern within the wall. When we were done, I had to admit, it looked a whole lot better than the sloppy job Rives and I had done. This time it would hold, no question.

As Charley and I left the freshly repaired A-frame, I sensed the City sliding back into Nil normalcy, where survival and escape were equals. We'd survived today's threat, so we could play Nil's game again tomorrow—or worse, in an hour. Nil loved nothing more than a second round of fun.

Pushing Nil from my thoughts, I focused on the good. On Charley, who stood mere centimeters away. I breathed easier having her close. It gave me a fighting chance to keep her safe.

"So," I asked as we rinsed our hands in the ocean, "are you, like, some beach volleyball pro back home?"

"Not so much. I just play a little indoor ball." She cocked her head at me. "You held your own pretty well. Is volleyball one of your hidden talents?"

"Maybe."

"Well, you're definitely athletic," Charley said. "I bet you're a heck of a snowboarder."

Moments flying over white felt distant, like they weren't mine. Grabbing the last memory before it faded, I reveled in the rush, feeling the icy air bite my cheeks as I breathed it in. Snow had a distinct smell, pure and clean, like nothing else on the planet. Like nothing on Nil.

"I wanted to go pro." My voice was quiet.

"Wanted?" She looked curious. "You don't anymore?"

I shrugged. The memory was gone. All I could smell was salt and sea.

Charley waggled her finger at me. "Oh, no. That's the Dark Side talking. You could catch a gate tomorrow and be back on the slopes in forty-eight hours. You never know."

You could catch a gate tomorrow.

I didn't want to leave Charley tomorrow. And part of me—the terrified part that kept me awake at night—whispered that I didn't want to leave Charley *ever*.

That feeling hit me harder than the quake. Then like an aftershock, I realized I was lucky I hadn't lost her already. A gate could've snatched her yesterday. I swallowed, knowing I was a fool. Knowing I'd wasted time, the most precious commodity on Nil.

"What is it?" Charley asked. "Are you okay?"

"Just thinking. Listen, we're a little behind in your island tour package, and if I've only got forty-eight hours, we've got a full schedule." I grinned. "Are you game?"

"Hmm," Charley mused, even as she stifled a grin. "What did you have in mind?"

CHAPTER
29

Thad and I sat on driftwood, waiting for the tide to come in so we could close the doors of the fish pools. Then we'd fish, or so he said. I prayed we wouldn't go back empty-handed.

"Why are you staring at me?" I asked, self-consciously wiping my cheek. Nil had no mirrors, which was a major pain.

"I'm taking your advice. Focusing on the good, and the gorgeous." Watching me, he laughed. "Which is *you*, by the way."

"That's what being on a semi-deserted island does for you," I said. "It's worse than beer goggles."

"Look." Thad's grin vanished as he spoke. "If anyone's sporting Nil goggles, it's you. I don't know whether the guys back in Georgia were blind or too scared to ask you out or what, but you're the most beautiful girl I've ever met. More than that, it just clicks with you. Half the time, you say what I'm thinking, or what I would've said if my thoughts weren't so messed up around you." His lazy grin was back. "You do things to me, Charley with an *e-y*."

I was quiet. Natalie's words echoed uncomfortably in my head. *Thad's never paid attention to any girl here . . . until you.*

"What?" He frowned. "Right now I have no clue what you're thinking."

"It's just—are you sure you're not just feeling the days? I mean, feeling like time is short?" I paused, hating what I was about to say, but I had to put my nagging fear out there. "Doing something you normally wouldn't do?"

Thad tilted my chin to look at him. "Oh, I am most definitely feeling the days. Time *is* short, and I'm definitely doing something I wouldn't normally do."

His admission crushed me. I closed my eyes. *Live in the moment*, Thad had said at the Nil Night. Does that mean live without fear of the future or regard for it? Because while Thad might be ready for an island fling, I wasn't. Not with the only guy I'd ever wanted, not with the one guy I might not be able to keep. My mind flew through the Dark Side and nearly shut down.

"Open your eyes, Charley," Thad whispered. His fingers cradled my chin. "Look at me."

I did. His sapphire eyes held mine. "Back home, I would've never told you how I feel, not yet, anyway. I would have played the game, trying not to get burned." For a second, he looked unsure. "Then again, maybe I would've told you, knowing the burn was worth the risk. Because you're just that amazing." His blue eyes blazed with an intensity that I'd never seen—not in Thad, not in anyone.

"But we're not home, we're here," he said softly. "And I've got nothing to lose telling you how I feel, nothing but time. You're right, Charley. Nil does change the way you see things. Nil makes everything more clear. What's important, what matters. And for me, that's you. This might sound crazy, but I feel like I've been waiting for you. Not just here, but in my life." He smiled, his lazy smile that made my breath catch. "Told you it sounded crazy."

It did sound a little crazy, because I felt exactly the same way. And I was too shocked by his admission to find words.

"Don't you feel it?" he asked, his eyes searching mine. "The connection between us? Tell me you feel it. Tell me I'm not crazy, or at least tell me I'm not alone."

"You're not alone," I whispered. *And neither am I.*

Leaning forward, I kissed him.

Thad's lips were salty and sweet, and kissing him felt like the most natural, most perfect thing in the world. In *any* world. Reaching up, he pulled me closer and crushed my lips to his, his hands cradling my cheeks, his thumbs caressing my jaw, then his fingers slid into my hair and there was no doubt *he* was kissing *me*. It was still not enough; he trailed kisses along my neck to my shoulder, and then his lips were back on mine.

Several kisses later, Thad pulled away. "I've been waiting for that," he said, his voice ragged. His finger traced my cheek, my jaw, my collarbone.

"Me too," I whispered, my skin tingling from his touch. "I got tired of waiting."

"I'm glad. I like a take-charge kind of girl. Have I mentioned that I like everything about you?"

"You don't know everything about me," I teased.

"So tell me," he said. "Something juicy." Thad made little circles on my shoulder with his finger, which was turning my mind into mush.

"Like what?"

"I don't know," he whispered. "Surprise me."

I was struggling to think when Thad's face darkened.

In one fluid motion, Thad whipped me to my feet behind him, pulled out his knife, and faced the trees. One second later the most emaciated squirrel I'd ever seen poked out; its tail looked worse than

Charlie Brown's Christmas tree. I felt Thad relax as the critter scampered up a tree.

"Nasty buggers, those Nil squirrels," I said. "Thanks for the protection."

"Hilarious," Thad said, then kissed my forehead. "Something dragged off the dead warthog, and it was definitely not a squirrel."

"Gotcha," I said. "Lions and tigers and squirrels, oh my."

"And you've left the poor zebra out again," Thad said. "The thing is, there're a lot more animals on Nil than people. Bunnies, mice, squirrels, you name it. Lots of little stuff, but it's the big things that worry me."

I shivered. "Like the tiger. But no one's seen him lately, or heard him. Rives thinks he's gone."

"He might be," Thad said. "But if not, the good thing for us is that as long as you stay out of his way, chances are, you'll be fine." He smiled. "Seriously. Tigers usually avoid people. They go after wildlife first, and there's plenty here. It's just that quakes spook the animals, and spooked animals can be scary."

Thad obviously got a good look at my face, because he kissed me, hard, then held me tight. "Don't worry. C'mon, let's collect dinner and head back."

Moving with ease, Thad dropped the reed doors, then tossed in a twine net. When he pulled it up, the net seethed with fish, their silver bodies flashing like mirrors in the fading sunlight. Two minutes at the pools, and all three nets were full.

"Wow," I said, taking in Thad's catch. "I can't tell you how many days I sat in the water, trying to catch fish. I never caught one. And believe me, I tried."

"What were you using for bait?"

"Me. I just tried grabbing one." I shook my head at the idiocy of it. "I know, it sounds stupid."

"No, it sounds difficult. The only person I've ever seen catch a fish by hand is Talla. She was a competitive swimmer before she landed here. I swear she's half fish."

Talla. The girl Thad went to avenge. The girl who worried about Thad being a mess. The girl who Bart insinuated was more than Thad's *friend.* And the girl who bore an eerie similarity to a feisty five-foot-tall cheer captain named Stacia.

Thad held out his free hand, smiling. I hesitated, then took it. But Thad noticed my teeny delay.

"Having second thoughts?" he asked.

"No. I just—" I looked Thad squarely in the eye. "What about Talla?"

"Talla?" Thad looked confused. "What about her?"

"I got the idea from Bart that you and Talla were an item. I just want to know if there's a history between y'all. I don't care, but I want to know."

Thad's expression darkened. "First of all, don't listen to Bart. Second, there's nothing between me and Talla. Never was, never will be."

I raised both eyebrows, wishing I could only raise one.

Thad made an exasperated sound. "Look, I'm serious. Talla is"— Thad gestured widely—"Talla. A friend, nothing more. She's not who I dream of. She's not who I think about twenty-four seven. There's only one girl I think about, and that's you."

"I believe you," I said. "But part of me says this can't be happening. Literally, it's like someone peeked inside my head and figured out my dream guy—and it's you. It's too perfect. Like it's too good to be true."

Emotion flickered in Thad's eyes, like a ghost. "Don't you see, Charley? That's part of Nil's fun." He laughed, but it sounded choked. "That's part of what I needed to get my head around this past week.

The fact that I'd met the perfect girl, here, in the one place where there's no future. Where the only given is that we can't stay." The pain in his voice was back.

"That's why I stayed away from you, hoping it would change how I feel, but it didn't. You were all I thought about. I always knew where you were, heard your voice in my head. I barely slept. And then I decided that even if Nil ripped my heart out and crushed it, I'd rather spend my remaining hours on Nil with you than without. With the girl who survived twelve days solo in Nil's house of horrors, with the girl who channels MacGyver for a little island ingenuity, with the girl who makes me forget I have an expiration date even for just a minute. That's you, Charley. And that's why I've been killing myself to get the City ready to run without me." He swallowed, hard. "Because I want to spend my last days here with you."

Thad's take was jaded and a little depressing, but I got what he was saying. But it was what he didn't say that stood out the most. He'd chosen to hope, even if it hurt.

"I told you," I whispered, reaching up and laying my palm gently against his chest, over his heart. "I've always wanted my very own island guide."

Thad grinned, his lazy smile that made me melt, and lowering his head, he kissed me. This kiss wasn't crushing; it was tender and sweet, and full of so much pain that my chest ached in response, because like Thad said, if we had a future, it sure wasn't here.

CHAPTER 30

THAD
DAY 290, TWILIGHT

Charley insisted on carrying one net; I carried two. But it was the fit of her hand in mine that made me feel like shouting, that and the taste of her on my lips.

Made-to-order perfection, I thought. Dropping my nets, I kissed her again, cupping her face in my hands. Despite knowing we needed to get back, it was nearly impossible to stop. She looked as dazed as I felt.

"Wow," she breathed, opening her eyes slowly. "I could get used to this."

"Me too." I whispered, my lips inches from hers, my thumbs caressing her jaw. "Clearly being an island guide has its perks. I'm going to incorporate lots of this"—I brushed her lips with mine—"into our schedule."

"I thought our schedule was full," Charley said with a straight face. "Or are you upgrading the tour package?"

"More like fine-tuning," I said. "Like I said, it's my first run as an island guide. Your satisfaction is my top priority."

"Well then, by all means. More kissing." She blushed, making me laugh. Of course I kissed her again. Gently, then urgently, totally shell-shocked by the intensity of it all. By my feelings, by hers, by the moment.

Reluctantly, I pulled away. "We need to go."

Walking again, hands tight together, I thought Charley finally understood how I felt about her, but something told me she still didn't see how twisted Nil was. The yin and the yang. For every good there was something bad; we were pawns in Nil's game. Nil gave me Charley, but surely there'd be a cost. I just didn't know what it was—yet.

And I prayed it wasn't Charley who'd pay the price.

Jason jogged up as we got close.

"Welcome back, man," I said. "What's the word?" *Tell me Nat made it, and that she's gone.*

"Nat's restocking. We saw a double, but it was too far out." Jason looked upset.

Damn, I thought.

"Don't worry," I said, gripping his shoulder. "She's got time."

Jason shook his head. "It's not Nat. It's Li." He paused. "She went renegade."

And just like that, my Charley stoke dulled. It was a harsh reality check, no doubt perfectly island-timed.

"What do y'all mean, she went renegade?" Charley said. "Where'd she go?"

Jason ran his hand through his curly hair, which was wild and crazy carrot-top-looking after long days on Search. "She took off while her team was sleeping. She left her groundcover folded, with a single flower on top. Like a good-bye."

"Why?" Charley's face paled. "Why would she leave?"

"Sometimes people want to spend their last days alone," I said quietly.

"Like Kevin," Charley said, her eyes on mine.

"Like Kevin."

For a second it was just me and Charley and the God-awful tick-tock in my brain.

Jason broke into our world. "Quan's so upset he didn't talk the entire way back. I'm worried, man. What if he leaves the City now that Li's gone?"

"Quan?" Charley frowned. "Who's Quan?"

"Li's shadow," I explained. "Problem is, Quan doesn't speak a word of English, and his vision sucks."

"Li talked for him," Jason added.

"And his vision's bad?" Charley's expression turned horrified.

"Yup," Jason said. "He's fast, but blind as a bat. He almost walked into a ravine once. You know, the whole glasses-don't-come-through-the-gate thing."

"So because Li's gone, Quan might not make it either?" Charley asked, unable to shake the look on her face. "How long does he have?"

"I'm not exactly sure," I said. "He showed up a few months after me. Where's Nat?"

"Over there." Jason pointed to the firepit, where two rabbits hung over the fire. Upwind of the smoke, Natalie stood with Jillian and Talla. Nat's hands moved so fast they blurred.

Natalie's group was not the only one with extra intensity. An electricity crackled in the air, potent and familiar. The people changed, but the vibe never did; it slicked in with the return of the last Search team, the one that came back short a member but without word of a gate. The City hung on edge, waiting. For news of Li . . . for new teams to head out . . . for change, because that was the one constant on Nil—that and the fact that no one ever celebrated a one-year anniversary.

Holding Charley's hand tight, I turned to Jason. "Talk to me about Search."

The next hour flew by as we took advantage of the fading light. I debriefed every team just back, cataloguing what they'd seen and heard, grateful the quake was minor and no one got hurt. I spoke to everyone with Priority, shoring up their choices. When I was confident the new teams were balanced and prepped, I whistled.

Conversations stalled like a gate dropped from the sky; all heads turned to me.

"So here's where we stand. Nat's back, ready to roll out tomorrow. She's got time." Silent nods, fierce faces.

I took in the stoic group. "As you might have heard, Li's gone. Today was her last day. So let's all keep her in our prayers." More nods, even more eyes closed as silent prayers flew skyward.

After a thick moment, I cleared my throat. "Okay, here's the latest. Jason says Nil's home to an ostrich now, and he brought back another goat." I pointed to the pens, where two goats kept company with the cow. "Li's team saw a trio of wild horses. No one's seen the rhino lately, but who knows. There's also a pair of hippos. Hippos usually find their way to the mudflats. I saw one there last month, so we might have three. Keep your eyes open. I'm no hippo expert, but like everything else, they can get mean when cornered, eh?"

"True dat," Bart said. I ignored him.

"Last but not least, no word on whether the tiger's still around. Stay alert, take care of each other." I took a sip of water. "Next up: teams. New ones launch tomorrow. Morning or afternoon, team Leaders make the final call on departure and support. So here goes: Elia as Leader, with Johan as Spotter and Cassie and Julio as support. Miguel, with Jillian as Spotter, Sy and Macy as support. Nat, with Jason as Spotter, Charley and me as support. I nominate Rives to Lead while I'm gone. All hands yea?"

A dozen hands shot up at once. As he raised his hand, Sy looked guilty. Beside Sy, Bart's arms stayed crossed, his expression furious.

"Okay." I nodded. "Let's get busy, and get lucky."

The buzz was back. If anything, it had jacked up a notch.

I looked around for Charley. She wasn't in sight. I wondered what she was up to, but before I could find out, Talla came up, asking about gliders. Jillian had concerns about supplies, and Johan was on Jillian's heels, with news about one of the crops. Questions and problems, answers and guesses. Bart strode up as Johan moved away. *Problem*, I thought, taking in Bart's hard face.

"Did you tell Miguel not to pick me?" he asked.

"No, Bart," I said, working to keep my voice steady as I highlighted his lack of basic courtesy, "I asked him to name his team. And he did."

Bart's voice rose like he'd sucked down helium. "Well, I've helped him find wood to carve, and he said he'd pick me. He *promised*." Now he sounded petulant. And seriously annoying.

"Look, that's between you and Miguel. All I know is that he named his team, and you weren't on it." Even though I'd spoken the truth, I regretted my bluntness. "Maybe next time," I offered lamely.

He launched into a new argument, decibel level set at full whine. Then like a switch flipped, Bart stopped. "Well, I may not be on this Search, but I have more time than you." His smug smile erased my small shred of sympathy. "A lot more, like Charley. Think about that."

I fought the urge to slam my fist into his face. "True. But if someone picks you, don't forget you're *support*. Priority rules. Otherwise, you're on your own." I returned Bart's smile.

"People are getting tired of you and your rules," Bart insisted. "You'll see."

"Not my rules," I shot back. "City rules. And you're either in or out." Without waiting for a response, I left Bart, found Rives, and unloaded my Bart frustration in a near growl.

"Has anyone been banished for being a slacker?" Rives asked in a low voice.

"I've never known anyone to get banished, period. But if he doesn't pull his weight, no one will pick him, and he's pretty much screwing himself. Gates don't drop in the City very often."

Rives nodded, but he still looked troubled. We changed topics, and as Rives left, Charley's hand slid into mine.

"You've been busy," she said. "Is there anyone you didn't talk to?"

"You."

For a moment, we stood without speaking, staring at each other, which should have been weird but wasn't.

Slowly, savoring each second, I lowered my head and kissed her. Long and soft, but I felt the heat and ached for more. With super-human effort, I made myself break away.

Watching her eyes flicker open to firelight, I asked, "Can I walk you back?"

"Definitely," she said. "Especially with those crazy Nil squirrels on the loose."

"Insane rodent protection, at your service." I grinned.

"So we head out in the morning?" she asked.

"Dawn." I nodded. "Island adventure awaits."

Charley smiled, then gave an odd laugh. "You know something funny? My dream was to travel. Back home, I have a huge world map across one wall. I'd sit on my bed, staring at the map, dreaming of all the exotic places I wanted to go."

"Let me guess. Nil wasn't on your map."

"I don't think Nil's on anyone's map."

"True." I thought of the island, nonexistent yet real, and of Li, out there alone.

"But it's exotic, that's for sure," Charley said. "So, where're we headed tomorrow?"

"The black lava field, the south one."

"There's two?" She frowned.

"Yeah. They bracket the red flow, the one where you found your clothes. Different colors, different flows."

"Exactly how many hot spots are there?" she asked. "Places where gates flash the most?"

"We're not sure. The current Nil software is a little dated." I grinned sideways at Charley. "Right now people seem to be having the best luck in the lava fields and by the base of the mountain. I'd add Black Bay to the list, too. It's a moving target, but it's all we've got." Frustration made my words sharp, but my beef wasn't with Charley, it was with Nil. With the whole marionette game.

Three seconds later, Charley's A-frame was right in front of us. I hated to leave; the idea of waking with Charley in my arms was killer. But something told me Nat needed Charley's company more.

Another day, I told myself. *I've got time*. Right.

Outside her A-frame, I pulled her close. "I hate to say good night, but I don't think Nat should be alone. But," I tucked her hair behind her ear, "as your island guide, I think this moment calls for a good night kiss. As part of the tour package, of course."

"By all means, let's stay on schedule," Charley whispered.

As her hands wrapped around my waist, I kissed her, losing my fingers in her hair and my mind in the process. We broke apart at the same moment.

"Good night, Mr. Island Guide," Charley said, smiling. She took a step, then stopped, surprise registering on her face. "I just realized something."

"What?"

"How is it that I feel like I know you better than any guy I've ever met, but I don't even know your last name?"

"Because it doesn't matter. But since you're curious, it's Blake.

Thaddeus Blake." Smiling, I tucked a wisp of hair behind her ear. "What's yours?"

"Crowder."

"Charley Crowder," I said, savoring the words. "I like it."

She laughed, shaking her head. "You're a mess."

"Only with you," I said, brushing hair away from her eyes. "Always with you."

She squeezed my hand. "You're definitely a mess. A hot mess. Now you'd better get some sleep. You've got a big trip tomorrow, Thaddeus Blake."

When I went to bed, I felt like I'd just swept the men's finals by a landslide, the rush was just that good. Charley's feelings echoed mine, feelings that went beyond the borders of Nil.

If Nil lets them.

I sucked in air. The same fear I'd been fighting for days sliced deep, only sharper, and more concrete. Bart's snide comment had struck a nerve. He was right; my time was dwindling.

Eyes wide open, I lay in the darkness, shockingly aware that my fate tracked Kevin's—a boy waiting on the other side, with a heart as hopeful as mine—if I was lucky. And after 290 days, no one had to tell me that luck was as tough to come by on Nil as a gate.

CHAPTER 31

The second I entered the hut, Natalie sat up. "I'm so glad you took my advice and kissed Thad."

"How do you know I kissed him?"

"Please. I think everyone saw that kiss by the fire. And it's about damn time." She smiled, then she looked down. Twisting her covers between her fingers, she spoke quietly. "I know this sounds old school, but don't waste a minute. Not one. Time flies here, faster than you're ready for. No regrets, okay?"

"Okay." I nodded.

Natalie looked up. "So if you want to stay with Thad tonight, I understand."

I felt slow, realizing Thad had already considered it and decided against it. "The thought hadn't occurred to me," I admitted.

"Well, don't feel like you have to stay with me. My feelings won't be hurt, I promise."

"It's okay. Really." I smiled as I curled up on the bed across from hers. "I'm good."

I meant it. I wanted to be with Thad, but I also needed a minute to ground myself. Plus, Thad had sensed Natalie could use some company.

"You sure?" she asked.

"Totally." I nodded. "I know how lonely this hut feels with only one person. I hate being alone, especially at night."

"Seriously? You made it eleven nights by yourself in the creepiest place ever."

"Barely." I shivered. "At one point, I lost it. I mean really lost it. Bawled like a baby."

Sometimes I thought there was something wrong with me because I rarely cried. I didn't even cry at my granddaddy's funeral, even though we were close and I missed him terribly. When I thought tears should fall, they didn't. But I'd cried here, when I realized I was totally alone. And I hadn't cried since.

Natalie was staring at me. "Honey, I lost it the minute I woke up. And for the next few weeks, I kept freaking about stupid stuff, like all the school I was missing, and how behind I would be when I got back. Then I realized I'd be lucky if I got back." She shook her head. "Don't feel bad about losing it. Nil has a way of getting to everyone, sooner or later."

I wasn't exactly sure what she meant.

"So you and Thad, huh?" Natalie grinned, a wicked Em grin. "I like it."

"Me too." I couldn't help smiling. "You know what's crazy? I didn't even know his last name until tonight."

"What is it?"

"What?"

"Thad's last name," Natalie said. "What is it?"

"Blake," I answered, surprised.

"Kevin's is Radford. Mine's Bourdean. Natalie Bourdean."

"Charley Crowder."

"It's nice to meet you, Charley Crowder." She chuckled, but under the laugh, she sounded exhausted.

"I'm glad you're back, but I'm not, ya know?" I said.

"Yeah." Her voice was small. "I know."

"How many gates did y'all see? Jason said one flashed near the rain forest, but too far away to catch."

"So far away I didn't see it, but Jason swears it was there. It doesn't matter." She sighed. "I didn't catch it."

"It just means that gate wasn't yours. You'll catch one, Natalie. You'll make it."

"I hope you're right."

Me too, I thought, but I said, "Did you see any others?"

"One, the first day, near the hills. A bird flew into it, and it collapsed."

"Any inbound?"

"Nope."

I nodded, taking mental notes.

"Natalie, the big carving, the one by the Arches. Thad calls it the Man in the Maze. He said there's an identical one across the island, only that one has a woman instead of a man."

"There is."

"So what do they mean?"

"Who knows?" Natalie yawned. "Maybe someone had a lot of time on their hands."

"But the carvings are so precise, they must be here for a reason," I insisted. "Maybe someone was trying to leave us a clue. Maybe Nil is the maze, and the carvings tell us how to escape."

Natalie looked thoughtful. "It's a nice thought, but I don't see how."

"I don't either, but I think the carvings are important. I just don't know why." *I'm missing something*, I thought. *But what?*

The night breeze wafted in, making me shiver. I missed being warm at night, which made me think of Thad and our kiss by the fire. Nothing missing there.

"So when you get home, what's the thing you'll miss most about Nil?"

"Nothing." Natalie's voice was flat.

"Really? Nothing? What about the sunsets, the black sand beaches? The coconut soap?" I joked.

"Nope. I'm over it. The stress, the running. The merry-go-round of noon. I've seen too much death, too many noons. All I'll miss is the people, but if you think about it, that's not really Nil."

"I guess," I lied. Because for me, the people *were* Nil. I realized that even though we shared this hut, Natalie was in a different place—one I hoped I'd never see.

We stopped talking as Natalie dozed off. I curled into a ball under the thin covers, trying to get warm. Despite the moonlight, darkness crept in, cold and complete, like the dying whisper of a gate. But it was the darkness in my head that was the hardest to shake. For the first time, the darkness had a name. It was the daywatch.

Thad had seventy-five days.

CHAPTER 32

CHARLEY
DAY 25, DAWN

Light peeked inside the hut, a perfect streak of gold. My first thought was *Thad*.

He had seventy-five days left. Exactly seventy-five noons.

Then I thought of Natalie, who had even fewer. Beside me, her bed sat empty. I had the weirdest flash of home, of Em's empty bed hugging the other wall in my room. But while Em was probably out hunting the perfect fake ID, Natalie was out hunting gates.

And I was supposed to be with her.

I threw on my sandals, grabbed my satchel, and flew outside. The fire ring smoldered without flame. Two fresh logs sat on top, waiting to burn. And like my first morning here, Thad stood at the Wall, running his hands across the wood. His fingers traced carvings, which now I knew were names. His hand hovered over my name, tracing the *e-y*.

I kissed the back of his neck.

"Morning, Mr. Blake."

"Morning, sleepy." He turned and kissed my head.

"Why didn't you wake me?"

"Because you needed the rest. If you'd slept much longer, I would've woken you, but now you're up. Let's get you set and then we'll roll."

Talla jogged over as we met up with Natalie and Jason by the Shack. "It's good to have our Leader back," she said, shooting a pointed look at me. Then she gave Natalie a fast hug. "Good luck, Nat! Run fast." Stepping back, Talla snapped a nod at the three of us. "Watch her back, okay? See you soon."

Watching Talla trot away, her back ramrod straight, her intensity barely contained, understanding dawned. *Talla is Talla*, Thad had once said. I'd finally figured her out. She was a fighter. More than competitive, she was determined to win—to beat the island odds, and she needed a strong Leader to do it. And that Leader was Thad. Talla and I didn't always click, but I finally understood her.

Rives pulled Thad aside, gesturing past the A-frames. Thad listened intently, and after clasping Rives's shoulder, Thad walked back, his eyes scanning the City perimeter.

"Let's pack and roll," he said as he hefted his pack.

"And hope the gates roll, too," Jason said. Spear in hand, he started after Natalie, who set a brisk pace. We followed, heading south.

"What was Rives talking about?" I asked Thad.

"We lost the cow last night. Something broke down the pen. The hyena was finishing it this morning, but we think something else got it first."

"Who had watch?"

"Sy." Thad's expression was frustrated. "But apparently he didn't see a thing."

"Interesting," I said.

"Yeah." He snorted. "I still wish we hadn't lost the cow. The goats are missing, too, but they'll come back." He gave me a sideways grin. "But until they do, we're back to coconut milk."

"My favorite." I grimaced.

Thad laughed. But his eyes stayed sharp.

We passed through familiar territory and beyond. By late morning, we'd made it to our destination: a black lava field, a different one than I remembered. This one looked aged. Drier, grayer, and with more fissures and cracks. Red gleamed to the north.

Plunking down our bags, we took a break. Today's snacks were fresh, and our gourds full. From what Thad said, that wasn't always the case, especially toward the end of Search. While Thad was stretching, I turned away, quietly working on my secret project.

"What's that?" Thad asked, pointing to my hand.

"Paper I got from Jillian." I made one final mark, then tucked it away.

"I see that," Thad said dryly. "Are you writing me a love letter?"

"A poem, actually. Nothing like a little island pentameter." Then I hesitated. "Okay, seriously, it's a map. I'm pretty good with directions, and I've started mapping the island. You weren't the only one who stayed busy when you were getting your head straight."

"Cool." He snuck my paper back out. "Looks good," he said as he studied my sketch. I'd used charcoal sticks from the fire. More sticks were tucked deep in my satchel, carefully wrapped in leaves and twine.

"What are you using for a measure of scale?" he asked.

"My big ole feet. I mark off the distance as I walk."

"They're not big, they're perfect," Thad said absently. He pointed to a trio of tiny black circles. "What are these? Gates?"

"Yup. I've marked locations of both entry and exit gates in this radius." I traced an arc with my finger. "Entries are solid; exits are open circles. And if it's not on the map yet, it will be. I've got another piece of paper where I'm keeping track of entry and exit sites I haven't mapped. Once I've mapped the entire island, then I can transfer over the gate info."

Thad was still studying the map.

"I'm not so good at making soap," I said. "So I thought I'd make maps. My contribution to Nil."

Thad looked up, his eyes flush with blue hope. "It's not a gift to Nil, it's to us. To the City."

He yelled before I could stop him. "Jason! Nat! C'mere! You gotta see this!"

"Stop," I said, embarrassed. "It's not much to look at, not yet."

"You're wrong," Thad said quietly. "It's hope."

I explained my maps and charts to Jason and Natalie, who grew as excited as Thad.

"Okay, there's one more thing," I said. "I keep hearing y'all talk about hot spots. Like the Flower Field, Black Bay, the lava fields, and the meadow by the base of Mount Nil, where Thad landed. All of those are open areas, and I think that's the connection. I'm not sure if more gates really roll through those spots, but I do think they're easier to see."

"And easier to catch," Jason said, nodding.

"Right. But there may be actual hot spots, places where gates are statistically more likely to flash. Where *exit* gates are more likely to flash. And I'm hoping if we can put all the exit gates onto one map, maybe we'll see—something. Something that'll increase the odds of getting off Nil for everyone."

"How far are you going back to get your gate info?" Natalie asked. "Won't that skew the charts?"

"I don't know. I've thought about that, about whether I should try to start from two weeks ago, or even a month. But I think we should just get all the information we can, from anyone and everyone. The most important being where people caught exit gates, or at least saw them, and for that, let's go back as far as we can remember. See if there's a pattern."

Natalie nodded. "We need to go down the Wall and tell you where people we know caught gates."

"Uh, I hate to break up this powwow," Jason said, "but time's up. If Nil's sending a gate, she's not gonna wait. Look." He pointed to the sun. "We need to move."

Thad was already on his feet. "Jason's right. Let's get away from the tree line, into the open."

"Easy lookin', easy runnin'." Jason smiled.

"Easy for you to say," Natalie said. But she was smiling, too.

We walked in a loose line. It was a weird feeling, watching and hoping, waiting for something that might never show. It was how I imagined a blind date would be, only this was way worse. Because if a blind date never showed, you could just walk away, no harm done. Here, if a gate never showed, sooner or later, *you* were done. I still wondered exactly what happened to you on your last day if you missed the gate. I prayed I'd never find out.

Not helping, I told myself. *Not helping Natalie.* I pulled my mind back from the Dark Side and scanned the ground ahead, looking for any sign of a shimmer.

It was agonizing.

After an eternity of waiting, Jason spoke. "That's it." His voice dripped disappointment. "I was so sure it would flash here today." He looked at Natalie. "Sorry, Nat. Bad idea. You shouldn't have listened to me."

"How do you know noon's passed?" I asked.

"We just know," Thad said, his jaw hard. "The sun, for one. A feeling, for two." Natalie was nodding, but Jason looked upset—with himself.

"Jason," I said hesitantly, "I don't think you're wrong. I think you're early."

Everyone turned to me. "I have a theory. I've been looking at my chart, where I've listed all the gates—the confirmed landing sites and exits, including gates people saw but didn't catch. We know inbound ones come anytime, anywhere. There's no pattern, and I think it's because the pattern is determined on the outbound end—back home. But if you look just at the exit gates"—I pulled out my last paper, the one with a rough map and marked only with outbounds—"I think they roll north in a constant wave, hitting a different latitude each day, but always north of the last one until the entire island is crossed. I have no clue where the wave starts, or even if the starting place is always the same. But we know gates never appear in the same place two days in a row, and I think it's because they follow a sequence, from south to north. So based on Samuel's gate on White Beach ten days ago, which is north of us, we might not see a gate here for another day or two." I shrugged. "It's a total guess. But if you factor in the flash that Jason missed on the day I met y'all, and Sabine's, and chart the other gates people have seen, well, it kind of fits."

They were all staring at the map.

"Why didn't we ever see this?" Thad sounded frustrated.

"Because we never tried to map the timing." Natalie said. "We just knew they rolled north after they flashed."

"Charley, this is amazing." Thad stared at the map, the one with the charts.

"I wouldn't go that far," I said quickly. "Like I said, it's just a theory, maybe more like a guess. And before we get too excited, there're some gates that don't fit; they flash out of order. Like the gate Jason saw by the rain forest, about the same time Samuel caught his on White Beach. From what everyone's told me, the rain forest lies on a latitude south of White Beach, so either one was an aberration, or my theory is junk."

"A rogue set," Thad murmured.

"A what?" Natalie frowned.

"A set that breaks farther out from where all the other waves are breaking. It's called a rogue set."

"Maybe," I said. "Or maybe I'm just forcing something that doesn't fit."

"It's better than nothing," Jason said. "Which is what we had. I say we try Charley's theory and see if it helps." He looked at me. "So where to?"

I was shocked that the three veterans looked at me like I had a clue. "Uh, I don't know. I just think the next gate will be coming from that direction." I pointed south. "So maybe here tomorrow, or the next day." *Or maybe not at all*, I thought.

"So either we stay or walk north." Natalie looked thoughtful. "We go through the red, to the next black."

"No," I said quickly, "not that far." All three looked at me, and I shrugged. "Or maybe yes. I don't know. I'm just guessing here."

"Stay or go?" Jason asked.

"Stay." Natalie's voice. Natalie's choice.

"Stay it is," Jason said.

"Okay," Thad said, "we've got twenty-four hours to explore. Let's help Charley fill out her maps. We'll walk north, toward the red field, pacing it off. Sound good?"

Plan in place, we worked our way across the black ground. With each step, I had flashbacks to my first day on the island. I wondered what happened to the zebra.

Jason took point, constantly scanning ahead. It occurred to me he was searching for gates—inbound ones, the kind that bring warm-blooded creatures, like us. I had flashes of Rory, falling out of the sky, red as a lobster, then Rory on the ground, red with blood.

I flinched. Beside me, Natalie sucked in her breath.

"Don't look," Thad said sharply.

Too late.

For the second time in two weeks, I saw a dead body sprawled on the ground. Only this one wore a handmade lei.

CHAPTER
33

"It's Li," Natalie whispered. "She didn't make it."

"She made me a lei once," Jason said to no one in particular.

Charley's face was pale, but she said nothing.

I was the only one not staring at Li.

"Okay," I said, desperate to defuse the very bad karma of finding a body the first day of Search. "Let's close our eyes and bow our heads." For the first time, I wished Nat had chosen Johan as Spotter instead of Jason. Johan, with his rich words and humble prayers that flowed like water. But without Johan, Nat was stuck with me.

We joined hands in a tight circle. Bowing my head, I spoke quietly. "Heavenly Father, you know our needs before we do, and here on Nil we have many. Today we pray for Li. We ask that her soul rest in peace. And for her family back home, we ask You to give them peace. Be with Li, and be with us all, her family here in Nil. In Your name we pray, Amen."

Whispers of "Amen" echoed around me.

"Okay," I said, letting go of Jason's hand, then Charley's. "Now let's bury her."

"How?" Jason frowned. "This rock is tougher than asphalt."

I looked at him. "I never said we'd dig."

Ten minutes later, I carefully laid Li's body on the bottom of a wide hollow in the rock, fully dressed. As valuable as her clothes were, I was not about to pull a Sy and strip a dead body. We covered her with rocks, making a black rock tomb. As the others stepped back, I pulled out my bag of bleached coral and crafted a cross, white on black.

"Rest in peace, Li," I whispered.

Natalie made a strangled choking sound.

"Nat?" I asked, standing. "You okay?"

"I just remembered something," she whispered, her eyes fixed on Li's coral cross. "That creepy song Ramia sang on her last Nil Night." Dropping into Ramia's odd cadence, Nat said, "To Nil we come, from Nil some go, and some like me will stay. The clock winds down, our time runs out, and Nil will have her way." Natalie lifted her haunted eyes to mine. "If you change 'me' to 'Li,' it fits." She started to shake. "Why did I remember that now?"

Because Ramia knew, I thought. *Somehow Ramia always knew.*

NO. My brain balked at the thought. *Her predictions mean nothing*, I told myself. *Absolutely nothing.*

Consumed by my mental sparring, I froze, and Charley stepped up before I could. She clasped Natalie's hands and held them steady. "Natalie, it's okay. You've got plenty of time. Weeks. Plus"—Charley's voice was confident—"you've got us."

Natalie held Charley's hands so tight that Natalie's knuckles turned white. Bloodless, like Li's face.

And some like me will stay.

"Natalie, look at me." Charley's voice turned fierce, strong enough to pull me back, too. "You're not Li. You're *Na-ta-lie*," Charley's drawl dragged out Nat's name, "and we're going to get you home. So please, don't fall apart on us, okay?"

Natalie nodded. Taking a deep breath, she faced Li's rock tomb. "Good-bye, friend," she said. "Thank you for the beauty you brought into my life. I'll never forget you. Rest in peace."

"Where to?" I asked Natalie.

"Anywhere," she said. Despite the sun, her teeth chattered.

I thought fast. "I know just the place." I hitched up my pack, keeping my hands away from Charley, not wanting to touch her since I'd just touched death. "To the tubes."

"To the tubes," Jason echoed.

We walked in silence. The funeral hangover threatened to make me sick.

Another death on my watch.

It was a relief to spot the tubes. South of the Arches, a web of tunnels carved from old lava flows sat open to the sky. Glistening with fresh water and heated daily by the sun, the tubes were perpetually warm. Not as hot as the showers Charley dreamed of, but a marked change from the icy Cove.

Even better, South Beach lay on the other side. A wide black beach stretching down the western coast to the southern tip, someone before my time had slapped it with the generic name, and it stuck. Seeing the setup for tonight, I relaxed. Not totally, but enough. Enough to stay sane one more day, enough to hold the possibility of sleep. Camping near the sea beat crashing deep in the island any day. One less side to guard.

I turned to Charley. "You'll like this. It's Nil's version of a warm bath."

For the next few hours, the four of us lounged in the tubes, elbows out, faces to the sun, chilling like we were in a hot tub at a ski chalet—only this was Nil. And not for one minute did I forget. Judging by Nat's face, neither did she. Death hung with us like a fifth wheel.

When the air cooled, we foraged. I fished, Charley harvested redfruit, and Jason and Nat gathered firewood. Charley might have been green, but our team purred with island efficiency, enough to dispel the aura of death. Action was always the best Nil antidote, a fact I'd forgotten in the wake of Li's burial. While Natalie cleaned the fish, I showed Charley how to make fire using my bow. Rub and blow, coaxing the wisp of smoke to burst into flame. The brittle tinder caught within minutes. The blaze was not just for warmth; it was for protection. Animals disliked fire.

As the fire burned and the sun set, I took first watch.

Natalie was already asleep, or lost in thought with her eyes closed. Jason was sacked out beside Nat. Beside the fire, Charley lay in my arms, her back resting against my chest, her face tilted to the clear Nil sky. Even with the crappy day we'd had, I felt guiltily content. I'd buried a girl today, and now I held the perfect one in my arms. It was the yin and yang of Nil, and it was totally twisted.

Charley had been quiet for so long that my gut said she wasn't thinking about the stars.

"Thinking about Li?" I asked softly.

"I can't believe she didn't make it." Charley's voice was subdued. "One thing's for sure, I'll never look at black rock the same. I hiked all over piles of that stuff my first day here, and for all I know, I was walking over dead bodies. Like a cemetery." She shuddered.

"Well, I've never buried anyone in black rock before, if it makes you feel better."

"It doesn't. Because you and I are just the latest drop-ins. Look at the Wall. It's covered in names. There're hundreds on there."

"I know," I said.

Charley's face was still tilted toward the stars. "Do you think we're here for a reason? I mean, on Nil?"

"I don't know. But"—I kissed her head—"right now there's no place I'd rather be."

"Same." She smiled, then looked straight at me. "Who's Ramia?"

"Ramia?" I replied, startled.

"Natalie mentioned Ramia, and that name sounds familiar. Who is she?"

"A girl. She left a few weeks after I arrived."

Charley's eyes stayed on mine. "She didn't make it, did she?"

"No."

"And she's the one who carved that creepy bone bracelet I heard about?"

"Yup."

It's bone, Ramia had said, her fingers stroking the cuff in an eerie caress. *Bone of an animal that never left. Bone of an animal I chose not to eat. Soon it will be bone on bone.* She'd paused, her eyes on the cuff. *I'm not leaving, Thad. My journey ends here.* Then she'd looked at me, her eyes shrewd, an odd smile pulling at her lips. *As does yours. You'll Lead, but you'll never leave. Because you do not see. The blind leading the blind,* she'd cackled. *The blind leading the blind!*

Then she'd stopped abruptly, her eyes wide. *Or will you?* she'd crooned, her eyes traveling my face, searching. *If you want to live, you must give up what you want the most. Open your eyes, Thad. Will you open your eyes? Will you see?* Rocking, rubbing that creepy cuff, she'd just kept repeating *open your eyes* and mumbling about the blind leading the blind.

You'll never leave.

I'd never told anyone her prediction for me. *Because it doesn't matter*, I told myself. *It means nothing.*

But her prediction haunted me. And it changed me; it was the moment I'd decided my mid-season break was over and that I'd do all I could to get the hell off Nil, no matter what some crazy chick predicted. I was leaving.

Until Charley.

Now Nil would have to pry me away.

"Speaking of creepy," Charley was saying, "did you see Li's lei? It was made of black rock, like she knew she wouldn't make it." Now Charley turned, regarding me thoughtfully. "You used to wear a necklace with a single black rock. But now you wear a shell." She pointed to my neck, where a smooth shell as gold as Charley's eyes hung from a piece of twine.

"You're very observant, Ms. Crowder." For months, I'd worn black rock, my way of mocking Nil. Black rock, dead rock, spit from Nil's gut. But the day I'd met Charley, I'd found this shell and ditched the black.

I'd actually found two.

I reached into my pocket and withdrew a necklace. Same twine, different shell. Her shell was gold, too, but flecked with blue, like the ocean was buffering the darkness of Nil. I'd been waiting for the right time to give it to her; maybe that time was now. She could use the buffer.

"I found this shell when I found mine," I said. "In case you wanted some island bling."

"It's beautiful." Smiling, Charley tied it around her neck before I could help. "Thanks," she said, one hand touching the shell at her neck. "I love it."

I love you.

The rush of emotion hit me so hard, the words stuck in my throat.

Unable to speak, barely able to breathe, I twisted my fingers in her hair and pulled her lips to mine. Then, breaking away, I held her tight. No words, no expectations, just Charley in my arms and my eyes wide open.

CHAPTER 34

CHARLEY
DAY 26, LATE MORNING

We were back on black as noon approached. I felt weird because everyone this morning had looked at my charts like they meant something, and for all I knew, they were just chicken scratch. But I wanted them to mean something: I wanted them to mean a gate was coming for Natalie.

"Showtime," Jason remarked, his eyes dancing across the dark field.

Even without Jason's warning, I sensed noon was close. It was like the longer I was here, the more I understood the island. Or maybe I just wanted to think I was getting a clue, because so much was unknown. I stopped thinking about all I didn't know, because my charts were on that list, full of holes. And yet here we were, riding the hope they offered. It was totally stressing me out.

Natalie's face was anxious, making me forget about me.

I squeezed her hand. "Run fast, sweet friend." To say good-bye felt so final—plus I was afraid to jinx it. Like if I said good-bye, a gate wouldn't show.

Trees spread to our right, black stretched before us, and

chunky red curved to the left. Everyone's eyes scoured the ground. The air crackled with waiting, and wanting. The intensity gave me chills, and with a start, I realized everyone was looking south. I shivered.

At the precise moment I noticed the air was slack, Jason shouted.

"There!" he hollered, pointing right. Near the tree line, the ground was rippling, then stretching, into a shimmering wall reaching for the sky. The edges grew dark and defined; the air inside writhed with translucent color and no color at all. No longer rising, now the gate was rolling. North, like we expected.

Natalie was already running. The gate glittered a football field away.

We dropped back, pacing Natalie, giving her space as she chased the gate. She was sixty yards out and sprinting. Thad and I kept quiet while Jason barked directions.

Please make it, I thought, watching Natalie race against noon. *Please catch this shimmer. Please let this be the last noon you have to see.*

Thirty yards to go.

Then, like a bad B movie, two figures darted from the trees. A pair of girls, naked and screaming, running side by side as they streaked—literally—straight for the gate. For Natalie's gate.

"Not good," Thad murmured.

"Run, Natalie!" I yelled.

But I knew it was over. She was too far away, with too much competition. The girls' trajectory would intercept the gate well before Natalie could.

The scene slowed but didn't. The naked girls flying over the black rock, their four legs like two as they converged on the gate; Natalie on her own, too far behind. Natalie was still a good fifteen yards away when the two girls hit the gate as one.

The air flashed blinding white, like a mirror reflecting the sun.

Instinctively, I shielded my eyes, and when I looked back, the gate was gone. The air was clear, unwavering blue; the island breeze was back. One girl lay on the ground, as still as the rocks.

And the other girl was gone.

"Did you see that?" Jason said as the three of us broke into a sprint. "She flew back, like she was shocked."

"Or repelled," Thad said, his face hard.

"Have y'all ever seen that before?" I asked.

"Never," Thad said. "But I've never seen two people try to catch the same gate either."

We caught up with Natalie as she kneeled beside the motionless girl. With practiced ease, Natalie pressed her fingers to the girl's wrist, checking for a pulse.

"Is she breathing?" Thad asked.

"Barely. I'm not sure what happened to her."

"Me either, but I think it's pretty clear that two peeps shouldn't go for the same gate." Jason looked at the girl, who looked Indian, or maybe Pakistani. Naked as a jaybird, she was stick-thin. "Man, I never thought I'd say this, but I'm getting sick of naked women."

"Just when they look like corpses," Thad said grimly. "But she's not dead. And we've got to help her." He was already pulling objects from his magic pack.

"Totally." Natalie covered the girl with her extra wrap. "Even if she did crash my party." But she didn't sound upset; she sounded weirdly upbeat, which seemed odd given the circumstances.

"Are you okay?" I asked Natalie. "I mean, that gate. You could've made it."

"Not my gate. And unlike her, I'm totally fine." She glanced at the girl, worried.

"Still, I'm glad you're not upset."

"Upset? I'm not upset, at least not about the gate." She laughed.

"Don't you see? Your charts work, Charley! A gate was just where you thought it would be!"

Her praise made me uncomfortable. "Natalie, it could've been pure luck. Let's not get too excited, okay?"

"Nope." She kept grinning. "They work. Because there's no such thing as luck on Nil."

CHAPTER
35

Another day on Nil, another round of lugging an unconscious person back to the City.

Looking at the girl on the slapped-together-piece-of-island-crap stretcher, I hoped she fared better than Rory. But I had to admit, it didn't look good. We'd been walking for hours, and the girl hadn't opened her eyes or made a sound. At least she was breathing. Taking in her ashen face, I thought, *Whoever you are, please don't die.* I was sick of death and burials.

Charley walked beside me, her eyes straight ahead. She'd been quiet since Natalie missed the gate. Something had gotten to her; I just didn't know what. *Nat missing her shot? The girl on the stretcher, the newest Nil contestant? Or Li's death, haunting us all?*

Maybe all of the above, or maybe she just couldn't fit a word in around Natalie, who wouldn't shut up. About an hour ago, Natalie had dropped into rapid-fire Nat-speak, babbling about teams and timing, strategies and gate waves. As much as I liked Natalie, right now I wished she'd just stop. She was borderline Nil nutty.

"Nat," I breathed, "give it a rest, okay?"

"Please," Jason muttered.

"Okay. Sorry. I'm just really excited about Charley's charts and the idea of a gate wave. I've just never thought about the order and the spacing, or the timing between each gate or sets of gates. It's like they always come at noon, but I never really thought about the gap between gates that flash in the same place, like the ones at Black Bay, so—"

"Nat," I broke in, wondering how Nat talked like a machine gun and still managed to breathe, "please."

"Okay," she said, "but you gotta admit Charley's theory is awesome."

Nat fell silent, and no one filled the gap. Charley's eyes hugged the ground.

"Crowder," I said, "you okay?"

"Yeah," she answered.

No, you're not, I thought, reading her face. But now was not the time to press. Not with an audience, not with a girl clinging to life in our hands.

"Hang in there" was all I said. For a second, I wondered exactly who I was talking to. Charley, the girl, me. Or all of us. Then I focused on walking and not dropping the girl. My legs burned, my arms shook, but I refused to take a break.

Near the City, smoke drifted into the night like a beacon. I sent Jason ahead, and as we staggered into camp, Rives came running.

I filled him in on the girl.

"Where're you gonna put her?" Rives asked.

"With me," Nat said. "It'll be tight, but we'll fit. Or"—now she smiled at Charley—"you could always bunk somewhere else. There's someone I know who doesn't have a roommate anymore." Natalie winked at me, then turned back to Charley, beginning a new round of questions about the charts.

While Natalie monopolized Charley, I slipped into Nat's A-frame and gently laid the girl on a bed. Nat had one of the smallest houses; I had the other. The bigger A-frames could bunk up to six, but our max was two.

Back outside with Rives, I cut right to the chase.

"We found Li. She didn't make it."

"Damn." Rives blew out a hard breath. "You know, she was the first person I met on Nil. Where was she?"

"The black field, near the tubes. We took care of her. I gave her a coral cross."

Rives nodded, then glanced toward the Wall. "I'll carve for her. And I'll tell Quan."

"You sure?" I asked.

"Totally." He looked back, his face set. Dark planes in a black night, touched by Nil's demons. "You've been taking care of us for a long time, bro. Now take care of yourself. You hear?"

I nodded. "Where's Jason?"

"Crashed out. Said he took second watch last night. I bet he's already asleep."

"Good." I squeezed Rives's shoulder, then went to find Charley. The City was quiet, like it always was when a large group had left on Search. Charley sat by the fire, alone, watching the flames. She didn't look up until I stood right beside her.

"Where's Nat?" I asked, taking a seat.

"Getting supplies for the girl. And talking to Talla about my charts." Charley sounded less than enthusiastic.

"Hey." I took her hand in mine; her fingers were chunks of ice. "You've said three words all afternoon. What's wrong?"

"I think I made a mistake telling y'all about my theory. I shouldn't have said anything, not until I really know something. I mean, I've been here all of three weeks, and y'all looked at me today like I had the answers to the final exam, ya know?" Charley tried to smile, but it came out a wince. "But I don't. I only brought up my idea of how the gates might roll in sequence because Jason looked so darn upset when a gate didn't flash, and I wanted Natalie to have a ray of hope. But she ran with it like it was solid, like it was more than a theory."

I chuckled. "That's Nat. She tends to get a little excited."

"But that's just it. Now I feel like I've given her false hope. Like I've given *everyone* false hope. Thad, my maps are rough, and my wave idea is just a guess. What if Natalie misses a gate? Because of me?" She bit her lower lip.

"Look, no one's expecting you to swoop in and save the City. Your maps are great, and your theory is, too. And yeah, it's just an idea. But it's a starting point, and it gives us something to work with. To prove right or wrong, okay? You gotta understand. Your wave idea beats the shotgun approach any day, which is all we had. Your idea can't be any worse."

Then I winked. "But hey, if you want to sit here and beat yourself up, go right ahead."

Charley rolled her eyes, but stayed quiet. I realized she had a point.

"Tell you what. Over the next few days, we'll toss around your theory and gather gate information from everyone. Make it a City effort, not just a Charley effort. Would that take the pressure off?"

"Okay." She sighed. Reluctantly, she unrolled her main map and weighted the edges with pebbles from her satchel. The island's rough outline looked like a fat diamond. "Rives described the east coast, just to give me a starting point, but it's not to scale yet, not even close. And I know that the southeast portion has the active volcano, behind Mount Nil. Lava's not shooting up in the sky, but it's flowing, dropping into the water and cutting off the coastline. Rives told me it looks like thick tar with a layer of fire. Plus, there's steam and active vents. So the southeast corner is out of bounds."

I nodded, and she continued. "And from what I hear, the northern tip has cliffs and rock beaches. No sand. Tough for running. Past the north shore, due east, past the hills, the rain forest is here." Her finger dropped a little. "While it's great for gathering twine and other stuff, it would be tougher to see a gate because of the growth. Not to mention you'd have to be there on a day it was sunny *and* due a gate, so it lowers your odds even more. The sun is always shining when a gate flashes, right?"

"As far as I know," I said.

"So, from what I can tell, the best place to catch gates—and still eat—is this area." Charley swept a large arc around the City. "The west coast—White Beach above Nil City, south to Black Bay, South Beach below the Arches until the South Cliffs—and then inland: the lava fields, the meadow, the hills, and possibly the groves. It's basically what you've been doing. I guess all I'm saying is that heading to the northeast corner—the rain forest—is a three-day hike, and I'm not sure it's worth it. And Jason says that coastline is narrow. No running room."

"I hear you. But people have caught gates near the rain forest, so it's not hopeless."

"Not hopeless, just harder. Again, just guessing here." She shrugged.

For a minute we stared at her map.

"I wonder how long it takes for the gate wave to cross the entire island," I said. "From tip to tip."

"I've wondered the same thing. And does it cross the whole island every time or just sweep across part? The only given is that once gates flash, they roll on straight longitudinal lines, always north." She paused. "We know gates never flash in the same exact spot two days in a row, and I'm guessing they don't even flash on the same *latitude* two days in a row. Hence the wave. But how many days before a latitude is repeated? Could be three weeks, could be two, could be four. Or more. And what's the gap between different latitudes? Take the beach at Black Bay. Two gates, one day apart. Same beach, different latitude. Maybe even same longitudinal line, or does that change daily, too? And did I even see a gate at all?" She looked unsure. "And Rives said there hadn't been a gate at Black Bay in months, but I also know it doesn't mean one wasn't there. It just means no one saw it, at least no one we know. Then, after Jason missed, the gate wave jumped north, above the Arches, to the beach at Nil City, where Sabine caught it." She sighed. "I'm also not sure how far apart the individual gates of a noon set are. I think it varies, and I don't know why. Does it relate to the speed of the gates? Or something else?"

She chewed her bottom lip. "My gut says it takes around two weeks to cross the island before the wave starts over, but within that stretch there might be clumps and rogue sets, which could affect the overall timing. Ugh." She looked frustrated. "Don't you see? I don't know anything. I'm trying to make the pieces fit, but I don't even have all the pieces. And maybe they won't ever fit. My whole idea might be junk."

"Then we'll figure it out."

She looked at me.

"We'll walk Nil, mapping the island and charting gates. We'll time the gates, test your theory. It'll help everyone, including us." Leaning back, I pointed to the pebbles scattered around the map and smiled. "Nice rocks."

"Thanks. I found them in the Cavern, on the way to Black Bay." She pointed to one that looked like a dirty ice cube. "That one's my favorite. It reminds me of the island. It's murky, like something mysterious hides inside. But others are clear, like diamonds."

I chuckled, picking up her favorite and holding it up to the firelight, trying to see it through Charley's eyes. "They *are* diamonds, Charley. Raw, uncut diamonds. But unlike us, they're not going anywhere."

CHAPTER 36

CHARLEY
DAY 26, NIGHT

Thad was like an atomic heater. I wriggled closer, feeling warmer than I'd felt in weeks. I'd finally relaxed, now that he'd stopped talking about my gate wave theory and started playing with my hair.

We lay together, fully clothed, or at least as clothed as we ever were on Nil, which meant Thad's chest was bare, except for my arm resting across it. Lying in bed with a boy was a first for me. Feeling his body resting against mine, and mine against his, feeling safe and wanted. It was comforting and electrifying, both at once, or maybe that was because it was Thad. And it made me wonder about Thad's past, of which I knew nothing.

"Have you ever had a serious girlfriend?" I asked.

"One." He paused. "Mallory. It was over before I got here."

"What happened?"

"She wasn't who I thought she was."

When he didn't add anything to his very vague statement, I said, "What does that mean? She lied to you?"

"That too. She cheated on me with my best friend, then lied about it."

"Wow. That sucks. Sounds like you could use a new best friend."

Thad grinned, a lazy grin that made my breath catch. "Got it covered." He swept my hair off my shoulders, making my scalp tingle, then slowly traced my collarbone with his fingers. "What about you? Ever had a serious boyfriend?"

I faked a serious look. "Just one."

"Oh?" Thad's fingers stopped for one noticeable second.

"Yup. But it didn't last."

"What happened? Did you break his heart?"

"Doubtful. We were in the sixth grade. Jack Rodgers passed me a note asking me to go with him. There were two boxes. I checked no."

Thad chuckled. "You crushed that boy for life!"

"Nah." I smiled. "I just wasn't ready to get serious."

"And now?" he whispered, his sapphire eyes intense.

"If Jack Rodgers passed me the note now, I'd still check no." Thad groaned as I laughed. "But if you passed me the note, well, that's a different story."

He kissed me, first sweet and warm, then urgently. Then he pulled away, abruptly.

"What's wrong?" I asked.

"Nothing." Thad's breathing was ragged. "Absolutely nothing."

Reaching up, I touched the scar over his left eyebrow, the one that looked like a tiny mountain. He closed his eyes, and in that minute, he looked seventeen and relaxed. A rare sight.

"How'd you get this? Snowboarding?"

"Nope." He didn't move, letting me trace his scar. "Skateboarding. Flipped off a rail."

"Do you ever get scared when you snowboard?" I pictured the Winter X games in my head. "Afraid you might crash?" My finger left his scar and traced his eyebrow, then his cheek.

"Never." His eyes stayed closed.

"Not afraid of anything, are you, fearless Leader?" I teased.

Thad's eyes flew open. He stared at me, and the carefree seventeen-year-old was gone. "Losing you," he said, his voice rough. "Before we've ever had a chance. That's my greatest fear."

"Then you have nothing to be afraid of," I said. "You'll make it. So will I. We've got plenty of time."

Then I kissed him, as urgently as he'd kissed me, and in that moment, I tasted fear. *Thad's* fear. It was powerful and real, and for the first time, doubt crept in.

Plenty of time, I'd said. *But is it enough?*

CHAPTER
37

THAD
DAY 293, DAWN

Sunlight creeping in, Charley in my arms. It was the best morning on Nil yet. For the first time in weeks, I'd actually slept. No dreams, no nightmares. Just sleep.

Watching Charley sleep, I thought again of my greatest fear, the one I'd admitted last night. I thought I'd loved Mallory, but I was wrong.

The idea of losing Charley was unbearable.

You'll make it, Charley had said fiercely last night. *And so will I. We've got plenty of time.*

I hoped Charley was right.

And that Ramia was wrong. That thought shot from nowhere, making me jerk, and the movement woke Charley up.

"Morning." I kissed her forehead. "How'd you sleep?"

"Great." She smiled, turning away to yawn. "Best night ever."

"Did you miss your socks?"

"Socks?" Charley looked confused.

"You said you miss socks. That your feet freeze at night. So I'm wondering if you missed socks."

Charley laid her hand on my chest, over my heart. "I didn't miss anything," she said softly. "Not one thing."

"Good to hear," I said, kissing her forehead and alternately wanting Charley closer and desperately needing space before I lost control. "We'd better get some food before we miss out."

Natalie sat with Talla by the fire, a bowl of cut pineapple between them. It looked untouched.

"Morning, ladies. Dibs on the pineapple?" I asked.

"All yours," Talla said. "The pit's full of fish wraps. Good ones, too. Seasoned with lime and sea salt. You can thank Rives and Jason for that."

Nodding, I grabbed two wraps and gave one to Charley.

"There's fresh coconut milk, too," Talla offered.

Charley made a face as she sat. "Thanks. I'm good with water."

"How's coma-girl gate-crasher?" I asked.

"Six feet under," Talla said.

"What?" Charley said as my stomach dropped. "She *died*?"

"We buried her last night," Natalie said in a small voice. "Me, Rives, and Talla." She looked at me, guilt coating her face. "And it's all my fault!"

"Huh?" I frowned. "How do you figure that?"

"I let you put her in my bed!" Natalie cried. "I didn't stay with you, and when I went inside the hut to check on her, she was dead."

"What does your bed have to do with it?" I asked, not following.

"Ramia." Natalie's voice was anguished. "She warned me, but I forgot! I was so obsessed with Charley's charts, I totally blanked. And now the girl's dead. Ramia warned me, Thad. And I blew it."

"No." I said sharply. "I don't know what she told you, but it means nothing. Ramia was a fruit loop, Nat. You know that."

"Was she?" Natalie asked, suddenly quiet, her eyes intense. "She sat with me, Thad. By the fire, the night before she left. I wished her good luck on Search, gave her a hug, and when I pulled away, she stared at me, like she was looking *through* me. 'Keep your luck,' she said. 'You need it. You will lose the one you love, and when you try to save another, she will die. Dead in your bed." Natalie shivered, twisting her hands. " 'Dead in your bed,' she told me. Rubbing that stupid bone bracelet! And now the girl is dead! And she died *in my bed*!" Natalie's rising voice now bordered on hysterical, and her hands shook.

Ramia's singsong voice echoed in my head. *Dead in your bed. Open your eyes, Thad. The blind leading the blind. Will you open your eyes?*

"Nat—" I faltered, not sure what to say.

Charley gave me a long look, then reached over and clasped Natalie's hands, holding them steady. "Natalie, I never knew Ramia, but she sounds like a complete whack-a-doo. My nana likes to say that you'll find what you're looking for, and no offense, but right now you're looking for the weird. You're looking for something to fit her crazy predictions, and if you look hard enough, I guarantee you'll find it. But it doesn't make it true. And it doesn't make you responsible for that girl's death." Charley paused. "Besides, it wasn't your bed."

Natalie head jerked up.

"It's just borrowed," Charley continued. "Temporary, like everything else on Nil. Like your separation from Kevin. You're just another Nil visitor, living a temporary time-out from home. Nothing here is yours. Not your A-frame, not your bed. So if I were you," Charley said softly, "I'd let it go. But that's just me."

Natalie launched herself into Charley's arms. "Have I told you lately how glad I am that you were the one who found Kevin's clothes?"

Me too, I thought, choking up, watching Charley comfort Natalie.

And that somehow I found Charley. And that she found me, even the part that had been lost.

In my peripheral vision, a black furball crept into sight. When I saw the paws, I grinned. Burton.

He slunk close enough to shoot me his evil cat eye. "Good to see you too, buddy," I said, tossing him my last hunk of fish. "I figured you'd turned into a Scooby Snack by now." Burton hissed, but barely. He snatched up my offering, without hesitation.

"Do you always feed stray cats?" Charley asked. Wiping her eyes, Natalie looked at me curiously.

"Just Burton."

"Burton?" Charley said.

"Yeah. He hung around long enough that I finally gave him a name. It made him seem less puny." I watched Burton inhale the fish, then lick his white paws clean. "I doubt he's got many of his nine lives left. He's a serious pain in the butt."

"Uh-huh," Charley said, in that same tone of voice she uses when she sees through my crap but doesn't call me out on it. "Sounds like he's a survivor." She tossed him a piece of fish.

Burton hissed so loud that Charley jumped back.

"I think he likes you," I said, grinning at Charley. "But we won't know for sure until he brings you something dead."

CHAPTER 38

CHARLEY
DAY 27, MORNING

"Did you let me win?" I gasped. Hands on my hips, I glared at Thad. "Because it felt like you slowed. On purpose."

"Nope." Thad looked shocked. "You just had more gas in the tank than I did."

I studied his expression. "Really," I said. "I beat you. Running."

"Seriously." He nodded. "I think I should've eaten two wraps this morning. Or maybe not tossed so much to Burton." He smiled, but it was weary—like him.

Because now that I looked, Thad was the poster boy for exhausted. Half moons hung under his eyes, and even his sapphire blues looked dull. *No wonder*, I thought. He'd carried a girl miles back to the City yesterday, along with his pack. We'd all helped, or tried to, but there was no question that Thad did the heavy lifting. Typical Thad, helping everyone but himself, even grumpy cats. With a sinking feeling, I realized he'd looked this tired ever since Rory's death.

"Well, then," I said, taking his hand. "Let's get you something to eat."

Johan's team was back, with a new addition. A boy. Tall, thin, and heavily inked, he had quarter-sized holes in his earlobes that I assumed used to hold piercings. His overall look screamed lead singer of a rock band; all he needed was black eyeliner and skinny jeans, but instead he sported a loincloth. He sat by the firepit in an awkward crumple, his pale skin glaringly white where his tattoos weren't. His ashen face registered one emotion: shock.

Heesham intercepted us halfway to the fire. "S'up, guys. Charley, is it okay if I steal your boy for a minute?"

As Heesham smiled, for a heavy second, I thought of Sabine. I knew he missed her. Hopefully he'd find her soon—on the other side of a gate. If they found each other here, surely they could find each other back home.

I realized the boys were staring at me, waiting.

"Y'all go ahead." I smiled at Heesham. "But a little fyi. Thad here's pretty hungry. He let me beat him in sprints, so I know he needs to eat."

Thad protested as Heesham laughed. "I'll take care of him," Heesham promised. Still grinning, he steered Thad away, talking low.

By the fire, the pale boy still sat alone, looking as pitiful as ever. Remembering my freaky first days, I went over to our newest lost soul.

"Hey," I said, trying not to stare at the ginormous holes in his earlobes. I could see straight through them. "My name's Charley."

He lifted his eyes to me, bewildered. "I'm Dex."

"You hanging in there?" I asked, sitting beside him. Dex didn't respond. Judging by his expression, I'd guess he wasn't quite sure himself.

"Where were you when the gate hit?" I asked.

"Walking out of a mate's house in Manchester. I'd left some goodies in the car, needed a bit more. Then the air fried me up like a crispy chip." He looked at me, surprised, like he was seeing me for the first time. "Is this a trip? Or am I totally mental?"

"It's definitely a trip." I smiled, going for reassuring. "But you're not imagining it, if that's what you're asking. It's real. Well, as real as a freaky island in some parallel dimension can be."

Dex stared at me like I was nuts. And to tell you the truth, it did sound a little crazy.

"Look," I said, adopting Natalie's soft-but-steady tone, "I don't know what this place is. No one here does, at least no one here now. And it doesn't matter."

"It doesn't matter?" he repeated blankly.

"No. It doesn't matter what Nil is, and there isn't time to figure it out. All that matters is survival and escape." *And the number of days you have left*, I thought. Observing Dex's empty stare, I wondered if he had any clue how long he'd been on the island. "Dex, when the team found you, did they ask you how many days you've been here?"

"Yeah. I think a week." Dex sounded unsure. "I'm not certain what day it was when I left. We'd been cooked for days." He sighed. "What a bloody mess."

"Well, I'd err on the side of caution. Go with ten days, just to be safe."

He nodded. "Brilliant." Then he sort of laughed, sort of choked. "The big bloke spelled it out. I've got a year to ring up a gate or stay tripping here for good."

"Um, you don't exactly 'ring' them up," I said. "The gates, I mean. They appear at noon like clockwork, somewhere on the island. We haven't figured out a pattern, not yet, anyway. But we're trying. And we do know when you see one, you run like crazy, because if you catch it, you're outta here."

"Fantastic," Dex said miserably. "I'm screwed. I don't even know what a bloody gate looks like. I never saw it, just felt it. I thought I'd taken a bad hit, like I was burning up from the inside, but it was the gate thing, not the smack, right?"

"Right."

"So what does it look like?" Desperation gave his eyes life. "The gate? To get back?"

I looked at Dex, recalling my first day in the City. I remembered the shock of arrival, the unending blur of new faces, and the sense of joining the merge one day too late. I remembered the horrific moment I'd learned my days were numbered. Counting the days was my new normal.

Suddenly I felt like an old-timer, which was crazy.

Dex was staring at me, with an odd mix of hope and denial.

"Look," I said, speaking as gently as Em, "I know you're freaking out. Everyone does at first. And to answer your question, look for shimmering air rising from the ground. But don't worry. If you stick around, you'll figure it out. And you'll have backup to help you."

"Backup," Dex repeated in a hopeless monotone. "Shimmering air. Running. Death." Dex closed his eyes. "Got it."

"Hey, look on the bright side. At least you're not naked anymore, right?" I said, smiling. Dex jerked his head up so fast I thought he'd given himself whiplash.

Before Dex could speak, Thad reached out his hand.

"Hey, man. I'm Thad."

Dex stared at Thad's hand, then grasped it. "Dex."

"Welcome to Nil City," Thad said.

Dex looked absolutely miserable. "Thanks."

Thad chuckled. "Hang in there, dude. Get a bite to eat, you'll feel better. Do you like fish?"

Dex nodded like a robot.

"Good. Here's a wrap. You can eat the leaves on the outside, too." Dex took Thad's offering as Thad turned to me. I noticed he carried two wraps, along with a mango. "Ready?" he asked.

I nodded. As we walked away, Thad grinned. "Were you trying to put that poor guy into permanent shock? When you smiled at him, I thought he might have a heart attack right then."

"Funny," I said, punching Thad in the shoulder.

"Ow." Rubbing his arm, Thad laughed.

"I just feel bad for him," I admitted. "He's pretty freaked out."

"Most rookies are," Thad said. He turned to me. "Except you."

I shook my head. "You didn't see me on night five."

"Doesn't matter," Thad said. "I saw your shelter by the Bay. You weren't freaking; you were surviving. Now eat." He handed me a wrap, just as we left the trees behind.

The beach hummed with activity, preparations for tonight's Nil Night. One person stuck out, only because he should be missing.

"Miguel's back?" I turned to Thad. "I thought he was on Search."

"He was. Jillian hurt her ankle, so they bailed early. She's okay. Just a sprain. And Miguel's got time."

I wasn't sure if Thad's last line was for my benefit or his.

"What are they cooking?" I asked, sniffing the air. "It smells weird."

"Rabbits and an ostrich. Heesham killed a big one on the way back."

"Ostrich?" I made a face. "People eat those?"

Thad laughed. "Jason says they taste like beef. And after two hundred ninety-two days of fish, trust me, ostrich sounds pretty appealing."

Two hundred ninety-two days.

Seventy-three noons left.

Is this how it starts? I wondered. How the daywatch creeps into the days? One unexpected moment at a time?

"What is it?" Thad asked.

"Nothing," I lied.

Thad whispered in my ear. "Plenty of time, remember?" He

brushed a kiss against my temple, then grinned, his lazy grin that stole my breath.

Rives appeared by Thad's side.

"Thad." Rives kept his voice low, but I easily overheard. "The Shack was hit again last night while we were taking care of that girl. And this time, no chance it's an animal." Rives paused. "The metal knives are gone. All of them."

CHAPTER 39

CHARLEY
DAY 27, TWILIGHT

Thad was a man possessed.

Rives's news had made him furious. Maybe because there might be a traitor in the City's midst, maybe because the thefts happened despite all the efforts he'd made to prevent them, but either way, Thad had been on a tear ever since he'd spoken with Rives. He and Rives searched the area around the Shack, making it known exactly what they were hunting for. While they stomped around the woods, I spotted Jason slipping into Bart's hut, no doubt on a covert knife-recovery mission. But Jason came up empty, like Thad and Rives. The knives were gone.

Like today's noon.

It passed quietly, without a gate. The lack of a gate meant nothing, at least as far as my theory and charts went. All it meant for sure was that no one around the City caught one.

After noon, a group of us went surfing. I managed to actually stand up for more than two seconds without falling off. Talla and Rives cheered; so did Jason and Natalie. Thad just smiled, like he'd known I could do it. But my favorite part was simply floating on the open water. It was a nice contrast to the stress of noon.

And now it was night.

A Nil Night, to be precise. My second, only this one was very different from the first. Now Dex was the newcomer, not me, and veteran Li was dead, buried in black rock. And rather than Thad, tonight my escort was Natalie, or maybe I was hers, because ever since the mystery girl's burial, Talla and I had made sure Natalie was never alone. Natalie had agreed to bunk with Talla, which was a huge relief since she hadn't stepped foot inside her A-frame since Rives had carried out the dead girl, and I knew Natalie wouldn't catch a wink of sleep there if she tried. Good sleep meant a good Search, or so I'd heard. Maybe it was some wacky island version of an old wives' tale, but if it could help Natalie, I was all for it. And after last night's midnight burial, Natalie definitely needed some good sleep.

So Talla and I had struck a deal. I'd promised Talla I'd look out for Nat on Search if Talla looked out for Nat tonight. *She'll have her own personal watch*, Talla promised. *I'll pull an all-nighter if it makes her feel safe.* As usual, Talla's response was extreme, but it made me feel better. Looking over at Natalie, the sweet girl who'd watched over me on my first night in the City, and whose time was running out, I sure hoped I kept my end of the bargain.

As we broke through the trees, twilight was falling. The sun hung low, brilliant and orange; torches in the sand flickered with firelight, less brilliant than the setting sun but powerful enough to cast shadows on the sand. The beach scene looked exactly how I remembered it from my first Nil Night, and the strange déjà-vu took me back. Recalling Rory hanging in the shadows, observant and wary, I glanced toward the trees, half expecting to see his ghost. Instead I spotted Rives making out with a girl I didn't know. Her blond hair trailed down her back, and with a start, I realized it was Talla. *Dang,* I thought with surprise. I hadn't seen that twosome coming. Then again, maybe it was just a casual hookup.

Near the food table, Thad was talking intensely to Miguel. Behind them, an island band of homemade strings, reed pipes, and gourd shakers cranked up, and they didn't sound half bad. The two large drums sat silent. It took me a minute, then I remembered the missing drummer was Samuel. Samuel, who'd caught a gate, giving us something to celebrate. Only there were fewer flower leis worn tonight, because Li was gone.

By the fire, Jillian sat stiffly, her ankle wrapped in white cloth. Dex sat beside her, his skin as pale as Jillian's ankle, except for his tattoos. He reminded me of a lost puppy. Granted, one that was over six feet tall and skinny, but despite the pierced zombie look, he seemed oddly vulnerable.

When she saw us, Jillian waved.

"Hey, Jillian." I gave her a hug. "Sorry about your ankle."

"Me too. I'm just glad I didn't break it." She shuddered, and our eyes caught. *Because then you can't run*, I thought.

"Hey, Dex," I said. "How's it going?"

"Fine, I guess." His disinterest didn't feel rude; it was like talking to a shock victim. Only now he stared at the drums, rather than the fire.

"Do you play?" I asked, pointing to the drums.

"Yeah. Me and my mates have a band. The Dead Reapers."

The name sounded a little redundant, but I wasn't about to debate his band's name. "Well, if you want to play, go ahead. It's a free for all around here."

Confusion flickered across Dex's face. "Really? I thought there were rules. The big bloke mentioned a contract?"

"Covenant." Natalie spoke up. "It just means that if you stay in the City, you agree to support the Search teams and pitch in. You can hunt gates by yourself, but it's easier with a team as support."

"Totally," Jillian said. "What if I'd fallen when I was out by

243

myself? Sy practically carried me the whole way back. It can get crazy here."

Dex studied the fire. "Yeah. About that. Uh, I'm not quite sure, because I was still bent, but . . . the day I landed, I saw a big cat, with spots. Like a leopard." He seemed bewildered. "I don't know if it was real, but if it was, how bloody scary is that? I mean, there're bloody leopards out there?" He pointed toward the island's interior.

"No idea," I said, "and even if there was, there's no guarantee it's still here. Animals come and go just like people. But to make you feel better, there're no snakes."

Dex looked stunned, like he'd never thought about reptiles.

Thad whistled, drawing everyone's attention. He raised his cup. "First, to Li. In her honor, let's have a moment of silence."

Heads bowed, and for a long minute, only the ocean made a sound.

"Now, to Samuel." Hoots and hollers split the air. "You made it, man. Cheers." Thad raised his cup. Everyone did the same, except Dex.

"And we've got a rookie." Thad turned toward us. "Dex, welcome to Nil. We're glad you're here, even though we're sorry you're here." Dex managed a wobbly wave, his empty hands shaking.

"To business," Thad said. "First up, Search. Three teams leave at dawn. Elia's heading out with Johan as Spotter, Raj as support. Miguel's heading out with Bart as Spotter, Talla and Heesham as support. And Nat's heading out with Jason as Spotter, Charley and me as support."

Looking supremely confident, Bart high-fived Sy.

Thad's face darkened, a change evident despite the black Nil night. "Second. The Shack was hit last night, and the metal knives are gone. All of them." His eyes roamed the group. "Animals don't steal weapons; people do. If it's one of us, stop. Put the knives back;

that's all that matters. And if it's not one of us, then whoever takes watch at the Shack, stay awake." He glanced at Bart, who didn't flinch. "We can't afford to lose any more supplies."

Thad took a deep breath. "Last thing. I'm stepping down as Leader. I nominate Rives to Lead. He's been a great Second. Any other nominations?"

Bart's hand shot up. "Sy."

Thad nodded. "Anyone else?"

The fire popped in the silence.

"Okay," Thad said, "All in favor of Rives as Leader, raise your hand."

Over a dozen hands filled the air.

"Hands down." Thad said. "All in favor of Sy, raise your hand."

Bart's hand flew up. Sy's weakly followed. No other hands moved.

"Hands down. That's it." Thad tipped his cup to Rives. "It's all yours, bro. Who do you pick as your Seconds?"

Rives stood. "Heesham and Talla. And Sy." Sy looked shocked; Bart looked confused.

Thad nodded. "Okay, that's it. Take care of each other. Focus on the good, live in the moment. To now." As Thad raised his cup, so did the crowd, and the echo of "to now" was deafening.

As the City cheered, I realized Thad hadn't mentioned the nameless girl, the one Rives and Natalie buried in the night. The omission made her even more lost. No recognition here, and no going home. Despite the fire, I shivered.

"Speaking of now, Macy's cooked up a little something, just for tonight." Thad nodded to her. "When you're ready."

"Thanks!" Macy beamed. "Okay, people, I'm gonna try something here. If I were you, I'd back up." As everyone stepped back, I felt Thad's arms slide around my waist.

Macy nodded to Heesham, who threw her a stick about three

feet long. Each end was wrapped in something thick, like twine or vine. She dipped each end in the fire and then twirled the stick like a baton. Flames swirled in the darkness, forming a circle of light. Macy tossed the stick in the air, caught it, and twirled it until the flames crawled toward her hands. When the flames kissed her fingers, Macy tossed the stick into the fire. As everyone hooted and clapped, she bowed, laughing.

Later, as Thad and I left the beach, Macy's act played in my head: a ring of fire swirling against the charcoal night. The flaming circle reminded me of a gate, a moving target full of heat, one that everyone was dying to catch.

Like Thad, who had seventy-two days—to catch a gate, to save himself.

And like Natalie, who had even less.

If I was going to help them, time was running out. My charts were full of gaps and guesses, and I couldn't shake the feeling that I was missing something. That we were *all* missing something.

And I'd no clue how to find it, or if I even could.

CHAPTER 40

THAD
DAY 294, DAWN

The City was hopping.

People running, people packing. People praying. Johan led a group in worship, making me wonder if it was Sunday. But the day of the week didn't matter; the day count did. And prayers were good anytime.

Spying Heesham packing food, I strode over. "Sham, got a minute?"

He nodded. "What's up?"

"Last night Dex told Charley he saw some kind of big cat, with spots. He was jacked when he landed, so the details are foggy, eh? He's not sure it was real." I paused. "But this is Nil, so I wanted to give you a heads-up before you went out."

"Appreciate that, bro. You tell Johan?"

I nodded. "Stay safe."

"Got my protection right here." He patted his thick wooden knife. Miguel had carved it for Heesham, and like the boy who held it, the knife was a beast. "You stay safe, too."

"Absolutely."

Heesham strode to Miguel and clapped him on the back. Bart

stood by Miguel, shifting his feet anxiously. *No surprise there*, I thought. Bart hadn't been on Search in weeks, and now that someone had finally picked him, he was a nervous wreck. At least Miguel had Heesham and Talla as support. Heesham and Talla would pick up any Bart-slack. And the truth was, as much as he annoyed me, Bart had stellar vision. He could spot a gate meters out, which was the point. *Pull your weight,* I thought, catching Bart's eye and nodding. *For Miguel.*

Talla was deep in conversation with Charley, then the two girls shook hands like conspirators. As Charley hugged Heesham, Talla gave me a fierce nod. Then, looking *past* me, her face softened. Two seconds later, Rives picked Talla up, swung her around, and kissed her, hard. Then Rives just held her. To my surprise, Talla actually let him.

Good for you, man. I couldn't see Talla's face, but my gut told me it mirrored Rives's, which was full of quiet emotion.

Heesham whistled. He waved one finger in a quick circle and tipped his head toward Miguel. Talla let Rives go; Bart trailed Heesham like a puppy. Elia's team gelled in thirty seconds flat.

All three teams rolled out, each heading in a different direction. As we parted ways, I had the eerie sense that no team would come back intact. Hopefully that would be a good thing. The teams were balanced, which was good. And all three Spotters were sharp, which was even better.

But like I'd told Heesham, this was Nil, and you just never know.

CHAPTER 41

"This is where I woke up on my first day," I told Thad.

We were standing on one of the tallest peaks, gazing at the sea of red. It struck me that the rocks were the exact color of Georgia clay back home. There was my mushroom rock, looking smaller than I remembered. There were the rocks as big as buses, and there was my blood, camouflaged on the red, but I knew it was there and remembered the pain. There was my hidey-hole, where I'd cowered in fear, and there was the path I'd taken when I'd chosen to run. To chase the last shimmer, only to fall short.

I'd never been so happy to fail.

"What're you thinking so hard about?" Thad asked.

"That I'm lucky I didn't catch that shimmer my first day here. Because if I'd caught it, I never would have met you."

"Meant to be." He smiled, tucking a strand of my hair behind my ear. "So which way?"

"East." I pointed.

Thad nodded. Cupping his hands, he shouted, "East!" Then he pointed. Natalie and Jason were just below us, and when they heard

Thad's shout, they gave a thumbs-up. We trekked down the rise and moved out as a team.

"So this is where you found Kev's clothes," Natalie commented.

"Yup." I smiled. "Waking up here was totally freaky."

"Wasn't it?" she agreed, nodding.

Something awful occurred to me, and I couldn't believe I hadn't thought of it before. "So we'll wake up naked on the other side? Back in the world, who knows where?"

"Probably," Natalie said. "It's not like these clothes go with you, right?"

"Fantastic," I mumbled. "Good times."

Beside me, Thad laughed.

Jason was quiet. It was too close to zero hour for him to chat. The sun was high, and my gut tingled with an awareness of noon.

I'd had six days to refine this tingle. When we'd left the City, we'd headed southeast, hoping to intercept gates. We were operating under the assumption that gates flashed on latitudinal lines, then ran north, longitudinally. Yesterday we'd finally spotted one in the southern black lava field: a single, too far away to catch. It was the first gate we'd seen.

So after noon yesterday we'd changed tactics, and directions. Now we were chasing gates. We'd gone north, hoping to hit the next latitude, and in the end, we'd settled here. The red lava field, an open hot spot, where it would be easy to spot a gate if one decided to show.

I wanted a gate for Natalie so badly it hurt.

"Your sandals tight?" I asked Natalie.

"Strapped and ready." She grinned.

"Be careful." I felt like I was talking to Em. My words tumbled out—anything to give her an advantage. "This rock is a pain to run on. It shifts under you, especially the little pieces. Watch for cracks. Look for flat spots, okay?"

She hugged me tight, saying nothing.

I hugged her back. She had to catch a gate today, because today was the last day of this Search. Our supplies were dangerously low. So after noon today, regardless of what happened, we would head back to the City. But being in this field today—where it had ended for Kevin—felt right.

Jason stopped. The field was eerily silent, just like I remembered. No air moved.

"There!" Jason shouted, pointing. "Sixty yards, rolling left! GO!"

Natalie was already running. The wall of writhing air shimmered in the Nil sun, drifting left.

"Go, Natalie!" I urged. But I didn't yell. Jason was her guide, not me.

Ten yards left.

Natalie sprinted, hurdling cracks as she ran toward the gate. Then she slipped. Her foot slid, she tumbled forward, and then hit the ground hard, landing between a pair of jagged rocks.

"I'm stuck!" she cried, yanking on her foot.

By the time we reached Natalie, she'd worked her foot loose. Scratched and bloody, her foot looked better than her sandal. It lay in pieces, torn in half. Yards away, the outbound collapsed and winked out.

Her gate was gone.

"Well, this sucks," she said. "My sandal's trashed." Tears filled her eyes.

"Take mine." I rushed to get mine off, then I thrust it in her hand. "It's big, but it's better than nothing."

She looked at me, numb.

Her hair lay flat; there was no wind to push it around.

"Hurry!" I shouted, bending to help. The rush of urgency made me shake. "That gate was too slow to be a single! *C'mon!*"

As Natalie scrambled to strap on the sandal, Jason yelled, "Gate at nine o'clock, rolling left. Forty yards!"

Natalie jumped to her feet, then broke into the same awkward sprint I'd done naked. The moment was slow and fast; the past mixed with the present. She flew erratically over the rocks, shooting for flat spots as she gained on the shimmer.

And then Natalie was there.

Two feet in front of the shimmer, close enough for the gate to illuminate her face. She smiled, glittering tears running down her face. She waved, then stepped back into the gate, and the iridescent wall of air washed over her as quickly as the gate had washed over Sabine. Natalie flickered and faded. Then the gate collapsed.

Natalie was gone.

All that remained was a pile of clothes and two sandals. One sandal was hers, and one was mine, like two halves of a surreal island BFF charm. She was the best friend I'd had on the island, and I'd miss her. But I still had Thad.

Thad.

His hair rustled against his shoulders; the wind was back. Not whipping but gentle, barely noticeable unless you were looking for it, which I desperately was. Because I'd just realized that if another gate flashed right now, it would be Thad's, and as much as I wanted him to catch a gate, to lose both Thad and Natalie in one day would be both awesome and terrible. I'd never considered we might have minutes instead of months, and the reality that I might lose him right now was shocking.

The wind stayed steady.

I couldn't breathe.

Jason's voice broke the awful moment. "That's it. It was so slow, I thought it was a triple, but no dice."

I shook. With relief, with guilt, with happiness, with sadness, with too many emotions at once. I stood there, eyes closed, fists clenched, hating that I wasn't prepared for this moment. I couldn't stop shaking.

"You did good, man," I heard Thad tell Jason.

Then Thad's arms wrapped around me. "Hey," he whispered in my ear. "It's okay. Natalie made it because of you."

"No," I said. "It wasn't because of me. It was luck. But"—I bit my lip, furious with myself for not being ready to say good-bye to Thad—"never mind." Taking a deep breath, I hugged him fiercely, then pulled away.

Thad looked at me, frowning. "You're wrong," he said. "Your charts are good. Your theory works."

I was too shaken to argue.

Thad reached for my hand. "Let's get Nat's stuff and go."

"I'll get it," I said. Without waiting, I followed in Natalie's invisible footprints, leading to her clothes. As I lifted my sandal, an object fell and struck the rock with a brittle *crack*. It was Natalie's white shell bracelet, the one she wore 24/7.

I picked up the bracelet, picturing Natalie twisting it as she asked, *You didn't find anything else with the clothes, did you?*

Now I understood exactly what she'd hoped I'd found. When I'd snatched up Kevin's shorts, something white had gone flying. Something as white and fragile as the bracelet in my hand.

"Kevin made that for her," Thad said. He'd come up beside me.

"And he had one, too," I said, knowing it was true. "Like you made our necklaces." I swallowed, knowing one day I would pick Thad's necklace off the ground, keeping him close until I could meet him on the other side.

And it could have been today.

Willing my hands not to shake, I slipped Natalie's bracelet into my satchel. Then I gathered her clothes, packed them next to my maps, and turned to Thad, knowing there was something I had to do. One last thing to keep my promise to Talla, because it's what Natalie would have wanted.

"I'm ready," I said. "Can I pick the route?"

"Lead on." Thad gestured for me to go first.

Turning around, I retraced the route I'd first walked thirty-three days ago.

Thirty-three days.

Thirty-three days was nothing, and yet it felt like a lifetime. Thad had sixty-six days, and it seemed like nothing. We'd be lucky to have sixty-six days.

For all I knew, all we had left together was twenty-four hours.

CHAPTER 42

THAD
DAY 299, AFTER NOON

Seeing Nat catch that gate had weirded Charley out. I knew her well enough now to distinguish an easy Charley silence from an anguished one, and this silence was anguished. I figured she'd stew until we were alone, then spill.

Charley led us through the red rocks. Hiking through the rubble was no picnic, and I couldn't wait to hit the black.

Just shy of a massive crack, she stopped. "This is where I found Kevin's clothes."

She pulled out Natalie's shell bracelet and held it tight. Then she dropped it into the deep crevice. The bracelet flashed white, then disappeared. "When I picked up Kevin's clothes, his bracelet fell into that crack. It just seemed like the two bracelets should be together, you know?" She shrugged. "And now they are."

The simple goodness of her gesture surprised me, and the rightness of it, too. I realized Charley understood Nil more than I realized, even the dark part.

Especially the dark part.

I slid my hand into hers. "Let's go."

When she didn't move, I asked, "Charley?"

"Thad"—she spoke slowly, like she was thinking out loud—"you said the sister drawing of the Man in the Maze was near the rain forest. Was it carved in black rock?"

"Yeah."

"And you landed by the base of that mountain?" She pointed to Mount Nil.

"Yeah." I wondered where Charley was going with these questions.

"Did you see any carvings there?"

"No."

She looked thoughtful. "But you weren't looking for one either, right?"

"Right."

"I want to head that way. Track the black lava field to the mountain and fill out my maps, checking out any large rock formations for carvings along the way. If we ration it, we have food for one more day, and plenty of water. What do y'all say?" Her face dared me to refuse. For his part, Jason looked curious. I think he was just happy to be included.

"Okay," I agreed. "There's a cave about ten meters above the mountain base, overlooking the meadow. It's small but safe. We can crash there tonight. But unless we find food, we have to head back first thing tomorrow." Watching Charley nod, my gut told me this impromptu trek was about more than just mapping and carvings. Something was eating at her. And maybe more than one thing.

We veered southeast until we intercepted the southern black flow, then turned inland, toward the mountain. The farther east we went, the greater the wildlife. Clumps of trees cropped up. One copse sheltered a nervous giraffe. A pair of wild dogs spooked a rabbit, which was disappointing since I would've liked to have caught it for dinner. On the upside, the dogs left us alone.

Every rock formation we passed was just rock. No carvings, no clues. If Charley was disappointed to find nothing but rock, she hid it well. But the black rock tour slowed us down, and as daylight faded, we were well short of the cave.

"Time to stop," I said reluctantly. "We need firewood and a secure spot, because we won't make the cave before dark."

As Jason frowned, I eyed the last clump of black rock. Dropped by the volcano in a rough semicircle, the chest-high rock offered marginal protection from wind and wildlife. Not ideal, but better than nothing.

"There," I said, pointing.

The mountain loomed over us as we camped for the night. We collected wood, made a fire, and shared a beggar's dinner of dried fruit and nuts. Then we hunkered down as the stars popped out. Jason took first watch.

Charley and I sat by the fire, close to Jason but out of earshot.

"You've been quiet all day," I said. "I know you'll miss Natalie, but she made it, eh?"

"It's not that." Eyes on the fire, Charley toyed with her shell necklace. Keeping quiet, I didn't press, and after a long moment, Charley continued. "For a second, I thought it was a triple," she whispered in a constricted voice. "That a third gate would flash, after Natalie's. And it would be yours. I'd never considered I might have to say good-bye to you right then. In minutes, not months." She looked at me, her expression fierce. "I wasn't ready, not yet. But I promise, the next time noon rolls around, I will be."

In minutes, not months.

I stared at Charley as her words sank in. Months weren't long enough. Minutes were a joke.

"Oh, my gracious," she said, watching me with wide eyes, "you didn't think of it either! You didn't consider that if Nil sent a triple, the third gate was yours, Mr. Leader with Priority?"

"Not really." *Not at all.* And I couldn't believe I'd missed it.

She nodded, looking at our hands entwined together. "I just—I want to have a proper good-bye. I want—" Charley broke off, shaking her head slightly.

"No regrets," I whispered, filling in her blank. "Nothing left unsaid."

"Exactly." She lifted her face to mine. "No regrets."

Her hand in mine, we sat tight together, cloaked in darkness, just us against the clock. And in that quiet moment, I knew exactly where I was headed, I just had to work through the best route to get there.

"My dad and I had a fight," I said quietly. "My last morning in Whistler. A blowout after breakfast, right after I told him I was dropping out of school."

I closed my eyes, remembering. My dad had grabbed my helmet, holding it hostage as he forced me to listen. *Drop out?* he'd roared. *For this?* He'd shaken my helmet in my face. *You want to throw away your future FOR THIS?*

I'd snatched my helmet and held it high. *This IS my future. Not a windowless cubby, crunching numbers, eating what-ifs for lunch.* Then I'd turned my back on my dad, grabbed my board, and stormed out, too furious to make my case. Instead of telling my dad that my future was boarding, built on a present packed with daily coaching and private tutoring, I'd left him with hateful words and a cheap shot to boot. I knew I needed to apologize, but I was too pissed off to go back. I figured I'd set things right later, giving myself time to cool off, giving him time to come around.

Later never came. Regret was an ugly bastard, one I'd lived with every day since.

"And?" Charley prompted gently.

"I screwed up. The thing is, my dad quit the pro skiing circuit for school when my mom got pregnant with me. He's an accountant, and he hates it. Going pro was his dream, and I know he regrets giving it up. But I'm not him. I'd planned it out. I had a tutor lined up, and I was actually going to graduate early, but he never gave me the chance to tell him. And I planned to go to university in the off season. But after ten months of cooling off, I realize *I'm* the one who walked away. I had a chance to tell him my plan, but I didn't. I walked out."

"But—" Charley started.

I placed a single finger over her lips. "My point is," I whispered, for her ears only, "I was waiting for the perfect time to lay out my plan, and I missed it. I waited too long. I won't make that mistake with you. I keep assuming you know how I feel, even though I don't say it. There is no perfect time, especially not here, where every moment could be our last." I smiled, still blown away by the one girl who made me feel more alive than I'd known was possible, especially in a place where death was king.

"I love you, Charley. More than I've loved anyone ever, more than I knew I could. I've loved you since the first day I met you, when you strode out on the sand looking like a seriously hungry badass, worried about your goat when you should have been worried about yourself. I've loved you for weeks. It just took me some time to realize it." My voice was raw. "So now you know."

Charley smiled. Reaching up, she traced the tiny scar over my eyebrow. "I already knew," she said softly. "You've shown me a million times how much you love me, constantly protecting me from this." She swept her hand around us. "And while you've been busy being the best island guide ever, with full Nil-protection services, I've been protecting you here." She placed her hand against my chest, over my heart. "Because I love you, too. More than I've ever loved anyone ever, more than I knew I could. I've loved you since the first time I saw you walking down my beach, guarding Jason from scary wild things like me. I've known it since Day One." Charley grinned.

"And," she said, "if we're practicing a proper good-bye, then I think it needs a kiss, don't you?" She smiled her sly Charley smile, the one that made me feel like we just might make it after all.

"If you insist." I grinned. As I moved to kiss her, a massive roar split the air.

I leaped to my feet alongside Charley.

"We're screwed," Jason called. A few meters away, he stood rigid, his back to us, spear raised as he scanned the darkness. "We're sitting ducks."

"Charley," I said, sweeping my eyes around the darkness, "make sure the fire doesn't go out."

No one slept. The night burst with noise and silence, and the three of us were caught in the dead zone, trapped inside our black rock prison. *Rats in a maze*, I thought. A hyena cackled, dogs barked, and faceted eyes glittered in the darkness. Backs to the fire, Jason and I lobbed rocks at the eyes and the darkness using cloth slingshots, with Charley feeding us rock ammo. Finally, one rock connected. From the whimpers, if I had to guess, I'd say a wild dog went down. The keening death cries and intermittent roars rubbed our nerves raw.

The eyes retreated but the sounds remained, and when we weren't launching rocks, we waved torches at the dark maw of night. It was like trying to stop an avalanche with an umbrella, hoping to be breathing when it finally stopped.

Dawn broke before we did.

"Well, that was fun," Jason said, stretching.

"I'm sorry for dragging y'all out here." Charley looked miserable, but we probably all did after last night's crappy no-sleep-a-thon. "This was a mistake. Give me a sec to do my business, then I'll be ready to head back." She walked over to a large rock, the one resting alone near where the trees thickened, like a marker for a trailhead. A black behemoth sporting green groundcover, the mountain's slope began a stone's throw away—if you threw hard, which for me right then would have been tough. My shoulder ached from last night's artillery.

I followed Charley, knife out, unwilling to let her out of my sight. Privacy took a back seat to safety. But as she approached the back rock face, I scanned our perimeter. So far, so good. *All quiet on the southern front.*

"Thad!" Charley's voice snapped my focus. "C'mere!"

She was frantically ripping vines from the rock, and soon I understood what drove her. Flat and etched, the rock bore another carving. Same maze, same *12* at the top, only this carving had two lines bisecting the maze, placing the man dead center in the target. *Bull's-eye,* I thought.

Charley practically glowed. "This is what I was hoping to find! Another carving!" She pulled a sheet of paper from her satchel and placed it over the carving. The thin paper was almost translucent, nowhere near the thickness of our clothes; it made me appreciate Jillian's mad skills with paper trees. Using charcoal, Charley rubbed the paper, pressing until her paper turned black and the white maze leaped out in sharp relief.

Something bumped my ankle. I pivoted to protect Charley, already in motion even as my head canceled the threat.

A black kitten wobbled near my leg. I thought of Burton, wondering how he was faring in the land of hidden hyenas and wild dogs. *Maybe he's home,* I thought, *wherever that is. Maybe he's even in Canada.* Burton on snow made me smile.

Charley misinterpreted my expression.

"I know! It's so cool, right?" She rolled up her rubbing and tucked it away with her maps. "Let's go. I want to make it back before nightfall, and if there's time, go by the Arches."

Jason barely glanced at the rock carving. "I'm on board with Charley's plan to bail. I found a dog carcass, and I don't want to be lunch."

And that was that. We took the straight shot back. As the day progressed, there was no more talk of a detour to the Arches. Maybe Charley had decided against it, maybe she knew I'd shoot it down. All I cared about was food and a bed, and the Arches had neither.

By the time we made it to the City, it was dark. Charley held a torch while I carved Natalie's check. *Let the City wake to good news*, I thought.

Then, totally exhausted, we fell into bed.

I wrapped my arms around Charley. She laid her head on my chest, and tucked in the semi-safety of the A-frame, I'm not sure which of us fell asleep first.

CHAPTER
43

My dreams were twisted, full of mazes and screams, packed with wild cats and hunters with no faces. I woke at dawn, restless and edgy. From my dreams, and from the day's reality.

Today was Day 300.

It felt like a turning point. I was on the backside of the mountain now. Flying too fast, maybe out of control.

Charley's eyes were closed, her breathing soft and even. I knew if I lay here much longer, my head would explode or I'd twitch, waking her either way. I also knew Charley needed her rest.

Careful not to wake her, I slipped out. My first order of business: check in with Rives. I'd no intention of mentioning Charley's latest discovery or her fascination with the carvings. For me, yesterday's find was solid confirmation that each of us had a bull's-eye on our back and Nil held the gun. End of story.

I found Rives on the beach, eating a mango.

"Sweet news on Nat," he said, thumping my shoulder.

"Definitely." I grinned. "So what's the report?"

"Johan's team came back two days ago. Never saw a gate, Raj saw the tiger on night two, and on day three, their camp was hit. Food stolen, weapons too. Even extra clothes. Gone."

Animals don't steal weapons, people do. And naked people steal clothes. "Did they see who?"

"Two boys. Skinny, young."

"But no one got hurt." My statement held a question.

"Right."

"That's good." I wondered if the raiders knew about the gates and the time limit. And I wondered if they were the ones who had hit the Shack.

"That's not the good." Rives smiled. "The good is that Quan didn't go renegade, the knives are back, and we have another newb. Sergio. He's Italian, and get this: his dad was a carpenter, and he can make anything. With wooden nails." His grin grew.

"Handy," I agreed. But I was still thinking of the knives. Their return said it wasn't raiders; it screamed inside job. *All that matters is that the blades are back,* I told myself.

Rives was on a roll.

"I'm thinking animal traps. Maybe a new glider. We could make oars, shore up Julio's cracked A-frame . . ." Rives spoke as fast as his missing twin, Natalie.

I clapped Rives on the back. His to-do list felt oddly remote. "Sounds like you've got it. Let's run, eh?"

Rives looked at me. "Yeah. Let's run." He didn't mention his projects again.

I ran intervals with Rives as long as I could, but my legs were beat from yesterday's hike, and I bailed early. Plus I was starving. And I missed Charley.

By the fire, Jillian was tying Charley's hair into twin ponytails.

"Morning, you two." I grabbed a hot wrap and sat beside Charley. Her shoulders were relaxed, her head slightly tilted as Jillian gathered her hair into a thick roll and held it tight.

"Okay, Charley," Jillian said, reaching for a piece of twine, "don't move."

As if Charley would. I smiled to myself. Charley loved it when I combed her hair. Watching Jillian, I felt a stab of envy.

"Just so you know, Jillian, that's my job." I shot Charley a lazy grin.

Jillian laughed. "So you're a hairstylist now?"

"He has hidden talents." Charley's tone was serious.

"Geez, I'd say get a room, but you two already have one." Jillian smirked. "Done." She shifted her feet and winced.

"How's your ankle?" I asked.

"Better," Jillian said. "Just stiff. I'm guessing I can run in a week or so."

Julio and a new boy passed by, their arms stuffed with green leaves, the kind used for wraps. I guessed the new kid was Sergio, then with a start I realized it was Dex. Dex, who had looked like a strung-out vampire when we'd left. He looked like he'd gotten fresh blood or a dose of Nil sun. His skin no longer glowed pasty white; he actually looked alive. But his ears still looked weird.

"Huh," I said, watching Dex.

"What?" Charley asked.

"Dex. It looks like he's joined the land of the living. No more vamp camp for him."

Jillian nodded. "It took him a couple days to snap out of it, but he's actually a decent guy. Handy, too. Dex's been on his own since he was fifteen, so he knows how to cook. And unlike some rookies, he was smart enough not to get totally fried his first week here."

I nodded. More than one new contestant had gotten sun poisoning, and it was never pretty. The sickest one in a long time was Bart.

Bart. He was currently on Search, supporting Miguel.

"Did you hear that?" Charley said, craning around.

Tuning out the ocean, I listened. Then I heard it: a high-pitched wail. Faint and human. I jumped to my feet behind Charley. Jillian stood and immediately faltered on her ankle.

"Stay," I told her. "Better yet, find Rives."

Charley was already running toward the sound. Taking off after her, I heard the cry again. A thin scream, shouting a name. I didn't recognize the voice, but I recognized the name.

Rives.

CHAPTER
44

"Rives!"

A girl's voice, laced with panic. The pauses between shouts were as terrifying as the shouts themselves.

Thad caught me as the trail widened. Our legs matched each other, stride for stride, and I knew if we kept going, eventually we'd hit the valley, the one before the rain forest. But I also knew we'd never get that far—that we'd find something first. Or someone.

A girl staggered from the trees. No, two. One was Asian, with slick dark hair, tiny like Li but younger, with eyes full of fear. The other girl was Talla. Bloody and unconscious, her head lolled like a rag doll as the smaller girl half dragged, half carried her up the path, crying for Rives.

The instant she saw us, the tiny girl collapsed, shouldering Talla to the ground.

"Want me to help find Rives?" I asked as we closed in on the girls.

"No. Stay." Thad's voice was clipped.

Talla's arms and face were scratched, and a jagged, bloody gash slashed up her forearm and wrapped around her elbow, exposing bone. Her left arm hung at a funny angle. She needed a hospital, but all she had was us.

The whimpering girl seemed to have shrunk. She rocked Talla on the ground, tears staining her childlike face. "Do you speak English?" Thad asked gently.

She nodded.

"I'm Thad," he said, using the same soft, steady tone. "What's your name?"

"Mi-Miya." Her word jerked through tight breaths.

"Okay, Miya. Do you know what happened?" Thad pointed to Talla, who was unconscious.

"Wolf. She save me from wolf."

Where's Miguel? And Heesham? And Bart? Where's her team?

Thad was obviously thinking the same thing, because he asked Miya, "Did you see anyone else with her? Boys?"

She shook her head.

Rives came running, with Jillian limping behind. It turned out Jillian's mom was a physical therapist, and Jillian was now the de facto head of island medicine. "I don't know crap," she said, her voice shaking. "But her shoulder looks dislocated to me." Gently, Rives lifted Talla, his face drawn.

Back in the City, Thad and Rives reset Talla's shoulder. Her scream was bloodcurdling, then she passed back out, which was probably good. Jillian took over when Thad left. Rives refused to leave Talla's side.

Feeling helpless, I brought Rives a plate of pineapple. "Rives, you need to eat."

Rives didn't move. I set the plate on the small table.

"Can I get you anything else?"

"Deadleaf," Rives said. "We're out."

His eyes never left Talla.

"Where do I get it?"

"Closest strand is near the groves." Rives turned to me and, for an instant, purpose replaced desperation. "It's a haul, I know. Don't go alone. Take Thad, or Jason. And don't touch the leaves."

"Why?"

Jillian answered. "Because your hand will go numb. The leaves weep white juice; it's an instant anesthetic. Sabine's the one who taught us about it. If you crush the leaves, they make a numbing compress. When you harvest, one person cuts, and one packs. Don't touch. And don't eat the fruit. Not that you'd want to—it smells terrible—but the fruit's poisonous."

I stopped. "It smells bad? Like throw up?"

"Yup." Jillian crinkled her nose. Rives was intent on Talla. He held her hand, watching her closed eyes.

"Are the leaves super shiny green?" I asked Jillian.

"Yup." She nodded.

"I think I know where a bush is. Be back soon."

Outside Talla's hut, I grabbed Jason and told him about the bush at the end of Black Bay, the one I suspected was a deadleaf plant. Sure enough, it was a deadleaf orphan, growing out of place. According to Jason, they usually grew in clumps on the eastern side of the island.

The leaves smelled grassy when cut, but like Jillian warned, they oozed milky juice, making them hard to pack. On the other hand, the fruit smelled awful, and the odor intensified when plucked. The smell was overpowering, almost suffocating.

"I thought the fruit was poisonous," I told Jason, swallowing repeatedly as Jason packed the fruit in a separate satchel.

"It is," he said, sounding nasal as he breathed through his mouth. "But maybe we can use the island's defenses to our own advantage." Now he grinned. "Thad's idea. We're going to sow some seeds around the City. See what grows."

Sacks full, we headed back. It was frustrating to be so close to the Arches and not visit, but Talla came first.

She was still unconscious.

"I've got a bad feeling about Talla's team," Jason told me and Thad as we hung our newly washed satchels by the Shack to dry. "A wolf attack is not a good sign."

"And getting separated from your team is even worse," Thad added, his voice grim.

A crashing noise echoed through the trees.

Thad spun in front of me and crouched, knife in hand. Jason raised his spear. I stood there, empty-handed, feeling helpless. What could I do, throw my sandal at the wolf?

A long moment later, Heesham stumbled out of the trees. Dirt streaked his face, arms, and clothes, and he was swearing. With a start, I realized it wasn't dirt that coated his skin; it was dried blood.

"Talla," Heesham gasped as he stormed closer. "Is she here?"

"Yeah." Thad answered. Heesham's relief was obvious. "What happened? Word is a wolf attacked. Was it a pack? Where's Miguel, and Bart?"

I pressed on Thad's arm. "Heesham," I said gently. "Let's get you something to drink, then you can talk." Heesham looked ready to fall down, or fall apart. I'd never seen him like this, and it threw me.

Thad looked embarrassed. "My bad. Charley's right. Are you hurt?"

"Nope. Not my blood." Heesham looked even angrier.

I grabbed a water gourd, which Heesham emptied in a quick minute. Striding to the clearing, he plopped down on a rock—the same rock where Sabine had sat on my first morning here.

Then he leaned forward, his massive hands clenched. "Talla and I were getting firewood. Miguel and Bart were tracking a rabbit. We hadn't made good time. We were still near the rain forest, instead of where we'd planned to be that day. So we were hustling to restock fruit and game, getting ready to launch the next morning. Next thing I know, Bart's flying at us, telling us to run. Says a giant monkey thing with a ghost face jumped Miguel, that it dropped from a tree and landed on Miguel's shoulders, and that more animals came out of the trees and took Miguel down."

Heesham swallowed. "I lit into him right then. I wasn't buying his pack-of-monkeys story. There aren't packs of anything on Nil, except us.

"I made him lead us back to where he said Miguel was attacked, but Miguel wasn't there. Then Bart changed his story, kept insisting we couldn't find Miguel because he was gone. Said a gate flashed and took Miguel and the monkey thing through it but he hadn't told us because he didn't think we would believe him because gates rarely flash in the rain forest."

"So he lied," I said.

Everyone jerked their heads to me.

"Sorry," I said to Heesham, feeling rude, "but two things can't take the same gate. Remember that girl? The one who died after an outbound zapped her?"

"Two people can't go, but I don't know about a person and animal." Thad frowned.

"No, he lied," Heesham said, his voice hard. "We started hunting in circles, spreading out, calling out to each other to stay in range. Then Bart stopped answering. Talla and I hooked back up, but Bart had disappeared. So had our food and maps."

Everyone was silent, listening. The breeze had even slowed.

"Now it was just me and Talla. We kept looking, and next thing you know, we found a dead monkey. Big sucker, with white around its eyes and nose. It'd been stabbed." He looked at us. "The monkey thing with a white face that supposedly took Miguel through a gate was dead. And Miguel's knife was stuck in its gut.

"So now we knew Miguel was around. We called for him, tried to follow blood trails, but we'd walked so long we were turned around and night was falling. Plus, for all we knew, Miguel was walking in circles, too, and we were missing each other. So we stopped. That night, Talla and I stayed put, alternating watch. The next morning, we walked a tight grid, searching for Miguel. We found him, leaning against a rock, barely alive, his face messed up. One eye gone. The baboon did a number on him."

Heesham looked at Thad, his face furious. "Bart left him there, bro. Bart was Miguel's support, and when Miguel needed him, he bailed."

Thad's jaw ticked.

"Miguel couldn't walk, and he was really out of it," Heesham continued. "So I picked him up and started back to the City. We'd been walking for maybe an hour, when we heard a girl scream. A little girl scream, you know? At first I thought it was another monkey, a trick of my head. Then we saw a girl, running naked. She was fast, man, like the wind. Then we saw the wolf. Mangy-looking thing, it was after her. It happened fast. I had Miguel; Talla's hands were free. She took my blade and went running. I didn't know what to do. I didn't want to leave Miguel; he couldn't protect himself. And I didn't know if Talla could handle the wolf, and it was too late to follow." Heesham took a deep breath, visibly struggling to hold it together.

"So I tracked toward the City. Alone for hours, carrying Miguel and keeping him talking. Then like a gift from Allah, an outbound flashed four meters out. I ran, said a prayer, and threw Miguel in. He's gone."

Everyone sat silent.

The moment was surreal.

The blue sky, free of clouds. The gentle breeze, making the trees sing. The ocean roaring, the fire crackling, the fish baking. Talla bloody and unconscious, Heesham bloody and furious. Miya, bloody and fragile, a wounded bird, curled by the fire. Miguel bloody and gone. Bart missing.

Julio came up from the beach, soaking wet. "Miguel made it?" he asked.

"Yeah." Heesham's face was blank.

Throwing his fist in the air, Julio shouted something in Spanish. Still grinning, he asked, "And Talla's back?"

As Heesham nodded. Julio frowned, looking over our group. "Where's Bart?"

"Don't know," Heesham said. "But when we find him, I get him first."

"Take a number," Rives said, appearing by the fire. His face was stormy. "Talla's got a fever."

CHAPTER 45

CHARLEY
DAY 35, TWILIGHT

Please let Talla's fever break tonight.

I'd never thought about what it would be like to be sick on Nil, and Talla was worse than ever. Floating in and out of consciousness, her skin burned hotter than a gate.

The past two days had been awful. Jillian packed Talla's wound with deadleaf, but her fevered sleep stayed restless, and none of us knew how to brew Sabine's deadsleep tea to help ease Talla's pain. Too strong and it would kill rather than soothe; it was a risk no one was willing to take. Sabine's loss had never been more apparent. Without the tea, both Rives and Jillian worked in shifts to keep Talla cool and comfortable, but Rives's frustration was evident.

We need a doctor, Rives vented to Thad after dinner tonight. *A real doctor, with real meds.*

Thad had gripped Rives's shoulder. *We're doing all we can. And she has you, and our prayers. The rest is up to her. Talla's strong, Rives. Don't count her out.*

Thad's words made me feel better. If anyone could beat the fever, it was Talla. After all, she'd survived Rory, she'd fought the wolf, and she'd saved Miya.

Now she had to save herself.

CHAPTER 46

THAD
DAY 303, EARLY MORNING

Talla died last night.

She just didn't wake up.

Bart. I wanted to beat the coward into the ground, make him pay for Talla's death. But he hadn't come back. Maybe the traitor was too afraid to show his face, no balls to own up to what he'd done. Maybe he'd caught a gate. Maybe something had caught him.

I couldn't help thinking that if he hadn't bailed on Miguel, Talla might be alive. Miguel might never have been hurt, and Heesham would've been free to help Talla. A dozen other choices, a dozen other outcomes. But like Charley said weeks ago, the what-if game went nowhere.

I was so sick of the games. Nil's games, head games.

Dead games.

"Ready?" Charley asked.

"No," I said, taking her hand and walking anyway.

The burial ground sat at the edge of the Flower Field. We trekked as a silent group, all dressed in matching dingy white funeral wear. Our mourning clothes were our morning clothes, and our afternoon clothes and our night clothes. There was no getting away from them, unless Nil tossed a little luck and a gate your way.

Talla's luck had run out.

Dressed in burial white, she rested in Rives's arms, her eyes closed forever. Rives looked both stormy and empty, like he'd lost something he'd just found. Next to Rives, Johan's head was bowed in prayer.

Once we were gathered, Rives nodded to Jillian, who was already crying. She placed a lei of flowers around Talla's neck. "Sleep well, my friend," she whispered. "I'll miss you."

As Jillian stepped away, Rives kissed Talla's forehead, then looked up at Johan, tears streaming down his face. Seeing Rives's pain, I nearly lost it myself.

Johan's deep voice drifted over the group. "Heavenly Father, we gather to honor Talla, and in our hour of need, we call on your words. *The Lord is my shepherd; I shall not want . . .*"

Rives gently laid Talla in her grave. Heesham, Jason, and I began covering her with dirt, and as the black Nil ground swallowed Talla forever, pictures of past funerals flickered through my brain.

Today's burial was so much worse.

"*He maketh me to lie down in green pastures . . .*"

Wrong! my gut screamed. Talla's death was wrong—out of order. She should have said good-bye to me, not the other way around. But with nine months left on the clock, Talla was gone, claimed by Nil forever.

The grave was level, a raw island wound. Quan had carved a sleek wooden cross as a marker. It made me thankful Quan had chosen to stay. But it was Rives who placed the cross on Talla's grave.

"*Yea, though I walk through the valley of the shadow of death, I will fear no evil: for thou art with me . . .*"

The shadow of death. It loomed larger than ever. I held Charley's hand, holding tight to the goodness in my world—the goodness that had nothing to do with Nil's shadow and everything to do with Charley. Because Nil was evil. Fate had brought Charley here, but it was Nil who would rip her away.

I watched Rives fall to his knees and sink into the fresh dirt at the edge of Talla's grave. As he bowed his head, my blood went cold. *Will Charley have to bury me? Please, God, no.* And I prayed I wouldn't have to bury her. I didn't think I could survive it.

I prayed that I'd make it.

And that she'd make it.

And that somehow we'd live happily ever after on the other side.

But fairy tales were for little girls in polyester princess getups, not for seventeen-year-old boys daring to hope. And Nil was no fairy godmother, that was for damn sure. Still, I hoped, because I had to.

I tuned back just in time for Johan's *Amen.*

"Amen," Charley murmured. Her "A" sounded strong, like she sent her prayers up with a little extra power. Beside me, Jillian sobbed quietly. Rives stayed on his knees.

Charley dropped my hand. "Be right back," she whispered. She walked up to Rives and touched his shoulder. "Come," she said softly. "I'm not your twin, or your Talla, but I hate to see you hurting. We miss her, too."

Rives looked at Charley, his eyes shockingly empty. "I'd just figured out who she was. It was like we always played each other, you know? But she'd finally let me in. I knew her, Charley. Talla was my girl. I can't believe that's her." He pointed to the fresh grave.

"It's not," Charley said, kneeling. "She's here"—Charley touched Rives's chest, then his forehead—"and here. And you're still with us. Take a minute, say your good-byes. Then come with us, okay?"

Rives looked at Talla's grave. Slowly he lifted his fingers to his lips, then reached out and touched her cross.

My chest was so tight I could barely get air. Grief for Rives, grief for Talla, fear for me and for Charley, all twisting into one massive life-sucking terror. The shadow of death had never felt colder. Or closer.

"Thanks," I told Charley when I could finally speak.

"For what?"

"For what you said to Rives. He's solid."

She slid her hand into mine. "He told me the same thing about you once."

As a tribute to Talla, the girl who loved the water more than anyone, we grabbed boards and the group of us hit the water together. With each stroke, I thought of Talla. Of how she owned the water and dreamed of Olympic gold. *I'm sorry, Talla. You deserved more time.*

Don't we all, the waves murmured, full of their adrenaline rushes. *Don't we all.*

The swell pitched, rising like a mountain. Vaulting to my feet, I rode the line, going for speed, racing away from the shadow of death. Water flew under my board, then like a fast run downhill, the ride was over. The wave closed out, and as the foamball churned, for a second it looked like I was riding snow.

Then the wind kicked up, onshore and cross. Soon the sea looked like a washing machine, like the water was protesting Talla's death, too.

"This sucks," Rives said. "I'm going in."

"Right behind you," I said. I looked to my right, where Charley sat on her board. She'd gotten better, but she'd bust it bad in this chop. "Let's bail, Charley. It's getting rough."

Sy flagged me down the minute we left the water. "Thad, got a second?"

Not really. "Sure."

"Listen . . ." Sy fidgeted on the sand. "I know you're not Leader anymore, but there's something I have to tell you. It was me!" he blurted. "I messed up the Shack and took the knives. It was Bart's idea. He thought that if enough people doubted you as Leader, that we could nominate someone else." Sy looked sick. "I'm sorry. It wasn't right. I already put 'em back, but I just wanted you to know." If possible, Sy looked even sicker.

"Thanks for coming clean," I said. "That took guts. But from here on out, I'd be a team player and then some if I were you."

Sy nodded like his neck was rubber.

As he took off, I weighed his confession. He wasn't Bart; he was better than Bart, I realized. Younger, more honest. Sy might just make it after all.

"Everything okay?" Charley asked.

"Yeah," I said, my eyes on Sy's retreating back. "I think so."

Charley and I caught up with Rives and Jason at the Shack. As we racked our boards, we were a quiet group. The only noise came from Heesham. He rumbled around the Shack, testing the weight of the remaining knives, grumbling about the small handles.

Then a twig cracked, loud and crisp, in the identical spot where Heesham had appeared two days ago.

The wolf, I thought, pulling my knife. *It tracked Heesham. It followed the blood.*

Armed with a spear, Rives flanked my right side. Jason and Charley had my back.

As I raised my knife, the tallest, blackest boy I'd ever seen stepped out from behind a tree. Wearing leaves around his waist and holding a homemade spear tipped in black rock, he saw us and stopped. "Whoa." Nature Boy took a step back.

The odds ran through my head, the same ones no doubt slamming through his. *Four to one.*

"I'm Thad." I held up my hands, splaying my fingers, even though I still held a blade. "Don't freak." As an afterthought, I asked, "Do you speak English?" Based on his "whoa", I'd have guessed yes, but on Nil, nothing was a given.

"Yeah. I'm Ahmad." He lowered his spear. "Where am I?"

"Nil City," I said.

"You're on the island of Nil. It's some kind of parallel dimension," Charley chimed in with a casual wave. Then she plucked the knife out of my hand and slid it into the sheath at my waist. "I'm Charley."

Ahmad stared at her: Dex-shocked, but less vacant.

"Rives," Rives said with a nod.

"Heesham." He'd popped out of the Shack.

"Where you from?" I asked.

"The Sudan. But I live in Minnesota." The boys sized each other up. Ahmad gave Heesham a run for his money. Taller and not as thick, with longer arms and legs, Ahmad looked like a first-round draft pick for the Timberwolves.

"Where were you when the gate hit?" I asked.

"Gate?" He frowned.

"The wall of moving air," Charley offered. "The one that burned and knocked you out."

Now Ahmad nodded. "Back in the Sudan. We were visiting relatives."

I asked him about the days and the date, and learned Ahmad had landed on the north shore. He'd been here twenty-eight days. Straight up, I broke the news that the gates were his ticket home.

"Wait a second. You're saying those gates, they take us back?"

"Yup. They're the *only* way back."

Ahmad threw back his head, laughing. "I've been running from those things for weeks. Thought they were bad, man. Evil, like the devil."

No, that's Nil, I thought.

"Sick spear," Heesham offered.

And just like that, we got our fifth rookie in two weeks. It was a Nil record.

CHAPTER 47

CHARLEY
DAY 37, AFTER NOON

When I was ten, my parents took us to see the Blue Angels fly over Jacksonville. At the start of the show, six planes took flight, then one peeled off, leaving a gap in the formation. My dad told me the maneuver was to honor the Blue Angel pilot who'd died after his plane crashed the day before during a routine practice flight. He called it the missing-man formation.

That's what I thought of when we paddled out to surf after Talla's funeral and there was a gap in the lineup. That's what I thought of when we sat to eat lunch and the space beside Rives was empty. Talla's presence had always been powerful, and her absence was just as big. She was our missing man.

Not just missing, I had to keep reminding myself. *Gone—forever.* The most competitive survivor on Nil was dead.

Time had never felt more fragile.

With nothing to lose but minutes, I grabbed my rubbings and went to find Rives. I figured he could use a distraction, too.

I found Rives with Jason and Thad. The boys were sprawled on the black beanbag rocks where I'd first shared breakfast with Natalie and Sabine, whittling greenwood spears. *Perfect*, I thought. Exactly the three I wanted to see.

"Okay, y'all, I need your brains. Especially yours, Rives, because you've got fresh eyes."

"At your service," Rives said. He didn't smile, but at least he'd answered.

Unwrapping the rubbings, I spread them out.

"Rives, you probably recognize this one"—I pointed to the Man in the Maze—"but I doubt you've seen this." I pointed to my newest rubbing, the maze pinned by bisecting lines. "We found it near the southern lava flow. Thad calls it 'Bull's-eye.'"

"It does look like crosshairs," Rives commented, studying the paper.

"But I don't think they are," I said quickly. "Thad told me once he thinks the carvings mean we're rats in a maze. And I think he's partly right."

"We're rats?" Jason asked curiously.

"No." I shook my head. "Not rats. But I think the maze represents the island. Only I think on Bull's-eye, the lines relate to the island, not the man. Like the island is broken into four parts." I paused. "And I think there's a fourth carving, I just don't know where, exactly."

"Why?" Thad asked.

"Because the Man in the Maze sits west, its sister drawing sits east, and Bull's-eye sits south. So it follows that there's a drawing in the north. We just have to find it."

"Again, why?"

Before I could answer Thad, Ahmad's voiced boomed behind me. "There *is* a fourth carving. I camped near it for a week. It was almost totally buried by a rockslide when I found it."

"What does it look like?" I asked.

"Like Bull's-eye." Ahmad pointed. "Only it has numbers at the bottom and top, and the man is outside the maze, not in the center."

"Do you remember the numbers? And can you sketch it?"

"I can try."

I offered Ahmad my last sheet of blank paper and a piece of charcoal. He drew a circle, two bisecting lines, and a stick figure near the bottom right, outside the lines. At the top of the maze, just outside the circle, he added the number twelve, then he turned the tip of the vertical line into a double arrow, which pointed at the twelve. Underneath the drawing, in deliberate strokes, he wrote "3-2-1-4."

"Three, two, one, four," Thad read aloud. "Like a countdown? Three, two, one, boom? Three, two, one, dead? Why four?"

"Four quadrants, four seasons," Rives offered. "Maybe the countdown is to the one-year mark. You've got four seasons to leave, or your number is up."

"And the arrow points to twelve," I said. "Noon, I'm guessing. The most important time on the island."

"What are y'all looking at?" Macy asked. She'd appeared beside Ahmad, along with Dex.

"Island mazes," Thad said.

Macy peered over my shoulder. "Those aren't mazes. Those are labyrinths."

"Maze, labyrinth. Same difference," Thad said.

"Oh, no." Macy shook her head emphatically. "They're very different. Mazes have twists and turns, and dead ends. Labyrinths follow a path. There's only one way in and one way out."

"Like Nil," I said. Rives was nodding.

"But there's more to a labyrinth than that," Macy said. "My uncle walked one last year, out in Texas. There're famous ones, like the one with the Minotaur, but there're tons in churches, too, because walking a labyrinth is a spiritual journey. Both the walk in and the walk out. Some believe it's to get closer to God; some say it's a journey of self-discovery. Either way, it's personal."

"So being here is a spiritual journey?" Thad quirked one eyebrow. "We're here to find ourselves?" His voice was mocking.

Macy took Thad's negativity in stride. "I can't answer that; no one can." Her tone was kind. "The way I see it, you've got to connect the dots for yourself." As Thad snorted, Macy pointed to the rubbings. "Where'd these come from?"

I explained quickly. "Macy, once you told me you believe we're all here for a reason. Do you think the reason is related to these labyrinths?" I realized it was kind of Thad's question, kind of not.

Macy answered slowly. "Maybe. I do believe I'm here for a reason, that we're *all* here for a reason. But"—she looked up—"I'm not sure we're all here for the same reason. Does that make sense?"

"Totally," I said, feeling the tendril of understanding blossom in my brain, too ethereal to grasp.

"Nope." Thad cut in, his voice sharp. "We're here because a gate dumped us here, plain and simple. And we already know there's only one way in and one way out: a gate. Grab one at noon and you're gone. That's what these tell us, nothing more." He jabbed his finger at the drawings.

"Maybe," Macy said agreeably. "But maybe not."

Rives tapped Ahmad's sketch. "What's with the numbers?"

"Tick-tock," muttered Thad, crossing his arms.

"They relate to the lines, I think," Macy said slowly. "It's a sign of four. The lines divide the labyrinth into four equal parts, and there are four numbers evenly spaced, with four being last." She traced the first number on Ahmad's sketch. "Three always represents the trinity. It's a divine number, and here it's first in the sequence, giving it priority. Not sure what the number two represents, but the number one could be us. The individual. The guy or the girl who has to go into the labyrinth, because on this drawing, the figure's near the entrance, like he's ready to go in." She pointed, and sure enough, the man on Ahmad's sketch was positioned outside the maze, in the bottom right corner— not directly in front of the opening, but slightly above it. His placement was peculiar, yet my gut said purposeful. And no doubt important.

I stared at Ahmad's drawing, at the man *outside* the maze. And then it clicked.

"That's it!" I cried. "That's what I've been missing! The start of the gate wave! It always starts in that lower right quadrant, on the eastern side. I can't believe I didn't see it before!" I pointed at the entrance, the entry point I'd always assumed was just symbolic. But everything on the drawings had significance; I saw that now, more than ever.

"And the numbers," I continued, speaking fast. "Maybe they relate to the number of gates in a set? A triple, then a double, then a single, and occasionally a quad? I'm guessing here, but these numbers relate to the gates, I just know it."

Rives looked thoughtful. "Quads are so rare that I can't believe the four stands for a quad."

"Four often represents balance," Macy said. "Four seasons, four elements, four directions, four chambers of the heart. And four often represents Earth, the balance to the divine. These two crossed lines"—she pointed as she spoke—"make the sign of four, and four here is last in the sequence, after the one, which makes four the most powerful number of the group, like the sum."

"Like it's the goal. The final destination." Jillian's quiet voice was sobering.

Everyone stared at the rubbings.

"I call bullshit," Thad said, breaking the heavy silence. "I say three, two, one, represents the countdown, ticking off until you make it home. To *our* Earth, in our dimension."

"Maybe," I said, using Macy's tone. "But I think there's more to it. And I think these drawings give us a definitive starting point on the gates." I tapped the lower right quadrant. "Then gates move north, just like the double arrow tells us. These drawings might help us time the gates better."

The next hour of discussion focused on gates and timing and quadrants. Ahmad offered to take a team to the north shore to make a rubbing of his sketch, which now, thanks to Thad, everyone called "Countdown."

Talla was not forgotten, but the labyrinths were a definite distraction. Thad took Jason on sweeps, checking the perimeter from the air. I didn't need to be a rocket scientist to know he was avoiding the City—and the labyrinths.

He didn't mention the drawings until we went to bed.

"You did it again," Thad said. "Gave the City hope, or at least something to think about other than death."

"Just trying to put pieces together. Anything to give us a better shot, you know?"

"I know." He paused. "But like you told Nat once, you'll find what you're looking for. We can look at those mazes twenty-four seven and see what we want to see—symbols and karma and cosmic mumbo-jumbo or whatever. But I think we're better off focusing on your maps and your charts. On something definitive that will help us get off this rock. And it's not those mazes. They don't lead anywhere but back here."

Reaching up, I traced the scar over his eyebrow. "I hear you. But I can't help but think these labyrinths represent something meaningful and that we need to figure them out. Maybe they exist to tell us to catch a gate—and that gates are the ticket home, as you told Ahmad. Maybe they even show us a pattern to catch them. But maybe, just maybe, the labyrinths suggest something more. I just don't want to miss anything important."

"I won't let you," he whispered. Then he pulled my hand to his mouth and kissed each of my fingers, one at a time. Gentle, and highly distracting.

"Before I forget," he murmured, "we're set for dawn. Jillian volunteered as support. Jason too." More kisses.

Search. Support. Jillian and Jason. Thad's words finally registered: tonight was our last night alone for days.

Thad tapped my nose. "Earth to Charley. What are you thinking so hard about? My half-naked body?"

I laughed, although he was partly right. "Just thinking."

"About what?"

You. Us. Our last night alone.

We'd fooled around, but we hadn't done the deed. Talla's death was a painful reminder of how little time we had, and I'd never felt more determined to make each moment count. Maybe tonight was *the* night.

"Charley?" Thad tilted my chin up and searched my eyes. "What's going through your head right now?"

"I was thinking about us, and wondering if tonight is the night." My cheeks grew hot.

"The night?" He looked lost.

"*The* night. Where we, you know . . ." I trailed off, embarrassed.

Thad sighed. "Charley, I wish. You have no idea how much I want that. But we can't."

His quick dismissal stung. "Why?" I asked.

"Because. We just can't."

"You have to give me a better reason than 'just because.' That sounds parental."

"Okay. Because it won't end well. Because we have no protection here. Because you still have ten months on the island." Thad's flat voice turned tortured. "What if you got pregnant? What if something happened to you during delivery? We have no doctors, no hospitals. And I won't be here to help; that's a given. And if you did have the baby here, remember only one person goes through the gate. One. You or the baby, not both."

The horror of that thought sank in.

"And what if you're still pregnant?" Thad wasn't done. "Could you both make it through?" He ran his hand through his hair, and in that moment, I knew he'd thought of all these nightmare scenarios before, probably more than once. "I don't know. And say you both make it, and you have the baby back home. What then? What if I didn't make it? Now you're a single mom? At seventeen? I can't do that to you—"

"Stop!" I said, my voice tight. "That's the Dark Side talking. You'll make it."

"I'm just saying, we can't." His voice was flat again.

"Fine. We can't." My tone matched his.

I lay with my head on his chest, listening to his heartbeat. "Don't talk like that," I said finally. "Like you won't make it. Don't even think like that."

"Look, I believe I'll make it," Thad said, but the lie in his voice stung. "But not everyone does. There's a chance I won't. So we have to take that into account. Plan for it, eh?"

"No." Anger tinged with frustration made me snap. "That's not planning for the worst; that's giving up. *You're* the one who balked when I joked that eighteen was overrated. *You're* the one who looked horrified that I was quitting. So don't you dare give up on me now, Thaddeus Blake. Not when you have sixty-two days left and at least that many chances." I dared him to argue, but he stayed silent, which was worse.

"Tomorrow we'll go on Search," I said, determined to make him see reason. "We'll finish mapping the island and chart gates. We'll use the mazes, follow our patterns, and if we see a gate, you'll run your butt off to catch it, you hear?"

"I hear," Thad said, breaking into a smile. "I love you, Charley."

"I love you more." And then I kissed him, more fiercely than he'd ever kissed me. Because I knew Thad could be gone tomorrow, and that he would definitely be gone in sixty-two days.

I didn't need the labyrinths to tell me that.

CHAPTER 48

THAD
DAY 311, ALMOST DAWN

Charley was asleep. Considering it was still dark, I wasn't surprised.

It was my turn on watch. I sat with my back against the rock, blade in my hand. So far there'd been no sign of raiders or big cats on this Search, which was good.

And there'd been exactly one gate, which was bad.

We'd been gone for seven days. In seven noons, we'd seen one exit gate. A single, too far away to catch. Equally surprising, it was Miya who'd spotted the gate. Now officially the youngest person in the City, she'd latched on to Jason after Talla's death and refused to leave his side, so our team had gained a plus one. But it didn't help.

I was still here.

And I had fifty-four days left.

Charley's words from a week ago ran through my head. *Don't you dare give up on me now, Thaddeus Blake . . . not when you have sixty-two days left and at least that many chances . . .*

But she was wrong. If you averaged my odds, I'd be lucky to spy one gate a week. And with just under eight weeks left, I had maybe eight shots. Twelve at best. It wasn't the Dark Side talking; it was Nil reality.

Only six hours until today's noon.

Tick-tock.

CHAPTER 49

I woke, alone.

The bed beside me was cold, and for one terrifying second, I thought Thad was gone. We'd gotten back last night, after nearly two weeks on yet another fruitless Search.

"Hey." Thad's voice rang from the doorway. "I didn't mean to wake you. The waves are pumping. Want to come?" The rising sun shadowed his eyes, and I didn't like it. "But no pressure," Thad was saying. "If you want to sleep longer, just say the word."

"No." I jumped up. "I'm awake."

Outside our A-frame, two boards lay on the ground. By the fire, Dex was carving a spear, his back to the Wall. Only now there were two walls, which felt both right and strange.

Sergio was carving the island map in wood, right next to the Naming Wall. When finished, the Master Map would live on, long after the paper maps disintegrated and the ones who made them were gone.

Like me, and like Thad.

As we passed the Wall, Thad's blank space stood out like a sore thumb. Other blank spots held more meaning than ever. Jillian. Rives. Jason. Macy. All had spaces waiting to be filled, belonging to real people I knew and cared for.

Bart's space was blank, too, and for all I knew, it might stay that way. The consensus was that he'd either caught a gate or run into trouble. No one gave him much credit for survival, and no one seemed to care.

There was a new name, Naomi. Her accent reminded me of Sabine's, only less buoyant. She'd been here six days.

I'd been here sixty-four.

And Thad had been here 330.

Trying not to freak out so early in the day, I focused on the dawn. As the rising sun kissed the water, the day's promise was so fresh, so raw, it gave me hope.

We glided through the channel, with the breeze at our backs. I pulled up on my board, and in that perfect moment, Natalie's words floated back to me. *Time flies here, faster than you're ready for.*

Natalie was right. The last few weeks had flown by, too fast to count—and yet we did. Twenty-six days, twenty-six noons. Fourteen days with no gates at all. Three inbound: one brought a deer; another, a chicken. The third came and went, with no rider at all. Five outbound. Two singles, both moving away, too fast to catch. Two doubles. One was close, so close Thad said he felt the heat, but it collapsed before he made it, almost on top of the Woman in the Maze carving, which of course I'd made a rubbing of to add to my collection. The other double was so distant it may have been wishful thinking. And two days ago, we'd seen a triple, close enough to identify, but too far away to catch. That noon was the worst. To miss three chances was a huge loss, because triples were rare. No wonder Thad doubted my quad.

And I was doubting my charts. The gate wave started in the

lower right quadrant of the island—that I believed. It made sense. It fit with the charts and the labyrinths. But after that, gates flashed without a definitive pattern. Like I'd already figured out, they never flashed in the same place two days in a row, or even on the same latitude. But they jumped around, and days would pass without us seeing any gates at all. Something was missing.

No, *I* was missing something. We all were.

And now that I'd seen the Woman in the Maze for myself, I was more convinced than ever that the carvings provided not only the start of the gate wave, but something deeper, something more personal. Something each person had to figure out before he or she could leave. That part I didn't voice to Thad. On the subject of the labyrinths, his mind was closed.

He floated beside me, studying the horizon. I traced his profile with my eyes, committing the lines of his face to memory.

"I absolutely, completely love you," I said.

"And I absolutely, completely love you." Smiling, Thad raised one eyebrow. "What was that for?"

"No regrets," I said.

"No regrets," he agreed. His blue eyes sparkled. Then he pointed. "Go, Charley from Georgia. Or you're gonna miss your wave."

I didn't move.

"You don't want your wave?" His lazy smile was full of challenge.

No, I want something else.

"There's something I need to ask."

CHAPTER 50

THAD
DAY 330, MORNING

Charley and I had the ocean to ourselves for a while, then the easy waves brought company. Rives and Jason paddled out; Miya too. Unlike Heesham, Miya was feather-light. I knew the board could float her if she just managed to stand up. She did.

The waves were fresh and frothy, and for a few adrenaline-filled minutes, I forgot all about the days.

I had thirty-five left.

Waking up in the City today was harsh. Not quite full-on suckage, but close. The stakes were high, and I knew it; my internal Nil clock woke me up. The tick-tock, the urgency. The sense that I'd better catch a gate, and soon. Charley's charts were solid, and I knew they'd up my odds. They already had. But in the end, it was up to Nil and how she wanted to play the game.

When I'd passed the Wall this morning, my tired space screamed at me. Holding steady between two crosses, it begged for a check, like Kevin. *I'm trying*, I thought. God, was I trying.

The triple tease Nil had sent two days ago was her latest cruel call. Three gates, three sprints. I'd never even been close enough to feel the heat.

Shoving that memory aside, I blinked to clear my head and searched for Charley. She was paddling out. Water slicked across her board, caressing her skin like I dreamed of doing every second of every day.

Like an icy slap in the face, Charley's words from an hour ago crashed back.

Thad, what we talked about, before we went on Search. I asked for something, and you said no. Do you remember?

I'd sat there, feeling my blood chill, trying not to throw up.

I remember, I'd said. *Like I could forget.*

I thought about it all the time, not that she'd know that. I thought about it during the day, when she smiled, making my heart race and body ache. I thought about it at night, when lying next to Charley was exquisite torture. I thought about what it would be like to be with her, knowing it would be better than anything I'd experienced ever, because this was Charley. And it was exactly because it was Charley that it wouldn't happen. It couldn't happen—not here, for all the reasons I'd told her before.

I want you to reconsider, she'd said, her golden eyes determined.

Why? I'd asked, wondering why she was testing me, like I hadn't weighed the risks a million times over and always come down on the cruel side of no. *Why take the risk?*

Because I don't want any regrets, she'd answered. *I want you to be my first.*

I'd stared at her, stunned, wondering when she'd decided our happily ever after wasn't meant to be.

So you don't think we'll both make it. My voice had been flat.

NO! she'd said. She'd looked shocked, which had surprised me. *It's just—I want—*She'd looked away. *Never mind. Forget I said anything.*

Charley, look at me. I'd worked not to beg.

She'd turned back, and the desperation in her eyes killed me.

I love you, I'd said. *More than you can imagine. More than I've ever loved anyone ever. And I'd love to give you what you want—God, you don't know how much I want that—but we can't.* Her lips had parted, like she was about to say something, then closed.

Charley—I'd slowed, holding her gaze—*if you really believe in us—that we'll both make it—it doesn't matter if we wait.*

She'd stared at me, lips parted but not saying a word, and the awful chill had rushed back. My knuckles had tightened on the edge of my board.

Don't quit on me, Charley, I'd thought. *I'm barely hanging on. I want us to make it so badly I hardly sleep. And when I do, I feel the heat of a gate in my dreams, knowing only one of us can take it. I dream of you, of gates, of being with you somewhere other than this plastic paradise, and sometimes it's all I have to get through the day.*

Don't quit on me.

Because if she quit on us now, I didn't think I was strong enough for the both of us.

Charley? I'd prompted, keeping my face blank.

You're right, she'd said, forcing a smile. *It doesn't matter if we wait.*

Liar, I'd thought, watching her golden eyes flicker. But I didn't say it. Something told me she was as scared as I was, that the fairy-tale ending we desperately wanted would crumble for sure if we brought our fears to light. Like Nil would feed off them, making them real.

So I'd said nothing. Neither had Charley.

But I still felt cold, even now.

"Hey, Thad!" Charley shouted, pulling me back to the present. "Did you see that? I tried that cutback thingy, and I didn't fall off!"

Watching Charley celebrate, I almost broke. The pain in my

chest was so great, the swell of want so potent that I could barely breathe. Forcing a breath, I focused on Charley's latest victory, which had everything to do with Charley herself and absolutely nothing to do with Nil.

"You killed it, Charley. I knew you had it in you." As she paddled up beside me, I thought, *Please let me sleep tonight. Not forever, just for a night. I really need it, before I lose it for good.*

For the first time, I pretended the foam was snow. I missed racing so much it hurt like a bruise, one only I could see. I'd taught Charley to surf; I ached to teach her to board. My kind of boarding, flying on ice. It was part of my happily-ever-after, and lately no matter how hard I stretched, it seemed just out of reach.

But wanting to see Charley on snow more than I'd ever wanted anything ever—because that vision meant we both won, it meant we had a future without limits—I closed my eyes as I made the drop.

When we left the ocean, I was spent but still sane. I counted that as a win.

On the sand, Heesham and Rives were setting up the volleyball net, with an audience of hecklers. A cocker spaniel ran around the beach, barking at the waves. I wondered when the Nil pup had arrived. Pets didn't make it onto the Wall.

"I call Charley!" Heesham shouted when he saw us.

"Too late." I smiled. "She's taken."

"I call Ahmad!" Jillian said. He gave her a high-five, and with his long arms, he looked like a contender.

New teams, new day, but the result was the same: Charley was unstoppable. Charley spiked home the final point, splitting the line between Ahmad and Jillian. Both dove and missed it. Then she turned to me. "No regrets." She winked.

"No regrets," I said, then kissed her forehead.

As Charley laughed with Jillian, I scanned the audience. It

looked different. Familiar faces gone. Fresh faces I didn't know. And other faces, older and sharper.

Suddenly I felt stale and out-of-date, like those oldies on the slopes. Still shredding, slow and steady, but their mojo has been stolen by someone younger. Someone with more time.

"You okay?" Charley asked, poking my arm. "You look a little far out there."

"Yeah." I smiled. "Just tired."

She looked at me, hard, like she saw through my crap answer but decided not to call me out on it. *Thank you, Charley, for just being you.* I kissed her again. *No regrets.*

"Let's eat," Jillian called, waving everyone over.

"And reset the teams," Rives added, shooting me a look before winking at Charley. "Hey, Charley. Will you take pity on me for one game? And while you're thinking about it, I need another Second. With your maps and charts, you're a good fit. You game?"

His request hit me hard. *Talla,* I thought. She was Rives's missing Second. He hadn't replaced her, and Charley would be perfect. Charley with her fierce attitude, her island ingenuity and her killer charts giving everyone hope. But for some reason, I wanted her to say no. To not give up any more of herself.

Of course she said yes.

"I'd be honored," she said, looking solemn. Then she squeezed Rives's arm. "I miss her, too. Last time we ran, Talla beat the tar out of me. I still owe her a Sprite."

Rives nodded. It took him a moment to speak. "Thanks," he said.

We sat around, catching up. Ahmad was the life of the group. The dude was funny, I'd give him that. Like a stand-up comic, even when he was sitting down; he was just that tall. And after a few weeks in Nil City, he'd even added some weight.

But the biggest change was in Dex. Tan, with a few muscles, his tats looked menacing now, and his vacant look was gone. He actually looked human, except for the ears. Now he sported twine hoops through the holes with shark's teeth dangling like knives.

Jillian stood, covering her eyes as she looked out to sea. "Guys, do you see that? There's something in the water."

"Nothing ever washes up on Nil," Charley murmured, briefly squinting at the sea before sliding her eyes to me. "You told me that my first day here."

"This is a first," I said.

Jillian was right. Something *was* floating in the water. Something that didn't belong.

A body.

CHAPTER 51

CHARLEY
DAY 64, LATE MORNING

"Bart," Rives said. "Or what's left of him."

Even though I wasn't a Bart fan—and it was tough to find one after the Miguel debacle—it was awful to see him like this: pale and bloated, with one hand missing. I wondered how he ended up in the water, washing up here, and I wondered what killed him. It was another Nil mystery to add to the rest.

The fellas dragged Bart's body onto the beach. There was no blood, which seemed strange. Jillian stood beside me, her nose crinkled like she smelled something bad. All I smelled was the ocean, thank goodness.

"The last time I saw Bart, he was talking to Talla." Jillian paused. "Weird."

"Totally weird," I agreed.

Bart was dead; Talla was dead. And then there was poor Miguel, fate unknown. Heesham's Search team had turned out to be a dadgum mess, and the only one still standing for sure was Heesham. He towered over the body, his size casting an enormous shadow over Bart's corpse.

"Wonder what he ran from this time," Heesham said, frowning.

"What?" Rives said sharply.

"Did you see those cuts on his back? Something sliced him up, man. Something with claws. Bart was in full retreat when it got him."

"Now what?" Dex asked.

"Now we bury him," Thad said. "Since Johan's out on Search, same for Macy, I'll lead the service, unless someone else wants the honors." He looked around. No one volunteered. Not even Sy, Bart's former roommate. The silence was telling.

"Then it's settled," Thad said. "I'll handle the service."

Now Sy spoke. "Uh, maybe we should send him back out to sea." Now that he had everyone's attention, Sy looked like he'd just swallowed some unripe redfruit and was trying not to choke. "You know, like an ocean burial."

"You mean feed him to the fishes?" Rives asked, smiling slightly. "Make him shark bait?"

"No." Thad shot Sy a sharp look. Rives may have been Leader, but Thad was still in charge. "We bury him. What Bart did doesn't make it right for us not to treat his body with respect."

"Just not near Talla." Rives's voice was hard. And that was the end of the discussion.

Bart was buried in a very poorly attended service, outside the City lines. He got two crosses: one on his grave, one on the Wall.

It wasn't until later that I realized Bart had shown up at noon. If a gate had flashed, it wasn't around here. Or if it was, we were all too busy looking at the water to see it.

Thad had thirty-four chances left.

"Charley!"

Jillian's voice pulled me from my thoughts, and the Wall. I hadn't moved since Sy carved Bart's cross.

"Hey." I turned toward Jillian. "What's up?"

"You okay? You haven't moved in, like, an hour."

"Jillian—" I fumbled, trying to frame my question and not sound Ramia-looney, "Thad's certain that the labyrinths mean one thing: that there's one way on and off the island—a gate—and that catching a gate is like finding your way through a maze. But I can't stop thinking that the labyrinths mean something more personal. That we're here for a reason, and that it's up to us to figure it out."

I took a breath, primed to test my latest wild theory. "Sometimes I think that the key to how many gates flash in a set is tied to the personal journey part of a labyrinth, like we each hold the key, inside of us." I didn't mention that I'd seen a quad within minutes of landing; I'd no idea what that meant. "What do you think?"

It took Jillian a long time to answer.

"I think that we're all searching," she said slowly. "That being here has changed us all; I mean, how can it not? But"—she sighed—"is there some deep reason we're here? And does discovering it help us get home? Sorry, but to me it feels like a stretch. Back home, people disappear all the time and are never found. It's the mass disappearances that get attention, like ships or planes in the Bermuda Triangle, or entire families that vanish. I believe freak things like Nil exist without any hidden agenda." Her tone went from apologetic to firm. "Talla worked harder than anyone here to get home, and she didn't make it. Same for Li. So what didn't they figure out?" She shook her head. "Sorry, my friend, but I agree with Thad. We're here because each of us got swept up by an invisible storm. Wrong place, wrong time. All we have to do now is catch a gate to make the return trip."

I stared at Jillian, processing her words.

"What is it?" she asked. "Did I say something wrong?"

"No." I shook my spinning head. "You said something exactly right. Jillian, you're a genius!" I hugged her quickly, then dashed to my hut and collected all four of my rubbings. The paper I'd used was thin, more like tracing paper than parchment. I carefully spread out all four of my rubbings on the ground in front of my hut and stared at them. Soon I had an audience. Jillian, Rives, Thad, Dex, Jason, Macy, and Ahmad all peered over my shoulder.

"Okay, here goes. We know once gates flash, they roll north along longitudinal lines, and they never flash in the same spot—or on the same latitude—two days in a row. And we know the gate sequence starts here. I'm sure this is Quadrant One." I pointed to the bottom right quadrant, to the spot where the man stood outside the maze on the drawing Ahmad found, the one Thad called Countdown. "It's the only thing that makes sense. But I've been thinking it's a wave of gates, passing over the island, and I think that's where I went wrong."

Moving slowly, I gently laid one rubbing on top of another, using the number twelve at the top as a constant. The Man in the Maze lay on the bottom; Countdown sat on the top. The remaining two rubbings were sandwiched in the middle. All the number twelves were carefully aligned, their edges sharp. I stepped back, gazed at the rubbings, and like a hidden picture that leaps out after careful study, I saw precisely what I was looking for: the straight lines within the mazes faded, and the circular etchings took center stage. Swirling lines, spinning toward the epicenter, toward the center of *every* maze. Separately, the drawings were a labyrinth; together they were a guide.

Behind me, Rives sucked in a breath.

"It's not a wave," I said, my eyes still traveling the rubbings, "it's more like a storm—like an invisible tornado. Or a hurricane. It swirls around the island, mimicking the circular path of the labyrinth, starting here"—I pointed at the bottom right quadrant again—"in Quadrant One, then moving left, clockwise, hitting each quadrant in turn, no more than four times." I looked up. "That's what I was missing—the circular pattern. And I needed all four rubbings together to see it." I spoke out loud even as my thoughts gelled. "We rarely see the gates that flash first, because so much of the southeast corner is blocked by volcanoes; we usually catch the storm in Quadrant Two, the southwest corner. And I think the rogue gates that don't quite fit are like outer bands of a storm, slightly off latitude but still within the same quadrant." I paused. "What do y'all think?"

Dex spoke first. "It's bloody brilliant."

"I think you're a hell of a Second," Rives said, grinning. "I'm glad you're here, even though I'm sorry you're here." He looked at Thad, who was quiet, then to me. "So, you gonna hit Quadrant Two tomorrow?"

"I have to check with my island guide," I said, "but I'll let y'all know. I hear there's a storm coming." Smiling, I crossed my fingers; I couldn't help it.

Please let my latest theory be right.

CHAPTER 52

The day after I broke out my storm theory, we were riding high. Noon brought a gate, a gorgeous single. Flashing fast and furious across the southern black field, Thad didn't have a prayer of catching it, but it was there. And then it was gone.

And so the chase began.

We chased gates, and we chased noons, and the faster we ran, the faster time flew. Minutes drained like sand through a sieve, too many at once, too fast to stop. Each time I reached out to seize a moment, it was gone.

Day 331 turned into 332; 332 flew into 333. Sunrise, sunset—334, 335.

Three hundred forty.

Three hundred fifty.

Each dawn broke sooner than the last; each noon came faster still. *Stop!* I wanted to shout. But we couldn't stop the clock; we could only hope to beat it. Time only slowed during that excruciatingly long moment when we grasped that noon had passed and Thad was still here. That moment felt like an eternity, until a mix of guilt and regret and worry came to wash it away. Then time sped right back up, like pressure made the minutes fall faster.

Trying to relax, I focused on the ocean. Usually the waves were a sure-fire cure, peaceful and rhythmic. But not tonight.

Camped on the north shore, nights here were unnerving, creepier than nights near the City. With clouds to the east blocking the stars, blackness saturated the night, the sky, even the sea. Right now, the invisible ocean crashed incessantly against the rocks, furious and impatient.

Blocking out the sea, I switched to my charts, mentally reviewing my latest notes. Using the storm theory, our gate sightings had definitely increased. But it still wasn't enough. I knew it wasn't enough, because Thad was still here.

He should already be gone.

Instead, he lay beside me, one arm slung across my waist, eyes closed, jaw relaxed. Sleep softened his ever-present intensity. For countless minutes, I watched him sleep, forcing the moment to slow, trying not to freak out.

He'd challenged me, weeks ago. *If you really believe in us—that we'll both make it—it doesn't matter if we wait.*

I hadn't brought up making love again; neither had he. But I thought about his words, more often than he knew, because they went so much farther than just the physical. Wait to make love, wait to dream. Wait to plan. Wait to talk about the future, because lately it hurt too much.

He should already be gone.

The thought crept back in, persistent and disturbing.

What are you missing, Charley? Finding a gate was one thing; catching a gate was another thing altogether.

"We're doing everything right, aren't we?" I whispered. Silence answered me, punctuated by waves beating against the rocks, crashing like fear.

Aren't we?

CHAPTER
53

Using a wooden knife, Charley peeled the rind off a mango in a few slick swipes.

"Tell me again," she said, licking juice off her finger. "They say that the best way to memorize something is repetition before you fall asleep and again when you wake up."

I didn't need to repeat it; I had her address down cold. But I knew she needed to hear it.

"Charley Crowder. Eighteen Mountain Laurel Drive, Roswell, Georgia."

"Again."

I laughed, and repeated her address. "Now you."

Charley said my address, then handed me a slice of mango. "I'll call you as soon as I catch a gate." We both knew our cell phones were long gone. Lost, or canceled, or both. But families don't move, not when their kids are missing. "I promise." She grinned. "I've always wanted to see Canada. I've got a tack on Vancouver on my wall map. I just need to move it over a speck to get to your house."

"Speaking of maps, did you pack yours?" I asked.

"Got 'em right here." She patted her satchel.

"Let's pack and roll."

She smiled. "And pray the gates roll, too."

My gut clenched. Charley had switched the words from hope to prayers, revealing the desperation behind her casual reply.

Dropping my pack, I wrapped her in my arms. "They will," I whispered. "I'll make it."

"I know." Her voice was fierce. "You have to."

For a long moment, neither of us spoke. I didn't want to let Charley go, but we had around four hours until today's noon and a two-hour hike, give or take, to get to the meadow. Past the lava fields, past Bull's-eye, it was the same meadow that I'd woken up in exactly 351 days ago. According to Charley's charts, this latitude was due a gate, and the meadow was wide open, another hot spot ready to pop in the opening quadrant on the storm track. The only downside was that since the grasses were tall, you couldn't see the gate rising until it broke above the grass line. But, once it did, the meadow offered room to run. And although I didn't share the feeling with Charley, this spot felt tailor-made for me. I'd been snatched off one mountain, then landed at the base of another, and to me, it seemed fitting that if Nil wanted to let me go, she'd send a gate there. In the shadow of a snow-capped mountain that I'd never be allowed to climb.

"C'mon." I kissed her forehead, gently, because I still could. "Let's hike."

As we trekked, dainty Miya was as quiet as Nil. She glided over the ground, walking without a sound, and she rarely spoke, except to Jason. But judging by the way he smiled at her, Jason didn't mind.

I'd only been back to the meadow twice since I'd landed, including the sleepless night preceding Bull's-eye's discovery. I'd spent my time in the City, or in the arc Charley had identified as holding the best odds. But outside that arc, the meadow sat ready. Today we'd see how Nil wanted to play.

The hike took longer than expected. As we neared the meadow, I felt edgy and Jason looked worried. Gauging by the sun, noon was close. For her part, Charley looked determined.

The meadow sprawled like an open target. Tall grasses waved in the wind; trees were scattered to the left, Mount Nil rose to the right. But the rest was wide open.

"Watch the grass line," Jason said. His eyes were busy.

"Look!" Charley cried, pointing.

For one surprised second, I thought she'd beaten Jason to the punch, then I realized she was pointing to a pair of horses. Running in sync, their brown coats glistened as their hooves trampled the grass. The sound was a dull echo; we were too far away. Oddly ordinary, the sight was peaceful.

Miya spoke sharply. "Something moving in grass. There."

Following her finger, thirty meters out, the grass shifted in waves toward the horses, like ripples in the sea as a shark moves beneath the surface.

"We need to get over there." Charley pointed across the meadow. "The far end."

She took a step and I threw out my hand to stop her. "No. Something's in the field."

Charley shrugged. "Probably just the hyena going after the horses. Let's go. We can stick to the side."

Charley strode into the thick grass. I lunged forward and grabbed her elbow; at the same time, a massive tiger went airborne, skimming the top of the grass. It latched on to one of the horses' necks, taking it down in a clean kill. The horse's hooves swept the top of the grass line, then disappeared. Never slowing, the second horse galloped out of sight.

"I guess the tiger's still here," Jason said.

"Ya think?" I said. Back in the meadow, the tiger ripped into his lunch with gusto, making his stripes blur.

I turned away. "Okay, Plan B. We are not hiking around a hungry cat who's busy with lunch. He might think we're stealing his snack, and we don't want to be dinner. Let's go." As I started to walk, Charley stopped me.

"No," she said. "We need to be *there*." She pointed toward the far corner. "I know it." Her voice had that determined I'm-not-backing-down tone.

"Charley, we can't." My tone matched hers.

"Yes, we can," she said, her voice confident. "We can skirt the meadow's edge. We won't be close to the tiger. Let's go. Now!" Her last word was militant.

I stared at her, trying to figure out how to say *Don't be stupid* without sounding like a jerk.

"We have to go!" she snapped.

"No we don't." Jason's voice was dull. "Look."

"What?" Charley asked.

"Far end, rolling north." Jason pointed. "And it's a racer. A single for sure."

I peered across the field, seeing nothing. Then I caught the speeding flash of iridescence, and I knew Jason was right.

"We're too late." Charley's voice was bleak, and when she looked at me, I felt sick. Her face wore the same look I'd seen for the last two weeks when noon passed. Relief, then guilt, mixed with worry and fear—they swirled through her eyes, dimming the gold—and I hated Nil for that, too.

Noon was seriously starting to suck.

CHAPTER 54

CHARLEY
DAY 85, AFTER NOON

Natalie once said there's no such thing as luck on Nil.

She was wrong.

Luck is personal; we all have our own. Sometimes it's good, sometimes it's bad, but it's yours, and it follows you wherever you go—even to Nil. And luck can change, because as my nana always insisted, luck was a state of mind.

Chance, on the other hand, is different. Chance is a coin toss, chance is probability. My charts had increased Thad's chances, but it hadn't changed his luck.

And I couldn't understand why.

As we left the meadow, I pondered luck and chance, labyrinths and personal journeys, island mazes and carvings and the eternal question: *Why are we here?*

But mostly I pondered the most disturbing question of all: *Why is* Thad *still here?*

The next morning, I woke before Thad, a rare event.

By the fire, Miya sat alone, sewing a pair of shorts, her nimble fingers working the thin twine in an easy rhythm, her shoulders relaxed. I was struck by the change in her bearing. No more wounded bird, tucked in a ball. The most fragile soul on Nil had been saved by one of the strongest, and now Miya emanated a quiet strength reminiscent of Talla's inherent confidence. I wondered what Miya's future held for her once she escaped. Her gift for spotting gates rivaled Jason's, and my gut said she would make it. Talla's bravery had secured Miya's future, but the cost was huge. I wondered if Talla's cross haunted Miya or inspired her. It was not a question I'd ever ask.

Past Miya, Rives sat near the Wall, like he was meditating, only his eyes were open. Lately he'd become as obsessed with the Wall as Thad, but while Thad traced the carvings, Rives just stared, and never at the same place twice.

"Find anything new?" I teased, walking up to him.

"Actually, yes." Rives stood, grinning too broadly for this early in the morning. "Okay, what do you see when you look at the Wall?"

"Is this a trick question?" I asked, instantly annoyed. Now was not the time for games, not when Thad had only thirteen days left. "I see names."

"Exactly. Thousands of names, if you count both sides. And I have." Rives began to pace. "We know gates flash once a day on our end, at noon. So if we assume that gates flash once a day back home, that leaves three hundred sixty-five chances for people to show up per year. But we know that some inbounds have no riders, others pick up whatever happens to be there—chipmunk or cheetah, or a person. So I'm guessing worst case, one person gets snatched per week. That's roughly fifty people a year. Now, if you do the math and count backward, this Wall was built in approximately 1859." Rives raised an eyebrow at me.

"O-kaayy," I said, fighting impatience. "So it's old."

Rives shook his head. "Do you know what happened in 1859?"

Before I could say no, he said, "The biggest solar flare in history. That superflare sent a bunch of junk toward Earth, causing the largest geomagnetic storm ever recorded. Scientists call it the Solar Superstorm; I know because we studied it last year. All kinds of crazy stuff happened after the superflare. Telegraph machines caught fire; others kept typing after being unplugged. Weird stuff. And get this"—Rives paused, clearly for effect—"according to the British astronomers who observed it, the superflare happened just before noon."

Only slightly less dramatically, Rives continued. "Obviously, it wasn't noon everywhere, but the only dudes who saw that superflare—the only two, Charley!—both saw it at noon. How crazy is that? Two scientists, totally unrelated, working at two different observatories in the same time zone, and both record the superflare at noon. So, just like there're different quadrants here, there're different time zones back home, and the gate storm had to start somewhere, right?"

He stopped, his face animated. "I remembering you asking Macy why we're here. Well, I think it's possible we're here because of that massive solar storm. Maybe something happened back then, something cosmic that created this place or ripped open the gate to it. We'll never know, but it's possible it's related. And it was your storm theory on the gates that gave me the idea." Grinning, Rives waited for my reaction.

I wanted to scream.

Maybe that's why the island *is here, but it's not why* we *are here.* Different question, different answer, and Rives's answer didn't matter, because it didn't help Thad. Like I'd told Dex weeks ago, all that mattered was survival and escape, and for Thad, time was running out.

"It's a cool idea," I said, fighting not to snap, "but like you said once yourself, it doesn't help get us home."

Rives's expression softened. "I know. But it makes the place less freaky, at least for me." Stepping close, he wrapped his arm around me like he used to do with Natalie. "Keep the faith, girl," he whispered. "Thad's gonna make it."

He has to, I thought, biting my lip. *For both of us.*

CHAPTER
55

Today was my day.

I felt it—when I woke up, when we picked the Flower Field as the day's hot spot, and when Charley squeezed my hand a second ago. Today felt *right*. Or maybe I just wanted it to be right. Want, need, entwined in a blur of desperation, choking me so tight I was incapable of separating the two.

Charley's voice sucked me back from my mental black hole.

"Scan the field," she said, her eyes busy. "I've got the north edge."

Tick-tock. Seconds passed, then minutes. I felt noon slip when Charley shouted.

"There!" she cried, pointing.

Meters away, the writhing wall of air whispered my name as it rose. *Come, Thad. Run.*

"Run!" Charley yelled, pulling my hand.

I took off, Charley by my side, her hand tight in mine. The gate was glorious, winking with outbound perfection. Abruptly, clarity struck—as crisp and clear as the cloudless Nil sky—and in that moment, I knew: I couldn't win. Because even when I caught the gate, I would lose.

I would lose Charley.

Just run, I told myself. Charley's feet paced mine.

The gate rolled fast, skimming the north edge of the Flower Field. It was a racer, a single. Three meters away, the air glittered like sunlight bouncing off of snow.

I looked at Charley, certain I would shatter, even before I felt the burn of the gate. "I love you."

"As I love you." She grinned. "No regrets. See you on the flip side!" Then she let go.

In my peripheral vision, Charley spun out of gate range.

Heat leaked from the gate; it was like approaching an oven set on full broil, and I was about to throw myself in. As I braced for the burn, a sickly looking orange cat darted from the field, brushed my ankle, and shot into the gate.

Charley screamed as the cat shimmered; I fought to stop, windmilling my arms to get away before the gate zapped me to death. Millimeters from my nose, the gate snapped shut with an audible hiss.

It was gone. So was the cat.

And I was still right here.

"Well, that sucked," I said. I rested my hands on my hips as I fought to catch my breath. My quads trembled; I couldn't make them stop.

Charley threw her arms around me. "If you'd have hit that gate—" She shook her head, holding me tight.

I rested my head against hers. "But I didn't."

For a long moment, we just stood there. I had no clue who was holding who, and it didn't matter. We were together. And I was still alive.

"Holy crap," Charley murmured, her breathing almost normal. "That gate was yours. We were *right there*. And some crazy cat stole it and almost killed you in the process. What's up with all these frickin' cats?"

"You know how Nil loves to play with kitties. Gates are like catnip. It's weird."

"It's awful." Letting go, she sat on a rock. Her expression was half shocked, half furious. "To be so close only to have it stolen by something so random, especially something that looked half dead."

"Nothing like Nil to try to save a cat with one foot in the grave." My voice was bitter. Forcing a smile, I sat beside Charley and took her hand in mine.

"No," Charley said. "It wasn't Nil, it was random. Cats are like a wild card, literally."

That was when I knew Charley didn't get Nil. Maybe Nil hadn't found the chink in Charley's armor of goodness; maybe Charley didn't have one. Nil wasn't in Charley's head—at least not yet, and I hoped not ever.

Because I knew better.

This was Nil's playground, where Nil watched and cackled and called every last shot. She knew that cat was primed and ready to run, just like us. Nil flashed gates where she pleased, using gates to change the game, bringing new contestants and threats to add to her fun. Right now Nil was enjoying herself way too much with us to let me go: watching us hope, watching us struggle. Today's gate was a calculated Nil move. *Here, kitty*, she'd crooned, crooking her island finger and calling for trouble. *Run and I'll let you go. But you, Thad, will stay.*

Thinking of Ramia, I shuddered.

Watching me, Charley frowned.

"Maybe you're right," I said, unwilling to tell her she was wrong. I refused to give Nil any advantage, not when it came to Charley. The warmth in Charley's hand was a grounding force, a reminder of what was real and what mattered.

Charley looked at our hands. "I hate this. I mean, I'm so happy to have you for another day, but—that cat robbed you." Her voice went flat. "I was ready. I was ready to say good-bye, dreading it but ready, and you got robbed."

"I know." I rubbed my thumb over her palm. "I know."

For a minute, we just sat there, holding hands, not speaking.

"Did you ever see that old movie, *Groundhog Day*?" she asked.

I shook my head.

"Well, it's about this guy who lives the same day over and over. Noon is like that for me. We just keep saying good-bye, over and over. And then when noon's over and you're still here, it's great, but it's also terrible. And it's worse than that stupid movie, because when we wake up, it's not the same day, it's another day, gone."

I stared at Charley's hand in mine. "For me, noon is like that moment when I'm on the mountain, behind the start line and the horn's about to blow. I'm running through the course in my head. I'm amped and ready; I've got my head straight—and then it's like someone canceled the race. Without warning, they just said, 'Not today. Come back tomorrow.' And then I just get jacked up all over again, ready to fly, ready to *go*." I swallowed, hard. "Ready to say good-bye."

She nodded, then laughed, a weird hollow sound. "That word: *good-bye*. I get that, too. Because when you catch a gate, it'll be good. Better than good, it'll be great. But it's still a farewell." Charley paused. "The crazy thing is, when noon passes, it's like a gift. Another twenty-three hours together, guaranteed, that no one can take away." She looked at me, her face full of guilt. "I know I shouldn't be telling you this—I feel like I'm confessing, and I'm not even Catholic—but I'm totally dreading our good-bye."

Understatement, I thought. Charley had no idea how much I dreaded leaving her behind. Maybe I'd started out as her island guide, but along the way I'd become more like her shield, her protection against the darkness of Nil. And I feared that without me, she'd be vulnerable. But it wasn't my choice; it was Nil's. The cat was cruel evidence of that.

"Me too," I said, squeezing her hand. "But it's temporary. It'll all work out. Plenty of time, remember?"

Despair washed over her face, and my heart dropped. Her mind had leaped ahead; she'd already done the math.

Less than twenty-four hours until tomorrow's noon.

CHAPTER 56

CHARLEY
DAY 89, NIGHT

I'd lied to Thad today.

Okay, maybe I hadn't lied, but I hadn't been totally honest either.

I wasn't lying about feeling guilty when noon passed and Thad was still here, because it *did* feel like a gift, a wholly selfish present. But today was different. Today when noon passed, Thad's presence didn't feel like a gift; it felt *wrong*. That was the truth I didn't share with Thad.

And the more I thought about it, the more today's outcome felt like a mistake—a kink in Fate's plan. Today was *Thad's* day, bearing *Thad's* gate; we'd never been so close. But that stupid cat stole it, and now Thad only had ten days left.

As much as I was dreading it, the sooner Thad and I said good-bye the better.

And yet, I couldn't stifle the sense that we were missing something. That *he* was missing something—something that caused the kink.

We're all here for a reason, Macy had said. *But not the same reason.*

I watched Thad's eyelids flutter in sleep. *Do you know why you're here? Have you figured it out?*

His breathing was steady, like Thad himself, which was oddly reassuring. *Maybe he already knows*, I thought. But if he didn't, I prayed Thad dug deep, and soon. Because if Thad was right, and today's miss wasn't random, then he had exactly ten days to change his luck.

And my charts couldn't help with that.

CHAPTER 57

THAD
DAY 356, DAWN

The Naming Wall looked different now.

New names, belonging to faces I didn't know. Spaces filled by hands that weren't mine, on days I wasn't here. Quan had a check. It seemed to right the balance. Heesham sported a fresh check, too, which felt better than good. Elia had a cross, which sucked. So did Sergio. I wondered why. He had plenty of time. Or did.

One space looked exactly the same: mine. No cross, no check. The crosses around me looked sinister, like they were conspiring to birth one beside me, Nil jonesing to win her twisted version of tic-tac-toe.

No, I thought, glaring at the space beside my name. *You won't win.* Part of me had the perverse urge to carve a check next to my name right now, but it would accomplish nothing. It wouldn't bring a gate. It wouldn't guarantee that I'd live.

Then my eyes fell on Ramia's name. The rising sun hit her cross, setting it on fire, then I blinked and the illusion was gone. I stared at Ramia's cross, unable to look away.

"Come on." Charley's voice broke my Wall thrall. She gently drew me away. "Everybody's ready."

Behind her, Jason flashed me a thumbs-up. Miya stood beside him. Rives was talking to Dex, his new Second.

Charley's hand in mine, I walked over to the group.

Dex stuck out his hand. Tattoos covered his chest and arms like a long-sleeved shirt, dark and tribal. His outstretched forearm boasted a massive cross sprouting flames.

"Good luck out there," he said. "Run fast."

I stared at his burning cross as I shook his hand. "Will do," I said. Consumed by fire and fear, by flaming gates and burning crosses and by the infernal nature of Ramia's predictions, my brain threatened to implode.

Dex's strong grip brought me back. "I'm serious, mate. Run fast. Get yourself back home. For you, for all of us." He released my hand and looked at Charley. "Be careful, Charley," Dex said. "Protect your boy, and watch your back as well. It can get a bit crazy out there, you know?"

"I know." She smiled. "See you, Dex. Stay alert and take care of each other."

She'd be a great Leader, I realized, if Nil didn't steal her first, like Talla. Or Sergio. The firestorm in my head grew.

Jillian squeezed my arm. "You'll make it, Thad. I believe in you."

"Thanks." *But it's not up to me.* Not my game, not my choice. My destiny wasn't my own, and I hated it.

I was wired so tight I thought I might snap. Break, then shatter—into a million bone bits, doomed to stay forever, but I knew that's what Nil wanted, and I refused.

I would not crack.

And yet part of me wondered if I already had, at least a little. Nil was screwing with my head, like she'd been for almost a year—and yesterday she'd drilled a little deeper, hitting another nerve. At the Flower Field, for a minute, Nil let me think I'd escape. I'd actually believed I'd made it, only for Nil to snatch victory away using a half dead cat. I'd stayed up half the night wondering if Nil would spend the next ten days toying with me, only to claim victory in the end.

Charley was wrong about the carvings, at least about the lines. The target was on my chest, dead center, and I'd never felt more like prey. After all, that was why Nil brought us here. We were Nil's sport, Nil's fun. It was that simple.

As we loaded our gear, I took a final look at the Wall. Empty spaces taunted me, like gravestones hungering for a final date.

You'll make it, Jillian had said.

Staring at those empty spaces, I hoped we all made it. But I knew we all wouldn't. The Wall said it all.

Plus, Nil was full of all those damn cats.

CHAPTER 58

The night was silent and still. Thad lay beside me, and I prayed he was asleep. And I prayed we didn't have to go back to the City.

I'd barely been able to rip Thad away from that dang Wall. He'd stood there, running his hands over the carvings, only this time he was tracing crosses. I didn't want to ask what was running through his head. I was afraid I already knew.

After leaving the City, we headed north, marching toward noon. Watching and waiting. Then today's noon came and went without a gate, like a party popper that fizzled.

The rest of the day was weirdly shadowed.

We continued north, trying to get ahead of the gates. Thad's time was running out, and I was scared to death. I was scared *of* death—of Thad's death. If he died, it would kill us both.

He had nine days left.

How did the end get here so fast? My mind couldn't wrap around the pace, the frightening acceleration of time. It was like the more I wanted time to slow, the faster it sped up.

The entire island was mapped now. We'd skipped the mountain, because none of us had enough clothes to hike up there anyway, and so really, what was the point? We'd made gate schedules using the quadrants as a guide, and we'd identified every hot spot. Food sources, too, which was Thad's idea. The mango groves, guava stands, fish ponds, and shrimp spots—all were marked on a separate food map; the idea was to give future visitors the best chance to survive long enough to get home, just in case anyone forgot to mention to a rookie where they found something to eat. Back in the City, the Master Map was nearly finished. Dex took over where Sergio had left off, ensuring Sergio's legacy would live on.

Poor Sergio, I thought. Nil was not the place to get stung by a jellyfish. Jillian told me he'd died within minutes. Odd how something so small could be so deadly.

On the other hand, noon was killing us one day at a time.

Thad and I just kept saying good-bye, over and over, and I was terrified that the one day I forgot to say it would be the day he left. But that would be good.

Because that would be good-bye.

As I fell asleep, I prayed that tomorrow was Thad's lucky day.

CHAPTER
59

The last seven days passed so fast they blurred. Like cards flying through the hands of an expert dealer, flipping so fast you barely have time to spot the card's edge before it vanishes into the deck, gone forever—those were my last days on Nil. I caught only the edges, unable to make time slow down, not sure I wanted to anyway.

Nil was the dealer, and I was so damn sick of playing. And making the game extra fun, I'd developed insomnia. Raging, vicious, rip-your-eyes-out insomnia.

I wanted to sleep, but couldn't. And the more I thought about how much I needed it, the harder it was to fall asleep. It's like when you watch the clock at home, thinking, *If I fall asleep now, I'll get five hours of sleep. If I fall asleep now, I'll get four.*

There were no clocks on Nil, but I knew exactly how much time I had left.

Two days.

Two noons.

Two chances.

And if I blow those chances? Simple. It's checkout time.

Please just let me sleep, I begged.

Two days, Nil giggled in the midnight breeze. *In two days, you can sleep all you want.*

Desperate to shove Nil out of my head, I focused on Charley. On all that was good in my world. She lay curled against me, the one thing I wanted to live for more than anything else. And yet I couldn't stop thinking about the end. *My* end. It was coming like an avalanche, or maybe I was shooting toward it.

An old memory surfaced, one built on speed. I was seven. I loved skiing, the faster the better. I'd point my skis straight down the mountain, my only goal to get to the bottom faster. Frustrated by my apparent lack of caution, my dad had bought me a snowboard. He'd figured that if I had to go sideways, I'd have to slow down. That was when I'd discovered snowboard cross, and racing.

And now I was racing toward death.

Pictures of Nil's victims flickered behind my eyes, a cruel mental montage. Li. Talla. Bart. Older visuals. Thomas and Sara. Uta.

Ramia.

You'll Lead, she'd whispered, her eyes sharp, her fingers stroking that creepy bone cuff. *But you'll never leave.*

You don't know, I thought, my mental tone fierce. *It's up to Nil, not you.*

Holy shit, now I'm talking to a dead person—in my head.

Trying not to lose it more than I already had, I told myself that Ramia was a freak, an island anomaly. So what if she predicted her own death and a few others? My destiny lay with Nil.

Life or Death. Door Number One or Door Number Two.

I'd never told anyone—partly because I didn't care, partly because I refused to add fuel to the labyrinth fire—but for me, the number two on Ahmad's sketch represented choice. Life or death. Two options,

329

the ultimate choice. Only it's Nil's choice. Because the gates are always her call.

People die here, that's a given. But if Nil chose death, the how was unclear, another Nil surprise. *Will I just fade away? Or drop like a rag doll? Will it hurt? Burn like hell? Or will it be some fantastic ride?*

I couldn't shut down the mental rat race.

Charley had been asleep for at least an hour. I'd watched her the whole time, studying the curve of her shoulders, the set of her jaw, the bow of her lips. Nil's cruelty was complete. She'd given me a taste of the good life, just to tear it away.

I couldn't imagine a world without Charley. It was worse than a world without snow.

At some point, I obviously fell asleep, because Charley's honey drawl woke me up.

"Thad," she whispered, stretching my name into two syllables, "are you awake?" Charley lay beside me, one hand propping up her head, her dark hair falling around her shoulders like rain.

I blinked against the bright dawn light. "Yeah." I tried to smile, but it came out a yawn.

"I'm sorry," she said, looking guilty. "When I saw you move, I thought—"

"It's okay. I'm glad you woke me."

Now that I focused, Charley looked wide awake. Eyes clear, and worried.

"How long have you been up?" I asked.

"A while," she said, smiling. But her smile faded before it ever took hold. "I was terrified that when I woke up today, you'd be gone. Promise me you won't leave, not like Kevin left Natalie." Charley paused, her eyes fierce. "Promise you won't go renegade."

I nodded.

I didn't admit it, but I *had* thought about it. Not about leaving

Charley, but about Kevin's choice to leave Nat. I finally understood. I still didn't agree with it, but now I understood it. And Kevin's choice was not mine. I refused to leave Charley until Nil ripped us apart. Plus, I had Charley's charts, a shot at winning that Kevin never had.

Charley was frowning at me.

I reached up and tucked a strand of hair behind her ear. "I give you my word. I promise I won't leave you."

She nodded, then twisted her hair into a thick roll. The act struck me as nervous. "Thad, I keep thinking. About the carvings and the labyrinths. I know you think the personal journey angle Macy talked about is a bunch of hogwash, but—" she paused, avoiding my eyes. "Maybe you've already thought about it, maybe you've figured it out. But if you haven't, I want you to think about it. Really think. About why *you're* here. Because I agree with Macy, that we're all here for a reason, and the reason is different for everyone."

Wrong, I thought. *We're here for exactly the* same *reason: Nil needed new contestants. End of story.* "So why are you here?" I winced at the bitterness in my voice.

"To meet you." Her voice rang with conviction.

"Then I'm here for you," I said.

Her eyes searched mine, like she was digging deep, hunting for truth. *You know me*, I thought, feeling the familiar ache in my chest. *Better than anyone, ever.* But I didn't say it. Staying quiet, I watched her study me.

She smiled, a sad smile that hit me like a punch in the gut. "We need to get going if we're gonna make it to South Beach," she said quietly. She was already getting to her feet.

"Let's pack and roll." The words rolled out, like an auto-response. *Have a nice day. Good luck. May the Force be with you.* Rote and hollow.

Rives stretched, looking oddly comfortable for someone who'd slept upright against a chunk of black rock. Not many people could grab zz's sitting up, but Rives told me once he could sleep anywhere, anytime. Lucky him.

I watched them: Miya opening her eyes to Jason, Jason handing Charley dried fruit, Charley laughing at Rives, Rives reading Charley's charts. They'd take care of each other after I was gone, and the knowledge gave me comfort. Charley wouldn't be alone.

We reached South Beach by mid-morning. After chasing gates north, we'd turned and were now chasing them south into Quadrant Two. The gate storm should be swirling through here soon—unless we'd already missed it. And we wouldn't know until today at noon.

I felt amped and edgy, like I always did as noon approached. Lately the noon vibe was worse than ever, because now nausea was mixed in, just enough to throw me off my game. Off Nil's game.

Eyes wide open, Kevin's ghost urged. My eyes were so wide I barely blinked.

Jason and Rives hugged the tree line, pacing like soldiers. Miya drifted near Jason. She had eagle-eye vision, and was a great Spotter in the making. And of course Charley walked beside me. Her hand tucked tight in mine, her chin tilted up, daring Nil to defy her.

God, I love you, I thought, watching her face. I squeezed her hand, and just as she turned to me, Jason's cry split the air. "Gate! Eleven o'clock!" Whipping to look, I caught the shadow rippling across the charcoal sand. Fifty meters out, at most.

This was it.

Like someone had shot a gun, we all began hauling ass toward the gate, running as if our lives depended on catching it, which of course, mine did. The sand dropped, the air rose, and in a sweet twist of fate, the gate began moving—toward us.

"All out, Thad!" Rives shouted. "GO!"

Jason, Miya, and Rives dropped back. I refused to let go of Charley's hand. My fingers crushing hers, I kept her close.

"Love you," I choked out.

"Love you, too," she said, grinning, but her eyes were shimmering, like the gate I was dying to catch.

Please don't cry, I thought, fighting to run. *Because I'll lose it for sure.*

She didn't. "Almost there," she said. Now her eyes were on the gate. Her grip loosened, a tiny hint of what was coming: pain.

But the pain of the gate would be nothing compared with the pain of leaving Charley.

The gate rolled at us, fast. It was a single. It had to be; it flew like a rocket. The air glittered, reflecting rainbows and light, a million prisms, each one itching to tear me apart, more brilliant and roiling than I'd ever seen an incoming gate, or maybe I was already feeling the burn; the iridescence was blinding. Every fiber of my being ached as my brain screamed to let Charley go. Meters from the gate, I spun Charley out of range.

The luminescence dulled.

Behind me, Jason yelled, "Thad, something's weird! The gate's muddy."

"I see it!" I braked so hard I kicked up black sand. It sprayed into the face of the gate, where it disappeared like mist. Then it reappeared.

Black sand. Black mist. Blackness in the air.

"Back up!" I shouted, reversing in the soft sand and stumbling away. Breaking into a run, I grabbed Charley and dragged her away. "Incoming!"

Two gates—one entry, one exit—were flashing in the same space, something I'd never seen or even known was possible. And my gate was blocked.

As we sprinted away, I looked back in time to see the inbound gate flush completely black. To its left, the outside edge of the outbound gate shimmered. For an instant, two overlapping circles were clearly defined: one as black as night, the other iridescent crystal magic. The black one glittered like mirrored charcoal, confirming my fear: this inbound had a rider.

Person, thing, or animal.

One breath later, a massive bundle of brown fur fell from the air. *Animal.*

My gate kept moving, missing the creature by inches, still rolling toward us. On the black sand, the animal lay still.

"You have to go back!" Charley cried. "You can make it!"

She yanked her hand away, and ran toward Rives. "Run!"

"Charley—" I started. The creature stirred, lifting its head and baring its teeth. My answer was wrong: it was a thing.

"RUN!" she screamed.

I spun around and sprinted back toward the gate, feeling like I was playing Nil's sick version of Simon Says. *Nil says catch the gate. Nil says run away. Run back.*

The animal wobbled to its feet, swaying like a drunken boarder and grunting. It was a giant grizzly—and I was running right at him. The gate beckoned less than two meters away; the grizzly three. It was a catch-22, Nil style.

Oh, I didn't say Nil says . . .

The outbound collapsed, dissolving into a shimmering black dot.

It was just me, Charley, Jason, Miya, and Rives, and one seriously pissed-off bear.

Nil says run away.

"Go!" I shouted as I turned back around. Five steps later Charley's hand was in mine and I was pulling her, running, sprinting, holding her tight; it was amazing I hadn't broken her fingers by now.

The grizzly roared; we had his full attention.

Flying as a group, we sprinted past the tubes, gaining distance with each step. We knew Nil, and the bear didn't. He was also having problems with the sand, or maybe he was confused from his gate trip.

We hit the trees, Rives in the lead. The bear followed, swatting trees, roaring in frustration, and generally making enough racket to let us keep track of him. Running and cutting, we wove through the trees, toward the lava fields and away from the bear.

Eventually we lost the grumpy grizzly. After we hadn't heard any roars in hours, I felt decently safe. We made camp, then I pulled Jason aside.

"You still have a spear?"

He nodded.

"Okay. Take Miya and head back to the City. Tell them about the grizzly. Let everybody know Nil has a new toy. And check the gliders. Make sure they're reinforced before you go up, okay? Check every time. But don't forget the grizzly."

Jason looked at me. He knew what I was telling him. Guys suck at good-byes.

"They need to know," I said, gripping his shoulder.

"You sure?" he asked, his face twisted with emotion.

"I'm sure."

He stood there, then kicked a shell that wasn't there. "This sucks."

"Nil does," I agreed. "But hey, if it weren't for Nil, I'd never have had the chance to school you in the proper way to land a front-side air."

Jason nodded. "Yeah. You did, man, you did. Hey"—he looked up at me—"when I make it home, I'll look you up. You can teach me how to snowboard, and I'll—I'll"—Jason stumbled—"let you drive the tractor or something."

I grinned. "Sounds like fun. I've never had the chance to drive a John Deere."

"Kidde," he said abruptly. Almost fiercely. "With two *d*'s and an *e*. That's my last name."

I realized I'd never asked Jason his last name. He was always Jason, from Omaha.

"Blake. Thad Blake. Whistler, British Columbia. Near Vancouver."

He nodded, and I squeezed his shoulder before I let go. "You're the best Spotter I've ever met. You'll make it."

"So will you," he said. Still fierce, only now he sounded desperate.

"Hey," I said as he turned away. "Don't forget the grizzly."

"I won't forget," Jason said quietly.

"I know," I said, feeling sad and empty and pissed all at once. "Thanks."

Jason walked away, releasing his spear from his belt. He said something to Miya, who turned to me. She bowed slightly, then lifted one hand in farewell. Then Jason took her hand, and together they disappeared into the trees.

I realized I'd forgotten to wave back. Maybe I'd nodded reflexively, but right now I was too far in my own head to be sure of anything, especially common courtesy.

Rives was gathering tinder. Charley sat another ten meters away, out of whisper range, unpacking our food. Looking at the meager spread, it seemed fitting. There wasn't enough food for three people to last another day; there was barely enough for two. But this Search ended tomorrow, and regardless of how the end played out, I knew that by the end of tomorrow, this team would be short a mouth.

Mine.

"Rives." My voice was low.

He looked up. "Yeah, bro?"

"Listen." I paused, swallowing, not sure how to say what I had to say. "I sent Jason and Miya back."

Rives rose, his face resolute. "You want me to bug out."

"No." I shook my head, then glanced at Charley. She was slicing redfruit, her hair swirling around her shoulders, shielding her face. I looked back at Rives.

"I want you to stay. But I have a favor to ask. Two, actually."

CHAPTER 60

Please don't give up. Please don't give up. Please don't give up.

Because I feared he already had.

One second I was freaking out, then I'd turn mad, then hopeless and then bitter. It was a continuous loop of desperation, and I was stuck smack in the middle, alone—because even though I lay curled beside Thad, he felt far away. A secret lay between us now, and I hated it.

My mind flashed back to the conversation I'd overheard with Rives. Thad had kept his voice low, but my mom always claimed I had hearing like Superman, and she wasn't kidding. Although I couldn't see their faces, I'd heard every word.

I have a favor to ask. Two, actually, Thad had said.

Rives hadn't hesitated. *Anything. You name it.*

Okay. Thad had paused. *Tomorrow I want you to stay with us, but hang back. Give us space, but stick around, eh?*

Not a problem, Rives had answered. *I'm your wingman.* There'd been a smile in his voice. *What's number two?*

*If I—*Thad had stumbled here—*if tomorrow doesn't work out like*

I hope, I want you to look out for Charley. I don't want her to bury me— NO! I'd wanted to jump up and shake him, screaming, DON'T GIVE UP! but I'd been frozen to the rock, redfruit juice dripping off my knife like blood—*and I need to know someone's watching her back after I'm gone.*

Rives's voice dropped, and I'd strained to hear his next words. *You know I'll do it, but listen, bro. We won't be burying you. You'll make it.*

Promise me you'll look out for her, Rives. Thad's voice was hard. *I need your word.*

I promise, Rives had said, almost reluctantly. *Like I said, I'm your wingman. I've got your back.*

Not my back. Charley's. Promise me you'll have Charley's back.

I promise. Rives sounded resigned. *I've got Charley's back.*

Thad never mentioned his conversation with Rives, and I hadn't brought it up either. It was the first secret we'd had between us since Day 13, since he'd stalled on telling me about the year deadline. This secret was so much worse. Because now I not only heard his words, but I also heard his voice—full of pain and, worse, defeat.

I don't want her to bury me.

And he doesn't know that I know, I thought, feeling sick. Another secret, adding to the distance.

Thad's dark lashes fluttered, hiding eyes that I knew were the color of Nil's deep waters. He was either asleep or faking it well. I studied his face, memorizing every line, and in this bittersweet moment, I felt achingly thankful to Nil. Nil was like that crazy aunt who hooked people up at weddings. Where other than on Nil would I have had the chance to meet the most amazing boy from Canada, a boy who snowboards so well he made their national team? Sometimes I'd caught Thad staring at the mountain when he didn't think anyone was watching.

Right now his eyes were closed and still. His lips rested slightly apart, his jaw was slack, and in this moment, he looked exactly seventeen.

He's asleep, I thought with relief. It's harder to sprint when you're tired, and I believed that crazy Nil would give him a reason to run tomorrow.

I believed we were here for a reason, and I believed I was here to meet Thad. Maybe he was here to meet me, maybe not. Maybe he'd already figured out why he was here and didn't want to share it with me, yet another secret he'd chosen to keep. But it didn't matter if *I* knew why Thad was here; all that mattered was that *Thad* knew.

But is knowing enough? my worried mind whispered.

I thought of Talla and Li, of Sergio and Rory. People who'd stay in Nil's labyrinth forever. Had they figured out why they were here? And did the understanding—or lack of it—alter their fate? Maybe knowing wasn't enough, but not knowing might be a death sentence.

Maybe some aren't destined to leave.

My breath caught at the thought. As panic set in, I clung to one irrefutable fact: crazy Nil had given us each other, and the only future we had wasn't here. Thad would make it; he had to.

He had one noon left.

Please don't give up.

Wrapped in darkness and blanketed by secrets, I lay beside Thad, praying for one last gate. And as my eyes grew as heavy as my heart, I prayed he'd be there when I woke up.

Because even though he'd promised he wouldn't leave me, it felt like he already had.

CHAPTER 61

THAD
DAY 364, NIGHT

I'm going to die tomorrow.

A pervasive sense of calm accompanied that thought. Each minute marched on, counting down toward one inevitable conclusion: death.

The writing was on the Wall.

Did the inevitability of death trigger the calm? I wondered. Did everyone staring down the barrel of a gun feel peace in that moment? Or did the surreal calm stem from acceptance of one's fate? I'd finally given up trying to control something I couldn't. My fate was out of my hands, and giving up had never felt so good.

Tucked tight to my side, Charley fit perfectly, like a natural extension of me. I studied her profile, etching it in my memory. Eyes closed, lashes dark, one hand hiding under her cheek; the other resting gently on my chest.

I knew she was finally asleep. She'd faked it for a while; we both had. Words were too painful. We'd said good-bye over and over, and at this point, there was nothing left to say. The reality sucked; it was what it was. The truth was ugly. Like Nil.

I have one noon.

One shot.

One last roll of the dice.

It was the ultimate Nil game. For 365 days, we took our chances, racing toward noon, standing in open Nil air, hoping for lightning to strike. Some were lucky, like Natalie and Kevin. Others rolled the dice over and over, but never won, like Ramia and Li. And some, like Rory, barely got to play.

And then there was today. The inbound had dropped a bear bomb, screwing up my roll and changing the game. Changing the moment and ruining my chance.

Maybe my last chance.

Definitely my best chance.

Our fates were left to chance, but it was Nil who ran the tables. Even with Charley's charts, the deck was stacked in Nil's favor. It was her show, her rules. One gate. One person. One noon. One year.

And like I'd known since Day One, her rules sucked.

But for the first time, I finally understood them. Today's message was loud and clear.

I held Charley against me, knowing that tomorrow I'd go all in. I'd step up, and with everything I had on the table, I'd roll the noon dice one last time. And this time, I'd be ready. Ready to run, ready to die. Whatever hand Nil dealt, I was braced to face it on my terms. All I hoped for now was the chance to win.

Focus the breath, focus the mind. This time—for the first time—my coach's new-age breathing tip worked. My mind was clear.

Because this time I focused on Charley's breathing, not mine.

Breathe.

CHAPTER 62

CHARLEY
DAY 99, MORNING

I opened my eyes and squinted. Light streaked above the treetops. Thad was propped on his side, looking at me.

"Morning, sleepy." He smiled.

"I can't believe I slept." I was so mad at myself I scowled.

"Running from a grizzly will do that to you." His grin widened.

"But I lost time with you! Why didn't you wake me up?"

"Because I like watching you sleep. You're so beautiful, Charley." Thad's voice was ragged. His eyes traveled my face, eyes heavy with exhaustion, with sadness, and with defeat. And it scared me. He hadn't slept. Not enough, maybe not at all.

"You didn't sleep," I said. "You needed to sleep." I bit my lip, refusing to cry.

Thad just smiled. With one finger, he traced my eyebrows, my cheekbones, my jaw. I closed my eyes, feeling his finger drift to my collarbone. It was the sweetest caress, and yet it hurt, touching an ache so deep I thought I might break.

His finger drifted lower, making me shiver.

"Where's Rives?" I asked, remembering we weren't alone.

"Giving us some space."

Their secret conversation from yesterday roared back. I bit my lip again, harder this time.

"I want to spend my last hours with you," Thad whispered. "Just you."

"Not your last hours," I corrected. "Your last hours *here*."

"Right."

I stared at him. "Don't you dare give up on me," I said fiercely, holding his gaze.

"I would never give up on you." His blue eyes were so raw that it hurt. "Never."

"Not on me," I corrected. "On you. On yourself."

"Charley." Emotions flickered across his face like the iridescent colors of a shimmer, too many at once, shifting too quickly to read. "I'm just being realistic."

The bear, I thought. Yesterday had changed everything; I knew it. *I don't want her to bury me,* he'd said.

"No," I said sharply. "Don't do this. Don't give up."

"I wouldn't dream of it." He leaned forward and kissed my bottom lip, the one I'd been biting. "So," he said, cocking one eyebrow and smiling devilishly, "I've got an idea of how we can pass the time this morning. Something you asked for, and I said no."

"You want to fool around?" I asked, incredulous. "But—" I tried to make sense of his sudden change of mind.

And then he changed his mind again.

"Sorry," he said. "You're right. We can't. It's selfish of me. It's just—" He broke off. "I shouldn't have said anything. No brain-to-mouth filter today." He grinned wryly, but a shadow lurked in his eyes, darkening the blue. Something I couldn't read, but wanted to.

Slowly, I reached up and traced his scar, the tiny mountain over his eyebrow. "Tell me what you're thinking," I said softly. "Please."

He closed his eyes. "Charley." His voice broke. "I've been thinking about what you said yesterday. About why I'm here."

A roar cut the air, too close for comfort. Thad's eyes flew open, and he scanned the area around us.

"Mad grizzly," I said, taking a heavy breath.

"Yup," he said, getting to his feet. "Let's pack and roll." Clearly the time for talk was over.

I just nodded. Hope wasn't strong enough, and my prayers for a gate were already sent.

There wasn't much to pack. All we had left to eat was some dried fruit. I wanted to keep talking, but I wouldn't press, not today.

As we hiked inland, Rives was our shadow. A silent follower, lagging far enough behind that it felt like just me and Thad, but Rives never lost us, and we never lost him. I knew without asking that Thad wanted me to have company on the return trip.

I didn't share that I'd already planned it out. I'd take Thad's eight-inch blade, the one he wore on his belt. He wouldn't take it with him. I'd also take his necklace and wear it with mine. I already had his bow, the one he used to make fire. I knew how to work it, sawing until my hands grew tired and an ember glowed, and I knew to use coconut husks as tinder, the drier the better. I'd learned so much from Thad, skills I'd use to survive until it was my turn. And I'd head back with Rives, taking a different route, using my maps to avoid the grizzly. These were my secrets, the plans I didn't share with Thad.

His secrets, my secrets. Island secrets. They formed an invisible gulf between us, and I hated it.

"We're almost there," Thad said. His first words in an hour— they sounded forced.

Our feet touched black rock. Red blazed to the right. We'd decided last night to head to the newer lava fields, the ones I'd found my first day on Nil. Two different flows, two different times. One red, one black, straddling Quadrants Two and Three. Using yesterday's gate as a reference, we'd headed north, putting us in position for today.

At the junction of the two fields, we paused.

"Red or black?" I asked. It was Thad's call, and it was time.

"I'm betting on black," he said, a smile pulling at his lips. "A little Russian roulette, Nil style."

"That's not funny," I said. "It's not a game."

Thad's jaw ticked. "Right."

"You'll make it. You have to. Don't you dare give up." My voice dropped two octaves and my eyes stung. "Do. Not. Quit. Okay?"

He smiled, his eyes burning like blue fire, then he kissed me. Fierce but gentle, his kiss was so full of raw emotion that I almost cried right then. But I didn't. We had a gate to catch.

"We have to move," I said, pulling back. "The gate will come from the south, so let's stay close to the red." I pointed, reviewing the charts in my head.

Yesterday's gate had been southwest of where we were now but still fairly close, latitudinally speaking. Gates could flash close two days in a row; my quad and Kevin's outbound showed me that— same for the pair by Black Bay. Thinking of those gates, I thought of something. Something terrible.

I grabbed Thad's arm.

"Thad, we have to go back! Back to the beach! Remember how Kevin's gate and my quad came one day apart? The gates were both in the red field. And Jason's miss at Black Bay came one day after I saw a gate *on that same beach*. What if when gates flash one day apart, they flash along the same longitudinal line? In the same quadrant? Maybe that's what the number two represents! And if I'm right, then today's gate will be back on South Beach, not here! We don't have much time. We've—"

"Stop." Thad placed a finger over my lips. "Stop," he whispered. "We went over this last night. We took our time, we thought it through. We picked a latitude north of yesterday's gate, in the next quadrant on the storm track. And we picked the two most likely hot spots. The most open and the most overdue. That's here." Brushing my cheek with his thumb, Thad looked at me, his eyes full of assurance and love and everything else that made him Thad. "Let's stick with our game plan."

"You're right," I said, shaken. "I'm just—no, you're right. Let's stick with our plan." *But it's not a game.*

It never was.

Thad held out his hand, and together we entered the sea of black. Even with Thad's reassurance, part of me wanted to turn and run, to make us fly back toward the beach. But I kept walking, holding Thad's hand.

The charcoal ground was as black as asphalt, as black as the Target parking lot that felt a million miles away. A different world, a different me.

We swept the ground for movement. I barely breathed; noon was *now.*

Then the wind stalled.

Fifty yards out, the black ground wavered. Then the black rose and fell away, leaving a rippling luminescence, stretching high and glittering with life.

"Gate at three o'clock," I cried. "Go!"

Thad stood frozen. He stared at me, not the gate.

"Go!" I screamed, giving him a shake. "Run!"

"Sprint with me, Charley." Thad held out his hand. "One last time. Please." His voice broke.

Taking his hand, I ran—anything to make him move. We flew over the black ground, our strides in sync, running together for the last time. The gate writhed ten feet away, drifting north.

Soon we were close enough to see the sparkling prisms of light reflecting the sky, the ground, us. In the reflection, we were distorted silhouettes, and in that moment I knew.

Thad would live.

All my perfect words were trapped in my head, my good-bye lost in the moment. All that mattered was that *Thad would live.* I squeezed his hand and stepped away.

"Charley, I—" Thad's face was tortured, and as he raised his hand, the gate collapsed. For one long, horrible second, a tiny black hole hovered inches behind Thad's shoulder. Then the black speck winked out completely.

Thad's gate was gone. The wind was back.

And Thad was still here.

I gasped in horror, half expecting him to fall dead at any second. But he stood there, looking stunned and very much alive. Our eyes locked in mutual shock.

Then the air went slack.

I sensed the stillness, even before I saw the glimmer. Behind Thad, a gate stretched languidly into the sky, eight feet away, at most. It was a second chance—a final chance, and this time Thad's escape was guaranteed. The gate drifted toward us; he didn't even need to run. It was meant to be, like us. Thad's luck had finally turned, and Nil was giving us the chance to say a proper island good-bye.

I threw myself into Thad's arms, overcome by a profound sense of peace. "I love you. So much."

Thad held me close, not saying a word.

"I'll tell the zebra you said hi," I whispered into his shoulder. Then I pulled away, still holding his hands. "And I'll look out for Burton. Go."

The gate floated three feet away.

"Charley." Thad's voice cracked. He swallowed and shook his head.

"It's okay," I said. "I've got time. I'll find you. I love you, Thaddeus Blake. Now go."

Emotion swirled so thick in his eyes that it spilled out the edges.

"Go," I whispered, feeling renewed urgency. The gate hovered footsteps away, so close we were reflected as one. "It's your time. See you on the other side." My chest tightened with the coming loss, but the ache felt good. "I love you." Then I smiled, because this was it.

This was our good-bye.

The leading edge of the gate threw rainbows of color onto Thad's face; his eyes had never looked more brilliantly blue. "I love you, too." His voice was choked. "More than anything."

And then Thad did the unthinkable.

He lurched forward, grabbed my upper arms, and threw me backward into the gate. I twisted as I fell, trying to catch my balance and get out, already feeling the blistering heat.

"*No!*" The scream tore from my throat, but I choked on the heat. Boiling air wrapped around me like invisible sludge, pulling me deeper and trapping me inside.

I was burning, in hellfire.

Darkness licked the corners of my eyes. Nil flickered and blurred, then began to shrink, like I was peering through the wrong end of a kaleidoscope. My last clear vision was Thad, contorting as he spun to the side, his eyes locked on me.

"I'll find you, Charley!" he shouted, his voice cracking and fading. "I promise! I—"

Darkness closed in like the lid of a coffin; the blackness turned absolute. The heat vanished, and the blackness became ice, forcing its way into my soul and tearing it apart.

Then there was nothing.

No light. No air.

No Thad.

CHAPTER 63

THAD
DAY 365, NOON

Charley was gone.

I'd lost her, and yet I'd won.

"I beat you!" I screamed at Nil. Stoke shot through me like I'd posted a perfect run. Only it was Charley who'd swept the heat; it was Charley who'd caught the gate. It was Charley who'd live—and that was the rush. I'd embraced my destiny: I'd protected Charley to the end, made the ultimate bodyguard move. I'd rolled the dice, and I'd won.

Me, not Nil.

Laughing, I punched the Nil sky. My laughter echoed over the endless black rock, Nil laughing back at me.

That's when it hit me. *I should be dead.*

I'd never been with anyone on their last day. I'd assumed that a gate came and went—or didn't come at all—and then you just keeled over. Checked out. Done.

But I was still standing. And feeling sick, I suddenly knew how it would all shake out: I'd have to wait for midnight, suffering without Charley. I'd have to weather the twilight of my dying day alone, every minute a biting reminder of what I'd lost—and could never have.

"Why?" I shouted, pissed and bitter, fighting to keep my Charley-made-it high. In the distance, I heard Rives shout my name, but I was too wrapped in Nil hate to answer. I tilted my face to the Nil sky, choking Nil air in my fists. "WHY?" I screamed. "Tell me!"

The grizzly roared, the ground shook—and then I knew. *Because this is Nil, and she's cruel. And because she's not done playing with me.*

Then she whispered, *RUN.*

CHAPTER 64

My skin was stinging. No, burning. No, *freezing.*

I woke, shaking uncontrollably. From cold, from pain, from a horrible sense of loss. It was the only thing that came with me through the gate.

When I opened my eyes, a crowd of guys in parkas and goggles were bent over me; they wore helmets on their heads and confusion on their faces. And in some cruel twist of fate, the land around me was brilliant, arctic white. Stark naked, I lay cushioned on fine powder that burned like fire.

I lay on Thad's snow.

Thad! Every cell in my body cried for him, but there was no answer, just fading echoes. *I'll find you, Charley! I promise!*

But you can't, my heart cried. *Because I took your gate, your chance to escape. And now you're stuck, condemned to Nil forever.*

The men spoke quickly, murmuring in a foreign language I made no effort to understand. I didn't care what happened to me. I was fractured, shattered and incomplete. And there was no way to put me back together, because the part of me that belonged to Thad was gone, brutally ripped away as I passed through the gate.

I closed my eyes, willing the men to walk away. *Leave*, I cried silently. *Leave me here, on Thad's snow. He should be here, not me.*

Just . . . leave.

But they didn't.

Hands lifted me, and gently slid my arms into soft sleeves full of warmth. I heard a zipping noise, and warmth spread across my chest. Damp socks slid over my feet, followed by pants that moved up my legs. The hands handled me like I might break.

They didn't know I already had.

CHAPTER 65

CHARLEY
DAY 4, MID-MORNING

Here turned out to be France. Mont Blanc, specifically. I was found in an out-of-bounds area by a group of expert skiers who had "accidentally" veered off course into virgin powder.

Everyone kept telling me I was lucky to be alive.

Wrong, I'd think. If I were lucky, Thad would be here, not me. If I were lucky, I'd be on Nil, with a fighting chance of catching a gate and seeing Thad again. If I were lucky, I'd have been left for dead. That would have been kinder.

But instead I'd been admitted to a French hospital.

So far I'd spoken three words: American. Charley Crowder. The rest of the time I either shook my head or nodded, when I acknowledged the doctors at all. I kept my eyes closed, alternately clinging to my mental pictures or hiding from them. They were all I had.

When Mom, Dad, and Em rushed into the room, they looked as foreign as the nurses. The minute they saw me, their words gushed like tears.

My mom. "Charley! Oh my land, it's really you! You poor baby, I can't imagine what you've been through." *No, you can't.*

My dad. "Oh, shug, we'd thought we'd lost you." *Me too.*

Em. "Charley, I've missed you so much. When we got the call they found you, it was the best day of my life." *And it was one of the worst days of mine.*

They huddled around my bed, pouring out their stories. They thought I'd been kidnapped. My clothes were found in the Target lot; my dad's Volvo was discovered in downtown Atlanta, stripped and trashed. My purse and wallet were never found. It was clear that my entire family had expected to find me dead—not alive on a French mountainside. No one could figure out how I got there, but they didn't seem to care. They were too happy that I was alive.

More babbling. More questions. More. More. More. Too much. Too soon.

I closed my eyes, shutting my family out. I couldn't tell the truth; no one would believe me. So I did the next best thing.

I claimed amnesia.

CHAPTER 66

Walking into my room was surreal. It was like a time capsule from another time, from another girl's life.

Em's bed sat neatly made and empty, exactly as I remembered it. UGA had one more day of classes before Thanksgiving break, so Em was away at college, just like on the day I left. My bed was made, too, not as perfectly as Em's but made nonetheless. On top of my covers, my iPod lay near my pillow, exactly where I'd dropped it over a hundred mornings ago. The book I'd been reading sat beside my bed, bookmark in place, waiting.

Nothing had changed—except me.

I dropped my bag and turned on my computer.

At the Google prompt, I typed "Thad Blake, snowboarder." There were tons of archived stories, all documenting a promising Canadian snowboarder who went missing days after he was named to the Canadian National Snowboard Team. One had a clear headshot of Thad. Same blond hair, shorter than I remembered, same sapphire eyes, same lazy grin.

Reaching up, I touched Thad's cheek. It felt flat and lifeless, two-dimensional and cold like I knew it would.

With Thad smiling at me, I finally read the article. Then another. I devoured them all. Regardless of the article, the theory was the same: he was lost on the slopes, on expert terrain. His body was never found. *Duh*, I thought. One article speculated suicide, noting a devastating breakup with his girlfriend, but his family and friends rejected that idea.

"Thad would never commit suicide," his mom was quoted as saying. "He loves life more than anyone in this world."

Maybe in this *world*, I thought, fighting the hollowness inside. But Thad wasn't in this world, and hadn't been for a year. He'd been on Nil, where you lived like you were dying. And while Thad had sacrificed his chance to live, it wasn't suicide. *Suicide* was an ugly word. Selfish. And what Thad did was completely self*less*. But either way, the result was the same: he'd died. For me.

Thad smiled at me from the screen, cocking his lazy, knowing grin. *I love you, Charley from Georgia.*

I love you, too. With all that I have, with all that I am. I love you.

I wished that had been my good-bye, but in the end, our bye was anything but good. I stared at Thad's picture, aching to be with him. Abruptly, his image disappeared, replaced by my stupid screen-saver, which was, of all things, a tropical beach scene. I jiggled the mouse, bringing Thad back.

If only it were so easy.

Unwilling to lose his smile, I printed the picture, and when a tear fell, blurring Thad's face, I printed another one. Then I crawled into bed, holding Thad.

Salt on my cheeks, salt on my lips . . . a taste of Nil, it was all I had left. Tears soaked my pillow, but I didn't move. I lay there, drowning in loss and pain, desperately wishing Em were here and deeply relieved she wasn't.

That was the night I finally understood there were worse things than being alone.

CHAPTER 67

There'd been no news, no calls. Nineteen days of complete Thad silence. I was still counting; I couldn't stop, and last night I'd dreamed of the Wall. This time the space beside Thad's name was filled—with a cross. And I held the knife.

I'd stolen his gate. He'd pushed me, but I was the thief.

Rubbing my eyes, I minimized Firefox. Even my browser's logo seemed mocking. A warm-blooded fox, circling the globe, as fiery as a gate, as elusive as Nil. His eyes were shrouded, giving nothing away.

I'd spent the last four hours scouring news sites. I didn't bother with the Atlanta paper anymore. I started with Canadian ones, then went international, searching for news of Thad. But any specific search turned up articles I'd read a thousand times, and my generic searches turned up nothing. No news of a missing Canadian found anywhere, no word of a naked boy showing up somewhere strange. The only unusual story I'd found was in yesterday's edition of Britain's *Daily Mail*. Titled "Rhino Raises Hell in Helsinki," the article reported the capture of a rare black rhino found charging down the streets of Helsinki. Local zoos denied responsibility, claiming all their animals were accounted for, and the incident sparked a national outcry demanding investigation into the exotic animal trade. "People shouldn't be housing rhinos in their backyard for sport," argued one Finnish man, whose bakery shop was damaged in the ensuing chaos. "What's next, tigers?"

Maybe, I thought. *But I'm still hoping for a naked person. Over six feet tall, blond, with brilliant blue eyes and a selfless streak a mile wide.*

I stared at the flaming fox, wondering what angle I was missing. Then an idea sparked. Bringing up a fresh tab, I typed the word *Nil.*

A flurry of results appeared. Most were definitions by online dictionaries and encyclopedias, followed by a few businesses that for some inexplicable reason had named themselves Nil. But one result caught my eye: a personal blog titled *Nil Nightmares.* Maintained by a South African man in his late twenties, the blog detailed his eerily familiar account of eleven months on Nil. He posted links to a private Nil survivor support group, various missing persons sites, and even a few crackpot wormhole theorists. The comments were scathing. Some questioned the man's mental health, others urged counseling, still more begged for details to get to Nil themselves. It was an abyss of information that confirmed my decision to claim amnesia. Better forgetful than crazy. And Thad was still lost.

With nothing left to search for, I turned off my Mac and climbed into bed.

Even though everything told me Thad was dead, I refused to accept it. Because even though everything about Nil screamed temporary, Thad and I had always felt permanent. I kept thinking that perhaps Thad had miscounted his days, or that somehow Nil had granted him immunity, giving him extra time before his clock ran out. I hoped that any day Thad would show up, flashing his easy grin, flesh and bone, in *this* world. But with each day that passed, my hope shrank, collapsing on itself just a little bit more, like the pinpoint black dot of a gate right before it vanished for good.

A soft knock intruded on my thoughts.

"Charley?" Em's voice. The door creaked open. "You have a phone call."

I sat up with a jerk. "Who?"

"A girl," she said, and just like that, my lingering hope died. Instantly, painfully. Irrevocably.

"She swears she's not a reporter," Em was saying, "and that you know her." Em paused.

"Her name is Natalie."

CHAPTER 68

Over the past fifteen days, I'd seen a neurologist, a psychiatrist, and a famous psychologist who specializes in victims of violent trauma. She'd actually made a house call after reading about me in the newspapers. Apparently it's not every day that a seventeen-year-old American from a middle-class family, on track for a volleyball scholarship and with no record of crazy behavior, disappears for months, only to be found naked in a foreign country.

I really needed to pay more attention to the news.

But that would have meant getting my hopes up, something I could no longer handle. I'd stopped my dates with Firefox, refusing to scour news sites for an article I'd never find. I also refused to see any more counselors. They'd all come to the same conclusion: whatever had happened to me was so traumatic that, as a protective measure, my mind had walled off all memories of the incident.

But I did remember. And as painful as the memories were, I'd rather die than forget.

The only effort I made was to go running. It made my parents happy that I actually left my room, not to mention my bed. I'd run for hours, reveling in my memories. *Thad running beside me, his hand wrapped around mine . . . Thad placing a lei around my neck, his sapphire eyes burning . . . Thad's lips on mine, warm and sweet, hungry and wanting.* I sifted through each moment one at a time, reveling in the joy and pain of it. I'd run until the fog of physical exhaustion settled over my brain. This morning I'd run sixteen miles, and I only came home because the drizzle became a torrent. I'd forgotten what it was like to get caught in the rain.

Then, feeling bold, I'd tagged along with Em when she went to the grocery store. Waiting to check out, I'd spied a wall of photocopied images, grainy black-and-white photos of missing kids, mostly teenagers. Lured by the faces, I'd wandered over to the bulletin board and studied the pictures. Some were girls, some were boys, most had bright smiles, all had their dates of birth printed in black ink. All were missing. Maybe they were on Nil; maybe they'd met an end worse than Nil. At some point, I started crying. Em had to drag me away, and drag me home.

That was two hours ago.

No longer crying, I sat by my window, watching the rain.

Silver drops speckled the window, each one a dazzling prism attacking the glass. I watched them glisten and fall, like if all the drops could run together they'd form a gate—a shimmering wall taking me back to Nil. But one by one, each drop slid down my window, out of sight, gone forever. Like Nil.

For one perfectly uninterrupted moment, I stared at the rain, aching for Thad, aching for the chance to go back and find him. But even if I could find a gate in the great haystack that was Earth, it wouldn't matter. Thad wouldn't be there, and Nil would be nothing without him. My world was here. A world full of silver and gray—and rain.

Thunder rumbled, abrupt and startling. It sounded like a quake.

Lightning flashed as a quick double knock rattled my door. My door opened, and my dad poked his head through the crack. "Hey, honey. Can we come in?"

"Sure."

My dad set a cup on the bedside table while my mom sat on my bed's edge. "I brought you a Sprite. A Big Gulp, with that crushed ice you like."

"Thanks." I managed a smile.

"It's good to see you smile, shug." He sat on the edge of my bed, looking as lost as my mom. "Charley, hon, I can't imagine how you survived what you did. But you're strong. You always have been. You'll get through this, love. I promise."

A promise means nothing, I thought. *It's a statement of present want, not future reality.*

My dad kept talking.

"Your mama and I are behind you, one hundred and ten percent. We checked with the school, and with all your fancy AP credits, you've got college credit. You can take next semester off if you want. Graduate early or get your GED. Travel, or not. Whatever you want."

I want Thad.

He patted my leg. "Think about it, hon. Think about what you want. If we can make it happen, we will."

"You don't have to tell us today," my mom said soothingly. "Take it slow," she said, repeating the last counselor's mantra. "There's no rush. You have plenty of time."

Plenty of time.

My mom's unfortunate choice of words hurt me like few phrases could, and the pain pushed me to act. I took a breath, picturing my sweet Thad smiling at me, and looked at my parents.

"There is something I want," I said, proud I was able to speak without tears. *No regrets.* With Thad's voice echoing in my head, I laid out my plan.

Five minutes later, my mom stared at me like I'd just told her I wanted to get a full-body tattoo.

"The University of Washington," my mom repeated. "You want to play volleyball at the University of Washington. In Seattle."

"Seattle." I nodded. "UW. The home of the Huskies."

My mom glanced at my window, and visibly brightened. "Honey," she said, employing her let's-be-reasonable-I-know-what's-best-for-you tone, "let's think this through. It rains all the time in Seattle. And when it's not raining, it's overcast. People go crazy because they don't see the sun." She smiled at me, confident she had a winning argument. "Think about it. Charley, you *love* the sun."

I just looked at her.

"Charley?" She frowned. "Let's think this through."

"I have," I said softly. *No sun, no shimmers. And no pretending.*

My mom shot my dad a pleading look.

He cleared his throat. "Uh, love, Seattle's just so far. What happened to good old UGA? Great college town, Saturday football games. You could room with Em again. And, shug"—now he grinned—"you know the sun always shines on Bulldog country."

"It sure does, Dad." *A girl disappeared in west Athens last month. All they found were her clothes.* I loved my dad fiercely, but my mind was set. "Seattle," I said gently. My voice didn't waver. "I want to go to Seattle."

"Seattle!" My mom's voice rose to a desperate wail. "That's practically in Canada!"

Exactly.

Dad winked at me, mouthed *I love you,* then gently guided a still-protesting Mom out of the room. I could hear her sputtering all the way down the hallway. "Seattle! My baby, in *Seattle!*"

Seconds behind Dad, Em breezed through the doorway, wearing

faded jeans and a university-grown confidence that both fit her to a T.

"Guess who's back?" she asked, beaming.

For a minute I thought Em meant me. Then Jen popped into the room. Her dark hair was chopped in an edgy pixie cut; it oozed Italian style.

"Charley!" Jen hugged me like a long-lost friend, which I was. She started crying, and squeezed me tighter.

In the background, Mom's wails rose to a crazy pitch, breaking the moment.

"Wow," Jen said, wiping her eyes. "Your mom's totally freaking out."

"Three thousand miles *is* a long way away," I said.

"She'll come around," Em said. "She just needs some time to adjust. The thing is"—now her voice cracked—"we just got you back."

Emotion welled, but I didn't cry. Because I didn't feel like I was back. I felt trapped in an unnamed place, caught somewhere between Nil and here, and I hadn't figured out yet how to pull myself out.

Jen squeezed my hand, and just like old times, the three of us sat on my bed. Em took my other hand, her fingers wrapping around mine.

"Charley." Her voice was tentative. "Do you remember anything yet? It's okay if you don't. It's just—you were gone so long . . ."

Em's eyes begged for understanding. I looked away, knowing Jen's face reflected more of the same: curiosity, worry, fear, hope. It was their hope that hurt the most, because I knew that to lose it was final, and devastating.

I took a steadying breath.

"There was a boy," I said quietly. "He saved me." I paused, fighting the emptiness inside. "His name was Thad."

It was the first time I'd spoken Thad's name aloud in days.

"And?" Jen said. "What happened?"

No more words would come; they were stuck, in that lonely in-between place. Maybe one day I'd tell Em and Jen the whole story, but not now, not yet. Not until I'd processed it all myself. Right now I needed the one thing this world offered that Nil hadn't—time.

I knew it was irrational, but one reason I wasn't ready to tell my story was that I wasn't ready to admit that it was fully written. That the end—*Thad's* end—was final. My heart simply refused to accept it.

Watching Jen's hopeful face, I slowly shook my head. *Not yet*, I thought. *Not yet.*

CHAPTER
69

CHARLEY
DAY 51, LATE MORNING

When my mom's taillights disappeared into the misty rain, I sagged against the bay window in relief.

I was finally alone.

Being alone meant I was free to remember, and being alone meant I could stop pretending. Stop pretending to be fine, stop pretending I didn't remember. Stop pretending I was whole. Because fifty-one days later, my heart still begged for Thad. I needed time to grieve and to heal—the kind of time only distance could provide.

That was a huge part of my decision to pursue a volleyball scholarship at the University of Washington, a school as foreign to my parents as Nil was to me. *If you're gonna be a dog, be a 'Dawg, not a Husky*, my dad had argued. But I was determined, and I'd won. I was also considering going out for the cross-country team, because running was the only time I felt alive, so I ran a ton, and I'd gotten pretty good. But no matter what I did in Seattle, I wouldn't have to pretend. And I'd feel close to Thad, even though he was gone.

Today was January gray, cool and wet. Not a storm, just gentle sheets of silver drizzle.

I watched it fall, oddly soothed by the colorlessness outside my window. And like I always did when I was alone, I thought of Thad, remembering us.

As I relived our last moment together, anger flared, slashing and painful, then the emotion fizzled as quickly as it had come. Fury had flickered lately in place of the numbness, fueling my latest runs. I was furious with Nil, with Fate, or maybe with both. Fate brought Thad and me together only to tear us apart, or maybe that was Nil; I couldn't tell where one ended and the other began. And I didn't understand why. *Why let me meet my soul mate, only to take him away? Was my purpose on Nil only to solve the mystery of the carvings, rediscovering knowledge that had been lost? And if so, why take me first, when my work on Nil wasn't done?*

I felt confident that I'd figured out the pattern to the gates, and I was grateful I'd shared my storm theory with everyone in the City. But I never figured out the numbers, not completely.

Maybe I wasn't meant to know, I thought, leaning my head against the cool glass. *Maybe the numbers are someone else's mystery to solve.* Like how Sabine shared the knowledge of the deadleaf leaves, but left before teaching anyone how to brew deadleaf tea.

Maybe I wasn't on Nil to meet Thad after all.

Every cell in my body screamed otherwise. The screaming reached a fever pitch, and in that instant, I was furious with Thad. I'd stolen his gate, but he'd thrown me in; his act was selfless, but it felt like quitting. On me, on us. And yet what he did was so perfectly Thad that my anger didn't last, because I couldn't be angry at Thad for being Thad. Sometimes I got mad at myself, wondering how I hadn't seen his slick move coming.

Don't you dare give up on me, I'd said. *Never,* he'd promised, his eyes burning with blue fire.

I'd misread him completely.

I rapped my head against the glass, then I let it go. I refused to play the what-if game. It wouldn't change the past. But while the past was over, it still shaped the present.

I missed Thad so much it hurt.

Out of habit, I touched my bare neck. All Thad's gifts were reduced to memories; the necklace, the lei, his kisses. Except one: me. His final gift was life. *My* life. To throw it away would diminish it, something I refused to do, because even though no one else would know, *I* would know. And I'd never forget.

My dad was right. I was strong; I would make it. I owed it to Thad, and I owed it to myself.

I'd just have to make it alone.

I thought about going for a run, but I was content to sit and watch the rain, knowing that for the first time in weeks, no one would ask me if I was okay.

The phone rang; I didn't move. I wondered if it was Natalie. She'd seen the news and found my phone number. When I'd told her what happened, she cried with me, stunned at Thad's choice. She was the only one who knew how I felt, and yet she didn't. Because she had Kevin, while I only had memories—memories that everyone else thought I'd forgotten. I loved talking to Natalie, but I hated it, too.

The phone fell silent. The rain kept falling. I caught the flash of someone in a slicker, then the doorbell rang, jarring and intrusive.

Like everything else unpleasant in my life, I ignored it.

Leaning my forehead against the glass, I watched the rain.

CHAPTER
70

THAD
DAY 365, NOON

The ground rocked under my feet.

"Thad!" Rives's voice was muffled by the quake. "On your left!"

I spun, and expecting the bear, I was shocked to see a gate rising twenty meters out.

RUN. Nil giggled. *Nil says RUN.*

I ran.

Everything wavered but me. The air roiled, the ground blurred. My feet flew over the shifting rock, but my eyes stayed locked on the gate. On my one last shot. Adrenaline pumped through my veins and death nipped at my heels; my quads burned and I made them burn more; I wanted them to burn like the gate I was dying to catch because the burn said I was still fighting.

RUN.

The noise was deafening, roaring like an avalanche as a massive quake shook the island. The gate glittered ten meters away, but the window to catch it was closing; I sensed it.

Noon was fading, like me.

RUN!

A giant crack split the black four meters out. Barely moving, the gate hovered just on the other side.

Come to me, I begged.

The gate crept closer, drifting toward the crevice. The seconds ticked in my brain, counting down. *Three . . . two . . . one . . .*

I ran for me; I ran for Charley; I ran away from the Reaper and toward the lazy gate, praying that I beat the odds, just this once. I ran without breathing; there was no time left.

I ran—and then I leaped. Because now the gate hung directly over the abyss: to fall meant certain death, but I was dead anyway.

For one instant, nothing shook.

Nothing trembled.

Time stopped; the air wrapped me in peace. I was flying and floating; I had nothing left. Then I was falling, and when the heat hit, I laughed.

And then I blacked out cold.

CHAPTER 71

Pressing the doorbell, I felt like I might burst; I'd been dying for this moment ever since I'd jumped into that gate like a man possessed. I'd woken up naked in Pakistan, finally made it home, and tracked down Charley with everything I had left.

My hands were shaking, so I set my backpack on the porch. I strained to hear footsteps over the rain.

There was no answer.

My heart sank, wondering if I'd screwed up the house number, knowing I hadn't. But maybe she wasn't home. Leaning close to the door, I called, "Charley?"

Two very long seconds passed, then the door flew open. Charley stood in the doorway, her dark hair tumbling around her face. Wearing jeans and a T-shirt, she looked as long and lean and gorgeous as ever, but her eyes were hollow, stealing my hello.

"Thad?" Charley's face drained of color.

"Miss me?" I said, breaking into a grin.

Charley didn't move. "You died. I stole your gate." Her lower lip was raw, like she'd been biting it for weeks.

"Nope. That one was yours." I grinned as Charley's eyes narrowed. "Mine was next. Nil offered up a triple dip." *Because I finally gave up what I wanted most—you.* My throat tightened. "And here I am."

"You are in *so* much trouble," she said, throwing herself into my arms. It was the moment I'd been living for: Charley in my arms, here in this world, and for an instant, the reality was as unreal as Nil. "What took you so long?" Her voice shook.

"I stopped for cookies," I whispered in her ear. "Chocolate chip. Sorry they're not homemade."

"I thought you'd died," she said, hitting my collarbone with her fist. "That I'd lost you. I thought—" Her fist pressed hard against me, she broke off, her voice full of hurt.

"I'm sorry," I said, gently covering her fist with my hand. "I came as fast as I could."

"Fifty-one days," Charley murmured into my shoulder. But she didn't move away. "Fifty-one days, Mr. Blake. Did you forget how to e-mail? Or use a phone?"

"My accommodations were a little sparse. No wi-fi and terrible guest services."

"Hilarious." She stiffened in my arms. "Fifty-one days, and all you can say is that you had bad guest services?"

"It's true. I woke up naked in Pakistan, and they didn't exactly roll out the welcome wagon." Flashbacks of a time darker than Nil slammed into my head, making me shudder. "And yesterday I called, but your dad thought I was a reporter. He hung up on me."

"Sorry," she said, relaxing. "He's a little protective these days."

"I don't blame him." I held her close, still stunned that Nil had given me this moment. "Am I still in trouble?" I whispered.

"Tons." Lifting one hand, she touched my cheek. Tentative, then exploring. "I can't believe you're alive," Charley murmured. "That you're *here*."

"Hey," I tilted up her chin so I could see her eyes. "I promised, remember?"

"I remember." She smiled, her eyes brighter than Nil's sun. "I remember everything."

"I love you, Charley with an *e-y*." Lowering my lips to hers, I kissed her, because I refused to waste a minute. Nil had taught me that. But Nil was then; Charley was now.

"Do you know what day it is?" she asked, wrapping her arms around my neck.

I grasped for the date, fighting Nil déjà vu. "January fifth?"

Laughing, Charley shook her head. "It's Day One," she said. "It's *our* Day One."

And with that, Nil's shadow vanished; the tick-tock was gone. All I felt was the sweet stoke of a future without limits.

"Day One," I agreed, pulling Charley close. "Of forever."

ACKNOWLEDGMENTS

Huge thanks to the following people that brought *Nil* into this world:

My amazing editor, Kate Farrell, for falling in love with *Nil*, for her spot-on insight, and for her sweetness and reassurance. I know how lucky I am. I can't imagine *Nil* without Kate's brilliant eye and guiding hand. Cookies for life are on me.

The entire Macmillan team for their kindness and endless enthusiasm, for my gorgeous book cover, and for all the things the Macmillan/Henry Holt powerhouse did behind the scenes to make *Nil* the very best it could be. I'm ever grateful.

My copy editor, Ana Deboo, who suffered through my painful Day time line and deserves all the hugs for her work.

Samantha Mandel, who helped pull everything together in too many ways to count.

My rock-star agent, Jennifer Unter, for taking a chance on me, for making my publishing dream a reality, for her encouragement and guidance, and for being the best agent-cheerleader ever. Jennifer, you are truly made of awesome.

Charles Martin, an incredibly gifted writer who kindly shared his time and wisdom with me early on, and who advised, "Write another book." I did—and that book was *Nil*. Thank you, Charles. I'm so grateful I had your advice to take.

My critique partners and writer friends: Jessie Harrell, who read *Nil* first and supported it from day one; Tonya Kuper, who shares my brain and read *Nil* almost as many times as me; Natalie Whipple, who is kind and gave *Nil* the push it needed; Jay C. Spencer, who made Thad more real and gave me Crispy Crunches; Laura Stanford, who loved the story and fought for the piglet; Lindsay Currie, who amazes me with her insight and saw things I didn't; and Becky Wallace, who reads as fast as me and is brilliant. I am so grateful that *Nil* gave me each of you.

My friends and cheerleaders: Kelly Anderson, Leigh Smith, and Christy Gillam, who read the (awful) early drafts of my first novel and still read more manuscripts later; Phaedra Avret, Gina Donahoo, Mary Claire Miller, Julie Cofran, Avery Williams, Kat Miller, and Marchie Surface, who read my second drafts and fueled my hope; Amy Grant and Sims Wachholz, who never doubted and who might be as excited as me; Allison, Lindsey, Virginia, Cathleen, Susannah B., Margaret, Heather, Susannah D., Mary, Natalie, Kasie, Erin, Nicole, Kim, Rebecca H., Michele, Debbie K., Annie, Rebecca C., Meg, Darden, and the sweet friend who I forgot due to writer's brain—I treasure every word of encouragement you've given me. I love you all.

The YA Valentines, for riding the 2014 debut roller coaster with me. I'm honored to be on this crazy train with you.

My teen readers, Mary Caroline Gillam and Porter Grant, who are the best.

My writer friends on Twitter, members of the #NILtribe, book bloggers, and my readers everywhere, for your incredible enthusiasm and support. You made *Nil* come alive.

My sister, Kristin Sziarto, who always believed. I love you, Ki.

My dad, who gave me my first Anne McCaffrey novel. I miss you, Dad.

My amazing family: Mom, Penny, Bev, Beepsy, Johnny, Jim, Grandma, Mark, Jill, Kerri, Blake, Ryan, Baz and Max, for loving me. I love y'all bunches.

My boys, Caden, Christian, Davis, and Cooper, for sharing me with Charley and Thad, and for making every day an adventure. I love each of you beyond measure.

And Stephen, my love-at-first-sight, my best friend, and my wing man, for reading everything I write and for being my biggest fan ever. I'm so glad I took Astronomy. I do, always.

NIL

BONUS MATERIALS

GOFISH

QUESTIONS FOR THE AUTHOR

LYNNE MATSON

As a young person, who did you look up to most?
My parents. They loved books and the outdoors in equal parts, and they instilled the same loves in me! They encouraged me to embrace the world around me and appreciate the beauty in everything, and they taught me that

© Ryan Ketterman

many of life's greatest joys are found in the smallest of moments. I think their philosophy helped me become the writer I am today. Even now, one of my favorite things in the whole world is reading a good book on the beach, with the soothing lull of the ocean in the background. Double win!

Did you play sports as a kid?
I did! I played a bit of tennis and golf growing up, and in high school, I ran track, was a cheerleader, and played some hoops. I love all sports—both watching them and playing them. Now I get to play sports with my boys (like tennis and basketball) and cheer them on from the sidelines, too, so I'm a happy camper. The one sport I wish I'd played in high school but didn't? Volleyball. I love watching beach volleyball in the

Olympics; it looks so fun! It's why I made Charley a volleyball player—she was inspired by Gabrielle Reece.

What was your first job, and what was your "worst" job?
My first job? During high school, I worked at a local sporting goods store in Georgia called Pro Appeal. The store sold tennis apparel and equipment, along with shoes and other general training gear. I loved sports, and the people I worked with were so nice that work was fun. It was a great lesson learned early on.

My worst job? I worked one weekend in high school as a shoe model for a company at a downtown shoe expo. I was a terrible fit for the job. Most sample shoes are a size 6, which I wasn't (I was a tall, gawky teen with still-growing size 8 feet at the time), and after a weekend of stuffing my feet into too-small shoes, I realized shoe modeling wasn't for me. Another life lesson learned for me: Don't try to be something you're not. Find what fits you (pun intended), and you'll be happy. :)

What book is on your nightstand now?
Just one? ;) I have a stack! *The Kiss of Deception* by Mary E. Pearson, *Throne of Glass* by Sarah J. Maas, and *Isla and the Happily Ever After* by Stephanie Perkins, to name a few. I'm currently reading *Partials* by Dan Wells. I read everything and anything I can get my hands on, but mainly YA.

Where do you write your books?
Everywhere and anywhere! I write heaps on my laptop, preferably either on our screened-in porch, or in our sunroom. I also write in our office, which has windows on three sides. Basically anywhere with lots of natural light. Light makes

me happy, although so do rainy days. Both sorts of days are perfect for writing.

What sparked your imagination for *Nil*?
I adore this question, because I can pinpoint the precise moment the idea for *Nil* fell into my head.

I had been in Hawaii (the Big Island) with my husband for all of thirty minutes. It was our first real vacation since the arrival of baby boy number four a few years earlier, and the lack of little Matson men under my charge was *huge*. It meant that as we got into our rental car, I didn't have to wrangle anyone into a car seat, point out a passing bulldozer, or drive one-handed while I blindly fished around on the backseat for a wayward sippy cup (note: don't do that; it's *not* safe.) It meant that, for once, I could just look out the window and relax. And think.

As we left the airport, we drove through miles of ancient lava fields. Broken red rock stretched endlessly on both sides, gorgeous and desolate. There were no roads, no buildings, no people—only the eerie sound of wind blowing over the rocks. The silence pressed against us, powerful and real. I remember thinking how much the landscape looked like an alien planet, and thinking how creepy it would be to wake up there, alone, without a clue to tell you where you were. And I specifically remember thinking, what if you were a teenager? And what if—because let's be honest, isn't this every person's worst nightmare?!—you woke up naked?

Nil was born in that moment. That barren-red-rock visual locked in my head, and that's what Charley sees when she first opens her eyes on the island of Nil. As soon as we checked into our hotel, I pulled out my laptop, and my very patient husband waited as I typed out the opening scenes of *Nil.* Those scenes never changed.

Are you a fan of shows like *Survivor* or *Lost*? Did either of them inspire the world of Nil?

I watched both of those shows! Mainly just the first seasons, though, and in my opinion, the first season of *Lost* was *brilliant*. While neither show inspired the world of Nil—as I mentioned above, Hawaii was the inspiration for the entire Nil world—I do think both shows indirectly influenced my writing of *Nil*. Both *Survivor* and *Lost* gave a fresh take on the idea of being stranded. Oh, and I should also mention that I watched a lot of *Gilligan's Island* when I was growing up.

Did you do any research while writing *Nil*? If so, what was the most interesting thing you learned?

I did tons of research. Writers tend to have very interesting Google search histories. I researched tiger behavior, warthog aggression, fatal knife wounds, ancient Polynesian customs, and solar flares, among other things. My most interesting discovery had to be when I stumbled across information detailing the Solar Superstorm of 1859. Also known as the Carrington Event, this storm was one of the largest geomagnetic storms ever recorded, triggered by a massive solar flare. These storms still happen today, and have the potential to cause massive worldwide disruption. In fact, in March of 1989, a severe geomagnetic storm in Canada caused the collapse of Hydro-Québec's power grid, leaving the entire province of Québec in a total blackout for days. Scary, and real. And for me, awesome fodder for developing the Nil world.

What can we look forward to in *Nil Unlocked*? (No spoilers, please!)

Rives. Skye. Answers and *feels*.

Which of your characters is most like you?
Good question. Probably Jillian. She's fiercely loyal and kind, and has a quiet strength I love. She gets more time and page space in *Nil Unlocked*, for which I'm grateful.

What makes you laugh out loud?
My boys! My friends, song parody videos on YouTube, Jimmy Fallon, perfectly delivered lines in books . . . so many things.

What's your favorite song?
I don't have a favorite song, but I have many favorite artists! Jack Johnson, Lana Del Rey, Coldplay, Snow Patrol, Thirty Seconds to Mars, Silversun Pickups, Jason Mraz, and Broods top my list, but I have many, many more I listen to as well. It depends on my mood, and what I'm doing—running, writing, or just chilling out.

But the theme song for Nil is without a doubt definitely "The Island (Part 1)" by Pendulum. It's haunting, creepy, patient, and melodic. . . . And how perfect is that title?! And if you ever have a chance to watch the video for this song, it's eerily similar to Nil, too. I discovered this song during revisions for *Nil*, and fell in love with it from note one.

What was your favorite book when you were a kid? Do you have a favorite book now?
My all-time favorite series is the Dragonriders of Pern series by Anne McCaffrey. I love these books so much, and have read them multiple times.

If you were stranded on a deserted island, who would you want for company?
Best interview question ever! I would definitely pick my husband, my four boys, and of course, Bear Grylls. He'd teach us

everything we'd need to know to survive and get rescued, even if it meant eating grub soup until we built the perfect seaworthy raft.

If you could travel in time, where would you go and what would you do?
Oh, time travel. So much potential for trouble! I'm not sure I would go back. What if I messed something up that changed my family's future forever, as in the worst butterfly-effect ripple ever? As cheesy as it sounds, I think I'd be better served learning from my past to create a better future and not tinker with what's already been done.

What's the best advice you have ever received about writing?
Read a lot. Write a lot. Revise even more. And never give up. If you don't believe in your writing and your stories, who will?

SQUARE FISH

DISCUSSION GUIDE

NIL

by Lynne Matson

1. If you arrived on Nil, would you choose to join the City? Why or why not? And if so, how would you see yourself contributing to the City?

2. Which character on Nil would you choose as an ally? Why?

3. What would be the hardest part for you about being on Nil? Would it be the difficulties on the island, or what you left behind?

4. Which character's view of the island resonates with you most: Charley's or Thad's? Explain.

5. What is the significance of the epigraph at the start of the book?

6. The title of the book is *Nil*. Analyze the meaning of the title in light of the entire novel. How do you think this single word captures the theme of the story?

7. *Nil* is told from a dual narrative. How do the alternating perspectives affect the story? What does the reader gain from having two perspectives rather than a single narrator?

8. How does Charley's view of the island differ from Thad's? Give text-based evidence to support your position. Over the course of the novel, does either character's view of the island change? If so, why?

9. Explain the significance of the Naming Wall for the teens who arrive on Nil. Why do you think the Wall was created in the first place?

10. One of the underlying themes of Nil is law versus anarchy. How do the "rules" of Nil—namely, that each person has 365 days to catch a gate or die and the "one person, one gate" limitation—impact that theme?

11. Thad states that "stealing someone's gate is island manslaughter" (p. 122). Explain what Thad means by his statement. Could stealing someone's gate ever be morally justified? Explain your reasons.

12. Throughout *Nil*, the idea of dangerous beauty is ever-present, as is the tension between paradise and doom. Could a Nil survivor ever appreciate true beauty or danger away from the island? Explain.

13. Describe what noon represents for the characters. How does the minute *before* noon differ from the moment *after* noon on Nil?

14. With the year deadline and constant arrival and departure of teens, the island is a revolving door. How does the constant turnover impact the retention—or loss—of island knowledge?

15. At the start of the novel, Charley hates to be alone. At the novel's end, Charley says that "there [are] worse things than being alone" (p. 357). What does she mean by this last statement? How did her time on Nil contribute to this realization?

Rives is the undisputed leader of Nil City, but keeping the City united is tougher than ever. Now Rives and a mysterious newcomer, Skye, must save the residents of Nil—but at what cost? And who will pay the price?

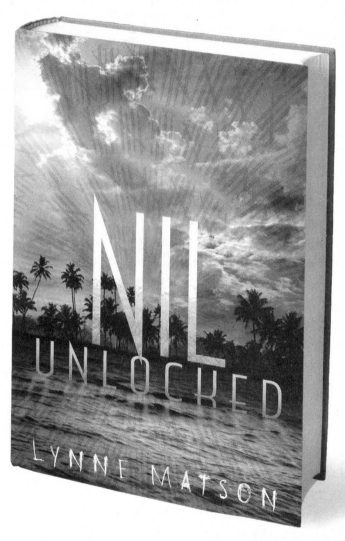

Keep reading for an excerpt of

Nil Unlocked.

CHAPTER
1

The ground shook, like Hades had lost his temper.

Or his favorite toy. Or both.

Given the last ten minutes of sheer insanity, I'd pick both.

Three gates, twin exits, and one massive quake, all packed into today's manic noon. Aftershocks tore through the black rock field as the island fought to win, and the battle seemed personal with the devil himself.

Right now I was doing my damnedest not to meet him in person.

Cracks tore through the rock, ripping the ground into a fresh jigsaw puzzle. One lava field away, red blurred like liquid rust. A buffalo lurched awkwardly in the distance, bracing against the very island that held it hostage. Quakes always scared the animals—me included. I scrambled over the trembling rock, aiming to retrieve Charley's gear and not kill myself in the process.

Nil wasn't happy—that was clear.

Another aftershock hit. The ground jerked; black rock splintered on my right. I shifted direction with the wind, already calculating a safer route.

The grizzly roared. I spun to place him. I'd forgotten he was my new sidekick.

I caught the bear in my line of sight and skidded to a sharp halt; my current vector put me on a crash course with the grizzly. He barreled toward me, erratic and unsteady, pointlessly trying to outrun the quake. It was a toss-up as to who was more terrified: me or the jacked-up bear. But it didn't matter. All that mattered was staying alive, a personal mandate that did *not* include me playing chicken with the grizzly.

I backpedaled, unwilling to take my eyes off the bear, and stumbled five steps before I tripped and caught myself one-handed on a large chunk of shifting rock. Three meters out, the ground where I would've been standing cracked into a cruel smile—one with teeth. Jagged black rock, dripping decay, lining a wide hole. The grizzly's eyes were wild, his pace uncontrolled. He hit a patch of gravel and slid—and then he fell. Sideways, into the chasm, a brown blur clawing at empty air. The island jerked, the toothy trap clamped shut. Rock crumbled into the dwindling crack as the island settled, then stilled.

No shake, no quake.

Done.

The only animal left was me.

The stillness was shocking. I gingerly let go of the rock and stood. Alone in the field of black, I marveled at the quiet. At the abrupt calm, which was as remarkable as the preceding fifteen minutes of mayhem.

Thad's shocking play.

Charley's escape.

The bear. The quake. Thad leaping toward a gate floating over a deadly black rift, Thad hanging in midair like a crazed long jumper, one heartbeat too long. But he'd made it.

Nothing like cutting it close, bro, I thought.

I exhaled a breath I'd been holding for days.

Days.

I had 124 left.

I took a breath, steady and deep, reveling in the feeling of being alive, then I turned in a slow circle, absorbing the look and feel of the island in the wake of today's noon. The red rock in the distance jutted crisply against the cloudless blue sky, all blurred edges gone. On my right, Mount Nil stretched high like an island sentinel. A near-vertical black rock peak slapped with patches of stubborn green, its tip speared the only clouds in sight. Wispy steam bleached the sky on the backside, visible if you knew where to look, where hidden vents released deadly pressure. Directly in front of Mount Nil sat the meadow, lush and green and more than a little deadly. I couldn't see the meadow from where I stood, but I knew it was there, just like the rain forest to the northeast and the City due west. So much of Nil was unseen. I understood that now more than ever.

As I stood alone in the wake of today's noon, the island looked exactly the same—and felt completely different. Foreign and new.

I gave a sharp laugh.

Of all the people here, you'd think I'd be the most accustomed to change as the constant, but then again, in my pre-Nil life, the places didn't change; *I* did. *I* moved; *I* traveled; *I* adjusted to new cities and countries as easily as changing my shirt. Here, *I* was the constant, forced to continually reassess the island and everything I knew, which made it impossible to get a handle on where I stood. Every time I thought I had something figured out, it changed.

And with the twin losses of Thad and Charley, things had definitely changed.

Welcome to Nil, Rives, I thought.

Again.

I'd just finished my full rotation when the breeze shifted. Dulled, as if interrupted. Or expectant.

Incoming, I thought.

I soundlessly fell to one knee beside the rock.

A moment later, a gate dropped a few meters away in midair and glittered, a writhing disco ball no one wanted to play anywhere near, especially me.

Perfectly still, I remained crouched by the boulder, once my anchor, now my shield. And I waited.

One second.

Two.

On three, every speck of the disco ball turned matte black. Deep black, the color of a night with no stars, the color of birth on Nil. This gate was an inbound, and now that it churned black, I knew it had a rider.

Friend or foe?

I'd barely finished the thought when the gate coughed out a flash of gold. An animal, with tawny fur the color of the waking sun and a thicker mane of the same, lay motionless on the black rock, his paws facing me.

Foe, I thought.

As the lion lifted his head, another gate popped a meter farther out and dropped. It, too, shifted into charcoal black, a dangerous aperture primed to open. One tick later, the second gate dumped another golden animal, only this one lacked a mane.

Lion number two rose to her feet as inbound gate number three appeared and instantly flashed black. Three gates, all inbounds. All with riders.

This time the newcomer wasn't a lion; it was a large, scrawny beast covered with dark splotches and a nasty mop of scraggly fur running down its back. It dropped out of the gate, rolled to a lifeless stop, and had barely stilled before raising its wobbly head. It sniffed once, swung its head around toward the lions—*and me*—and bared its teeth.

I didn't move.

With a high-pitched keen, it rose to its feet and took off after the lions at a blistering pace. Hyena, I guessed, although I'd never seen one so large. The trio sprinted away, toward Mount Nil and the meadow, the mangy mutt chasing the lions, an unsettling visual if ever there was one.

On Nil, even the king of the beasts ran in fear.

I stood, alone again.

Assessing again.

Charley, gone. Thad, gone. The grizzly, trapped in rock, lost for good. Three out, three in, the island's balance still intact, only today the Nil scales took a hard tip toward the deadly.

When the trio vanished from sight, I went after Charley's gear. Her clothes, sandals, and satchel lay in a clean pile. Inside the satchel, Charley's maps and fire bow waited, intact and undamaged. Thad's knife glinted like a dull gate, like life and power and something primitively badass. An island offering, just for me.

Thank you, Nil.

I took it all and didn't look back. The City was waiting.

I hoped it was still standing.